SALOME AND JUDAS IN THE CAVE OF SEX

SALOME AND JUDAS IN THE CAVE OF SEX

The Grotesque: Origins, Iconography, Techniques

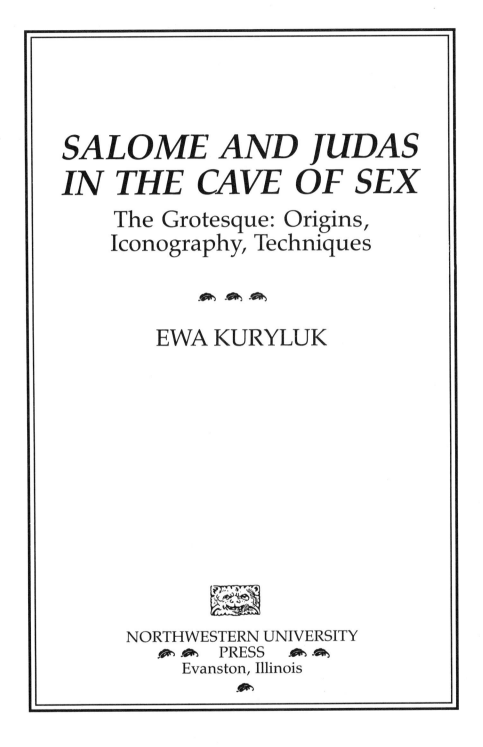

EWA KURYLUK

NORTHWESTERN UNIVERSITY PRESS
Evanston, Illinois

Northwestern University Press,
Evanston, IL 60201

© 1987 by Ewa Kuryluk
All rights reserved. Published 1987
Printed in the United States of America

Published with the assistance of
the J. Paul Getty Trust

Library of Congress Cataloging-in-Publication Data

Kuryluk, Ewa, 1946–
    Salome and Judas in the cave of sex.

    Bibliography: p.
    Includes index.
    1. Grotesque in art.   2. Erotica.   3. Art and
mythology.   4. Symbolism in art.   5. Arts.   6. Beardsley,
Aubrey, 1872–1898—Themes, motives.   I. Title.
NX650.G7K87   1986   700   86-23528
ISBN 0–8101–0739–2
ISBN 0–8101–0740–6 (pbk.)

CONTENTS

Acknowledgments

Ewa Kuryluk expresses her gratitude to Florence Stankiewicz, the first reader and editor of the manuscript, who not only canonized the author's slightly grotesque English but also encouraged her constantly in this fantastic undertaking. Warm thanks are extended to Frances Padorr Brent and Jonathan Brent for a critical reading and polishing of the text, and to a supporting team of "Rabbit's Friends and Relations," as they were called by Winnie the Pooh: Julia Przyboś, Klaudiusz Weiss, Marta Petrusewicz, Michael Kott, Wanda Rapaczyńska, Daniel Gerould, Jadwiga Kosicka, Jerzy Warman, Eva Hoffman, and Helmut Kirchner. Thanks to Jenny Gabbai for typing the manuscript, to Karin Mack for developing some of the photographs, and to Alma A. MacDougall for her careful copyediting of the book.

The execution of *Salome and Judas in the Cave of Sex* was promoted in its initial stage by a fellowship at the Institute for the Humanities at New York University, and in its terminal stage by the Hodder Fellowship at Princeton University.

List of Illustrations

Introduction

Searching in his *Aesthetics* for a metaphor which would reflect the nature of pre-classical and pre-rational humanity, Hegel came upon the image of the ancient sphinx, a mysterious mixed creature, half woman and half beast. The sphinx can also serve as a good symbol for the grotesque, a heterogeneous genre which presents many riddles. Wandering around the colossal woman-animal and the cave that shelters her, trying to relate the seductive smile on her lips to her paws and lion's tail, one feels small, stupid, and mystified—like a child. The more that is discovered about her, the more this sentiment seems justified. She forces her explorers to descend into the obscure past of humanity and into their own infancies where riddles different from those asked in the civilized, adult world must be answered. But how to pose them, being oneself part of a late and hyper-rational culture and not a member of an early society? This book attempts to cope with the difficulty by balancing itself between a proper scholarly approach and a loose, associative meandering in pursuit of two goals, one major and general, the other minor and particular.

Salome and Judas in the Cave of Sex strives for a general understanding of the ambiguity and complexity of the grotesque. It traces the origins, outlines the territory, studies the iconography, suggests a chronology, and indicates formal procedures which create strange and uncanny effects. However, it focuses in particular on the fin-de-siècle grotesque, a brilliant finale to this tradition, in which the English artist Aubrey Beardsley's extraordinary work provides a looking glass for the grotesque of previous ages and serves as a striking example of iconographic continuity. Thus, this book joins the stream of research investigating the diverse aspects of the grotesque and contributes modestly to the field of Beardsley studies as well.

General inspirations have been drawn from a number of books and dissertations.[1] But the author is particularly indebted to Wolfgang Kayser's study of the grotesque[2] and Mikhail Bakhtin's books on Rabelais and Dostoyevsky.[3] Kayser's chief contribution consists in his recognition of the important role that dreams, madness, and the unconscious played in the creation of the grotesque. Bakhtin's very different approach points out other equally essential sources of the grotesque: folklore and carnival. None of this can be disputed, but both theories have their limitations. Kayser's psychoanalytic perspective does not reach far enough, for he disregards aspects of the grotesque given form through ancient mythology, obscene literature and art, repressed eroticism, and the reverie of regression. He ignores the closeness of the grotesque to the heretical and sacrilegious as well as to destruction and death.

Bakhtin's greatest achievement lies in his locating the origin of the grotesque in popular festivals and their culmination, the carnival, and his tracing the relationship between the grotesque and the folk belief in an indestructible and material mother—nature. He gives an excellent analysis of carnivalistic practice, which debases and derides the serious routine of life, civil and religious authorities, established laws, ideas, and moral values. Furthermore, he suggests that this debasement corresponds to a fundamental desire to be integrated with earth, the cradle and grave of all living beings. Bakhtin is not interested in connecting this process of lowering and penetrating into the earth with the psychological phenomena of infantilism, regression, and death wish, nor does he link folklore and carnival to ancient mythologies, pagan religions, or secret cults. Exploring the symbolism of the earth, he does not touch upon that of the grotto.

Kayser is obsessed with the dark chaos that haunts an individual psyche; Bakhtin is fascinated with the collective chaos achieved during carnival, the abandonment of the spiritual and noble in favor of the material and vulgar. Taken together, their contradictory positions complement each other well: on one side, lunatics, phantoms, hallucinations, and dreams join their reflections in the circus, the commedia dell'arte, the puppet theater, and the drawings of Callot or Goya; on the other side, the Rabelaisian world of fleshly delights and horrors and the excesses of over-eating, over-copulating, and over-excreting meet with images from Hieronymus Bosch and the Brueghels.

My approach follows some of Kayser's and Bakhtin's ideas but also varies significantly from their positions. Although both writers identify the grotesque as being out of the ordinary, against the grain, they do not elaborate on this point systematically. Both speak about a world standing on its head, but the German scholar limits his view to a mental asylum, a theater stage, and a dream, and the Russian scholar confines his to the boundaries of carnivalistic monstrosities. I accept the validity of these anti-worlds but add further ones: the anti-world of femininity as opposed to the world controlled by men; the anti-world of childhood as contradicted by the world governed by adults; the anti-world of the hidden, forbidden, apocryphal, and heretical as different from the universe of the established and sanctioned, canonical and orthodox; the anti-world of Satan, hell, paganism, and damnation as distinct from the world of Jesus, heaven, Christianity, and salvation; the anti-world of sin, flesh, and death as divided from the cosmos of virtue, spirit, and the eternal life; the anti-world of darkness and corruption, down below and to the left, as distant from the world of light and purity, high up and to the right; the anti-world of apocalypse, war, and disintegration as contrary to the world of peace, order, and togetherness.

The grotesque encompasses all these anti-worlds and envelops a relatively stable subculture that can be defined, formally and iconographically, in relation to official or dominant European culture as it existed between the end of the Renaissance and the end of the nineteenth century. But, one might ask, why in this period alone? There are several reasons for this. First of all, the term "grotesque" and the appearance of a style denoted by this word dates back to the discovery of Roman "grottoes" in the time of the Renaissance and the subsequent imitation of paintings found there. The great interest in these frescoes stemmed from the fact that in them antiquity revealed its monstrous face, relatively unknown until then.

This discovery changed more than a perception of antiquity. Soon the ancient monstrosities were related to whatever strange and uncanny beings could be found first in art, later in life as well. Thus the old Roman and the new Italian "grotesque" were associated with the fantastic art of the Middle Ages—drolleries, diableries, gargoyles, and the monsters on the margins of illuminated manuscripts. All these phenomena were in turn connected with the "grottoes" and immersed in the symbolism of the cave. This stimulated a new awareness, an artistic and philosophical consciousness that was most explicitly formulated by the German satirist Johann Fischart (1545–91) when he subsumed under the "wundergestalte Grillische, Grubengrotteschische" ("the miraculously-shaped grylli, the cave-grotesque")[4] the mixed and heterogeneous creatures of antiquity, the horrible and ludicrous aspects of Ovid, Apuleius, Dante, and Giotto, the medieval representations of devils, sinners, vices, and of Saint Anthony's temptations, Michelangelo's Last Judgment, the visions of Rabelais, the excesses of the carnival, and his own fantastic work resulting from the derision of the Catholic church. Combining the notion of strange creatures with the remembrance of grylli (monsters engraved in ancient stones) and recalling frescoes painted in the ancient "grottoes," Fischart suggested that the distorted, fantastic, and grotesque belonged not only to each other but to the underworld as well. His perception serves as a point of departure for my own definition of the grotesque as a subculture that emerged at the end of the Renaissance and functioned in opposition to the official culture until the beginning of the twentieth century.

The distorting procedures used by artists of the grotesque can be traced back to humanity's earliest history and discovered in the artistic production of all times and cultures. However, what might have been perceived from the European point of view as a distorting and fantastic effect need not have been considered upsetting or ridiculous in the culture of its origin. There it could have been the norm: a perfectly familiar way of seeing and expressing the world. In primitive and exotic art, monstrosity does not represent a reaction to and a subversion of an orderly, balanced, and humanistic canon, such as had been established in Europe by the time of classical antiquity. It simply reflects a different symbolism and set of metaphors, another religion's concepts and way of life.

The problem of fluctuating norms is evident in a more restricted way even in one's own culture. The flow of time turns banalities into strange riddles. This affects, of course, the grotesque as well. One must assume that even the greatest monstrosities might have been considered less shocking at the time of their creation simply because people were more used to them. But the reverse can happen as well. A fantasy might become real, as did the homunculus-reverie of the alchemists when the first babies were produced from test-tubes. During the four hundred years of the grotesque tradition the standards did not remain universally consistent. Both the Church and the State gradually liberalized their attitudes and showed more tolerance of religious, political, social, and sexual dissent. But the grotesque was only slightly affected by these transformations because of its ahistorical, archaic, and existential character. Thus the core of the grotesque consciousness—a combination of the introvert and egocentric, at once pleasure centered and death oriented, infantile yet ironically and intellectually rebellious—was preserved until the beginning of the twentieth century. This relative autonomy and stability distinguished the grotesque from satire and caricature, which also feed on official culture, deride and debase it, using the same formal procedures as the grotesque. But satire and caricature sting momentarily; they react immediately to rapid changes and by being more dependent on the attacked subjects possess an ephemeral nature.

The grotesque can be distinguished from the fantastic products of Greek and Roman antiquity and other cultures as well as from European satire and caricature not so much by its form as by its subject matter. That is why it is necessary to concentrate on the iconography. Seen against the background of iconographic material, the problem of strange transformations can be better understood. Accordingly, the techniques which lead to distorting effects are discussed at the end of this book.

Not intending to offer a complete history of the grotesque, I have deliberately left out fields of research already covered by other scholars. I do not discuss in detail the origins and problems of fantastic medieval art presented in depth by Jurgis Baltrušaitis's excellent book.[5] A separate section, however, is assigned to Hieronymus Bosch (perhaps the most unconventional artist of the entire European tradition) and his vision of the world as an animated globe-grotto, a material paradise and hell in one. While the rather homogeneous Italian masters of the grotesque are treated as a group, a brief section is dedicated to another extremely original artist, Giuseppe Arcimboldo, whose pictures mirror better than anything else the principles of a heterogeneous assemblage and raise the important issue of metaphorical thinking as a source of the grotesque. These three sections of chapter 6 together point to the origins of the fantastic and grotesque in the following traditions: in the prehistorical, animistic symbolism of the primordial unity of all matter; in those mythologies of antiquity, or parts of them, in which this sense of belonging together had been preserved; and in the metaphorical way of thinking, which, by equating anything with something else, re-creates the frame of mind of pre-rational humanity and represents the oldest symbolic way of perceiving reality and one's place in it.

The words "fantastic" and "grotesque" are used in this book in a dual way, designating, on one hand the particular, on the other hand the general. The particular meaning of "fantastic" refers to the monstrosities of medieval art; the particular meaning of "grotesque" applies to Italian art created under the influence of the paintings discovered in the Roman "grottoes." The mixture of these two traditions led to the appearance of the "grotesque" which became the underground of European culture. The features of this new subterranean tradition are subsequently called "fantastic" and "grotesque" and are treated more or less as synonyms. However, when medieval features predominate, the word "fantastic" is used; when ancient monstrosity prevails, the phenomenon is described as "grotesque."

My study of the grotesque goes back to my earlier books on fin-de-siècle Vienna and the art of Aubrey Beardsley.[6] This interest in the late nineteenth century has certainly influenced my viewpoint and choice of subject. But there is more to it. Kayser noticed that the uncanny and absurd flourished in certain periods more vigorously than in others, and Bakhtin tied the grotesque to periods of spiritual unrest and crisis. Indeed, it seems that strangeness and exaggeration marked the state of transition at the end of antiquity, the Middle Ages, the Renaissance, and the nineteenth century—the agony of an old world and the birth of a new world. The transition into the twentieth century can be considered a turning point more radical than others, when not centuries but millennia of beliefs collapsed and were exchanged for a scientific and technological approach toward reality. Remains of ancient mythologies and religions have survived in and even dominated the ideologies of the twentieth century. But in Western Europe and in the United States Christianity has undergone an accelerating process of ossification since the end of the nineteenth century. This gradual fossilization of Christian beliefs caused the fin de siècle to be the last period in European history when the sacrosanct mattered enough to provoke sacrilegious attacks. But the disintegration of Christianity constituted only one aspect of the general cultural crisis. At the outbreak of the First World War Europe ceased to be the closed world which once considered itself superior to all other civilizations, standing proudly on its Greco-Roman-Christian foundations and consciously preserving its particular traditions. The generation of our grandparents was the last to read the Latin and Greek authors in the original in secondary school, to copy Roman and Renaissance statues at the academies of fine arts, and to have had in their bedrooms lamps in the form of Diana surrounded by her hounds. The current adult generation—not to mention contemporary children—finds it difficult to read properly the iconographic language which at the turn of the century was still spoken fluently not only by artists but even by educated children. This ignorance reflects the emergence of a new tradition, founded at the beginning of the twentieth century by the European avant-garde, which deliberately detached itself from its own past. The constructivists felt closer to machines than to Greek or Christian gods; the expressionists and cubists preferred African masks to those worn by the Muses.

In this respect the fate of Europe was by no means unique. Through transportation and communication even the oldest and remotest corners of the earth were opened up and their cultures exploited, mixed with others, and combined into one global collage. Thus every aspect of contemporary culture has become heterogeneous, and the chaotic and confused has become the principle of our time. The influx and assimilation of the exotic coincided with the rapid uprooting of old standards and traditions and (at least in the most developed Western countries) with the drive toward religious, ideological, and sexual tolerance. The moment a Baptist church and a synagogue, the quarters of the Communist party and the Ku

Klux Klan, a homosexual sauna and a lesbian cabaret all have the legal right to exist, it makes no sense to uphold the traditional notion of a cultural underground.

But nothing gets completely lost as long as humanity survives. One can still trace dim shadows of the traditional grotesque in twentieth-century visual arts and literature, theater and film. They remain, however, echoes of a world that is not with us any longer. The grotesque may be vaguely remembered and written about in scholarly publications, but it does not rule the imagination. Sphinx-like combinations and manifestations of the archaic and infantile can be clearly seen in dadaism, surrealism, neo-expressionism, collages, and happenings. Distortions and displacements represent, indeed, the most common quality of modern and postmodern art. But the application of these formal procedures was never unique to the grotesque. They were used in ancient and primitive art and in European caricature and satire as well. What made the grotesque a distinct subculture was not the use of distortion but the fact that it was used in order to oppose and subvert official Christian culture with inappropriate forms and shocking iconography or, when derision and demonization were sanctioned (as in the case of an artist's rendering of Satan or hell)—to depict a horrible, ludicrous, and dead wrong anti-world of devouring females, animalistic men, heretics, and Jews. Who knows or cares today about the animated cave of Venus-Salome and Amor-Judas, or worries about their enemies, the Christian saints. This iconography, forgotten or seemingly irrelevant—yet the very essence of the grotesque—no longer touches the heart of contemporary artists, nor does it inspire their visions.

The work of Aubrey Beardsley, the major subject of the second part of this book, is considered the most brilliant example of the last stage of the European grotesque. Representing the closure of a four-centuries-old tradition, his art reflects the grotesque of previous ages in a distorting and magnifying mirror that blends seriousness with parody and horror with delight. A true epigone, decadent and manneristic, as well as an artist of extreme originality, Beardsley replayed the great themes of the grotesque, clothed them in ludicrously inflated forms, and buried them in a grave of masks, quotations, obscenities, and sacrileges. Other artists of the fin de siècle engaged in this as well, but Beardsley alone recognized the grotesque as the essence of his art and dedicated himself to the excavation of that which is subterranean and embryonic. Combining formal inventiveness with the courage to transcend the limits of what was already permitted, he formulated with ironic clarity the erotic obsessions of his times.

Afflicted from early childhood with tuberculosis, Beardsley led the "grotesque" life of an invalid who had to be taken care of and knew that he was doomed to die young. He spent his days mostly resting or in bed, worked outside his home for only a brief period in his life, and stayed from birth to death under the protection of his mother, his older sister, and other female relatives. Although he did not receive much of a formal education, he had plenty of time to educate himself by reading books, looking at illustrations, and, whenever he felt strong enough, by visiting museums and bookstores. In rare texts and in curious pictures, in paintings, prints, and sculptures, Beardsley looked for reflections of his own fate: at times a quasi-fetal vegetation enveloped in feverish dreams about sex. Unable to participate in any practical activity, he lived in order to put his fantasies onto paper and to escape through them from his only reality—illness. He was an archeologist of the past and the unconscious, and a man of the night. Beardsley's crippled existence coincided with the general malaise and the apocalyptic mood of the fin de siècle, with its delight in the unhealthy and perverse, the subterranean and obscure. While Des Esseintes, the hero of Huysmans's novel *À rebours* (1884), transformed his house into an artificial cave, Beardsley was trapped in a grotto by destiny. He was therefore the ideal medium to utter the dreams of the dying European world—to express in his work a delirious *hypnerotomachia* which nobody, including himself, could take quite seriously.

The old grotesque is dead. But this does not mean that modern civilization, urban, computerized, atheistic, and ready to leave the globe for other planets, will not develop in the future some sort of underground culture, based, perhaps, on the remembrance and reverie of old mother-earth, abandoned, transformed, or even destroyed. It is possible that the materialistic and mechanistic consciousness of our age will result in an archaic and infantile-seeming subculture reminding us of the primordial unity of all things. This book, however, contents itself with the study of the past and does not venture into the future where a new sphinx, half human and half machine, may well await us.

Origins of the Grotesque

Chapter 1 · The Norm

"We must stop . . . mothers being misled by . . . and scaring their children by perversions of the myths, and telling tales about a host of fantastic spirits that prowl about at night." . . .

"It is not only to the poets therefore that we must issue orders requiring them to represent good character in their poems or not to write at all; we must issue similar orders to all artists and prevent them portraying bad character, ill-discipline, meanness, or ugliness in painting, sculpture, architecture, or any work of art, and if they are unable to comply they must be forbidden to practise their art."

—Plato, *The Republic*, 381 and 401, in H. D. P. Lee's trans.

 The meaning of the grotesque is constituted by the norm which it contradicts: the order it destroys, the values it upsets, the authority and morality it derides, the religion it ridicules, the harmony it breaks up, the heaven it brings down to earth, the position of classes, races, and sexes it reverses, the beauty and goodness it questions. The word "grotesque" makes sense only if one knows what the "norm" represents—in art and in life.

When the whites arrived in Africa, they perceived in the naked and tattooed blacks grotesque incarnations of medieval devils; but to the blacks, the whites in their boots, hats, and uniforms seemed like monsters from the moon. If the norm is white skin, black skin is regarded as a freak of nature, and vice versa; black fanatics tend to whitewash Satan.[1] Racists maintain that the color of their own skin is normal, original, and beautiful, while all others are abnormal, derivative, and ugly.[2] Similarly, the distant and exotic may easily be designated as "grotesque." However, the subject of this book is the "grotesque" in the narrow sense, when it contradicts the norms of European culture.

The extremely revealing etymology of the world "grotesque" captures its essence as if *in flagrante*. The term was coined in Italy at the time of the Renaissance when the overgrown ruins of Roman villas and baths were

11

excavated in the vicinity of Rome and Pompeii. The ancient remains were not properly identified but were believed, falsely, to represent "artificial grottoes" dug in antiquity for Diana and the nymphs.[3] This error determined the definition of the grotesque and outlined its territory, committing therein a mistake truly Freudian in character. Because the ruins were thought to be caves, the mural decoration preserved on their walls, or more precisely that part of it with which the Italians were completely unfamiliar, was called "grotesque" (coming from and belonging to the cave). This unfamiliar part consisted of frames or borders surrounding well-known mythological scenes. These frames, typical examples of late Roman style, were made from floral, animal, architectural, and human elements which, winding one around the other and growing into each other, formed a surprising and ambiguous whole. Before this discovery the Renaissance notion of ancient art was based primarily on knowledge of classical sculpture and architecture. Consequently, the newly discovered heterogeneous and chaotic frames contradicted the norms of clarity, balance, and harmony, features which were assumed to have governed the ancient mind.

At the time of its first appearance, the late Roman style was criticized by Vitruvius.[4] It must have been equally disturbing to Renaissance humanists like Alberti, who, in accordance with the Pythagorean-Platonic tradition, considered the beauty of both nature and art to be the product of three ideal proportions—the arithmetic, the geometric, and the musical.[5] Alberti expected every artist to strive for these proportions through a faithful study of nature and its laws. He defined the process of creation as a conscious activity subordinated to rational rules. Consequently, the art which resulted from it could be analyzed objectively. Of course great artists hardly ever conformed to this ideal, not even in the Renaissance. In the course of his life Michelangelo moved away from classical harmony and clarity toward convulsive dissonance and opacity. He appreciated the Roman grotesque,[6] and some of his colleagues truly delighted in it.[7] Stimulated by the late style of antiquity, Raphael developed his own fantastic designs as frames for the religious scenes which he painted in the Vatican.

Alberti's norm was opposed by the mannerist artists whom John Ruskin called "grotesque" and reproached for indulging in Medusan horrors and vulgar satire.[8] A disregard for rules, norms, and proportion was also expressed in the theory of the aesthetician Emanuele Tesauro (1591–1675), who suggested that all the arts have one thing in common: metaphor, which he defined as a poetical imitation by means of words, objects, or real actions.[9] But the classical period of antiquity and the Italian Renaissance remained an ideal until the late nineteenth century, and Alberti's doctrine had become the academic standard for European art schools, a standard which can be encountered even today in the most conservative institutions of that kind. However, the unexpected discovery of the Roman "grotesque" changed the perception of antiquity. Ancient clarity and harmony, so suitable for expressing the normative aims of a civil and religious order, could no longer be seen in absolute terms. Balanced figurative scenes formed only the center, which was surrounded by the fantastic and chaotic; under the sunlit surface of white marble extended an obscure grotto.

At the time of the Renaissance, paganism invaded the Christian world; the nakedness and liveliness of ancient figures promoted an interest in the realistic depiction of the human body. In order to prevent artists from dedicating themselves exclusively to the representation of pagan gods and goddesses, the Church had to show a certain liberalism about nakedness. Sensuality and eroticism entered Christian art, and soon analogies between biblical stories and pagan mythology were discovered: the Virgin with the Child, for instance, was seen from that point on in the mirror of love that once bound Venus and Amor. Although spirituality, so forcefully present in earlier Christian art, had to be sacrificed, the central and humanistic perspective of the Renaissance also offered certain benefits. It brought Christ and the Madonna into a new focus. Once viewed as the personifications of spiritual perfection, they now were regarded as the incarnations of ideal human beauty. In the light, abstract, and rational interior of a Renaissance church, the figures of Jesus and Mary could play a more important role than in the fantastically crowded medieval cathedrals. Thus the Church had good reasons to welcome the classical norm, which disturbed ascetic ideals but helped introduce the saints as true models for mankind.

The spirituality of early Christian art was achieved through a process of abstraction and formalization, through desensualizing the human figure and hiding the body under mounds of stiff folds. As soon as the artist worked from a model, that is, painted the Virgin after his wife and Jesus after his baby son, the sexuality which had emanated from his beloved was transferred to the image of the Holy Family. When divine and mystical love was translated into human experience, a certain degree of obscenity was bound to enter the sacred scenes. Although the Madonna or her mother, Anna, could fondle or display the genitals of Christ, and he, in turn, could caress his mother with the gesture of a lover,[10] there were limits to what could be represented. In no church, for instance, could Christ with a tail or Mary making love to Joseph be shown. The Christian ideal of immaculate love was slightly corrupted by the subjective intimacy inherent in every realistic representation, but the overflow of subjectivity and eroticism was controlled by the classical norm. This norm required that the supreme gods be represented in an idealized, harmonious, and balanced form to be derived, as in antiquity, from a study of well-shaped men and women. Ugly, defective, distorted, and beastly human features were reserved for the devil and his helpers.

During the Renaissance the norm established for the representation of virtue and sainthood in religious art combined the aesthetic ideals of classical antiquity with Christian canons. Artists were allowed to depict a certain degree of sensuality and nakedness but still had to conform to the core of Christian doctrine, which prescribed that the good be shown as superior, central, and edifying; evil, on the contrary, was to be depicted as debased, marginal, and monstrous. While the holy figures could be shaped after heroic pagan gods and noble ancient goddesses, the devils, witches, and sinners were modeled from satyrs, sirens, and cripples (fig. 1). A large reservoir of monstrosity could be found in the immediate past— the late Middle Ages. Baltrušaitis traces fantastic medieval art to distant ages and regions—to ancient Egypt, Mesopotamia, Persia, India, and China—as well as to "monstrous" Greek and Roman antiquity (fig. 2),[11] in which the dark and bestial "other side" both opposed and complemented the light and humanistic face. Baltrušaitis argues that the two faces that together had once formed a unity were broken apart by Christianity, which separated good from evil and, by condemning the latter, repressed and subordinated the fantastic. But the uncanny lived subterraneously, ready to surface whenever circumstances turned favorable. An explosion of the fantastic took place at the end of the Middle Ages. In the late Gothic style the figures of saints and sacred events represented on the altars, tympanons, and pages of illustrated books are surrounded by the freakish and indecent.[12] Outside the Gothic cathedrals an army of gargoyles sparks with brutal popular humor and obscene memories of paganism; inside, even the metaphysical colored light is "framed" by the chimerical creatures jumping from the walls, ceilings, columns, arches, and floors. The fantastic flourished in the late Middle Ages with the vitality of tropical nature. Every inch of the stonework appears animated, seems to pulsate and to breathe.

Although omnipresent, the fantastic remained at the periphery; the middle of every church was reserved for the cross, the Savior, the Virgin, the Holy Trinity. However, the periphery played a marginal role more in theory than in practice: the eye could not help being attracted away from the center; it marveled as it moved from one "shapeless shapeliness" to another "shapely shapelessness," as Saint Bernard of Clairevaux called the fantastic.[13] He disapproved of it as much as Vitruvius and worried that the nonsensically sculpted stones might exercise a corrupting influence upon the monks, making them "prefer to read the marbles rather than the books."[14] His words certainly expressed the view of the Church, which disliked the fantastic not only because of its formlessness and absurdity but because it represented a link to demons of the past which had survived in popular traditions. Religious authorities realized that they had to live with the drolleries just as they had to tolerate the remains of pagan beliefs and rituals in superstitions and folk festivals. But the Church never recognized in the presence of this older world anything but the reflection of human imperfection—a dark side of human nature which it hoped to eliminate by means of Christian illumination.

When the Roman frescoes were discovered and the term "grotesque" was coined for them, there already existed the fantastic art and architecture of the late Middle Ages. Both traditions shared many formal and icono-graphic similarities as well as the ambiguous and rather inferior status of the "underground" and the "frame" as opposed to the central, officially approved mode of representation; they stood for peripheral, aesthetically and morally dubious decoration.

Comparing the Roman frescoes with medieval fantastic art, one of course discovers differences. The ancient grotesque appears altogether lighter in tone, more playful and relaxed. One senses behind it an erotically permissive world, with strictness applied more to architecture than mo-rality. The fantastic production of the Middle Ages reflects the repression and banishment of what is sensual, sexual, and pagan. The craftsmen sculpting the gargoyles and the monks decorating the margins of illustrated books must have felt that they engaged in a slightly suspect activity when, instead of glorifying the virtue of the Virgin, they delighted in monsters, which according to the faith were meant to be destroyed, not immortalized (fig. 3). Whenever some Saint Bernard questioned the dragons and volup-tuous females seated among the branches of a colorful tree, the monks probably reacted in a way similar to my Polish publisher. In the Central Committee of the Communist party he was asked why he was bringing out a book on the grotesque, the most decadent Western swinishness, instead of, for instance, a volume on the victorious October Revolution. He answered: to fight evil we have to know it; and then, in a brief tête-à-tête with each of the strictest guardians of the Socialist morality, he prom-ised to present them with a copy of my book, which he assured them they would "prefer to read." Nothing excites the imagination more than the forbidden; and the cat-and-mouse game between one's interior and exterior censors may be quite pleasurable, provided that the cat cannot or does not wish to catch the mouse. The late Middle Ages was a liberal period leading into the Renaissance. One could indulge in dubious dreams and create unorthodox images without too much risk.

In every religion and ideology there is a place reserved for the ridic-ulous, demonic, and malicious. Oriental exoticism, Greek and Roman mon-strosities, caricatures of pagan divinities, and horrible distortions of human features were welcome in the Christian depiction of hell,[15] of satanic temp-tations, and in illustrations of the Revelation. The devil and the world governed by him were traditionally represented to the left of the judging Christ and more generally on the left-hand side of altars, paintings, and sculptural compositions as seen from within the picture (i.e., to the right of the viewer standing in front of them) (fig. 4). This pattern had been defined in the early renditions of the apocalypse, of which the oldest dates from the end of the third or the beginning of the fourth century, and in the equally old images of the Original Sin. The earliest representation of the Last Judgment shows Christ seated on a rock in the manner of a philosopher, with his right hand welcoming eight sheep, with his left hand repulsing five goats (fig. 5).[16] There is nothing obviously demonic in this picture, and one has to know the symbolism of the sheep (good) and the goats (evil) as well as the meaning of the numbers (eight representing resurrection and life, five standing for crucifixion and death)[17] to understand that it exhibits a moral judgment. The composition presupposes an animal symbolism[18] inherited from paganism and presents good and evil as existing together rather than in contradiction; both are represented as familiar beasts cared for by the shepherd. However, as bucolic as it may seem, the relief introduces the still common image of a goat-like, horned devil as set against Jesus, John the Baptist,[19] and other martyrs—lamb-like victims of demonic cruelty. In early Christian art a lamb changes water into wine and raises Lazarus;[20] it hangs, with crown and nimbus, on the cross. Because we have lost track of the old norm we find these animalistic incarnations of Christ monstrous and fantastic. Apparently they did not please the Church either: in A.D. 692 a council decreed that henceforth Jesus could not be rendered in the shape of a sheep.

Worlds separate the first Last Judgment, quiet and restrained, from later representations of this theme. From the Romanesque period onwards, the division of good and evil is portrayed as absolute. Artists indulge in the fantastic and horrible visions of John the Evangelist; crowds of the damned float and fall down to the left of the avenging Christ on the altars of Jan van Eyck or Hans Memling. The old animalistic setting is forgotten, at least in official religious art. But, not accidentally, it is remembered in a grotesque engraving by the Renaissance artist Giovanni Antonio da Brescia, who offers a satire of the sacred theme by replacing Christ with a fantastic Pegasus.[21]

In depictions of the Fall, Eve stands to the left of Adam (i.e., to the viewer's right), with the snake turning toward her.[22] Occasionally, the viper has a female head and looks like the mirror-image of the first woman (fig. 6). This order reflects the traditional hierarchy of values in which man comes first, woman second. Because we read from left to right, it appears natural that Adam is encountered by the eye before his wife (even today in most documents the man signs on the left or on top, the woman on the right or underneath). However, this order fixes the place to the left of Christ, Adam, the tree and the cross as the side of the female who succumbs to the temptation of evil. To understand the severity of the moral judgment implicit in the pictures of Original Sin one has but to recall that the tree of life was imagined as the one out of which the cross of the Savior was made (fig. 7). This automatically puts Eve with the serpent on the side of the accused, who will be mercilessly judged when the final day comes.

Thus, the wrong way is linked in Christianity to evil and femininity as well as to death.

Philippe Ariès observes that in the late Middle Ages death, which until then had been taken as the natural conclusion of every human life, began to acquire increasingly demonic features.[23] Chambers of the dying were invaded by Satan and his army of monsters, who tempted those passing away and waited to snatch their souls. A battle similar to the one to be fought on the last day was carried out against the intimate background of personal agony. This demonization of death was accompanied by its eroticization. The paintings of Hans Baldung (d.1545), for instance, depict sexual intercourse between the living and the dead.[24] Ariès believes that these macabre representations originated from a changed attitude toward death, which was then regarded as a rapture, similar to orgasm, rather than as a natural phase in the cycle of life.[25] This interpretation, however, disregards the fact that death was already eroticized in many medieval depictions of the Last Judgment and hell. In the paintings of Bosch, hell is the seat of copulation and conception, birth and death, where monsters unite with each other, creep out of broken eggs, and are immediately devoured. Baldung's skeletons embracing young girls are a new formulation of the old Christian pattern which has always married evil and death to sexuality and femininity. However, this could be rendered more suggestively by means of a style which gradually liberated itself from the abstract, hieratic, and schematic and adopted a naturalistic means of expression. Fantastic medieval art, like the Roman grotesque, is grounded upon a careful observation of nature. The increasingly concrete and therefore more shocking forms of the erotic danse macabre were promoted not so much by a new attitude toward death as by an increased interest in the human figure: by the study of living models as well as of corpses and skeletons in the dissecting rooms.

The visual arts translated Christianity's moral dualism into the polarity of the "right" and "left," the "up" and "down," the "male" and "female," "life" and "death." The symbolism of the good and evil way was projected onto already existing religious and philosophical patterns. In the Jewish bible the polarization of right and left already had a ritual and theological significance. In Greece the gods lived on top of Olympus and the road to Hades led underground. The symbolism of the crossroads and the two possible ways of life is incarnated by the letter Y. It is said that Pythagoras regarded Y as the symbol of human life (fig. 8). Several Roman poets refer to this, and two lines of Persius (iii.56–57) seem to imply that there existed an older form (γ) written from right to left. The straight road was seen as the difficult one, the deviating line as the easier path of vice.[26]

Christianity was based on the glorification of a male trinity, and thus femininity was pushed down and to the left. The exception made for the Virgin did not prevent misogyny, though it helped to establish some kind of distinction between good and wicked women. For instance, on the medieval triptychs representing the life of John the Baptist, the Virgin, who stands to the right of Christ, is opposed by Salome, the terrible personification of femininity, standing to his left (fig. 9). The pictures of female martyrs and saints correct the unseemly images of womanhood as well. But the depictions of female virtue did not possess enough power to efface or even balance the fact that Eve, the first woman, was represented, together with the snake, to the left, where hell and the crowds of the damned were to be found. She remained thus an omnipresent symbol of female corruption which caused the fall of humanity: her figure was visibly associated with the tragic descent into darkness, underground, and death (fig. 10); and it stood for nature's imperfection (fig. 11).

It is essential to recall that in medieval art the fantastic was relegated to the frame and the margin; that the producers of the "shapely shapelessness" derived their inspirations from the pagan (i.e., wicked) past; that their strange creations were not received with great sympathy by the religious authorities, but that monstrosity was welcomed by the Church when applied with the intention to demonize and deride the forces of evil; and, finally, that the fantastic occupied the left side of the altars, as seen from within the picture, or their lower part. This side, down and to the left, corresponded to femininity, which the ancient and universal mythological equations identified with earth and matter, with darkness and night, with the underworld and hell, and opposed to the male symbols: sky and spirit, light, day, and heaven. With all this in mind, one realizes the symbolic consequences of the mistake that linked the strange frames winding around the mythological tableaux in late Roman frescoes to the excavated "grottoes" of Diana and the nymphs and established the word "grotesque." One begins also to understand why the Roman grotesques could be, and indeed were, related not only to fantastic medieval productions but to everything that on the one side displayed some monstrous features and on the other was to be encountered off center and to the left, in the underground and in the closet, in the darkness and in the night. Through the discovery of the "grottoes," the entire fantastic art, which shared some similarities with the late Roman style, became associated with the subterranean, connected to the pagan past, and attached to femininity, which was present in the "caves" in manifold ways.

Chapter 2 · The Cave

The notion of the cave is central to the proper study of the grotesque. Nevertheless, its importance has usually escaped the attention of scholars or been only alluded to. Most recently Geoffrey Harpham referred to caves—and their mythology—as sources of the grotesque,[1] but in spite of many illuminating remarks he remains on the threshold of the problem, turning back too far through history. Instead of focusing on the Roman and Greek caves which were responsible for the etymology of the "grotesque" and which had a well-established position in European art, literature, and mythology, he discusses prehistoric caves which were discovered only in the course of the twentieth century. Dealing with them helps, of course, to understand the complex symbolism of the cave, but it shifts the emphasis unnecessarily to a particular subgroup that has barely any relevance to the term "grotesque" or the fantastic territory it inhabits in the European tradition. In order to understand the grotesque one has to analyze the appearance and meaning of a cave as such, and then to remember the particular character and mythology of European caves.

The grotto is a cavity inside the earth, either natural or artificial in origin (fig. 12). Natural caves come into existence by tectonic displacement or by the action of water. Artificial caves have been dug by humans since time immemorial. Both natural and artificial caves have served humanity as shelters, homes, hideouts, storage places, temples, and tombs. In ancient Greece, oracles were located in the grottoes, and diverse cults and mysteries were celebrated in them. Artificial caves were built for Artemis and the nymphs; Apollo and the Muses, originally nymphs of the water springs, were worshiped in the caves (fig. 13).[2] Orgies were celebrated in the grotto of Pan and the nymphs on Mount Parnassus.

Both the natural and the artificial grottoes are dark, cold, and damp. Their entrances may be visible and easy to find, but they may also be almost inaccessible, naturally or artificially hidden. Similarly, some caves can be crossed without difficulty; others turn out to be labyrinths from which, as in the legend of Ariadne's thread, a male explorer can escape only when a female is prepared to help him. The ambiguity of the cave arises from the fact that it offers protection but imprisons as well, that it rapidly turns from a shelter to a trap. These features of the subterranean correspond to the perception of woman as one who, carrying the embryo, nurtures as well as imprisons it. Birth liberates the baby from the body of the mother; but when a child does not emerge in time, it dies inside. Thus, the woman appears as a vessel of life as well as death. Fertile femininity is traditionally adored, but we find that contacts with women are feared by primitive men throughout the world.[3] This anguish is reflected in taboos imposed on women in early societies and in myths which recall the imprisonment within the female body. In those legends the danger of being captivated concerns not only real men but also diverse symbols of masculinity, as, for instance, the sun, which in the evening descends into the earth and in the morning has difficulties ascending from her womb.[4] The weakness felt by men after sexual intercourse has probably contributed to the legend of the female vampire and the vagina with teeth.

Because of the association with the womb and the cave, all closed spaces tend to be perceived as female and are associated with both protection and threat. Every closed space can be transformed into a cave-like shelter or prison by being isolated from the outside, painted black and darkened. The interior decoration of many bedrooms is clearly intended to give them the intimate shape and character of a motherly vessel. Studios and bathrooms also occasionally display the features of grottoes. A cave-like atmosphere is the rule in brothels, catacombs, and other secret meeting places. But also museums, wine cellars, hothouses, stores, libraries, and archives may be modeled after grottoes, and, in general, all dark, hidden ruins and solitary enclosures where some forbidden or unknown activity takes place are frequently referred to as caves.[5] In architectural imitations of real and artificial grottoes, chandeliers, lamps, vases, and columns are fashioned after stalactites and stalagmites; marbles and precious stones suggest the veins of the earth and geological layers; basins, fountains, and bathtubs are often shell-shaped. Grotto-like architecture shows a fascination with the subaqueous and oscillates, as do some natural caves, between a subterranean hall and an aquarium.

Natural and artificial grottoes may display enchanting and even artistic beauty as well as disgusting ugliness. The interior of the body has been universally perceived as the residence of the soul. In the Greco-Roman tradition the soul was addressed as female (psyche, anima) and represented as a maiden with bird or butterfly wings, or as a butterfly.[6] Jung's concept of man's female soul (anima) can be traced back to Apuleius's tale of Amor and Psyche, a lovely girl kept by the god of love in a splendid subterranean chamber. But a cave can also incarnate the foul, smelly, and contaminated texture of disintegrating flesh and of feces. Just as the ground is fertilized by dead bodies, "homo" and "humus" are related to each other.[7] The inside of the human body can be visualized as the charming bedroom of a young girl, but it can also be imagined as Pandora's box or a leaking sack filled with liquid impurity. In particular the anus and the vagina of a sick or old woman have always been among the favorite subjects of dirty jokes that compare them to sinks, cesspools, and latrines, or to the devil's kitchen.

This kind of humor is based on comparisons of eating, digesting, and excreting with sexuality, conception, and birth on the one hand, and with the creating of an idea or a work of art on the other. The image of God making humans out of the dust of the earth is repeated in the experience of a child molding clay or sand and in the efforts of a sculptor. But we also make our excrement, and it is well known that children and mentally disturbed people attach to excrement the importance of creation.[8] Because of the nature of human anatomy, with the genitals situated next to the anus and the urinary tract, even the most sublimated fantasies of the mystical interiors of love are constantly threatened by the shadowy presence of the dirty, obscene, and ridiculous. Likewise, secret rituals that are celebrated in the subterranean moisture of a cave have always been suspected of involving some excessive, unclean, and forbidden form of sexuality.

Darkness reigns in the cave. Sunlight is completely kept out of the subterranean halls and corridors, which can be illuminated only by artificial light: a fire, a torch, a lamp. The absence of light reduces humans to the blind existence of moles. Absolute blackness represents a terrible punishment—it foreshadows death. Sunlight animates through its warmth; seeing forms leads to an understanding of their meaning. Light is universally equated with life, with reflection and consciousness, and with growth and development. The dark grotto seems to sleep or to vegetate in semi-consciousness or without consciousness. Its silent obscurity provokes another comparison with the condition of woman as the dumb, uneducated, and inarticulate sex. As true as this observation might appear at first, it must nevertheless be considered with caution. It is contradicted, for instance, by the ancient figure of the blind prophet or hypnotized shaman who receives illumination exactly because of his blindness, which protects him from the distractions caused by fleeting appearances and the thoughts stimulated by them.

One must remember that in antiquity the insight obtained through divination was more highly prized than the systematic knowledge of a philosopher. In *Phaedrus* Plato distinguishes between the "sane" form of divination and the "insane" one; the first consists of a cool interpretation of certain signs in accordance with certain rules; the second is worked by a prophet who, possessed by the deity, in a temporary seizure utters mystic speech under divine dictation. The most influential Greek oracle, the oracle of Apollo in Delphi,[9] was of the second type. The god there spoke through a woman known as the Pythia, who resided in the Corycian cave and was in early times a virgin, later a fifty-year-old matron attired as a maiden. The afflatus reached a climax when she seated herself upon the phallic tripod and, inspired by a vapor that arose from a fissure in the ground, uttered some probably incomprehensible words which were then edited and set to verse by the priests. At Argos, the prophetess of Apollo Pythius attained divine possession by drinking the blood of the lamb that was sacrificed to the god in the night. At the Aegean oracle in Achaea, the prophetess at the shrine of Ge drank bulls' blood for the same reason. No less popular was divination by incubation. In order to attain communion with a god or the spirit of a dead man, usually a hero, the person chosen as a medium lay down to sleep or awaited a vision in some holy place, often in a sacred grove or a grotto. A state of unconsciousness and sleep was by no means regarded as inferior; on the contrary, it was valued more than clear and rational thinking.

The Muses, whose voices the poets heard in the depths of the grotto, the lovely figure of Psyche, the passing shadow of Diana, the friendly demons consulted in sleep and trance, the fertile ground and the motherly home, the museum rich in memories—the complex positive symbolism of the ancient grotto—were transformed by Christianity into the negative image of the underworld as the country of the damned dead, that is, hell. Hades, the Greek god of the underworld, had a gloomy appearance, but both his name, derived from Αϊς and Αιδης (invisible, making invisible), and his frequent representation with a cornucopia reflected a mixed attitude toward his subterranean kingdom. His land was certainly feared (the name of Hades was often replaced by euphemisms), but it was also regarded as the storage place of mineral resources and as the cradle of life. In the *Odyssey* Hades is described as an unappealing but not particularly horrible cave: ". . . the cavern of some rifted den, / Where flock nocturnal bats, and birds obscene" (24:9–10). Homer calls it also "the dusky land of *Dreams*" (24:18) and "the regions of eternal shade" (24:232).[10] The passages concerned with the underworld are permeated by the sentiment of sadness, sorrow, and regret; the flow of metaphors is diffused by the sense of vanity. But the Homeric Hades is not a hell.

The Christian demonization of the underworld is foreshadowed by another great epic poem of antiquity: the *Aeneid*. Virgil worked on it until the very end of his life and left it unfinished at the threshold of the Christian era (he died in 19 B.C.). His visions of Hades epitomize the transformation of the ancient world; they reflect the fact that the previous unity broke into two antagonistic extremes even before the arrival of the new faith. Virgil sees the underworld not only in terms of a dark and evil empire but also as a territory dominated by terrible femininity, the deadly enemy of male energy and spirituality. The entrance to his Hades resembles "a cavern, yawning wide and deep, / . . . below the darkness of the trees, / Beside the darkness of the lake." Virgil stresses that no bird, the ancient symbol of the soul, the spirit, as well as of the phallus, "could fly above it safely, with the vapor / Pouring from the black gulf." The country that stretches out below links reminiscences of the terrible places on earth (hospitals, lunatic asylums, wretched brothels) with memories of mythological monsters (Furies, centaurs, Scylla, Chimerae, Harpies, Gorgons), the majority of which is female. Virgil's hell smells of forbidden and dirty sex: "sons of gods" descend into it to snatch the "queen from Pluto's chamber";[11] and it smells of putrid and corrupt flesh, of worn-out vaginas and dirty anuses. This disgusting, carnal hell was inspired by the negative symbolism of the cave. In turn, it might have influenced some of the obscene humor of antiquity at its end, such verses as, for instance, those by Nicarchus, a poet of the first century A.D. who likened the division of an old prostitute among her three clients to a visit in the underworld:

> Of her, I myself got her white sea to dwell in;
>   we divided her up, one part for each, no switching.
> Hermogenes got her broad "hateful abode,"
>   finally stealing into the secret place
> where are the shores of the dead, and windy wild fig trees
>   whirl in the blast of shrill-screaming winds.[12]

Christianity moved Virgil's subterranean monsters to its own hell—a mouth and a vagina dentata (fig. 14). But devilish phantoms escaped from it in order not only to pursue ordinary mortals but to molest with particular delight the Christian ascetics. The pattern was set by Christ himself, who on his return from Jordan was led into the desert and, staying there in solitary confinement and without any food, was tempted by the devil (Luke 4:1–13). Saint Anthony (b. ca. 250) followed in the footsteps of the Savior, spending not forty days but twenty years in the Egyptian desert, during which time he was constantly visited by the most horrible and charming incarnations of Satan. Anthony not only withstood the temptations but became the founder of the monastic movement: a group of men who settled in neighboring grottoes.

The first monk has become associated with repressed sexuality and the flood of erotic hallucinations caused by it. His torments form a basis for the approach toward monastic seclusion which ever since has been suspected of hidden, imagined, or real obscenity. It is not a coincidence that as an artistic and literary subject the temptations of Saint Anthony were greatly favored by the masters of the fantastic. He was drawn and painted by Bosch and the Brueghels, and their depictions inspired, among other writings, *The Temptations of Saint Anthony* by Gustave Flaubert,[13] who wrote three versions of the Egyptian monk's erotic hallucinations and viewed this text as a greater achievement than *Madame Bovary*. With respect to the impact *The Temptations* made on his contemporaries he was certainly right. The book was read as a Bible in reverse, and the powerful women introduced in it (in particular the queen of Sheba, who in all her splendor visits Anthony's humble cave) were viewed, together with the queen of Carthage in his *Salammbô* (1862) and Herod's wife in his *Hérodias* (1877), as prototypes for the fin-de-siècle icon of voluptuousness.

While Saint Anthony was tortured by erotic dreams, the Renaissance monk Francesco Colonna composed out of his sexual reverie a fantastic novel entitled *Hypnerotomachia Poliphili* [*The Dream of Poliphilo*]. His text, illustrated and published anonymously in 1499 in Venice, was translated into English and French and has ever since delighted and inspired lovers of the rare, obscure, and erotic. *Hypnerotomachia Poliphili*, called by one of its scholars the *Finnegans Wake* of the fifteenth century,[14] is most suitable for the study of the grotesque in literature. It begins in the very setting that has supplied the name "grotesque": amid ancient ruins where the hero of the novel wanders ready to escape from the responsibilities and rigors of adult life into subterranean depths filled with pleasure and love. Colonna leaves no doubt that the beloved whom the hero seeks behind the door inscribed "Mater Amoris" is his own mother (fig. 15). Moreover, he finds her in the personification of Venus, whose hymen he perforates in order to gain access to the ultimate cave, her womb. But the desire to return to an embryonic state is accompanied by fear of death: the incestuous defloration is followed by a vision of the Mother of Love, in the attitude of a Madonna, nurturing the baby Amor (fig. 16). Ultimately the mother and her son turn out to be dead; they are just stone figures seated on top of a sarcophagus. Colonna's underworld is the seat of the pagan past and of death—of sexuality, conception, infancy, sleep, and dream; thus it contains the utmost delight mixed with inconsolable sorrow. This paradise-grotto is devoid of signs of hell. The Venetian monk has proved to be truly a man of the Renaissance; liberated from medieval repression, he made the garden of Venus grow in the grotto of the nymphs and did not admit any of Saint Anthony's monsters to his cave.

Chapter 3 · Alchemy

One of Jung's pupils has written about *Hypnerotomachia Poliphili* as an alchemical treatise.[1] Although Colonna's novel cannot be reduced to alchemy, the connection is most interesting and points to the imaginary relationship between the underground and alchemy, a secret science, and between the cave, the womb, and the hermetic bottle in which life was supposed to be hatched.

In the narrow sense of the word, alchemy was the art of making gold; in the broader sense, it was a theory of transmutation and a magic, pre- or pseudo-chemical activity aiming at artificial creation.[2] The word "alchemy" seems to be of mixed etymology. The prefix "al" is the Arabic article, and the second part probably comes from the Greek χυμεία (pouring, infusion). But it has also been traced back to "khem" or "khamé," the Egyptian hieroglyph "khmi," which signifies black earth as opposed to infertile sand. Various myths describe the origins of alchemy in different ways, but the beginnings are usually attributed to the Egyptian god Hermes (Thoth), the inventor of the arts and sciences. Tertullian refers to "Hermes Trismegistus," the Egyptian Hermes, as the chief scholar of nature, and later alchemists called their work "hermetic." (The seal of Hermes which they put upon their vessels is the source of the phrase "hermetically sealed.") Zosimus of Panopolis, an alchemical writer from the third century, claimed that the secret art was revealed by fallen angels to the women whom they married (Gen. 6:2) and was written down in a book entitled *Chema*. The earliest Greek manuscripts from the third and fourth centuries are filled with references to oriental traditions, and the philosophers' egg, as the alchemical bottle or vessel is also called, can be found as a symbol of creation in Egypt and Babylonia. The Greek alchemists believed that the egg contained within itself the four Aristotelian elements (earth, air, fire, and water) and perceived in it the symbol of art and of the universe. In Babylonia two other alchemical notions were formulated: the conception of man, the microcosm in whom all parts of the macrocosm were present (fig. 17), and the identification of metals with planets. Alchemical treatises were written in Greek,[3] Syriac,[4] Arabic, Latin, and later in modern languages as well.

Alchemy was concerned with creation and with the origins of life, and its adepts (some of whom Colonna must have known), while mixing and cooking substances in their philosophical eggs and relating the microprocesses to the positions of the planets, could not avoid formulating sexual analogies (fig. 18). They projected the experience of sex and the ancient erotic symbolism contained in legends and religious beliefs onto their theories and experiments (fig. 19). This made alchemy, together with astrology, an important source of the fantastic and obscene in the European tradition—an arena of daring erotic dreams. Jung recognized this, and his understanding of alchemy as a reflection of psychology still retains its validity, though one may disagree with his particular interpretations which occasionally tend to be dreams of their own.[5]

Because of their endeavors with artificial creation, the alchemists saw themselves as extremely powerful; they identified at the same time with god as creator and with woman giving birth, therefore knowing no limits to the fantastic and absurd speculations they spread throughout the relatively closed and secret world of the adepts. They had to remain in obscurity because of the Church, which was fond neither of their experiments, which questioned the very doctrine of divine creation, nor of the erotic tenor of their language, the sexual metaphors and indecent illustrations (fig. 20). When the alchemical symbolism is not understood, many pictures may seem pornographic because the opposite elements to be united with each other are usually shown in the form of a male copulating with a female. But alchemical intercourse is also unsurpassed in its grotesqueness: the couple copulates, for instance, in a cave or a pond surrounded by vegetation, with the sky occasionally visible above; and the whole scene is enclosed, like the embryo in the uterus or a dream in a dreamer's body, in the alchemical bottle—the philosophers' egg (figs. 21, 22).

The alchemical laboratories, the alchemical bottles, and the alchemical minds were indeed caves of the uncanny: of the forbidden, heterogeneous, and chaotic. Everything there, from the tiniest to the biggest, was related to each other. The exterior and interior organs of the human body were likened to the planets and to metals and then connected through a chain of endless poetic associations to landscapes, plants, animals, temperatures, seasons, hours of the day, numbers, chapters of the Bible, etc. In the underground and at the margin of society, fantastic anti-worlds were constantly being reorganized and replaced by each other. But their core never changed: it remained erotic. Although the alchemists did not manage to make gold or create a homunculus, they should be regarded not as failed scientists but as great writers and artists of the fantastic genre. As inventors of poetical metaphors and visual images they influenced important works of literature, such as the *Roman de la rose*,[6] *Hypnerotomachia Poliphili*, and Goethe's *Faust*,[7] as well as paintings and drawings by Bosch (fig. 23), the

Brueghels, and Albrecht Dürer; and through them many other artists from Arcimboldo to Beardsley. They were not precursors of chemistry, but they preceded Goethe's studies in the chemistry of emotions,[8] and they pointed steadily to the mysterious and fantastic territory "in the back of the mind" that Freud termed the unconscious.

Alchemy undermined Christian norms not only by asserting the omnipresence of sexuality but also by its peculiar use of biblical symbolism. The alchemists likened the marriage of the opposite elements in the philosophers' egg to the conception of Jesus within Mary's womb. They associated, for instance, a certain phase of their opus with the Crucifixion, and went as far as representing the Savior in the form of a snake fixed to the cross.[9] These images are of course only read as fantastic if one is aware of the dogmas they upset; thus alchemy represents an excellent example of the sacrilegious aspect of the grotesque and its marginal, subterranean existence. The alchemists took their fantasies as seriously as the Church took its own doctrine. The alchemical uncanniness is therefore of a different character and order from the extravaganzas produced by conscious derision through caricature, satire, and parody when applied to religion and its institutions.

Alchemical and astrological illustrations (fig. 24) influenced the designs of plates in early scientific books and encyclopedias and those, in turn, stimulated the later grotesque artists. The paradoxical and hilarious character of many of those plates is mostly unintended and caused by the sheer impossibility of representing in a drawing the temporal sequence of events, simultaneity, light, energy, translucence, etc. But the curious and ridiculous also result from the fact that early science was in many ways overshadowed by magic.

Often the absurdity of a scientific setting or a machine becomes apparent only through the presence of human figures in the work. Large-scale technology, requiring masses of tiny people, undermines the anthropocentric perspective and brings to mind the terrible Last Judgments and the disturbing paintings of Bosch and the Brueghels. In these pictures, as in many scientific illustrations, humans are reduced to the size of monks in Chinese landscapes, deliberately portrayed as ants, hardly visible in the immensity of nature. This perspective has been associated in Europe with the overpopulated oriental world, which has little respect for the concept of individualism. Thus until the nineteenth century the pictures of technical devices, a pump or a crane, for instance, looked frequently like satanic instruments of torture in medieval representations of hell or like the interconnected vessels of the alchemical laboratory—the "devil's kitchen."

Chapter 4 · The Anatomical Theater

In alchemy grotesqueness arises from an overall sexualization and marriage of heterogeneous elements. In anatomical depictions it results from dissection, decomposition, and disintegration, processes which lead to the ultimate fusion of death in the common ground of nature. The dissecting room shares some features with a battlefield or a mass grave, but the way corpses and anatomical parts are displayed in a prosectorium has also a slightly theatrical character. Hence the name "anatomical theater," which in itself must have attracted the artists of the grotesque. In this scientific grotto of curiosities the inside is turned outside and dark secrets of the organic become disclosed as the bodily cave is opened up (fig. 25).

Halfway between a macabre theater and a tomb, the dissecting room heats up the imagination. Thus it is surprising that this locality and its reflection in anatomical illustrations have not been considered by scholars of the grotesque as important sources of fantastic associations. Kayser and Bakhtin noticed that wars, sieges, massacres, plagues, diseases, and hunger have supplied the raw material of the horrible grotesque, the type associated with Goya, and these have promoted visions of a world distorted and dismembered by deprivation and cruelty (fig. 26). Similarly, both scholars acknowledged the influence exercised upon the literary and visual grotesque by commedia dell'arte and puppet theater. But the anatomical theater, an intermediate stage between the natural and the artificial performance of death, escaped their attention (fig. 27).

We know that anatomical theater became important for students of both medicine (one of them was Rabelais) and art at the time of the Renaissance. Leonardo da Vinci worked in one, and we can assume that some of his strange drawings of half-human, half-animalistic creatures hinting at disintegrating flesh might have resulted from the visual grotesque with which one is constantly confronted in the dissection room. There bodies of people and animals are cut apart and reassembled in the strangest ways.

Cut-away ears touch the penis, a hand supports the open heart, a liver lies on a foot, female genitals crown the brain of a man, a skin hangs on the wall (fig. 28). The hands of the demonstrators play with the entrails inside the visceral cavity; doctors present to the students a dead foot and, with theatrical gestures, tear apart the tendons. Because certain organs are better visible in animals than in humans, the anatomical demonstrations and illustrations link both worlds by juxtaposing the male embryo and the gravid uterus of a cow; the head of a woman and that of an ox or a lamb. The embryo growing inside a pregnant woman is depicted as a flower (fig. 29). The development of a fertilized egg resembles that of a bean-seed (fig. 30). And the death of an unborn infant is recalled in the image of a tiny skeleton (fig. 31). The *Anatomical Bundle* (1493)[1] includes, for instance, the illustration of a seated woman with her body opened to show the reproductive organs. In Berengario's introduction to anatomy (1522)[2] people with ordinary faces cheerfully display their muscular structure by holding back flaps of skin. Cadavers and skeletons are frequently set in a bare landscape or, as in Andreas Vesalius's *De humani corporis fabrica* (1543), against the background of overgrown ancient ruins. Occasionally a skeleton may contemplate, in the pose of a personified vanity, a skull placed on top of a sarcophagus that bears the inscription: "Vivitur in genio, caetera mortis erunt" (fig. 32). In such images, as in *Hypnerotomachia Poliphili*, a work certainly inspired by anatomical theaters and books, death equals the past, which lives on in the ruins and in the common cemetery of nature.

Living misfits (fig. 33) were occasionally paraded in the anatomical theaters as well, adding to their monstrosity. Thus one could easily imagine this location as hell where sinners were punished. Indeed, on a satirical anatomical print, devils dissect Judas (fig. 34). Similarly, one is not surprised to learn that the emperor Nero had allegedly had his own mother cut up (fig. 35).

FIG. 1 Andrea Mantegna (1431–1506), Vices.

FIG. 2 Centaur-like creatures, sarcophagus, ca. A.D. 230.

FIG. 3 Monk-scribe astride a dragon, German,
Rhenish (Cologne?), late twelfth century.

FIG. 4 Last Judgment, French Ms, 1519–28.

FIG. 5 Sarcophagus lid symbolizing the Last Judgment, fourth century.

FIG. 6 The Fall and expulsion from Paradise, in Hans Holbein's *Imagines mortis* (1547).

FIG. 7 John Hagerty, *The Tree of Life*, 1791.

FIG. 8 Y or the Two Ways of Life, in John Comenius's *Orbis pictus* (1657).

FIG. 9 Rogier van der Weyden (ca. 1400–1464), *Triptych of Saint John the Baptist*.

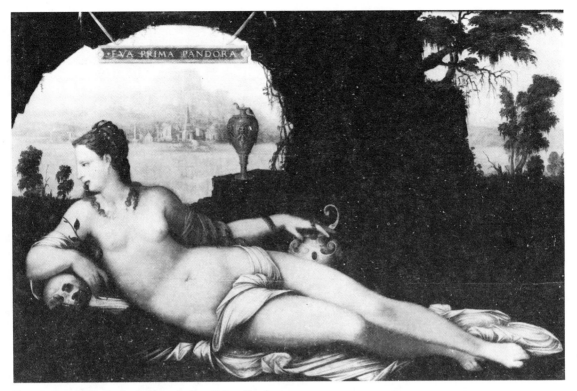

FIG. 10 Jean Cousin (1500–1590), *Eva Prima Pandora*.

FIG. 11 Perfect woman in imperfect nature, French Ms, 1527.

FIG. 12 Hubert Robert (1733–1808), *The Mouth of a Cave*.

FIG. 13 Hubert Robert, *Le bosquet des bains d'Apollon, Versailles*, 1804.

FIG. 14 Last Judgment, French Ms, thirteenth century.

FIG. 15 From *Hypnerotomachia Poliphili* (1499).

FIG. 16 From *Hypnerotomachia Poliphili* (1499).

FIG. 17 Sun as Man with the cock and Moon as Woman with the chicken, in
Michael Maier (1568?–1622), *Secretioris naturae*.

FIG. 18 The making of gold is symbolized by the birth of Pallas Athena out of
Jupiter's head, in Michael Maier (1568?–1622), *Secretioris naturae*.

FIG. 19 Rebis, the alchemical hermaphrodite, is being born out of two mountains, Mercury, to the left, and Venus, to the right, in Michael Maier (1568?–1622), *Secretioris naturae.*

FIG. 20 (opposite) Scene of castration. Saturn castrated and killed his father Uranus and ate his children. But thanks to Rhea, who substituted a stone for a child, Jupiter escaped this fate and castrated and murdered his father in turn. This cyclical development was for the alchemists a reflection of their opus, a series of deaths and rebirths. Latin codex, fifteenth century.

F. SOLVTIO PERFECTA III.

F. PVTREFACTIO IV.

FIG. 21 Copulation in the alchemical bottle, symbolizing the ''perfect solution,'' in *Pretiosissimum donum per Georgium Anrach*, seventeenth century.

FIG. 22 Copulation in the alchemical bottle, symbolizing putrefaction, in *Pretiosissimum donum per Georgium Anrach*, seventeenth century.

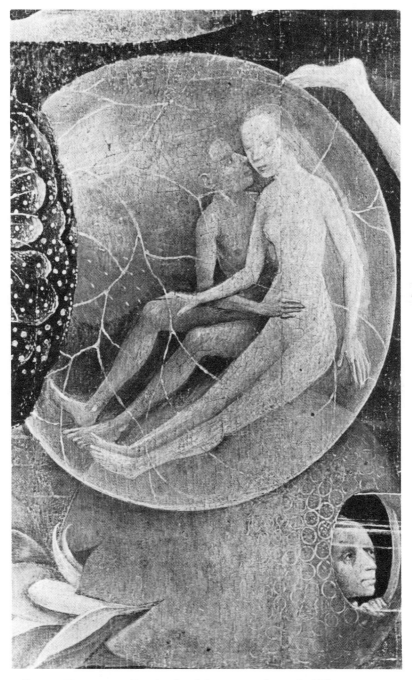

FIG. 23 Hieronymus Bosch, detail from central panel of *The Garden of Earthly Delights*, ca. 1500.

FIG. 24 Saturn with Capricorn as Man, with a burning torch in his hand and the Sun as his sex; Venus with Cancer, the horn in her hand and the Moon as her sex, in Johannes Nas's *Antastrologo* (1567).

FIG. 25 The anatomical theater, in Andreas Vesalius (1514–64), *Icones anatomicae*.

FIG. 26 Antoine Caron (ca. 1521–99), *Massacre of the Triumvirate.*

FIG. 27 Woman skinning a man, in Thomas Theodor Kerckring's *Opera omnia anatomica* (1729).

FIG. 28 From J. A. Kulmus's *Anatomische Tabellen* (1725).

FIG. 29 Anatomical engraving, in Adrian van der Spieghel's *De humani corporis fabrica* (1627).

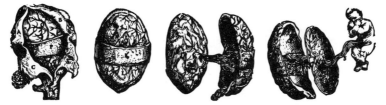

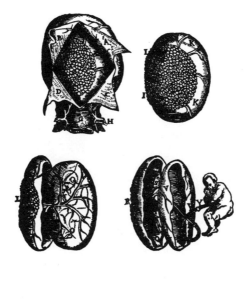

FIG. 30 Anatomical illustration, in Andreas Vesalius (1514–64), *Icones anatomicae*.

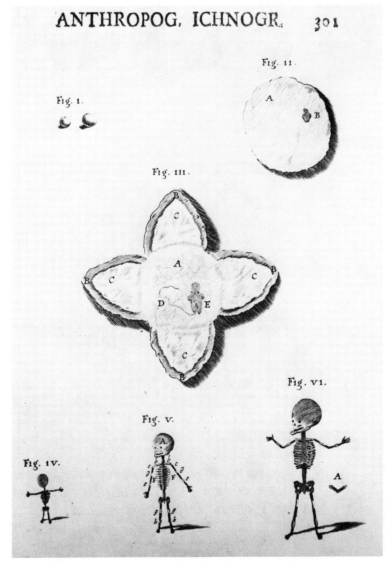

FIG. 31 From Thomas Theodor Kerckring's *Opera omnia anatomica* (1729).

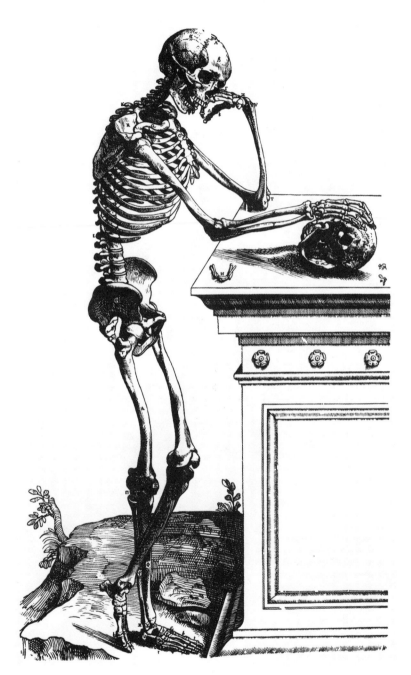

FIG. 32 From Andreas Vesalius (1514–64), *Icones anatomicae*.

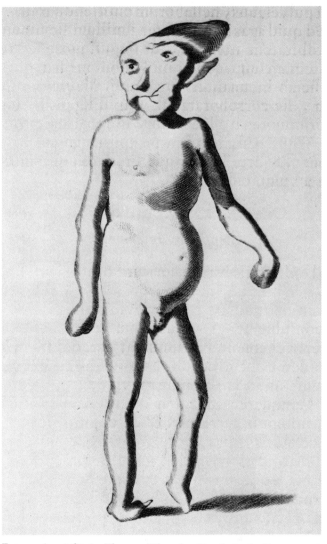

FIG. 33 A misfit, in Thomas Theodor Kerckring's *Opera omnia anatomica* (1729).

FIG. 34 *Judas the Archscoundrel*, engraving, Salzburg, 1695.

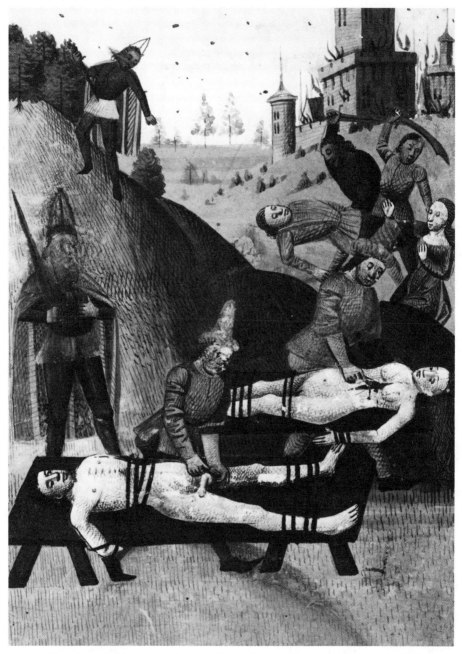

FIG. 35 Dissection of Nero's mother, an illustration to Laurence de Premierfait's French translation of Boccaccio's *De casibus virorum et foeminarum illustrium libri IX* (1472).

Chapter 5
Satire, Death, and Traveling

Recognizing the features that the anatomical theater shares with the art of the grotesque, one discovers that the latter is closely related to death. An obsessive preoccupation with death characterizes many great masters of the fantastic, including, paradoxically, the wittiest among them. This seems to confirm an old truth that the most brilliant jokers and clowns are often sad and tragic people who with verbal bravura, hilarious grimaces, obnoxious gestures, and outbreaks of laughter defend themselves against melancholy, depression, and death, which haunt them everywhere.

Bakhtin sees in Menippean satire the source of the "grotesque realism" of European literature and links the work of Menippus, Lucian, and their followers to the carnival and periods of crisis and transition.[1] He realizes, of course, that death represents the ultimate crisis and transition of human life, but, focusing on the interplay of birth and death, a typical trait of the carnival as well as many grotesque phenomena, he does not fully assess the enormous power which death alone exercised on the imagination of the very satirists he is concerned with. Menippus himself, a Greek slave, moneylender, Cynic, and satirical writer who mixed prose and verse, derided serious subjects, and made fun of the Epicureans and the Stoics, ended his life with suicide. Although none of his texts has been preserved, they exercised a remarkable influence upon later literature and greatly inspired Lucian, the chief exponent of the ruthless ancient satire whose dialogue *Menippus* (which carries the subtitle "A Necromantic Experiment") resembles a work ascribed to Menippus. But Lucian's entire *oeuvre* can be interpreted as experimental necromancy because it conveys his obsession with death and simultaneous refusal to take seriously the death of others, the death of himself, and of his world.

Lucian's disillusionment mirrors the agony of antiquity (he lived in the second century A.D.), the breaking down of traditional beliefs and norms, the flourishing of strange cults and superstitions.[2] His books provide an image not of balanced antiquity but of one that has gone crazy; a world given to folly and orgy in which even philosophers care more for a "fatter fowl"[3] than for truth. Lucian is greatly concerned with lunacy, impotence, and self-delusion, with religious mania, spiritualism, and excessive eroticism as ways of escaping reality. He deals with despair and fear and captures the typical expressions of life experienced as an inner exile: he dreams about journeys to the moon, that symbol of night and sleep, of femininity, madness, and death; he envisions the embryonic cave—in the dark and warm belly of a sea monster; he visits the Fortunate Islands of the dead.

Lucian called his description of the journey to the underworld *The Voyage Home*, a title that is doubly revealing. It connects the death wish to infantile regression and also presents death itself as a journey. This conforms, in principle, to Greek mythology, but Lucian considers the entire body of legends, including those of Homer, Hesiod, and Ctesias, as belonging—with magic, witchcraft, devils, ghosts, quack doctors, charms, exorcism, and divination—to a species of lies, and thus he mocks them all. *The Voyage Home* begins with the complaint that Charon's boat has been kept waiting for some important ghosts and from there develops into an unrestrained parody of gods and heroes not unsimilar to the witty sarcasms of his *Dialogues of the Dead*.

Lucian's writings oscillate frequently between straightforward satire or caricature and fantastic travelogue. The most successful example of this combination occurs in his *True History*, a lengthy narrative in two books that set a pattern for later writers and stimulated the artists of the absurd (fig. 36). *True History*, one of the most astonishing products of ancient literature, describes a voyage to the moon in a ship that sets out from the "Pillars of Hercules" and reaches the limit of the expedition of Heracles and Dionysus. Contrary to the heroic and tragic flight of Icarus toward the sun, the journey to the moon is successful but anti-heroic: the ship lands on a round island a little above the moon, and the travelers are captured by huge "horse-vultures" and brought as captives to the "man in the moon," who turns out to be Endymion (in Greek mythology the lover of the moon-goddess Selene). Endymion is engaged in a war with King Phaëthon, the ruler of the sun, and they battle over who should be given priority to colonize the planet Venus. A long and droll description of the inhabitants of the moon ends with a descent to the sea. The ship is swallowed by an enormous sea serpent and the travelers undergo comical adventures in the monster's belly; finally they sail out through the chinks between its teeth and arrive at the Fortunate Islands. There the astronauts meet with the spirits of the ancient heroes, philosophers, and writers, and Herodotus is chosen to continue Lucian's story "in his next books," a story that contains nothing but lies from beginning to end, as Lucian does not forget to stress.

True History, a forerunner of science fiction, has inspired Jonathan Swift's *Gulliver's Travels*, Rabelais's *Voyage of Pantagruel*, Cyrano de Bergerac's *Journey to the Moon*, and *The Adventures of Baron Munchausen*. But it also influenced the fantasies of countless travelers, their books and illustrations making the travelogue a reservoir of the bizarre. After the discovery of America, Europe was flooded with curious accounts and images of its inhabitants and their culture, of the distant and exotic flora and fauna (figs. 37, 38). Foreign races and primitive people were sometimes likened to the lost tribes of Israel, but more frequently to apes, monsters (fig. 39), and other animals. Later, studies in anthropology and the theories of Darwin suggested fantastic depictions of beastly creatures gradually transforming themselves into normal humans.[4] The pictures, and occasionally the texts, remind one of Ovid's *Metamorphoses*, a book about uncanny transformations that has delighted generations of fantastic writers and artists, fertilized the imagination of alchemists and astrologists, influenced the ideas of early anatomists and physicians (fig. 40), zoologists and botanists, and inspired illustrators of scientific treatises from the Middle Ages to the nineteenth century.

The accounts of travelers to exotic countries and the expeditions of anthropologists and archeologists revived in civilized, Christian Europe the suspect and obscene notions and images reminiscent of antiquity. Accounts of primitive tribes which practiced sodomy evoked the practices of Greek gods and goddesses who, lowering themselves to the level of humans and engaging in sexual intercourse with them, took the shapes of different animals (fig. 41). Pastoral settings found by the explorers reminded Europe of the coexistence of humans and animals in paradise or in Noah's ark, an unsurpassed metaphor for the solidarity of all living beings. Reports about headhunters or cannibals threw a new light on the figure of Salome. Unexpectedly, the exploration of new worlds led to the rediscovery of the past, and the study of primitive peoples' beliefs and habits foreshadowed a new interest taken in the fantasies of children, who, as though remembering their totemic ancestors, identify with animals or their representations and re-create in their rooms and play the feeling of primordial togetherness, abolishing distinctions between themselves and their puppies, teddy bears, and dolls.[5]

Confronted with the wild and infantile "barbarians" still living in the bosom of nature, the cultivated, adult Europeans began gradually to confront in a more profound way the animal and the child in themselves and to descend into the shadowy regions of the repressed and the unconscious. In this way, travel through time and space, steadily growing more possible since the Renaissance, prompted in the second half of the nineteenth century the journey inwards—across the mysterious territory of the psyche. This journey, like previous travels, stimulated the grotesque.

Chapter 6
The Fantastic, the Grotesque, and the Metaphorical

From the end of the Renaissance to the beginning of the twentieth century the European grotesque developed through the mixing, interwining, exploring, imitating, and enriching of three important traditions: the medieval bizarrerie, the work of Italian artists created under the direct influence of the excavated Roman frescoes, and mannerist art, indebted, among other things, to the dissections of anatomy and the paradoxical fusions of astrology and alchemy, of which Arcimboldo is the chief exponent. His paintings represent the best European example of heterogeneity derived from the agglomeration of metaphors, a procedure not uncommon in the art of the Far East (fig. 54) but rare in the European tradition.

Fantastic medieval art and the Renaissance grotesque were both inspired by the monstrous in antiquity. But while the Italians stayed within the framework of Greco-Roman iconography and consciously imitated the late Roman style, the artists of northern France, Germany, and, in particular, the Netherlands, developed a surprisingly original language suggested by diverse Christian heresies, alchemy, astrology, folklore, popular humor, and exotic travelogues. The difference between these two worlds can be best realized when one compares the work of Hieronymus Bosch with the paintings by Raphael, Pinturicchio, Giovanni da Udine, and Luca Signorelli, and with the grotesque ornaments in architecture.

The Globe-Grotto

Hieronymus Bosch possesses all the characteristics of an outsider. He was born circa 1450 in 's Hertogenbosch, a provincial town in North Brabant, and through marriage to a wealthy woman secured for himself financial independence and the opportunity to paint unhindered by the expectations of narrow-minded patrons. He worked largely for secret societies but also executed an altar for the local Cathedral of Saint John. The development of his extraordinary iconography was inspired by several contemporary heresies, in the first place by the teachings of Adamite eroticism adopted by the Brothers and Sisters of the Free Spirit.[1] The movement, spreading throughout western Europe from the thirteenth century on, had Gnostic origins and was related to the Adamite heresy of early Christianity. Epiphanius (*Panarion*, Haer. 72) derided the Adamites as moles afraid of the daylight because of their habit of gathering in underground heating vaults. Leaving their clothing with the doorkeeper, the Adamites entered the subterranean hiding places, "man and woman, naked as they had emerged from their mother's womb," and celebrated their rituals around the fire. Augustine (*De haer.* 31) repeats this report and explains that "the Adamites are called after Adam and emulate his paradisiac nakedness as it existed before the Fall. They reject marriage because before Adam sinned and was expelled from Paradise he did not know his wife. They believe that there would have been no marriages later either if no one had sinned. So men and women assemble naked; naked they listen to the readings; naked they pray; and naked they celebrate the sacraments. For this reason they regard their church as Paradise."

The Adamite doctrine was based on Origen's philosophy of the eternal return of all things to their beginnings. They linked the beginning of the world to its end, Adam to Christ, paradise to earth. Longing for a primordial unity, the Brothers and Sisters of the Free Spirit hoped to restore paradise in a spontaneous union of the sexes based on free love. They dreamed of the togetherness of all living beings and of androgyny, the ideal of perfection that has universally been imagined in the shape of a sphere. Spheres, complete or bursting with life, are a recurring motif in Bosch's paintings and drawings, and so are caves. In accordance with the Adamite doctrine, Bosch considered the earth (fig. 42)—and earthly enclosure—as the place of rebirth into a lost innocence that was to be attained through glorification of the flesh. He was obsessed with the symbolism of the womb, with visions of its penetration and insemination. In this he was greatly influenced by the pan-eroticism of the Adamites, as Wilhelm Fraenger has shown in his excellent study.[2]

In Bosch's paintings a general copulation is carried out in grottoes, eggs, fruits, translucent globes (fig. 23), bottles, baskets, boxes, houses, ponds, tree trunks, and innumerable other vessels. Inside them, conception and annihilation merge; physiology fuses with alchemy and cosmogony. This vision of paradise disregards all purity and abstraction. Not heaven, but unspoiled, fertile earth is yearned for; not divinity, but a community of humans is aspired to, humans restored to the age before the Fall, like infants, without any sense of shame and guilt, pursuing carnal happiness. In the Adamite garden of delights, asceticism not sexuality is regarded as a crime, an expression of egoism, hypocrisy, and sterility. The vision of hell is equally material: it originates in nature perceived not as a cradle but as a tomb, not as a source of life but as the container of poisonous impurities. In Bosch's paintings caves of pleasure are opposed to grottoes of horror filled with fornicating monsters.

Bosch's work also reflects his involvement with movements that foreshadowed the Reformation, such as the Brethren of the Common Life who came to 's Hertogenbosch in 1424 and called themselves Hieronymites.[3] They attempted to practice asceticism outside the organized monastic movement and to achieve salvation through pious deeds while fighting everyday evil without the intermediary of the Church. The Brethren of the Common Life fervently denounced the folly, blindness, and cruelty of ordinary people as well as that of secular and religious authorities. Their preaching made sinners see monsters rising from the darkness of their souls. While the Adamites indulged in fantasies of paradise on earth, the Brethren of the Common Life were obsessed with the Antichrist and his imminent arrival, with the world transformed into hell. They described what Bosch also depicted: that humans are animals capable of anything; that they are hungry only for food and sex; and that the bloodthirsty killers with their victims form a doomed lot (fig. 43).

Bosch upset all the prescribed patterns of Christian art. He blew up the familiar image of the world and reassembled the pieces in his own way, disregarding the former setting and its proportions, subordinating the entire design and every particular detail to a heretical vision of the universe, to a fantasy that ignored not only official religion but also the rules of common sense and the concepts of harmony and balance. A chicken egg is so large that a group of monks can hold a concert in it; a house is so tiny that it can serve as a hat for one of them. This method of dissection and fusion creates particularly shocking effects when applied to humans. The feeling of surprise and disgust is heightened because of the ancient European tradition of respecting and idealizing the bodies of men and women more than anything else. Bosch, however, dismembers and puts them back together, combining different people into one, leaving out parts of the body, letting human elements grow into objects, animals, and plants, and delighting in all that is unfinished, transitional, and embryonic. The world is seen *in statu nascendi* and reminds one of a corpse in an anatomical theater. The global monster is first dissected, then gathered into a new entity and animated.

In the universe of Bosch, as in the fertile ground of the earth, death as such does not exist. Creatures serve as food for each other. New life constantly arises from the disintegration of the old, which continues an existence in the intestines and blood vessels of another. Every enclosure is depicted as a uterus, every protruding shape as an inseminating phallus. Not only humans, animals, and plants, but also baskets, bottles, and knives want to fornicate and consume—each other. Guided by hunger and pleasure, this world lacks authority. Priests are corrupt and greedy, saints are surrounded by elaborate "flowers of evil," Christ and the Madonna are going under in a sea of bestiality. Pale, delicate, sad, they represent the exceptional dreams of the sublime, which monsters threaten to devour. Grotesque creatures force their way even into the humble hut where the melancholic Madonna shows her newborn baby to the Magi (*Epiphany Triptych*, Prado, Madrid); here, however, the siren-like birds with human heads remain in the margin, in the embroidered bands of the kings' rich clothes, and in the decoration of the precious presents they offer to the infant. Thus the child, pure and simple in its nakedness, in the very first hours of its existence comes in touch with the worldly—the ornamented and heterogeneous, the mixed and impure.

Besides heretical doctrines, Bosch's iconography is indebted to fantastic literature and illustrated books of magic, witchcraft, astrology, and alchemy; to such imaginary and real travelogues as, for instance, the Irish *Visio Tundali*, printed in 's Hertogenbosch at the end of the fifteenth century, Sebastian Brant's poem *The Ship of Fools* (1494), as well as descriptions of journeys to exotic countries. Tundal travels through hell, purgatory, and paradise, encountering strange animals and souls of the damned, that of Judas for instance, who on certain rare occasions is brought out of hell and chained to a rock overwhelmed with sea waves. In Brant's *Ship*, idiots, unaware of their fate, float to damnation. Camels, crocodiles, and giraffes can be encountered in Erhard Reuwich's illustrations of Bernhard von Breidenbach's *Die Reise in das heilige Land*.[4] Bosch's paintings astonish us because of the diversity of their sources and their unexpected combinations.

Virgin Surrounded by Satyrs

Compared to Bosch's work, the grotesque productions of the Italians seem monotonous and conventional (fig. 44). This perception is intensified by their symmetry, regularity, and use of repetition, features derived from the peculiarities of the original: the Roman frescoes served as architectural decoration and so were subordinated to the divisions and shapes of walls, ceilings, and the panels they surrounded. The main source of inspiration for the Renaissance artists was the ruins of the Domus Aurea in Rome. They did not know what the ruins represented and that the frescoes they so enthusiastically copied had been painted by Fabullus for Nero, an emperor renowned for his delight in monstrosity and voluptuousness.

To stress its grandiosity and luxury, Nero himself called his new residence a "golden house," and Suetonius (*Nero*, 31) described its perverse splendor: a dining room that rotated like the cosmos and had in its walls, which were covered with mother-of-pearl, jewels, and ebony, pipes that distributed fragrance and flowers. Like a real "Lustschloss," the enormous villa was surrounded by temples, nymphaea, and waterworks. Beside an artificial lake, a colossal bronze statue of Helios stood with features resembling Nero's. Today the Domus Aurea is crumbling, but thanks to the paintings and drawings of several Renaissance artists, some of the frescoes can be reconstructed. In all of them the playful and erotic prevail. The mythological tableaux show Amphitrite,[5] the ancient Greek sea-goddess, daughter of Oceanus and wife of Poseidon, who fled from her husband and was brought back by a dolphin. Works of art frequently render her driving with Poseidon in a chariot drawn by seahorses; in Nero's palace Triton, her son, with a trumpet precedes Amphitrite, whose name in poetry was used as a synonym for the sea. One of Fabullus's favorite figures was the winged Psyche; she is accompanied by peacocks, griffins, and other fabulous creatures, and her body occasionally ends in the tail-like shape of a plant. Nymphs gallop on strange beasts, young men ride horses, and ephebes float in the air holding vases between their thighs. Men and women hunt, girls are approached by centaurs, satyrs play flutes, and a group of naked youths direct their bows at a herm. Rapes, erotic surprises, encounters and farewells are depicted in a light, casual way: Paris meets Helen in the presence of Aphrodite and Eros; Hector and Andromache take leave of one another; Hephaestus discovers Ares and Aphrodite; and Zeus embraces Ganymede in the clouds. Wound round the figures and flying about are owls and sphinxes, dogs, horses, dragons, swans, and unidentifiable monsters. But their spontaneity is subdued by the architectural structure; the chaotic shapes are chained to each other and arranged into bands, squares, and circles; the fantastic is forced into a pattern, but even then it retains the ambiguous character of the shadow world.

Transient and transitional qualities obviously fascinated the imagination of the Renaissance painters who imitated and enriched the Roman grotesques. On the ceiling of the Domenico della Rovere palace in Rome provocative sirens are approached by dragons; a snake-like sea-god displays a shield with Medusa's head, her mouth wide open; a putto drives a "watercow." All this beastly eroticism comes from the brush of Pinturicchio, who did not hesitate to put the inappropriate motifs of naked putti, severed and winged heads (another popular motif of the Domus Aurea), and obscenely smiling satyrs on the illusionary architecture which encloses religious scenes in the Borgia apartments in the Vatican. Ghirlandaio painted the birth of the Virgin (Santa Maria Novella, Florence) against the background of the Roman frescoes, and, in the same church, Filippino Lippi used grotesque architecture to frame Saint Philip exorcising a demon. In Orvieto cathedral, Signorelli surrounded the tableaux of pagan figures and scenes with a veritable jungle of the grotesque, and so did Perugino, who in the reception hall of Cambio re-created both the erotic scenes of the Domus Aurea and its formal structure. But the light and frivolous atmosphere of Fabullus's decoration was most faithfully revived by Raphael and Giovanni da Udine in the loggiae and logettae of the Vatican; as in Nero's palace, creatures rendered swiftly and impressionistically dance on their walls.

The unique fantasies of Bosch combine the sublime visions of Christian heretics with the obscene humor of simple folk into an apotheosis of mother nature. In comparison, the Italian grotesque lacks humor and vitality; its *cochonnerie* speaks an aristocratic language, at once sophisticated and monotonous.[6] The erudite approach produces a sense of déjà vu. However, because of its decorative qualities, the Italian grotesque soon moved north (fig. 45) and remained extremely influential in architecture and crafts (fig. 46) all over Europe. Thanks to it the ancient monstrosities and indecencies were omnipresent up to the beginning of the twentieth century both in palaces and bourgeois homes—on pilasters, legs of furniture (fig. 107), vases, plates, jewels, embroideries, firedogs (figs. 47, 48), and wax reliefs (fig. 49). Art nouveau was still deeply rooted in the tradition of the Greco-Roman grotto and its new versions, developed after the Renaissance; and the entire fin de siècle can be imagined as a subterranean locale where incestuous and infantile sexuality flourished, where sodomy, necrophilia, and other Neronian delights hid in the corners. While all this was remembered even by the burghers, the fantastic creatures of Bosch were recalled mainly by the cognoscenti. From this reservoir of the fantastic, artists like Beardsley picked up the phallic monsters, the dwarfs, grylli (walking heads), and other transient embryonic, mixed and hermaphroditic creatures (figs. 50, 51). The decadents felt closer to the Italian grotesque than to the bizarrerie of the Middle Ages, although they shared with the late medieval artists their apocalyptic presentiments and an interest in the Antichrist and Satan.

The Metaphors of Arcimboldo

Writing about Arcimboldo (1527–93), Roland Barthes remarks that the Italian artist was dedicated, like a poet, to the play of metaphor, that he did not create signs but combined them, permutated them, deflected them, "exactly what a craftsman of language does."[7] This observation does not apply to Arcimboldo alone. The creation of metaphors in language corresponds to the formation of images in the visual arts, and every artist who does not simply reproduce a visible reality but conveys a symbolic meaning plays with metaphors. Vico considered metaphorical thinking the original mode of human expression which had once produced ancient mythology.[8] Indeed, neither the legends nor the art of antiquity can be imagined without metaphors. But Barthes is right to stress Arcimboldo's peculiar devotion to metaphors piled one on top of the other, his extreme poetical freedom that resulted in a unique absurdity. Arcimboldo disregarded conventional metaphors and did not restrain his taste for extravagance. He belonged to the species of true originals who in order to be tolerated have to play the king's fool, and he performed that role even as he worked for a select and enlightened public—the courts of Prague and Vienna, where rulers took an interest in astronomy, astrology, alchemy, and anatomy and, consequently, were not unprepared to appreciate his strange paintings. Admired for his entertaining qualities, Arcimboldo was never quite taken seriously. Until the twentieth century, his pictures, not belonging to the sphere of the solemn, led the shadowy existence of monsters and obscenities hidden in curio cabinets and rare books; often they were damaged or destroyed.

Although he painted the seasons as ludicrous and disgusting "heads" composed of objects which he associated with them, and he portrayed some of his patrons in that way, Arcimboldo imposed upon himself certain constraints in respect to subject matter. He, or one of his imitators, depicted Herod (fig. 52), the persecutor of budding Christianity, as a monstrous head formed out of naked infants, but he did not paint Christ's head by combining tiny sheep or crowns of thorns. With the exception of the two portraits of Herod which, according to recent attribution, may not even be by him, Arcimboldo avoided religious subjects, as if remembering that the leading theologians altogether distrusted metaphors. (In *Contra mendacium* Augustine disapproved of metaphors in general but defended the biblical ones, and Thomas Aquinas[9] regarded arguments constructed of metaphors as invalid.)

Arcimboldo's avoidance of certain territories raises the important issue of metaphors which are approved by authorities as opposed to those which are not. Even a child knows that to flatter the king one should call him a "lion" and to offend him a "pig." And adults understand the metaphor "Jesus is a lamb" as a canon and the metaphor "Jesus is an ass" as a sacrilege. Consequently, the image of a Christ-sheep is perceived as normal, that of a Christ-ass not only as absurd but also as obscene. As a matter of fact, I know of only one depiction of the second metaphor. Not accidentally, it dates from Christianity's early days and was scratched into the walls of a Roman house, presumably by pagans making fun of their neighbors—converts to the new faith (fig. 53).

But besides differentiating between metaphors of praise and metaphors of derision, on the one hand, and sanctified and sacrilegious metaphors, on the other, one has also to remember that a particular metaphor can be either illustrated in an ordinary way or rendered in an uncanny form. For instance the metaphor "the earth is a woman" has been traditionally represented by a female figure depicted against the background of blooming nature. This image is perceived as a stereotype and an allusion to the Madonna. However, Arcimboldo's *Earth* consists of a quasi-human profile put together from different animals, as in certain oriental miniatures (fig. 54), and the *Earth* of an alchemical illustrator depicts a naked, bottle-shaped female who has the globe for her belly, covered with the outlines of the continents (fig. 55).

Bosch and Arcimboldo represent two poles between which all grotesque artists oscillated. The first combined formal strangeness with subjects and figures that, in one way or the other, negated, ridiculed, and attacked established ideas and institutions, the commonplaces of religion and civil order. The second opted for an excessive formal heterogeneity and steered away from controversial topics. Bosch gave shape to apocryphal, heretical, and sacrilegious metaphors which debased the holy, high, and serious subject matter. Arcimboldo, on the other hand, offended only the defenders of established, trivial poetics and acted as the master of curiosity created by the peculiarities of his own metaphorical language.

Chapter 7
Grotesque Tendencies in the Late Nineteenth Century

The late nineteenth century delighted in the grotto and the grotesque and was fascinated with the subterranean, fantastic, and obscene, with irrationalism, spiritualism, mysticism, magic, occultism, satanism, and visions of the apocalypse. Scholars of the fin de siècle have found manifold reasons for this fascination, but it is not within the scope of this book to enumerate them all here. Instead only those facts and phenomena will be investigated which serve the immediate purpose of our analysis of the grotesque.

Capitalism had eroded the traditional structures of society, including the official Churches, and although there existed a strong need for religion, Christianity did not satisfy it any longer. Insecurity, reclusiveness, escapism, and extreme individualism became hallmarks of the era, producing dreams of a new spiritual community, at once cosmopolitan and hermetic. Humanistic sciences had excavated the past, discovered its traces in the present, and helped to promote an interest in prehistory, antiquity, mythology, and comparative religion as well as astrology, alchemy, and folklore, in black masses and heretic sects and, on a more popular level, in mesmerism, ghosts, and moving tables.

To the two most influential secret societies of the past, the Rosicrucians, dating back to the early seventeenth century, and the Freemasons, whose Mother Grand Lodge was inaugurated in London on Saint John the Baptist's Day in 1717, a new one was added: the Theosophical Society, founded in 1875 in New York by Helena Petrovna Blavatsky, who soon opened branches in London and Paris. The sect was based on the epigonistic, chaotic, and truly grotesque teachings of this Russian woman, who had traveled widely and was well read but had a rather confused mind. She intuitively grasped what mood and ideas were in the air and was able to take advantage of the popular longing for an unconventional and fantastic church, which made it possible for her to convert to theosophy people from all over the world and from vastly different backgrounds. Her person and her beliefs are presented here as symptoms of the malaise and as reflections of the bizarre social reverie prevailing in the last quarter of the nineteenth century.

At the core of Blavatsky's doctrine lies the notion that all religion, literature, art, and architecture have their origins in a common, archaic, and universal esoteric system, "the Sacred Wisdom-Science," which was supposedly written in a language once known to all nations but by her time intelligible only to a few adepts, of whom she was one. Thus she intended her teachings to become a key to the forgotten knowledge which at closer inspection turns out to be a mixture of Buddhism, Hinduism, Zoroastrianism, Gnosticism, Manicheism, Judaism, Christianity, and many other more or less obscure religions and cults, and of astrology and alchemy. Blavatsky quotes frequently, mostly from secondary texts, usually incorrectly and without acknowledgment, and she freely intermixes excerpts from the Egyptian Book of the Dead, the writings of Plato and the Mandaeans, the Kabbalists as well as Christian mystics and heretics; she deals with Darwinism and Catholicism, as well as biology, physics, and medicine. Her principal books, *Isis Unveiled* (1877) and *The Secret Doctrine: The Synthesis of Science, Religion and Philosophy* (1888) lack structure, method, or a clear message; they not only induce sleep but are full of errors and misconceptions, and at times remind one of automatic writing. But they were once widely read and admired and cannot be ignored. They mirror the mood of her age and a new phenomenon: an abundance of easily available printed material which popularized the distant, exotic, and hermetic and provoked the creation of analogies and of the most superficial syncretic systems. The influence exercised by Blavatsky's writings and the rapid spreading of the theosophical movement also corresponded to a general tendency to discover universal patterns hidden behind a particular figure. Regardless of its foolishness, her writing contains ideas which foreshadow those of Freud, Jung, James Frazer, Mircea Eliade, and many modern scholars of comparative religion and literature. She points, for instance, to the common Magna Mater type discerned behind the figures of the mothers of Krishna, Horus, and Christ, to the Sacred Flower behind the lotus, the water lily, and the rose, and to the fertile and bisexual sea monster of life and death behind the snake and the crocodile.

Theosophy provided a vision of an animated universe of curious metamorphoses, transmigrating souls, and omnipresent secret correspondences in an appealing attempt at transcending the divisions and separations of the mechanized and civilized world. It evoked a concept of the primordial solidarity of all living beings shaped after the myths of paradise, Noah's ark, and Buddhist saints who, believing that every insect might be an ancestor, let mosquitoes feed on their blood. Blavatsky called for a brotherhood of men and women of all races, nations, and religions. One can understand how, despite her shortcomings and fraudulent manipulations, she could enjoy genuine popularity not only among ordinary members of her society but also among some distinguished scientists, scholars, and artists. V. S. Solovyov reviewed *Isis Unveiled* with praise (his *Modern Priestess of Isis* appeared in English in 1895 in Walter Leaf's translation), and at the turn of the century the painters Frank Kupka and Wassily Kandinsky were counted among Blavatsky's admirers and introduced theosophical symbols in some of their early works.

Because of the many scandals surrounding Blavatsky's life (and eagerly reported in the newspapers), it was almost impossible to ignore her person and doctrine; she promoted a legendary account of her life, modeled after the apocryphal biography of young Jesus. Although married as a young girl, she presented herself as a virgin, and in her latter days used to call herself "Heliona" instead of Helena. Combining characteristics of a hysteric and a maniac with those of a prophet, femme fatale, and a clever businesswoman, the exotic Russian was in harmony with the atmosphere of the fin de siècle. And so was her theosophy, a pseudoscience and pseudoreligion, advertised in the metropolises but concerned with the primordial *urgrund* of nature, with forests and grottoes, witches and hermits, talking animals and dancing snakes—the many wonders described by Blavatsky in her travelogue *From the Caves and Jungles of Hindostan.* Written originally in the form of letters to a Russian magazine, the text appeared also in English, as a book published in London in 1892.

While Blavatsky escaped from Europe to India, some of the great dreamers of the late nineteenth century withdrew from the practicalities of life into an imaginary "Orient"—the inner mirrored cabinet of self-reflection and contemplation, where exotic splendor and terror would arise from fantasies and memories. Born into a late and relatively liberal culture, the representatives of the aesthetic or decadent movement—Laforgue, Mallarmé, Huysmans, and their followers, Oscar Wilde and Aubrey Beardsley—were no longer pushed underground or to the margin but removed themselves consciously as far as possible to the "left" where femininity, night, and hell have ruled throughout the ages and where they could play "the disciples of Satan" (fig. 56). From this followed their identification with the "evil woman" and imitations of her splendid and annihilating beauty in their works of art.

The late nineteenth century's fascination with dreams and grotto-like interiors was reflected in architectural design; in fact many private and

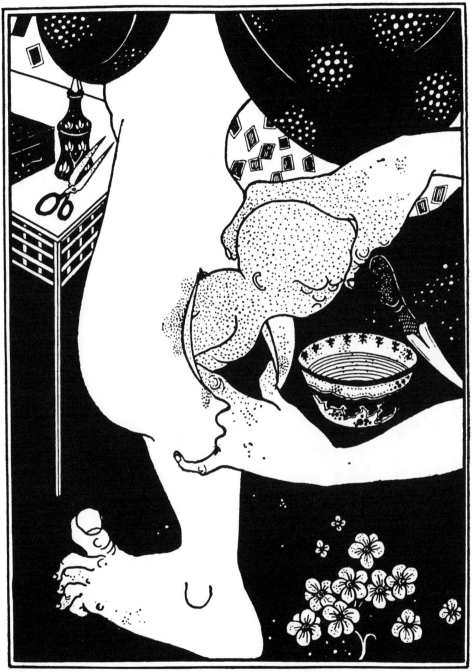

FIG. 36 Aubrey Beardsley, *Birth from the Calf of the Leg*, illustration intended for *Lucian's True History*.

FIG. 37 Strange rituals of the natives of Virginia, in Thomas Harriot's *Admiranda
narratio fide tamen, de commodis et incolarum ritibus Virginiae* (1590).

FIG. 38 A native woman of Virginia covered with tattoos instead of a dress, in Thomas Harriot's *Admiranda narratio fide tamen, de commodis et incolarum ritibus Virginiae* (1590).

FIG. 39 Monsters without heads from an island in the Indian Ocean, French Ms, early fifteenth century.

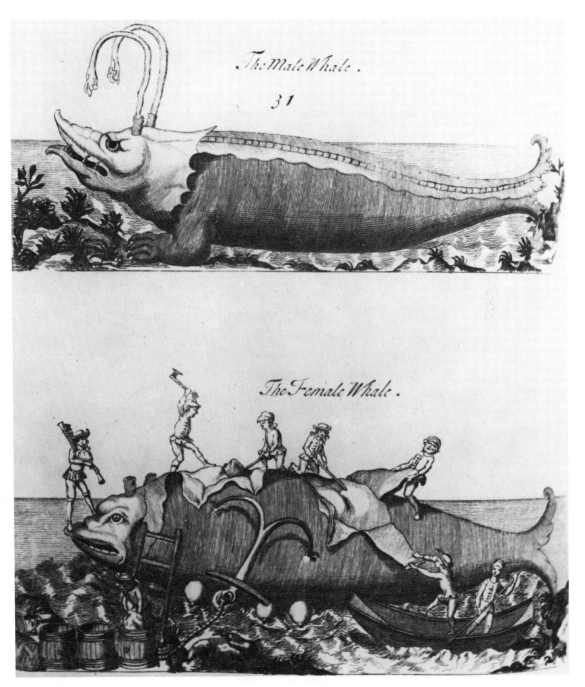

The Male Whale.

31

The Female Whale.

FIG. 40 From P. Pomet's *A Complete History of Drugs* (1748).

FIG. 41 Bacchiacca (1495–1557), *Leda and the Swan*.

FIG. 42 Hieronymus Bosch, the world on the third day of creation (Gen. 1:9–13), exterior covering of the triptych *The Garden of Earthly Delights*, ca. 1500.

FIG. 43 Hieronymus Bosch, detail from right panel of *The Garden of Earthly Delights*, ca. 1500.

FIG. 44 Grotesque frieze, Italian, early sixteenth century.

FIG. 45 Jacob Cornelisz van Amsterdam, *Adoration of the Magi*, ca. 1520.

FIG. 46 Severo da Ravenna, Marine
monster, Italian, early sixteenth century.

FIG. 47 *Firedog: Venus*, French, eighteenth century.

FIG. 48 *Firedog: Vulcan*, French, eighteenth century.

FIG. 49 Louis Clodion (Claude Michel, 1738–1814), *Nymphs and Satyrs, Playing,* wax relief, ca. 1765.

FIG. 50 Aubrey Beardsley, Vignette. FIG. 51 Aubrey Beardsley, Vignette.

FIG. 52 *Portrait of Herod*, in the style of Arcimboldo, sixteenth century.

ΑLΕΧΑΜΕΝΟϹ ϹΕΒΕΤΕ ΘΕΟΝ

FIG. 53 A crucified figure with the head of an ass
and a human body, inscribed "Alexamenos prays
to God," probably third century.

गुलवडर

FIG. 54 Mythical animal, Indian miniature, ca. 1725.

FIG. 55 From Michael Maier (1568?–1622), *Secretioris naturae*.

FIG. 56 Henry de Malvost, *The Disciples of Satan Trampling on Christ*, in Jules Bois's *Le satanisme et la magie* (1896).

public places, salons and boudoirs, coffeehouses, bars, brothels and casinos, dancing halls and theaters were fashioned after caves. Des Esseintes, the hero of *A rebours*, excluded daylight from his house, lit it by candelabras, and offered his friends a dinner that consisted of dark and predominantly marine food served by naked black women. Following his example Beardsley darkened his workroom and worked by the light of candles mainly during the night.

Sigmund Freud consolidated, focused, and interpreted many fin-de-siècle obsessions and mannerisms. He arrived at his theory of dreams and the unconscious by way of hypnosis, which he learned from Jean-Martin Charcot and Josef Breuer and then practiced himself. Drawing somewhat on the concept of divination, Freud formulated the theory of psychoanalysis on the assumption that the human psyche possessed a thus far neglected, obscure, and hidden dimension which shaped a person's life. He believed that knowledge of this dimension was accessible, but could be reached only indirectly, through the explanation of utterances made under hypnosis, the analysis of associated ideas, and the interpretation of dreams.

Freud started his career in a strange way: he put his patients, mainly hysterical young women, to sleep, discussed their dreams with them, and then related the material obtained in hypnotic and normal sleep to their psychological problems. During the psychoanalytic sessions the semi-dark, richly decorated rooms of the well-to-do Viennese bourgeoisie and Freud's own office turned into grottoes of wild reverie which deeply linked the doctor to the patient and, not surprisingly, led them to the discovery of eroticism. Freud, indeed, practiced a new kind of *hypnerotomachia* and, going further and further "down and back" in search of the first beloved, arrived at the door of the mother. Jung, following Freud and the ancient emperors, philosophers, and poets who had retired to their caves to meet the nymph of inspiration, found the anima in this inner darkness. Behaving like explorers of submerged continents and archeologists of a forgotten past, Freud and Jung tried to penetrate the female psyche as if it were a dark cave or the obscure residence of a sphinx whose riddles were to be deciphered by male intelligence. In this they occasionally succeeded but more often failed because of their inability to free themselves from the ancient mythology of femininity, to which they adhered as much as the grotesque artists of the fin de siècle.

Psychoanalysis and the grotesque shared visions and obsessions. Both were attracted to the subterranean, obscene, heretical and sacrilegious, and both responded to the repression exercised by the religious and civil institutions of established European culture. Thus Freud's theories, including those which are not considered valid today, can elucidate the grotesque production in general and the art of his times in particular.

In its terminal stage the grotesque was chosen by artists who openly declared themselves as against the grain and believed that their way of life and work protested "rabid Puritanism" and "finicking censorship" and that they contributed to "a little more tolerance and breadth of opinion," as Beardsley put it. More conscious of his *à rebours* position than most artists of his time, he knew the essence and value of his drawings and writings. "I have one aim," he said, "—the grotesque. If I am not grotesque I am nothing."[1]

Beardsley's Grotesque Iconography and Its Ancient Roots

Chapter 8
The Planet Venus

In Beardsley's drawing *The Toilette of Salomé II* (fig. 57) a woman, resting in her boudoir, is attended by her servants: a hairdresser, wearing a mask and the loose costume of a commedia dell'arte actor, and three hermaphroditic boy-girls, reminiscent of ancient eunuchs, with dissolute, daydreaming faces. The outlines of Salomé's skirt dissolve in the ground, turning her into a mountain. Cut flowers stand in a vase on her dressing table where phials and boxes are displayed. Prominently placed, a strange statuette with the head of an embryo stands in front of the princess, and one can read the titles of two books on the shelf: *La terre* and *Fleurs du mal*. The drawing synthesizes the entire scope of the grotesque and renders its playfully morbid essence by bringing the viewer to the center of this subterranean genre: the female grotto, where allusions to fertility and procreation mix with suggestions of luxury and vanity; where the erotic *theatrum mundi*, fascinating, ludicrous, and terrible, is performed in a heterogeneous setting that evokes all cultures at once and thus transcends them all. In Salomé's cave of love every detail and every gesture—the hairdresser's finger in her hair, the servant's hand caressing the column, the teapot's beak directed at the princess's breast—speaks of sexuality. This high concentration of eroticism must have been considered too indecent for the public eye, and consequently the drawing was not included in the first English edition of Oscar Wilde's *Salomé*. Instead, a more harmless version was chosen, *The Toilette of Salomé I* (fig. 58), a drawing in which explicit obscenity is replaced with hints given by the titles of books. They include *Nana* (the "golden fly," as Émile Zola called his heroine, a fabulous Parisian prostitute from whom no man was safe), *Manon Lescaut* (by Abbé Prévost, the story of another great courtesan), works by the Marquis de Sade, Apuleius's *Golden Ass*, and Paul Verlaine's *Les fêtes galantes*. Thus the different aspects of the "earth" and her "evil flowers" are brought together, suggesting love, play, and destruction.

The portrait of a passive and sleepy Salomé offered by Beardsley in *Toilette II* does not conform with Wilde's play about a hyperactive cruel princess. But the drawing coincides perfectly with Beardsley's Venus, the figure of a motherly goddess of love described in his unfinished novel, which was originally called *Under the Hill* (the "hill" being, of course, the mons veneris) and subsequently *The Story of Venus and Tannhäuser*.[1] She is the deity whom the *Toilette II* illustrates, which leaves little doubt that Beardsley imagined the Baptist's killer to be the personification of the dark side of the great earth-goddess. Her millennia-old mythology is given a wonderfully witty and obscene, as well as touchingly personal, interpretation in every single piece of Beardsley's work, but rarely do the visual and the literary complement each other so well as in the two *Toilettes of Salomé,* one demonstrating the fertile, the other the terrible face of nature. I have therefore taken the two renditions as the point of departure to survey a long tradition of legends, as well as works of literature and art, of which Beardsley is a late heir. I do not aim, however, at creating a compendium of iconographic motifs connected to the good earth and its evil flowers, a subject that could easily fill a whole library. On the contrary, I have chosen to signal problems rather than exhaust them, concentrating on texts and pictures well known in the nineteenth century; and I have limited my research to the most popular topics of the fin-de-siècle period. However, the few selected themes are illuminated from many different angles in order to convey their complexity and ambiguity and to show that the more archaic and elemental a motif, the more likely it is to contain not only a multiplicity of meanings, but also the coincidence of opposites.

Under the Hill

Beardsley's unfinished novel begins with Chevalier Tannhäuser arriving in the evening at the entrance to a cave (fig. 59), a place that "waved drowsily with strange flowers, heavy with perfume, dripping with odours." The mountain that he is about to enter breathes with "faint music as strange and distant as sea-legends that are heard in shells," and the sound is identified by him as "the Vespers of Venus" and "his cue for entry." "A delicious moment," thought Tannhäuser, "to slip into exile," and, "undoing a tangle in the tassel of his stick, [he] stepped into the shadowy corridor that ran into the bosom of the wan hill" (VT, pp. 25–26).

Beardsley's frivolous book offers a parody of ancient cave mythology. It makes fun of lovers, poets, artists, and aristocrats who in the depth of the earth search for muses and nymphs—poetic inspiration and unlimited pleasure. But there is something more serious in Beardsley's book as well. It speaks bluntly and with marvelous irony about the causes that make one go underground and "into exile." He exposes Tannhäuser's infantilism, his impotence, and his death wish. The garden of delights situated in the womb of the Venusberg is a paradise, a kindergarten, and an asylum where lunatics play Don Juans and Venuses, competing with each other in obscenity and perversion. Grossly exaggerating every minute detail of the merry-go-round, Beardsley alludes to and derides erotic art and literature as well as pornography. But he also makes the point that only by means of regression and infantilism is one able to get in touch with the most elemental desires and fears, the very fabric of life and art.

Beardsley's novel was inspired by the medieval legend of Tannhäuser as it was presented in Richard Wagner's opera *Tannhäuser*, though he might have heard the story from other sources as well. But to appreciate the novel one has to recall the ancient tradition on which it is based: the primordial cave which both opposes and complements the garden of paradise and as such belongs to the great subjects of fantastic reverie (fig. 60).

In the pseudepigraphic *Two Books of Adam and Eve*,[2] the parents of humanity are expelled from the garden and lodged in a grotto that is called the "cave of treasure." It is located below the garden that spreads out on the top of the mountain, and Adam and Eve consider it a narrow, dark prison. To bring some consolation to the desperate couple, God sends them tokens of their previous life to keep in the cave. The presence of souvenirs from the garden explains the name of the grotto. The "cave of treasure" functions as a secret and sacred primordial hideout where memories of the lost paradise are kept for future generations. When Adam dies, God orders his children to bury him in the cave, which thus becomes a catacomb.

The "cave of treasure" serves humanity as the first home and tomb. Like the Paleolithic caves of Lascaux and Altamira, it bridges the gap between the present and the past, the lost original and the copy, and represents the first museum. While open space evokes the danger of a journey into the unknown, during which one may lose one's way, forget one's origins, and abandon traditions, the cave, an intimate enclosure, suggests a protected, embryonic existence. Its inhabitants depend on God, as children would on a parent. (Indeed, Adam and Eve refer to God not only as father but also as mother.) Consequently, the cave is reserved only for the obedient ones. Cain, the "hater" of God, is expelled; he descends the holy mountain and settles at the bottom, becoming a restless wanderer in the "western plains," which symbolize human homelessness and corruption. But the "cave of treasure" reminds one also of the Platonic cave because the tokens from paradise are not dissimilar to the shadows thrown onto the walls of a grotto from a distant, perfect world.

The European symbolism of the cave as dwelling-place of mythical femininity, personifying the fertility and regeneration of earth and water, was established in Greece. Several famous passages in the *Odyssey* deal with caves: in Book 9 the cave of Polyphemus, in Book 15 the cave of Calypso, and in Book 13 the even more famous grotto of the naiads on Ithaca:

> High at the head a branching Olive grows,
> And crowns the pointed cliffs with shady boughs.
> Beneath, a gloomy Grotto's cool recess
> Delights the Nereids of the neighb'ring seas;
> Where bowls and urns were form'd of living stone,
> And massy beams in native marble shone:
> On which the labours of the nymphs were roll'd,
> Their webs divine of purple mix'd with gold.
> Within the cave, the clustring bees attend
> Their waxen works, or from the roof depend.
> Perpetual waters o'er the pavement glide;
> Two marble doors unfold on either side;
> Sacred the south, by which the Gods descend,
> But mortals enter at the northern end.
>
> (13:122–35)

The cave of water-nymphs, who produce the very fabric of life, is identified by Homer as a place of passage to another world, and, significantly, it has two entrances: the one, turned away from the sun and thus associated with death, is destined for humans; the other (likened to the immortal energy of the sun) is reserved for gods. Thus the cave appears also as the meeting place of the high and the low, the material and the spiritual, where shadows repose and beings made of light glide about.

Homer speaks of the elemental architecture created by nature and of life originating from it. His image inspires endless fantasy, as in Porphyrius's extensive commentary on the cave of naiads in the *Odyssey*.[3] The length of this mystical text conveys the significance Porphyrius attributed to the grotto as a metaphor for the spirit of the earth and the mysteries of procreation. The luminous gods, incarnations of sunlight and reason, visit the cave, but its permanent inhabitants are the shadow, the unconscious, and the female. Nature is a she and in her subterranean chambers dwell all Great Goddesses, like Venus and Diana. In Homer's *Hymn to Venus* the goddess tells Anchises that she will bear him a son whom the "Nymphs in their Caves shall nurse."[4] After death, the bodies of the mortals return to the caves and, thus, the goddess, worshiped at Delphi as ἐπιτυμβία (Aphrodite of the tomb), is responsible for them as well, her other epithets being τυμβώρυχος (grave-digger), μελαινίς (dark), and μυχία (of the depth). Similarly, Artemis, the goddess of birth and the hunt, has her refuge in a "cave, which no hand of man had wrought: but nature by her own devices had imitated art. She had carved a natural arch from the living stone and the soft tufa rocks. On the right hand was a murmuring spring of clear water, spreading out into a wide pool with grassy banks. Here the goddess, when she was tired with hunting in the woods, used to bathe her fastidious limbs in the pure water" (Ovid, *Met.* 3:157–61).[5]

The murmuring of the water in the depth of the earth was likened to the distant voices of the Muses—and to the flow of thoughts in one's own soul. "Muses" in Greek probably meant "thinkers" and "rememberers," and the ancient legends relate them to the past—to one's own memories and to the history of mankind as well as of the earth. Hesiod (*Theog.* 77) saw them as the daughters of Zeus and Mnemosyne (Memory); others described them as the children of Uranus and Ge. The Muses possessed the gift of prophecy, wore masks, and presided over the nine principal divisions of letters. The Roman poets identified the Greek Muses with the Italian Camenae, nymphs of springs and goddesses of birth, to whom a grove near the Porta Capena in Rome was dedicated by the king Numa, so that he might be able to converse with Egeria, one of them (Livy, 1.19). The presence of the Muses made the grotto a sanctuary of the arts: a museum. The ancients obviously believed that in the solitude of a subterranean location and in the presence of already created works of art, thoughts could be recollected and transformed into poetical images; visions could be born. In the shadowy Mediterranean caves music was played and the first theatrical performances were probably staged.[6]

The grotto of Psyche is related to the cave of the Muses. The chamber of the Greek soul, the beloved of Amor, is not dark but illuminated with its own inner light. "The walls were so solidly built up with great blocks of gold, that glittered and shone in such sort that the chambers, porches, and doors gave out the light of day as [if] it had been the sun" (Apuleius, *The Golden Ass*, 5:1).[7] Thus the home of Psyche is not a humid, earthly cave of organic life but a mine of gold and precious stones which, like the spirit, possesses its own light and so appears, as Walter Pater put it, "a place fashioned for conversation of gods with men."[8] It is an inner location that both opposes and complements the dark caves where the fabric of life is woven and disintegrates. The Platonic dualism of the body and soul and Apuleius's suggestive story of the beautiful young girl who, captive in the subterranean chambers, dreams and awaits her beloved have made European poets talk to their souls. Their incantations sound more mystical or more erotic depending on the gender of the word "soul," which in the Romance and Slavic languages as well as in German is indeed female.[9]

Directed against the mysteries and orgies of late antiquity, many of which were celebrated in caves, Christianity, once it had established itself (i.e., left the catacombs), did not promote subterranean localities. But because the cult of Venus had been transferred to the Virgin, caves continued to be dedicated to the Madonna in all Catholic countries. Besides, some of the great miracles of Christianity happened in caves, which were subsequently venerated by the faithful. It is interesting to note that the struggle between the old and the new gods involved caves which both pagans and Christians claimed for themselves. The fight for them is reflected in a letter that Saint Jerome wrote to Paulinus in A.D. 395, informing him about the statue of Jupiter being installed on the very spot where the Resurrection had occurred, and about a marble figure of Venus being put up where the cross had stood. Then, Jerome continues, "Even my own Bethlehem, as it is now, that most venerable spot in the whole world of which the psalmist sings: 'the truth hath sprung out of the earth' (Ps 85:11), was overshadowed by a grove of Tammuz, that is of Adonis; and in the very cave where the infant Christ had uttered his earliest cry lamentation was made for the paramour of Venus."[10] Once Christianity had taken over, Tammuz, the Babylonian god of vegetation, who was believed to die and to rise annually and was identified with Adonis, the lover of Aphrodite, disappeared.

The origins of the artificial cave, an architectural imitation of the real one, have to be sought in mythology, literature, and art, as well as in poetic reverie and in an understanding of their significance to the psyche. In southern countries the grotto represents a comfortable, cool retreat, and in general it is sheltered from the business of life and suited for daydreaming. Serving the pleasure of the happy, leisurely few, the artificial grotto is a highly aristocratic piece of architecture found in palaces and in the gardens of antiquity and again in those from the Renaissance to the twentieth century. Because of the important role played by water in real and imaginary caves, the origins of the artificial grotto are closely connected with that of a nymphaeum, a well or a fountain dedicated to the nymphs, which was later transformed into a bath.

Elements of artificial grottoes and nymphaea were combined into a luxurious and dreamlike whole in the design of the famous villa of the emperor Hadrian in Tivoli.[11] It consisted of baths and cryptoportici, pools, canals, vaulted temples, island theaters, a maritime theater, and an artificial grotto known as the Entry to the Underworld. The canal was built in memory of Hadrian's lover, Antinoos, who had mysteriously drowned in the Nile, and it was named after the Egyptian god Serapis. Hadrian held meetings in his villa with priests, scholars, and artists and indulged in poetry and music. There, perhaps, he wrote an incantation to his soul that sounds quite Jungian and was used by Walter Pater as an inscription for the eighth chapter of *Marius the Epicurean:*

> *Animula, vagula, blandula!*
> *Hospes comesque corporis,*
> *Quae nunc abibis in loca?*
> *Pallidula, rigida, nudula.*[12]

The artificial grotto became popular again in the Renaissance, when the overgrown ancient ruins were mistakenly interpreted as artificial caves, and some knowledge about grottoes and nymphaea was disseminated by *Hypnerotomachia Poliphili* (fig. 61). Because of the connection with water, femininity, and the origins of life, the scallop shell out of which Venus was born can frequently be encountered in these forms of architecture, both as a shape and as building material. In Alberti's description of an artificial cave we read that "Walls were composed of various Sorts of Sea-shells, lying roughly together, some reversed, some with their Mouths outwards, their Colours being so artfully blended as to form a very beautiful Variety" (*Ten Books on Architecture*, 9:4).

The shell is one of the emblems of the grotesque, not only in architecture but also in decorative arts. The predilection for it reflects both its inherent qualities and the universal reverie provoked by the miraculous creation of snails, which produce houses of their own substance—as if from nothingness. Being an intimate enclosure, the shell has been regarded as the symbol of the vagina and the uterus; hence it can be viewed as a miniature grotto. Gaston Bachelard writes beautifully about the shell's being a microcosm of its own and therefore regarded as a model of the world and of all creation (fig. 62).[13] Bosch and other fantastic artists of the late Middle Ages delighted in the depiction of shells with all possible creatures enclosed in or creeping out of them. As late as the end of the nineteenth century, the German painter Hans Thoma used the same image. He drew the world as a shell-like *orobouros*, a winged monster ready to devour a trumpeting, winged baby—the human soul singing in praise of its fragile life (fig. 63).

The white, perfectly symmetrical scallop shell has been especially popular in the European tradition. Among the Greeks, the female-shaped container was valued for features similar to those later attributed by the alchemists to the philosophers' egg: it was filled with the juice and the spirit of life. In the Renaissance the scallop shell was thought of as the cradle of Venus. Thus, in Botticelli's *Birth of Venus* the goddess is represented as floating on the shell or rising out of it. Sometimes the shell is not completely open and discloses only the deity's head and breast; sometimes the shell looks like wings. It protects the body of Venus and her purity. "A niche decorated with a scallop shell," writes Baltrušaitis, "throws onto the statue the light of immortality."[14] Like many other attributes, the scallop shell was transferred from the old to the new goddess of love and therefore appeared in the background of portraits of the Madonna. What had once served as the base on which Venus stood was elevated by Christianity to Mary's head or above it and functioned as a kind of nimbus. As if to stress the distinction between the two divinities, Botticelli, for instance, was careful to place the shell in the *Birth of Venus* turned with its mouth down, differentiating it from the shell with its mouth up in *Madonna En-throned with Six Saints* (Saint Barnabas Altarpiece, Uffizi, Florence). And Piero della Francesca recalled alchemical symbolism in depicting an egg hanging from the mouth of the shell that shelters the Madonna in his *Madonna with Federico da Montefeltro, the Duke of Urbino* (Brera, Milan).

Borrowing from the Christian tradition, Beardsley first associated the scallop shell with the Madonna and drew it above the head of his juvenile *Virgin with the Lily*. However, in his mature work the shell functions as an attribute of Venus and other voluptuous females. The cuffs on the sleeves of Venus's dress, her carriage, her mirror, and her flowerpots of rosebushes are all shell-shaped. In the drawing *Billet-Doux* a frivolous lady is shown in the depth of her shell-shaped bed, and *The Lodge* is ornamented with roses placed inside scallop shells.

In the seventeenth and eighteenth centuries, architectural grottoes were incorporated into baroque palaces and monasteries. The grotto salons became especially popular in Austria and Germany. They were usually situated beneath the hall, faced the garden, and were called "sala terrena." The setting and decoration of these terrestrial rooms evoke the symbolism of water and earth with the ambiguity typical of the grotesque—half joking, half serious.

The "sala terrena" in the Altenburg monastery (Lower Austria), for instance, can be regarded as an illustrated dictionary of grotesque iconography. The interior is dominated by water. Shells and vases filled with aqueous vegetation are painted on both sides of the narrow, winding staircase. At the bottom of the steps a Harlequin stands as if he were at the bottom of the sea. He holds a paper scroll showing a procession of his companions and seems to announce "a spectacle of theatrum mundi or a danse macabre."[15] On the walls of the first interior, tritons, seleni, nymphs, dolphins, and other sea creatures, together with shells and strange vases, constitute the allegory of terrestrial water. The paintings in the next room display an even greater richness and vitality of nature, alluding to water as the primordial element and the cradle of all being. They illustrate Ovid's *Metamorphoses:* Leda with the swan, Ceres, Prudentia and Diana accompanied by the unicorn. On the south wall the virgin huntress kills Orion; on the north wall she puts Endymion to sleep. The female principle dominates everywhere. But the seriousness of the mythological scenes is shaken by the paintings on the ceiling of the last room. There the announcement made at the entrance is at last fulfilled, and Harlequin's friends, Pantalone, Colombina, Mezzetino, and others, appear riding on fantastic birds. Surrounded by sea-monsters, they seem to flee the watery female element, escaping into the male sky.

In the "sala terrena," mythology is combined with play, ritual seriousness with a merry-go-round, ancient images with both commedia dell'arte and fashionable *chinoiserie*, of which there are several hints in the murals. This harlequinade reflects the sportive face of the grotesque. Its other, fearful side is revealed in the interior called the "crypt," of unknown purpose, situated not under the organ-loft but under the library of the monastery. The walls of this large, elongated hall are covered with representations of vanity and the danse macabre. Expired candles, sand-glasses, and bats unite with flagella and exotic birds in deadly arabesques. The impression of heterogeneity is reinforced by the contrasting images of living and dead matter: in front of a beautiful lady, serpents devour a female corpse. Water plays an important role in the crypt but not that of a life-originating element; here it is a destructive force. Thus, above a shell-shaped fountain that ejects a stream of water, a human skeleton leans its bony feet on an overturned amphora; skeletons of fish are stuck on Poseidon's trident. Hermes appears as a messenger from the underworld, and figures of hermits are shown hiding in the deep, dark caves.

An artificial cave of more modest dimensions was built in England by a poet. In order to communicate properly with his soul, Alexander Pope (1688–1744) constructed a small, personal grotto on his property in the village of Twickenham. The cave, as we know it both from his own description and that given by a visitor, seems to have combined the Homeric caves of the *Odyssey* (translated by Pope into English) with Apuleius's chamber of Psyche. "From the River *Thames*," writes the poet in a letter to Edward Blount,

> you see thro' my Arch up a Walk of the Wilderness to a
> kind of open Temple, wholly compos'd of Shells in the
> Rustic Manner; and from that distance under the Temple
> you look down thro' a sloping Arcade of Trees [lining the
> walk to the grotto on the garden side], and see the Sails
> on the River passing suddenly and vanishing, as thro' a
> Perspective Glass. When you shut the Doors of the
> Grotto, it becomes on the instant, from a luminous
> Room, a Camera obscura; on the Walls of which the ob-
> jects of the River, Hills, Woods, and Boats, are forming a
> moving Picture in their visible Radiations: And when you
> have a mind to light it up, it affords you a very different
> Scene; it is finished with Shells interspersed with Pieces
> of Looking-glass in angular forms; and in the Cieling
> [sic] is a Star of the same Material, at which when a
> Lamp (of an orbicular Figure of thin Alabaster) is hung
> in the Middle, a thousand pointed Rays glitter and are
> reflected over the Place.[16]

To this an observer from Newcastle adds:

> To multiply this Diversity, and still more increase the
> Delight, Mr. Pope's *poetick Genius* has introduced a

> *kind of Machinery, which performs the same Part in the Grotto that supernal Powers and incorporeal Beings act in the heroick Species of Poetry: This is effected by disposing Plates of Looking glass in the obscure Parts of the Roof and Sides of the Cave, where a sufficient Force of Light is wanting to discover the Deception, while the other Parts, the Rills, Fountains, Flints, Pebbles, &c. being duly illuminated, are so reflected by the various posited Mirrors, as, without exposing the Cause, every Object is multiplied, and its Position represented in a surprizing Diversity. Cast your Eyes upward, and you half shudder to see Cataracts of Water precipitating over your Head, from impending Stones and Rocks, while salient Spouts rise in rapid Streams at your Feet: Around, you are equally surprized with flowing Rivulets and rolling Waters, that rush over airey Precipices, and break amongst Heaps of ideal Flints and Spar. Thus, by a fine Taste and happy Management of Nature, you are presented with an undistinguishable Mixture of Realities and Imagery.*[17]

Pope's cave is a metaphor for the mind as an inner space onto which reality is projected and by which it is broken up into a myriad of particles: in the splinters of this inner looking glass the internal and the external combine into a fantastic world of imagination and poetry. His grotto celebrates the splendor of the mind as opposed to the outer shell of the body and closely resembles a philosopher's hideout, for instance John Locke's "dark room": "a closet wholly shut from light, with only some little openings left, to let in external visible resemblances, or ideas of things without."[18]

Though Pope presented his grotto as a place erected for the pursuit of truth and moral perfection (at the entrance, for instance, was placed a stone relief showing the Crown of Thorns), it served as a refuge for the poet, who was dwarfish, a hunchback, and a Roman Catholic at a time of religious intolerance. Pope's grotto also had female patronage: Egeria;[19] a sleeping nymph mentioned in an inscription that Pope found on an antique statue and translated into English; the nymph Calypso, whose grotto is represented in an engraving by William Kent that serves as the headpiece for Book 5 of Pope's *Odyssey;* and last but not least, the poet's mother. The obelisk in her memory with the inscription "Ah Editha! Matrum Optima. Mulierum amantissima. Vale" occupied the key position in the garden surrounding the cave and was the place where Pope used to grieve after her death.[20]

There are several references to caves in Pope's poetry. He speaks of a "Cave of Poetry" (*Dunciad*, 1:34), a "Cave of Truth" (*Dunciad*, 4:641) and a "Cave of Spleen" (*Rape of the Lock*). The description of this last cave exercised considerable influence upon Beardsley, who illustrated that "heroic-comical poem." The most startling of his drawings, *The Cave of Spleen*, corresponds closely to Pope's strange images. The grotto, crowded with phantoms of a highly erotic character, brings to mind the interior of Pope's own cave: a distorting mirrored cabinet and a kaleidoscope in which the differently broken and reflected particles of reality form grotesque pictures:

> *Now lakes of liquid gold, Elysian scenes,*
> *And crystal domes, and angels in machines.*
> *Unnumbered throngs, on ev'ry side are seen,*
> *Of bodies changed to various forms by Spleen.*
> *Here living tea-pots stand, one arm held out,*
> *One bent; the handle this, and that the spout:*
> *A pipkin there, like Homer's tripod walks;*
> *Here sighs a jar, and there a goose-pye talks;*
> *Men prove with child, as pow'rful fancy works,*
> *And maids turned bottles, call aloud for corks.*
> *Safe past the gnome through this fantastic band,*
> *A branch of healing spleenwort in his hand.*
> *Then thus addressed the pow'r—"Hail, wayward queen!*
> *Who rule the sex to fifty from fifteen. . .* "[21]
> (*Rape of the Lock*, 4:45–58)

In Beardsley's drawing the "cave of spleen" (fig. 64) looks like a mixture of hell, a fin-de-siècle den, and an alchemist's or anatomist's laboratory with homunculi or embryos kept in transparent vessels.[22] The illustration translates the whole fantastic and embryonic band of Pope's imagination into a visual grotesque.

An impressive complex of sea grottoes was constructed between 1731 and 1758 by the Margravine Wilhemine in Bayreuth. In her New Castle, for instance, there were two grotto-chambers made out of shells with a painting on the ceiling of a sleeping Venus with swans. They foreshadow the famous Venus-grotto built over a century later by Ludwig II of Bavaria in his park in Linderhof. His cave, made of cast-iron stalactites coated with cement, was to serve as a stage for the first act of Wagner's *Tannhäuser*. There, among all the other kitsch, a gilded shell in the form of a swan boat floats on a subterranean lake, a shell-shaped throne of the king stands in proximity to a waterfall, and garlands of roses hang about.

Wagner's opera contains the quintessence of the romantic reverie about the chthonic mother and the mysterious underworld of love and death. At the turn of the century this theme was both explored in an intense and serious way and derided and turned into a grotesque. Besides literature, art, and architecture, the fantasies were nourished by Darwinists pointing to the ancestors of humanity, who once dwelt in rock shelters and cavities; and by archeologists and anthropologists discovering sacred mountains and caves with many universal symbols of fertility and femininity, such as shells, spirals, and moons.

Turn-of-the-century literature, poetry, and art often express the fear of and the desire to drown in the black waters so frequently associated with Charon and Ophelia,[23] or to disappear into the mines, the empire of a "dark lady."[24] The motif of the grotto recurs in apocalyptic as well as blissful versions. Paths of "black corruption" lead to Georg Trakl's "blue cave" of infantile incest.[25] With the approach of the First World War, the cave of childhood ominously approximated a vision of mass graves and battle-fields with the trampled bodies of dead mothers, children, and embryos.[26]

Chevalier Tannhäuser, the hero of Beardsley's novel, was a historical figure—a medieval poet with a reputation as a womanizer and heretic. Born in Austria around 1200, he frequented the courts of Emperor Frederick II, his son King Henry VII, and Prince Frederick the Quarrelsome, and his poetry reflected the loose mores and the pleasure-filled lives of his pro-tectors. But Tannhäuser's vivid and colorful verses also mirror folk tradi-tions and, consequently, pagan rituals and the beliefs preserved in them. The Church fought them vigorously; it must have been highly disturbed by Tannhäuser's writings praising ancient sensuality and voluptuousness instead of virtue. This very animosity might have produced the legend, as J. Siebert has suggested: "Presumably the same circles which stamped the emperor Frederick II as Antichrist also invented the tale according to which Tannhäuser had lived for a long time with the pagan goddess Venus; when he finally left her, repented, and asked for remission of sins, nobody, including the pope, was prepared to forgive him."[27]

The multiple versions of legends about Tannhäuser coincide with the changing approaches to religion. In the oldest tales Tannhäuser weds Venus and thus condemns himself to eternal hell. In the fourteenth and fifteenth centuries, when mystical eroticism flourished, the fictional Tannhäuser was advised not to give up, but to pray for help to the Holy Virgin. Finally, during the Counter-Reformation, the stories included criticism directed at the pope, whose severity pushed Tannhäuser into the arms of Venus. Thus not only the poet but also the merciless pope was sent to hell. Obviously popular judgment favored Tannhäuser, who indeed mentioned Pope Urban III, an enemy of the Stauf dynasty, in his poetry. The legend survived in the German-speaking world until the nineteenth century and was made famous by Wagner. Originally entitled *Der Venusberg. Romantische Oper* [*The Mount of Venus. A Romantic Opera*], it was performed for the first time in 1845 under the title *Tannhäuser und der Sängerkrieg auf Wartburg* and appeared in 1861 in the repertoire of the Paris Opera House. In order to please the French gentlemen, who delighted in young girls' legs, Wagner extended the first scene, which takes place in the "Venusberg," by embellishing it with a ballet—in the form of a bacchanal. In 1892 Beardsley saw *Tannhäuser* performed at Covent Garden and he even drew Max Alvary,[28] who played the roles of both Tannhäuser and Tristan.

The first act of *Tannhäuser* takes place inside the Venusberg. Wagner describes the setting as a large grotto illuminated by dim light falling through a crevice. The landscape is dominated by water: from the top of the cave a greenish waterfall descends into the valley, giving birth to a stream that dissolves into the dark lake. From the walls of the cave ledges of irregular shapes protrude; they are covered with strange tropical vegetation. The stage description faithfully delineates the stereotype of the female cavity—dark, romantic, and filled with a great many natural wonders—as it is universally depicted in erotic literature.[29] This internal and subterranean landscape represents the womb of the earth and the home of man and is ruled by the goddess of love. When the curtain rises, Venus appears seated in her cave. Tannhäuser kneels in front of her, his head on her bosom, his harp at his side.

Wagner based his libretto on the version of the legend in which Tannhäuser is saved from eternal damnation by the intervention of the Holy Virgin. She puts a virtuous maiden in his way whose pure love tears him from the deadly caresses of Venus. Whereas the Wagnerian hero escapes the love-pit, Beardsley makes his chevalier return to the Mons Veneris, exclaim "adieu" and "goodbye, Madonna," and go underground.

Beardsley does not disclaim the inspiration he drew from Wagner's opera. Not only does he indicate that the mountain's breathing sounds like music, but, in an obvious allusion to the ringing of bells in a Christian church, he interprets the theme as the "Vespers of Venus." Upon hearing it, Tannhäuser strikes "a few chords of accompaniment ever so lightly upon his little lute" (VT, p. 26). The erotic tone awakens the moths sleeping on the "subtle columns" which flank the entrance. However, the gate through which he enters the "wan hill" is conceived not after Wagner's opera but after the sanctuary of love described by Jean de Meung toward the end of the *Roman de la rose* (21:228): it is hidden in a tower placed on two pillars, as if on two feet.

Inside the mountain, Tannhäuser finds not so much a grotto as an entire planet of love (fig. 65). In the morning "the re-arisen sun, like the prince in the 'Sleeping Beauty,' woke all the earth with his lips. In that golden embrace the night dews were caught up and made splendid, the trees were awakened from their obscure dreams, the slumber of the birds was broken, and all the flowers of the valley rejoiced, forgetting their fear of the darkness" (VT, pp. 43–44). The subjects of Venus adore "every scrap" of her body, and all her excrement. In the morning a young man waits under a rosebush to attend "Venus upon her little latrinal excursions" (VT, p. 67); for another "never . . . could her ear yield sufficient wax!" (VT, p. 67). Fanatic lovers collect her spit "and Saphius found a month an interminable time" (VT, p. 67). The passage, although it makes fun of sexual deviations, connects them simultaneously to primitive pan-eroticism, focused on the woman as on fertile and fertilizing ground.

Pleasure prevails "under the hill": theater performances follow ballets, and pantomimes concerts. But the narrative, sparkling with frivolity, also possesses a darker tone struck at the very beginning: evening has been chosen as the time for Tannhäuser's return to the Mons Veneris, and the moth is his guide. In the penultimate chapter of the unfinished novel the carriage in which Venus drives with Tannhäuser is almost overturned because the goddess is violently making love to her chevalier. Greatly upset by the accident, the lover at first refuses to continue the trip and, when he finally consents, the reader realizes that the incident was meant to hint at the more sinister part of Venus's world:

> The landscape grew rather mysterious. The park, no longer troubled and adorned with figures, was full of grey echoes and mysterious sounds, the leaves whispered a little sadly, and there was a grotto that murmured like the voice that haunts the silence of a deserted oracle. Tannhäuser became a little triste. In the distance, through the trees, gleamed a still, argent lake. . . . Around its marge the trees and flags and fleurs de luce were unbreakably asleep. . . . Sometimes the lake took fantastic shapes, or grew to twenty times its size, or shrunk into a miniature of itself, without ever losing its unruffled calm, its deathly reserve. . . . it was a wonderful lake, a beautiful lake, and he would love to bathe in it, but he was sure he would be drowned if he did. (VT, p. 71)

The sad grotto with a "haunting voice" and the dangerous lake that grows and shrinks like a vagina[30] cause Tannhäuser to imagine frogs, animals of earth and the underworld (and of Bosch's hell). He is frightened by the thought of "how huge the frogs must have become" when "the water increased" (VT, p. 71). Contemplating this deadly lake, inspired probably by Virgil's description of the poisonous Aornos at the entrance to the lower world in Book 6 of the *Aeneid*,[31] the lover of Venus seems finally to recall that nothing but the corpse returns to the mother earth, who, in this sense, feeds on her children.

The Rose and the Ass

> To Cyprian Venus, still my verses vow,
> Who Gifts as sweete as honey doth bestow
> On all Mortality; that ever smiles,

And rules a face that all foes reconciles;
Ever sustaining in her hand a Flowre
That all desire keepes ever in her Powre.
　　　　——Homer, "To Venus," in Chapman's
　　　　trans.

When Chevalier Tannhäuser was just about to step "into the shadowy corridor that ran into the bosom of the wan hill," a wild rose caught "upon the trimmings of his muff, and in the first flush of displeasure he would have struck it brusquely away, and most severely punished the offending flower. But the ruffled mood lasted only a moment, for there was something so deliciously incongruous in the hardy petal's invasion of so delicate a thing, that Tannhäuser withheld the finger of resentment, and vowed that the wild rose should stay where it had clung—a passport, as it were, from the upper to the underworld." (VT, p. 26).

As a flower of love and of Aphrodite, the rose was introduced into literature by Homer. In his *Hymn* to the goddess, he describes her falling in love with Anchises, leaving her residence in Cyprus, and flying to him in her "Gowne / Wrought all with growing-rose-buds."[32] She takes off this dress to embrace her beloved, thus making the flower indeed a passport to the delights of her underworld. Not surprisingly, the rose is found, like a stamp, in many of Beardsley's drawings (fig. 66).

Christianity transferred the rose, like other attributes of the goddess of love, to the Virgin and imbued it with spirituality and mysticism. However, in erotic literature and art the rose has never stopped functioning as a symbol of femininity in general and of the female mouth, breasts, and vagina in particular. In an Italian anthology of erotic texts a whole chapter was dedicated to this flower,[33] which had already drawn similar attention in the anonymous verses of antiquity, fragments of Asclepiades and Lucretius, as well as in poems dating from the Middle Ages to the late nineteenth century. The authors of the grotesque regard the rose as a debased form of a passive, vegetal femininity, which on closer inspection shows dangerous thorns; and they delight in playing with the ambiguity of the different rose-shapes and colors as well as with the notion of the fleshly rose of desire, hidden behind all the Platonic rosaries. White or slightly pink and still hiding the richness of its petals in the firmly closed bud, the rose stands for a young girl's boyish figure and her chastity. The subsequent stages of blossoming are associated with the ripening of the female body until it finally opens up in all its splendor and intensity, like the red rose in full bloom, a sign of utmost sensual pleasure which does not last long. The short-lived magnificence of a flower doomed to be gone tomorrow is easily associated with quickly changing passion and ephemeral beauty threatened by corruption. The transitional character of the rose makes it an ideal object of fantastic transformations. The flower seems to capture the very essence of nature simultaneously growing and decaying but never resting, of life as a sequence of strange metamorphoses. Although omnipresent in European imagery, the rose enjoyed particular popularity in late antiquity, the late Middle Ages, and from Romanticism to World War I. At the turn of the nineteenth century the decadents promoted the indecent symbolism of the rose with their favorite texts, the *Metamorphoses or the Golden Ass* and the *Roman de la rose.*

The popularity of *The Golden Ass* among the English decadents was partly due to Pater's *Marius the Epicurean* (1885), a novel set in the Age of the Antonines. But the "sensations and ideas" of Marius, its hero, are those of an English eccentric in the 1880s who identifies the sensibility and reverie of late antiquity with fin-de-siècle Europe. In declining Rome and in Victorian London there is a constant desire to "enjoy in a garden of roses,"[34] an image of sensuality and contemplation, eroticism and mysticism.

Marius experiences the world as a curious nebula of changing shapes and appearances which fluctuate among various initiations into sexuality, cruelty, and religion. The fifth chapter of Pater's novel is entitled "The Golden Book" and refers, of course, to Apuleius's book, "dainty and fine, full of . . . archaisms and curious felicities."[35] It is quite likely that Beardsley became acquainted with *The Golden Ass* through *Marius the Epicurean,* but even if he did not actually read Apuleius's book, he must have been aware of the importance attributed to it by Pater as well as by Huysmans in *À rebours.* It makes sense, then, to present *The Golden Ass* through Pater's summary, in which the most relevant passage, describing grotesque transformations that happen in the enchanted Thessaly, reads as follows:

> *The scene of the romance was laid in Thessaly, the original land of witchcraft, and took one up and down its mountains, and into its old weird towns, haunts of magic and incantation, where all the more genuine appliances of the black art, left behind her by Medea when she fled through that country, were still in use. In the city of Hypata, indeed, nothing seemed to be its true self.—"You might think that through the murmuring of some cadaverous spell all things had been changed into forms not their own; that there was humanity in the hardness of the stones you stumbled on; that the birds you heard singing were feathered men; that the trees around the walls drew their leaves from a like source. The statues seemed about to move, the walls to speak, the dumb cattle to break out in prophecy; nay! The very sky and the sunbeams, as if they might suddenly cry out." Witches are there who can draw down the moon, or at least the lunar virus—that white fluid she sheds, to be found, so rarely, "on high, healthy places: which is a poison. A touch of it will drive men mad."*

> *And in one very remote village lives the sorceress*
> *Pamphile, who turns her neighbours into various ani-*
> *mals. What true humour in the scene where, after*
> *mounting the rickety stairs, Lucius, peeping curiously*
> *through a chink in the door, is a spectator of the transfor-*
> *mation of the old witch herself into a bird, that she may*
> *take flight to the object of her affections,—into an owl!*
> . . .
> *By clumsy imitation of this process, Lucius, the hero*
> *of the romance, transforms himself, not as he had in-*
> *tended into a showy winged creature, but into the animal*
> *which has given name to the book; for throughout it there*
> *runs a vein of racy, homely satire on the love of magic*
> *then prevalent, curiosity concerning which had led Lucius*
> *to meddle with the old woman's appliances. "Be you my*
> *Venus," he says to the pretty maid-servant who has in-*
> *troduced him to the view of Pamphile, "and let me stand*
> *by you a winged Cupid!" and, freely applying the magic*
> *ointment, sees himself transformed "not into a bird, but*
> *into an ass!"*
> *Well! the proper remedy for his distress is a supper*
> *of roses, could such be found, and many are his quaintly*
> *picturesque attempts to come by them at that adverse sea-*
> *son; as he contrives to do at last, when, the grotesque*
> *procession of Isis passing by with a bear and other*
> *strange animals in its train, the ass following along with*
> *the rest suddenly crunches the chaplet of roses carried in*
> *the high-priest's hand.*[36]

What is of interest here is the obvious sexual relationship between the female roses and the male animal who wants to consume them. The very transformation of Lucius is caused by his desire to improve the chances of his promiscuity by becoming the "winged Cupid." Lucius is therefore terribly disappointed when he is transformed "not into a bird, but into an ass," not into the incarnation of a swift, attractive phallus but into the symbol of something comical and dull. Trapped in this ugly and ridiculous form, he hopes, nevertheless, for a "supper of roses," a meal that suggests defloration. All this makes sense. The metamorphosis results from sexual greed, and it represents a punishment. For intruding into the world of female magic, Lucius becomes an ass, an animal renowned for its foolishness, stubbornness, promiscuity, and subordinate position. (The ancient Egyptians depicted an ignorant person with the head and ears of an ass, and the Romans considered it a bad omen to meet a donkey. The fifth proposition of Book 1 of Euclid is known as the *Pons asinorum*, the "bridge of asses," and Thomas, the incredulous Apostle, was called by the medieval Germans "Thomasesel.") The German satirists of the emerging Protestantism developed a great liking for the beast as an instrument for their derision of Catholicism. Monks and bishops were represented as obscene asses and the pope was drawn as a hermaphroditic ass-monster, with many heads, tails, and horns.

In Théodore de Bry's *Album of Friends*, a dualistic ass framed by a Renaissance grotesque is depicted in process of choosing between virtue and spirituality (indicated to his right by a rosebush without thorns symbolizing the Holy Virgin and a dove incarnating the Holy Spirit) and worldly sin represented to his left by a thistle, a plant mentioned by God in his cursing of Adam (Gen. 3:17–18) and thus standing for sorrow and evil. Underneath the thistle, next to a bottle and a bowl filled with coins, hides the devil (fig. 67). The satirical picture is, of course, derived from *The Golden Ass* and Lucius's agonizing search for roses, which in the bewitched Thessaly grow in "shadowy valleys" and garnish the shrines of goddesses but are difficult to obtain for consumption and thus engender Lucius's hallucinations. Upon catching sight of "the grove of Venus and the Graces, where secretly glittereth the royal hue of so lively and delectable a flower," the galloping ass realizes that he has been misled:

> They were no roses neither tender nor pleasant, neither
> moistened with the heavenly drops of dew nor celestial
> liquor, which grow out of the rich thicket and thorns.
> Neither did I perceive that there was any valley at all,
> but only the bank of the river environed with great thick
> trees, which had long branches like unto laurel, and bear
> a flower without any manner of scent but somewhat red
> of hue, and the common people call them by the name of
> laurel-roses, which are very poisonous to all manner of
> beasts. (Golden Ass, 4:2)

The metamorphosis of roses which takes place here includes the transforming of their sex. Instead of being "tender" or "pleasant" in the way which is appropriate for a flower of Venus, they are given the name "laurel," a hard and masculine evergreen which is found in the wreaths of Hercules but not in the garland of the goddess of love. These phallic roses do not grow in a "shadowy valley" but at "the bank of the river environed with great thick trees," that is, in a completely different landscape possessing a rather masculine character. But the false roses not only have the wrong sex, they also seem to be close cousins to the "fleurs du mal" and all other poisonous and dangerous flowers of corruption, pestilence, hell, and death which became so popular in the poetic herbaries of the late nineteenth century. They represented the different dangers of sexuality: incurable venereal diseases as well as the mythological "vagina dentata," the feared organ of an aggressive, phallic woman. The name "laurel roses" conveys the threat of an inappropriate sexuality. In order to be satisfied, Lucius needs to "meddle" with women and not with men. Apuleius plays here with the dual gender of the rose—male when imagined as a closed bud, female when seen open—an ambiguity that for centuries has inspired both the vaguest and the most explicit erotic reveries as well as one that is alluded to at the beginning of Beardsley's novel.

Rose symbolism permeates medieval literature and art and can be encountered in many stories about the Christian saints. In the life of Saint Francis of Assisi (1181 or 1182–1226), for instance, an adversary thornbush is miraculously transformed into a gentle and wonderful rosebush without thorns. The legend, reminding us of Lucius's adventures, tells of Francis praying at night in his cell near the sanctuary of Portiuncula and suddenly being tempted to renounce his holy life. In order to overcome the temptation, he throws himself into a thornbush which at that very moment changes into a rosebush without thorns, the flower of Mary. The dried petals of these docile roses can still be bought today in the sanctuary; they are sold in tiny envelopes illustrated with a thornless rose branch and a picture of the saint caressing a lamb—his Lord—in a pacified rose garden.

The legend captures the intense preoccupation with roses that characterized Saint Francis's times. In the thirteenth century two great epic poems deal with the problem of gaining access to the rose garden. One of them is *Rosengarten*, written in Mittelhochdeutsch around 1250 and preserved in three different versions (which proves its popularity in German-speaking countries). The versified story is a heroic account of the battle between Siegfried and Dietrich of Bern (a name given in popular poetry to Theodoric the Great), who fought each other in Kriemhild's rose garden at Worms. The French *Roman de la rose,* started by Guillaume de Lorris between 1225 and 1230 and completed about forty years later by Jean de Meung, is, of course, better known.

Guillaume de Lorris conceived his *Roman de la rose* as the dream of a twenty-year-old youth who, after much wandering, comes across the garden of love surrounded by high walls and guarded by the enemies of love. Lady Idleness opens the door for him and Amor takes care of him, leading him to the fountain of Narcissus. At the bottom of the fountain there are two crystals that make it possible to see in the water the reflection not only of things close to the fountain, but of the entire garden with all its details. The attention of the young man is caught by the mirror image of the rosebushes. He is interested not so much by flowers in full bloom that will be gone by tomorrow but by tightly closed buds, and one of them in particular. When the god of love, who watches the young man closely, sees him single out a particular bud, he pierces his heart with six arrows. Gravely wounded, the youth capitulates and becomes the prisoner of Amor, who closes his heart with a key.

Though the lover is overwhelmed with desire for his rosebud, he cannot reach it because the rosebushes are protected by an impenetrable hedge. Assisted in his effort by Fair Welcoming, the son of Courtesy, the lover manages to get to the other side of the hedge only to realize that the rosebushes are well guarded by Resistance, Foul-Mouth, Shame, and Fear. Aware of the difficulties, Reason tries to persuade the lover to give up his desires and Fair Welcoming deserts him. Meanwhile Jealousy builds a fortress with a cylindrical tower around the rosebushes. Thus the rosebud and Fair Welcoming become imprisoned in this fortification.

The story of the rose was brought to this point by Guillaume de Lorris, a melancholic and ironic author interested more in the hardship than in the fulfillment of desire. He described the way to ideal love in accordance with the pattern of Hercules on the crossroads, who is confronted with nothing but obstacles after choosing virtue. What the lover pursues is not sensual pleasure but sublimity, suggested to him by the crystals hidden in the depths of the water. It is interesting that what he saw was not just the rosebud, but the entire garden of love. Thus the metaphor seems to combine Ovid's story of Narcissus with Platonism: the notion of an ideal that is out of human reach and can only be perceived as a reflection of reality.

The image of the rosebud is imbued with ambiguity as far as the gender of the flower is concerned; *bouton* (bud) is in French a masculine word, and the lover's rejection of all the open roses may be taken as a hint that he has little interest in the female sex. The rosebud can thus be understood as synonymous with the narcissus, a flower representing both self-eroticism and homosexuality. Such an inclination might explain why this lover of the rosebush is so slow, impractical, and unproductive even in the plucking of the flower.

Not much of this ambiguity is preserved in Jean de Meung's continuation of the story. His text is not written from the perspective of an idealistic and sexually undecided youth, but from the position of an experienced and realistic womanizer whose reflections on love and the female sex sparkle with satire. His *Roman de la rose* shocked and outraged its female readership, and he was accused, probably rightly, of male chauvinism. His hero, helped by an old procuress and Fair Welcoming, manages to take the fortress of love and to transform the bud into a rose in full bloom.

All this has to be remembered to understand why, upon awakening "under the hill," Tannhäuser "thought of the 'Romaunt de la Rose,' beautiful, but all too brief."[37] And why this reminiscence was immediately followed by a grotesque elaboration on a Christian saint:

> *Saint Rose, the well-known Peruvian virgin; how she*
> *vowed herself to perpetual virginity when she was four*
> *years old; how she was beloved by Mary, who from the*
> *pale fresco in the Church of Saint Dominic, would stretch*
> *out her arms to embrace her; how she built a little oratory*
> *at the end of the garden and prayed and sang hymns in it*

*till all the beetles, spiders, snails and creeping things
came round to listen; how she promised to marry Ferdi-
nand de Flores, and on the bridal morning perfumed herself and painted her lips, and put on her wedding frock,
and decked her hair with roses, and went up to a little
hill not far without the walls of Lima; how she knelt there
some moments calling tenderly upon Our Lady's name,
and how Saint Mary descended and kissed Rose upon the
forehead and carried her up swiftly into heaven.*

To leave no doubt about the tender feeling binding Rose and Mary to each
other, Beardsley drew a masculine-looking Virgin embracing Rose (fig. 68)
and added in a footnote: "All who would respire the perfumes of Saint
Rose's sanctity, and enjoy the story of the adorable intimacy that subsisted
between her and Our Lady, should read Mother Ursula's 'Ineffable and
Miraculous Life of the Flower of Lima,' published shortly after the can-
onisation of Rose by Pope Clement X, in 1671." (VT, pp. 56–57).

Hinting at the lesbian nature of the mystical love between the two
women, Beardsley derided nebulous rose-allegories and made fun of Christian mystics. His drawing of Rose in the arms of the Holy Virgin has a
sacrilegious purpose and could have been inspired by such erotic examples
of Counter-Reformation art as Bernini's statue of Saint Teresa, whose pose
and expression suggest orgasm. Beardsley took an interest in the autobiography of Teresa of Avila and might have fashioned his Saint Rose of
Lima, also a baroque saint, after the descriptions of mystical passion given
by Teresa.[38]

In the footnote, Mother Ursula, the nun invented by Beardsley, describes Saint Rose as a "slim, sensitive plant" (VT, p. 57n). The reader then
expects an "ass" to turn up as well. And indeed, the author does not
disappoint us. Between the account of Rose's sanctity and the detailed
footnote, he mentions a "strange pamphlet" Tannhäuser had found in
"Venus's library" entitled "A Plea for the Domestication of the Unicorn"
(VT, p. 57).

The motif of the Madonna in a rose garden, especially popular in
medieval German painting, was taken up by the Pre-Raphaelites as well
as by Beardsley. He also drew his own sacrilegiously reversed Annunciation
in *The Mysterious Rose Garden* (fig. 69).[39] Like Mercury in the alchemical
illustrations, the divine messenger wears winged shoes, and his girlish
face is made ironic by a tiny mustache. Instead of golden rays or a dove
flying to the womb of the Virgin, other phallic symbols appear: Beardsley's
annunciator carries a long stick, as if for lighting candles, and a lantern
which perhaps alludes to the virgins who "took their lamps and went forth
to meet the bridegroom" (Matt. 25:1).

Fascination with the rose corresponds to a pronounced sensitivity to the passing of time. The *leitmotif* of the *Roman de la rose* is the brevity of beauty and love. The same vocabulary occurs in endless repetition in the poetry of the fin de siècle:

> They are not long, the days of wine and roses:
> Out of a misty dream
> Our path emerges for a while, then closes
> Within a dream.[40]

Accordingly, Beardsley's Salomé dances on rose petals, and roses ornament her clothes; a rosebush grows next to the body of the Syrian who killed himself because of the Jewish princess's cruelty, and a broken rose floats in the air over his head like a symbol of death. The rose on the dress of Saint Rose clearly indicates her sex organ. The basket full of roses and the two boys playing with the flowers allude to defloration (fig. 89).

In some of Beardsley's drawings for *Salomé*, the roses form a dense and impenetrable ornament which sucks in the female satyrs, whose hair is turned into roses winding around the burning candles and imprisoning butterflies that look like tiny men in evening dress. This garden of love conveys the feeling of *horror vacui*, a spider's web, and hell overgrown with black, devilish flowers ready to devour the humans and half-humans trapped in them. Thus the roses on the title page and around the list of illustrations serve as a good introduction to the dark and cruel world of Salomé and her deadly passion. And they bring to mind primitive rituals, like the Aztec celebration of the god Tezcatlipoca's passion for Xochiquetzal, the goddess of love. The festival took place next to his temple, where the image of the goddess was placed, heavily decorated with roses; around it danced boys dressed as butterflies and hummingbirds.

Beardsley makes it quite obvious that he treats roses as a synonym for the female body. Consequently every single flower, as well as every rose garland and bush, is penetrated by or at least pointed to by sharp and elongated objects: candles, sticks, herms, trunks, columns, or obelisks. In the absence of roses the very same sticks aim at women's breasts and wombs. If they do not hit the sexual target literally, one has but to imagine the lines of all the mock phalluses extended, and almost invariably they meet at the female sex zones. We know that Beardsley used to work on a single sheet of paper, gradually eliminating the unnecessary lines; thus one may well assume that the "connections" between the male and female sex parts or symbols really existed at the beginning and were only at the end rubbed out. Possibly, at a certain stage the drawings looked like prehistoric sexual representations in which the connections are indeed preserved. In any case, the sexual relationship between the rose and the penis is indicated by Beardsley most directly in his novel, where we encounter "little Rosalie perched like a postilion [fig. 70] upon the painted phallus of the god of all gardens" (VT, p. 68).

Beardsley was inspired by the veiled allegories of sacred and profane love present in medieval paintings and poems and by the sentimental echoes of them contained in the works of the Pre-Raphaelites[41] and of Edward Burne-Jones, whom young Beardsley considered the greatest living artist of his times.[42] But in pursuit of his own grotesque vision, Beardsley left behind Burne-Jones's illustrations of the *Roman de la rose* and revived the Menippean monstrosity of *The Golden Ass*. Burne-Jones expressed the traditional degradation of femininity, which he depicted, for instance, in *The Pilgrim in the Garden*[43] as a beautiful, delicate flower approached by the spiritual wanderer dressed in heavenly blue. Beardsley undertook in his drawings a debasement of men as well, turning them into beasts possessed by "a certain arrangement of roses" (VT, p. 41).

In Europe the tradition of the female garden of love and the image of beasts surrounding Aphrodite go back to Homer.[44] Her evergreen residence is situated on top of the highest mountain of Cyprus, the island of eternal spring. It is surrounded by golden wire netting and has a shining copper gate. A grove stretches beyond the garden and only those birds which sing best are allowed to enter. To honor the goddess the trees interlace their branches amorously and erotes dip their arrows into two springs—one sweet, the other bitter. On this "wood-crownd Hill" the goddess gives birth to Aeneas, the son of Anchises, during the spring that follows their first encounter on Mount Ida. However, before Venus enters Anchises' oxstall,

> her Mother-Brests [she]
> Gives to the Preyfull broode of savage Beasts. . . .
> About her blessed feet Wolves grislie-gray,
> Terrible Lyons, many a Mankind Beare,
> And Lybberds swift, insatiate of red Deare—
> Whose sight so pleas'd that ever as she past
> Through every Beast a kindely Love she cast.[45]

Christianity transformed the garden of Aphrodite into the *hortus conclusus* of the Madonna, a place of fertility and life symbolically opposed to Golgotha, the bare mountain of death. Because of the Christian esteem for virginity, the inaccessibility of Mary's garden receives far more emphasis.

FIG. 57 Aubrey Beardsley, *The Toilette of Salomé II* (actually the first version).

FIG. 58 Aubrey Beardsley, *The Toilette of Salomé I* (printed version).

FIG. 59 Aubrey Beardsley, *The Return of Tannhäuser to the Venusberg.*

FIG. 60 Aubrey Beardsley, *The Landslide*, frontispiece to *Pastor Sang* (1893).

FIG. 63 Hans Thoma (1839–1924), The world monster.

FIG. 61 From *Hypnerotomachia Poliphili* (1499).

FIG. 62 *Nautilus Cup,* ca. 1600, engraved shell, Jan Rellekin, engraver.

FIG. 64 Aubrey Beardsley, *The Cave of Spleen*.

FIG. 65 Aubrey Beardsley, *The Man that Holds the Watering Pot.*

Fig. 66 Aubrey Beardsley, Hermaphrodite among roses.

FIG. 67 From Théodore de Bry (1528–98), *Emblemata nobilitati.*

FIG. 68 Aubrey Beardsley, *The Ascension of Saint Rose of Lima*.

Fig. 69 Aubrey Beardsley, *The Mysterious Rose Garden*.

FIG. 70 Aubrey Beardsley, *Juvenal Scourging Woman*.

FIG. 71 Bestiary with unicorn in the middle, in Johannes Marcanova (1410–67),
Antiquitates, ca. 1465.

FIG. 72 Fontainebleau school, *The Hunting Diana*, ca. 1550–60.

FIG. 73 Factory of Master F. R., Diana and Actaeon, dish, Maiolica, Italian, Faenza, ca. 1525.

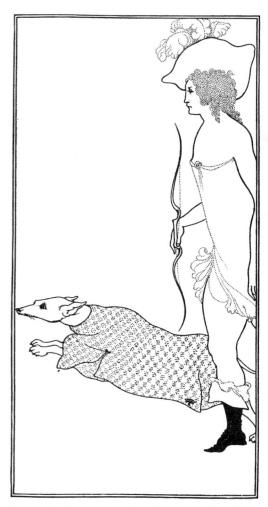

FIG. 75 Aubrey Beardsley, *Atalanta in Calydon*.

FIG. 74 Joachim Friess (d. 1620), *Diana Seated on Stag*, automaton.

FIG. 76 Aubrey Beardsley, *The Lady with the Monkey.*

FIG. 77 Aubrey Beardsley, Vignette.

FIG. 78 Aubrey Beardsley, design for the front cover of the *Savoy*.

FIG. 79 The cult of Priapus, in *Hypnerotomachia Poliphili* (1499).

FIG. 80 Aubrey Beardsley, *The Lacedaemonian Ambassadors.*

FIG. 81 *The European Race*, English engraving, 1738.

FIG. 82 Aubrey Beardsley, *A Footnote*.

The area is closed to all except her female servants (Venus's nymphs turned into decent maids), her animals, and the angel, the winged messenger from heaven who descends into the garden in order to announce the good news. The blooming spot, like Aphrodite's garden, is usually protected by gold wire netting with a copper gate, and among the beasts of the Holy Virgin one detects doves and rabbits, the sacred animals of the goddess of love. However, Mary has an especially intimate relationship with one animal, the legendary unicorn, which is frequently represented in medieval paintings with its head on her lap.

The mythology of the unicorn originated in the Middle and Far East.[46] The fabulous beast was usually described as having the head and body of a horse, the hind legs of an antelope, the tail of a lion or a horse, the beard of a goat, and in the middle of its forehead a long, sharp, and twisted horn. The unicorn was mentioned for the first time by Ctesias, who maintained that the Indian wild white asses had horns, colored white, red, and black, set on their foreheads. Moreover, he claimed that drinking cups made of these horns prevented food poisoning.[47] Aelian wrote (*De nat. anim.* 16:20) that the savage unicorn, usually rude even to females, at mating times becomes extremely gentle with his mate. This was repeated in the *Physiologus*, which describes the unicorn hunt: the fierce animal could only be caught by a beautiful maiden who, placed in its path, would make the unicorn come to her gently and put its horned head in her lap. Thus eroticism was added to the heterogeneous nature of the strange phallic beast, making the unicorn indispensable in medieval and Renaissance bestiaries (fig. 71).

If one takes into account that the horn has been universally associated with the male sex and remembers the purifying qualities mentioned by Ctesias, it is not surprising that the story of the unicorn was used in the Middle Ages as a symbol of Christ's conception[48] and more generally as a metaphor for love that renders gentle the rudest of men. In the poetry and painting of the late Middle Ages the unicorn stands for God the Father, Christ, or simply a lover, and is regarded as a symbol of purity. (It was believed that its horn, when dipped into water, turned it pure and sweet.[49]) The hunt for the unicorn was presented in several slightly different ways. Both the archangel Gabriel, who enters the "closed garden," and God himself may be regarded as hunters,[50] while the dogs that accompany them are supposed to incarnate different virtues. Christ is played by the unicorn, whom God chases straight into the womb of the Holy Virgin.

Fantastic, legendary, erotic, and religious, the unicorn was popular with the decadents. While Gustave Moreau's painting *The Unicorns* still evokes the atmosphere of a medieval fairy tale, Beardsley not only demystifies divine love but leads the ancient beast out of Mary's garden into that of Venus. Her unicorn is not a "Salvator mundi" but a pet by the name of Adolphe, "milk-white all over excepting his black eyes, rose mouth and nostrils, and scarlet John" (VT, p. 63). Like the god Priapus, the unicorn "had a very pretty palace of its own, made of green foliage and golden bars," was "proud and beautiful" (VT, p. 63), and knew no mate except Venus herself. There is, of course, no question of his hunting the goddess. Adolphe is completely subdued, roams in his "artful cage," and waits for Venus to satisfy his desires. This she does, however not without a certain sadism. First she feeds the animal and then pretends to leave the cage: "Every morning she went through this piece of play, and every morning the amorous unicorn was cheated into a distressing agony lest that day should have proved the last of Venus's love. Not for long, though, would she leave him in that doubtful, piteous state, but running back passionately to where he stood, make adorable amends for her unkindness" (VT, p. 63).

What follows is the only truly passionate love scene of Beardsley's entire novel. Not the overcivilized Tannhäuser and Venus but Adolphe and the goddess of love form the perfect couple—all sensuality and nature. "I have no doubt," writes Beardsley, "that the keener scent of animals must make women much more attractive to them than to men; for the gorgeous odour that but faintly fills our nostrils must be revealed to the brute creature in divine fulness. Anyhow, Adolphe sniffed as never a man did around the skirts of Venus" (VT, pp. 63–64).

Beardsley's unicorn is a completely passive lover who simply lies down, and "closing his eyes," waits for Venus to caress his member, likened to a "tightly-strung instrument." Consummating his pleasure, Adolphe bursts out in "venereal sounds," which signal the beginning of the day "under the hill." Only after Venus had "lapped her little aperitif" (VT, p. 64) were all of her other subjects allowed to sit down to their breakfast. Adolphe, an indispensable figure in her country, connects the human to the animalistic, the erotic to the culinary. Like a true masochist, he is without any aggressiveness and dreams not of capturing and possessing the Queen but of being devoured by her.

The quoted passage parodies all the famous female figures with beasts— Europa, Leda, and especially Aphrodite as sculpted by Scopas, who for the temple in Elis represented her seated on a voluptuous he-goat. Interestingly enough, this statue was both complemented and opposed by one sculpted by Phidias, which represented the other face of the goddess: a strict and proper woman with one foot on a turtle, presumably in this context the symbol of domestic virtues.[51]

The pre-classical Greek statues portrayed Aphrodite fully dressed, sometimes even with a veil. In the art of the fifth century B.C. she was frequently shown with a translucent chiton slipping down her chest. It is only from the time of Praxiteles and Apelles that she began to appear naked. The change perhaps reflects a relaxation of morality and the increased presence of beautiful *haeterae*, some of whom were worshiped as new Aphrodites,[52] painted and sculpted by the greatest artists, and immortalized in innumerable monuments. In Hellenistic times the Syrian Aphrodite, a goddess of prostitution, had her temples in the havens of Piraeus, Cythera, and Paros, and at the beginning of the Christian era the features of the Great Goddess appeared more obscene than ever. Thus, it is not difficult to understand why the adherents of the new faith fought so aggressively against her, defaming Aphrodite as a diabolical abortion of nature and a prostitute. In a tirade against the goddess, Clement of Alexandria states that "those lustful members that were cut off from Uranus . . . did violence to the wave," and then angrily continues: "And in the rites which celebrate this pleasure of the sea, as a symbol of her birth, the gift of a cake of salt and a phallos is made to those who are initiated in the art of fornication; and the initiated bring their tribute of a coin to the goddess, as lovers do to a mistress" (*Exhortation to the Greeks*, 2:14).[53]

Clement's insinuations remind us, strangely enough, of Beardsley's account of Venus and Adolphe, which reduces the story of the Virgin and the heavenly unicorn to its bare physical ingredients. The grotesque, indeed, is the language of polemical parody that well serves those who try to disarm the enemy by degrading their ideals. Connecting the cake of salt to the phallus, Clement attempts to show the men he addresses the meaninglessness of their love and their own reduction to mere sex organs. In opposition to him, Beardsley (who derides the mystical horn of god) extensively praises the penis of the unicorn and his song of love which "under the hill" announces the beginning of the day; church bells do the same on earth.

Beardsley animates the earth, the ancient landscapes, gods, and statues. Appalled by the pagan world, Clement wants to strike it dead:

> For even though there are some living creatures which do not possess all the senses, as worms and caterpillars, and all those that appear to be imperfect from the first through the conditions of their birth, such as moles and the field-mouse, which Nicander calls "blind and terrible"; yet these are better than those images and statues which are entirely dumb . . . incapable of action and sensation; they are bound and nailed and fastened, melted, filed, sawn, polished, carved. The dumb earth is dishonored when sculptors pervert its peculiar nature and by their art entice men to worship it; while the god-makers, if there is any sense in me, worship not gods and daemons, but earth and art, which is all the statues are.

Clement ends his condemnation of the ancient sensuality that was able to animate all of nature with an apodictical statement: "God, that is, the only true God, is perceived not by the senses but by the mind" (*Exhortation to the Greeks*, 4:45–46).

Artemis, another Great Goddess, and Atalanta, with whom she has been identified, appear in the company of animals as well. In the temple of Antikyra, a statue of the virgin huntress represented Artemis in a way that has fixed her for centuries: rushing forward with her dog, arrow in one hand, bow in the other (fig. 72). Christianity has reversed this image. It is God who hunts the virgin, and consequently the dogs belong to him and represent, in medieval pictures of the unicorn hunt, the divine virtues of Mercy, Truth, Justice, and Peace.[54]

The lap dog is a degenerate and domesticated offspring of Artemis's hounds (figs. 73, 74) and so are the doggish men licking the feet of fin-de-siècle beauties. Beardsley derides this tradition in his drawing *Atalanta* (fig. 75), which shows the racing goddess dressed in an outfit suggestive of underwear, with a bow in her hand, a large feathered hat on her head, and half-opened boots. The dog at her feet wears a flowery dressing-gown and reminds us of the gentleman in a nightcap who prays to a lit candle in one of Beardsley's illustrations for *The Rape of the Lock*.

Dogs in silk gowns look ridiculous, and so do amazons in underwear. In his novel *Mademoiselle de Maupin* (1835) Théophile Gautier offers a parody of the ruthless and energetic ancient huntress. Mademoiselle de Maupin, the new Diana, is an aristocratic lesbian who, to reach maximum freedom and independence, seduces a young girl, makes her a page, and escapes with her from her castle. Dressed as a man, the tall, slender, and strong de Maupin rides around, offering her stormy but short-lived passions to representatives of both sexes. Like the swift Artemis, who was occasionally imagined in the shape of a doe or a she-bear,[55] de Maupin attempts to escape all domestication. But she is too overdressed to be taken seriously, and the cultivated French landscape is by no means savage. Thus, the reverie of returning to an original wilderness—and greatness—is rendered grotesque by the inappropriate setting. In a Beardsley illustration, de Maupin is dressed in a costume that would be appropriate at a masquerade or a children's ball. However, both she and Rosette (one of her lovers) are drawn as petulant and domineering figures. The opposite sex, on the other hand, is represented by the subordinate and feminine Albert and by a tiny gentleman, a monkey in a tuxedo, whom Rosette holds on a leash (fig. 76).

The latter image makes one think of the masochistic fantasies so popular all over Europe at the turn of the century and still vital in the 1920s and 1930s when Bruno Schulz described, drew, and etched innumerable neurotic man-dogs begging for love and being stepped upon by huge females. Perhaps it was not an accident that he was from Galicia, the same part of the Austro-Hungarian empire that was the home of Leopold von Sacher-Masoch (1836–95), after whom masochism was named. Indeed, Masoch was a lover of antiquity and of Venus. His mediocre prose writings and his curious letters[56] attract interest not only from a psychological point of view; they also illuminate masochism as a tendency of the times. And they reveal the sources and patterns of masochistic reverie and its affinity to the grotesque. Besides dreaming about big women in leather boots and fur coats whose feet he could lick, Masoch also approached the subject from a philosophical and a historical angle and put his beliefs into the mouth of Wanda von Dunajew, the literary pseudonym of his wife Aurora von Rümelin and the name he gave the heroine of his best-known novel, *Venus im Pelz* (1870). There Wanda, a new Venus, confesses that "the ideal which I strive to realize in my life is the serene sensuousness of the Greeks—pleasure without pain. I do not believe in the kind of love which is preached by Christianity, by the moderns, by the knights of the spirit. Yes, look at me, I am worse than a heretic, I am a pagan."[57] Further, she condemns explicitly the "factitious" and "affected" religion "whose cruel emblem, the cross . . . brought something alien and hostile into nature and its innocent instincts," and ridicules the Madonna-stereotype resulting in "Holbein's meagre, pallid virgins" and "modern women, those miserable hysterical feminine creatures who don't appreciate a real man in their somnabulistic search for some dream-man and masculine ideal . . . cheat and are cheated . . . are never happy, and never give happiness . . . accuse fate instead of calmly confessing that they want to love and live as Helen and Aspasia lived."[58]

Not unlike the Marquis de Sade, Masoch proclaimed an unlimited Eros and the absolute fulfillment of desire. But he reversed the roles (the ruthless tyrant was to be played not by man, but by woman) and saw no possibility of partnership because of a basic inequality between the sexes: "Woman, as nature has created her and as man is at present educating her, is his enemy. She can only be his slave or his despot, but *never his companion.* This she can become only when she has the same rights as he, and is his equal in education and work. At present we have only the choice of being hammer or anvil, and I was the kind of donkey who let a woman make a slave of him."[59]

As we know, Masoch preferred to be an anvil and liked to be a donkey. Before marrying his "Venus in furs," he had her sign a contract that obliged her in their future relationship to use the whip frequently, while wearing furs on her naked body. But, interestingly enough, he recognized that in a world of emancipated women he could, perhaps, make love without animalistic submission.

Masoch's desires transcended the infliction of pain and the delight taken in suffering. His dream about "Venus in furs," not a passive goddess of love but a true Artemis clothed in the skins of lions, not only transported him to the bosom of nature and the golden age of humanity but also helped him regain the position of child vis-à-vis his wife. His letters to Wanda are a grotesque mixture of cruelty and infantilism. Their tone occasionally reminds one of baby talk. Descriptions of cruel baronesses swinging their whips are suddenly interrupted by tender questions about the health of Masoch's own children.[60] The dream of female domination helped him escape from the realities and responsibilities of his adult life into the protected chambers of a tyrannical but loving mother. There can be no doubt that this vision was influenced and nourished by the legends of the Great Goddesses described in detail in such scholarly books as *Die Griechische Mythologie* (1854) and *Die Römische Mythologie* (1858), both by Ludwig Preller, the head librarian of Weimar.

When femininity reaches the proportions of a planet, it is paired with a miniature male population of dwarfs, phalli, and animals. Images of homunculi adoring huge women are a stereotype of fin-de-siècle literature and art, but no one more successfully combined their infantile ludicrousness and terrifying deformity into figures of male grotesqueness than did Beardsley. His embryos who "survived the abortion" (figs. 77, 78)[61] and absurdly dressed dwarfs allude to the deadly secrets and dangers of sex, and are animated penises that make one think of the ancient earth spirits such as the Curetes, who grow out of the earth after a rainfall (Ovid, *Met.* 4:282), the Corybantes, whom the Greeks considered the first men and the original priests of Rhea, and the Idaean Dactyli.[62] The latter (from *dactylos*, "finger") were thought to be imprints of Rhea's fingers on the ground which she was clutching while giving birth to Zeus, or made of the dust that went through the fingers of the midwives helping her. Both in shape and origin, the Dactyli point to prehistoric times and the customs of primitive people who during fertility rites plant poles in the earth, thus repeating symbolically the penetration in the sexual act.

The Greeks worshiped the phallus in the form of Priapus. His statue is seen by Tannhäuser in the garden of Venus and commemorated by Beardsley in the name of "Priapusa," a governess of Venus. The cult of Priapus (fig. 79) was especially popular in the lush regions of the Hellespont and Propontis and also on Lesbos and other islands.[63] He was held responsible for the fertility of plants, animals, and humans and was the protective demon of gardens, vineyards, beehives, sheep, goats, and fish. In the mysteries of Bacchus, Priapus was celebrated as the god of regeneration, and for that reason his statues were erected on graves. In Lampsacus he was occasionally identified with Dionysus but also considered to be a son of Dionysus and Aphrodite, the son of the ithyphallic Hermes or of Hermaphrodite. Priapus was also regarded as the personification of the physical Eros as opposed to spiritual love. In antiquity this god "of all gardens" was represented in two basic forms, one slightly more grotesque than the other. As an object of worship he was shown on marble statues with the head of an old man and a large penis. But as *hortorum custos* he was the prototype of the scarecrow and consisted of a wooden pole with a huge member painted in red. He had a sickle or a stick in his hand, and his head was decorated with tubes and strings which, moving in the wind, made a noise and scared away the birds.

The images of Curetes, Corybantes, Dactyli, and Priapi are both phallic caricatures and symbols of male fertility magically connected to mother earth. Her ancient mythology, like a sexual reverie, transfers sexuality to all possible levels and domains of life and art. In Aristophanes' *Lysistrata*, one of the most hilarious comedies of antiquity, even peace and war are discussed from the point of view of promiscuity and abstinence. In Beardsley's illustrations of this play, the dwarfish anti-heroes carry their oversized penises like ridiculous weapons (fig. 80).

Realizing how profoundly the modern masochistic images have been influenced by ancient mythology, one has to remember, however, that the very same tradition, a century earlier, inspired sadism. De Sade was also against Christian morality and wished to promote the "natural" state of unrestricted pleasure. Sadism and masochism, although two sides of the same coin, are each linked to a specific time and a broader spiritual movement within European culture. The sadistic desire to torture and to destroy is connected to a belief in masculine power which can subdue the woman as well as the earth, while the masochistic dream of female dominance aims rather at a return to mother earth and a reconciliation with her. The first is related to progress, the other to escape and regression. Though sadism and masochism hardly ever appear in pure form, there are nevertheless periods when one trend seems to prevail over the other. Such a change of sensibility can be observed between the end of the eighteenth and the end of the nineteenth century. In the literature and art of this period, ruthless masculine heroes were often replaced by effeminate men, and accordingly the utopian idea of the conquest of nature and technological transformation of the entire planet gave way to dreams of a return to the earth's bosom.

The sexual aspect of the dream of masculine domination has nowhere been more forcefully formulated than in the writings of de Sade (1740–1814), while the concept of a superman who changes the face of the earth was given its fullest shape by Goethe (1749–1832) in his *Faust II*. The tragedy's second part, which Goethe worked on until his death, contains prophetic thoughts about the achievements and crimes to be committed by a humanity drunk with rationalism, atheism, scientific and technological progress. These reflections connect us to the transgressions of the Marquis de Sade. Both writers distill a masculine euphoria that occurs less frequently in the literature that comes after. It seems that the speeding up of technology and the quickening transformation of nature began to inspire skepticism and fear, and at the end of the nineteenth century a nostalgic humanity, tired of civilization, rediscovered nature as a mysterious refuge. Consequently the focus shifted from the conscious to the unconscious, reason was obscured and forward-moving activity frustrated.

In the second part of Goethe's tragedy, Faust plays the role of an enlightened, energetic entrepreneur of early capitalism who denies the existence of God, attacks nature and culture with his iron "fist," and behaves like the colonizers derided in an English engraving (fig. 81). He orders Mephisto, his animalistic helper and alter ego, to abduct Helena, the female personification of natural beauty and of Greek culture, and to set on fire the garden and home of Philemon and Baucis, a couple embodying perfect symbiosis with nature. Tannhäuser, who appears on the stage in the second half of the nineteenth century, is truly Faust's opposite: an anti-hero who, instead of snatching fire from the gods, desires to slip into the dark exile of the Mons Veneris. However, a subordinate but highly significant figure of *Faust II* expresses Goethe's ideas about the future man and is somewhat congruent with Tannhäuser. It is Homunculus, a super-intelligent hermaphroditic "man" whose power of reasoning surpasses the intellectual capacities of Faust. Homunculus lacks the experience of life, the richness and diversity of nature; therefore he is transported to ancient Greece and wed to the elements. The "wedding" consists of diving into the sea, the primordial female element and cradle of Aphrodite, the symbol of the indestructible fertility of nature which is praised in the famous hymn to "eternal femininity" at the end of *Faust II.*

In the figures of Faust and Homunculus, Goethe brilliantly renders the masculine ideals of two different ages. Faust, a powerful patriarch, stands for absolute exploitation of nature, unlimited progress, and the heroic, male-dominated world. Homunculus, "artificial," hermaphroditic and, like the poet Tannhäuser, an enthusiast of nature, foreshadows the future (fig. 82). By the end of the nineteenth century, the features of Homunculus, in Goethe's time only an imaginary creature speaking for his creator's visionary mind, had become recognizable in over-sophisticated, feminine writers and artists and in the decadent anti-heroes populating their works. All of this culminates in Beardsley's figures of embryos walking around in tuxedos, hiding in bottles, pots, and cages.

Architecture of Dreams

The temples dedicated to Venus, Diana, *the* Muses, *the*
Nymphs and the more tender Goddesses, ought in their
Structure to imitate that Virgin's Delicacy and smiling
Gaiety of Youth, which is proper to them; but . . . Her-
cules, Mars *and the other greater Deities should have*
Temples which should rather fill the Beholders with Awe
by their Gravity, than with Pleasure by their Beauty.
——Alberti, *Ten Books on Architecture,* 7,
3:141–42

Mythical and infantile, *The Story of Venus and Tannhäuser* has the free-
floating structure of a dream; it is loose, full of digressions and footnotes.
The erotic adventures of Tannhäuser and the diverse sexual relationships
that he observes in the Venusland are interwoven with allusions to works
of literature and art, to pieces of music, ballets and theater plays; to architecture, gardening, fashion, and cuisine. Beardsley cites existing writings and invents quotations; he describes with the same ease well-known
paintings and those only imagined; he derides his contemporaries and
himself. *Venus and Tannhäuser* is a book written by a sex maniac who laughs
at his obsessions and by an erudite man who never stops making fun of
erudition; it is a caricature both of erotic dreams and of the interpretation
of dreams which Freud began expounding at approximately the same time
(*Traumdeutung* appeared in 1900). Though psychoanalysis was unknown
to him, Beardsley wrote and drew as if he meant to parody dreams about
bottles with corks driven into them, dreams of keys and keyholes. Ridiculing his obsessions, he nevertheless remained possessed by them, and
this gives his work its freshness and authenticity. Borrowing and mixing
heterogeneous influences, he managed to create an architecture of dreams
that, at once stereotypical and individual, captures the essence of all fantastic buildings, imitating the richness of organic life as opposed to the
crystalline forms and rectangles of the manmade world. Beardsley's floral,
zoomorphic, and anthropomorphic constructions (pavilions, furniture,
fountains, and vases) coincide with the style of his time (remember the
iron "plants" of the Paris metro) and mirror a nostalgic return to the bosom
of the earth. They are indebted to the grotto, to the rose garden, and to
Hypnerotomachia Poliphili, whose author, Francesco Colonna, hid in an acrostic (how this must have appealed to Beardsley!) formed from the first
letter of each chapter: "Poliam Frater Franciscus Columna Peramavit."[64]

To realize the daring and sacrilegious character of this Renaissance
novel and the peculiarities of its fantastic setting, one has to recall Colonna's
biography, as far as it is known. The authorship of *Hypnerotomachia Poliphili*

is certified by a note dated 20 June 1512, which was found in the copy of the book belonging to the monastery of Saints John and Paul in Venice. The note has not been preserved but was still known in 1723. It contained the information that Franciscus Columna (also called Colonna, a Dominican monk from Venice) had fallen in love in Treviso with a certain Hyppolita, whose name he changed to Polia. The author of the note explained the acrostic and wrote that Colonna was still living in Venice, in the monastery of Saints John and Paul. The documentation gathered by M. T. Casella confirms these words.[65]

The *Hypnerotomachia* is illustrated with woodcuts by an unknown artist. For a time he was identified as Colonna himself, but there is no evidence for such an assumption. However, the author and the artist certainly collaborated closely, and it is possible that Colonna made sketches for some of the woodcuts, particularly those showing architecture and displaying topography.[66] In general the woodcuts are reminiscent of the work which came out of the studios of Andrea Mantegna and Giovanni Bellini.

The book describes a dream similar to that of Tannhäuser: of escape from the contemporary world of Christian virtue into the ancient land of Venus. Poliphilo, the autobiographical hero of the novel, falls asleep and dreams of a subterranean country which he enters through the door inscribed "Mater Amoris" (fig. 15). Behind it stretch gardens, blooming prairies, groves, and ponds. Beautiful naked nymphs await the dreamer, and one of them turns out to be Polia, his lost beloved. In a ceremony reminiscent of the alchemical marriage of elements, Poliphilo is wedded to Polia and subsequently meets the goddess of love herself. Against the scenery of this paradise for men (in the heaven of the Koran high-bosomed virgins serve refreshments), Colonna pursues super- and pseudo-erudite discourses on astrology, alchemy, archeology, sculpture, mythology, and literature which occasionally sound like parodies of academic pedantry. The flow of his narrative is constantly interrupted by digressions, and his Italian, extremely difficult to begin with, is additionally obscured by the interpolation of Greek and Latin words as well as Egyptian hieroglyphs (fig. 83). But in spite of his various interests, Colonna never loses track of the central concern of his novel: sex, and of the framework deliberately chosen for it: the dream, accidental and symbolic. He also emphasizes the motif of choice. Poliphilo does not simply enter through the gate of the Mother of Love, he chooses it as one of three, the other two being those of "Theodoxia" ("Gloria Dei") and "Cosmodoxia" ("Gloria Mundi"), guarded respectively by a distinguished-looking old widow and a fierce matron with a sword, a palm, and a crown. The episode represents, of course, a parody of Hercules at the crossroads, who had to choose between virtue and pleasure, as well as of Jesus teaching his followers to enter by the gate of asceticism (Matt. 7:13–14; Luke 13:24).

Acting as Poliphilo's Beatrice, Polia leads her beloved through the ancient underworld, animated, transient, and full of beasts and natural forms alluding to the constant metamorphoses and the undivided unity of all living beings. Pageants are organized in honor of Cupid, each dramatizing one of Jupiter's famous adventures of love with Europa, Leda, Danaë, and Semele. Passing the Elysian Fields and the pool of Narcissus, the lovers watch the triumphal parade of Vertumnus and Pomona, the divine couple of the harvest, moving around a marble altar on which the four seasons are depicted. On top, under a canopy made of leaves, a statue of Priapus stands and merry folk throw bottles at him filled with milk, wine, and blood drawn from the neck of an ass, in a ritual, at once carnivalistic and sacrilegious, alluding to fertility and destruction (fig. 79). The pattern presented here will be repeated many times throughout the book. Incorporated into the fabric of organic life, architecture becomes animated and eroticized, each construction reflecting the sexual play of phallic and vaginal elements, of fire and water. Poliphilo and Polia are married at a "miraculous cistern." During the ceremony, Poliphilo extinguishes Polia's torch in the pool, the blood of female doves is mixed with the blood of two male swans, and the altar is strewn with roses and seashells. This alchemical union infuses life into the stone: upon the altar grows a rosebush covered with flowers and roundish, rose-colored fruits which, when consumed, strengthen love.

In the landscape and architecture of dreams the individual mixes with the primordial. The newly married couple leaves for Cythera, the island of Aphrodite (modeled on Colonna's native Venice), covered with gardens, forests, and groves. At its center an amphitheater is erected to which Poliphilo and Polia, both wearing "rose-chains," walk in the procession of Cupid along the main avenue, which is flanked by rose hedges. In the middle of the theater, on a floor made of black obsidian, the fountain of Cupid's mother stands hidden behind a curtain with the inscription "Hymen." The god of love offers Polia a golden arrow with which to transfix the curtain before the fountain. When she hesitates, Poliphilo, burning with desire, snatches the arrow and tears apart the veil. The unveiled Venus forms a part of the architecture but she is also alive. She stands in a fountain, up to her hips in water, holding in one hand a shell with roses, in the other a burning torch. Doves flutter around her, and the steps of the fountain are covered with herbs that are useful at childbirth. On the right side of the goddess three Graces can be seen; at her left stand Bacchus and Ceres with snakes from which a secret fluid flows—figures frequently encountered in alchemical manuscripts. An arrow from Cupid's bow goes through Poliphilo's heart and stays in Polia's breast. Thereupon Venus sprinkles the couple with sea-water drawn from her fountain.

The ancient goddess, who so miraculously has come to life, subsequently falls back into death. The next station reached by the lovers is a rose arbor and the tomb of Adonis, whose sarcophagus is sculpted with scenes of his life and adorned by a life-sized statue of Venus represented as a young mother nursing Cupid (fig. 16). Moving like the alchemical opus between animation and death, Colonna's dream expresses the feelings and knowledge that the most intense passion entails when it is concentrated on the absent and dead for whom we search during many nights and whom we bring to life but for a brief duration, the bed of love turning cemetery in the morning, but then a fountain of love in the evening. Colonna's narrative follows, of course, such alchemical treatises as the medieval text by Nicolas Flamel:

> These two I say, being put together in the vessel of the sepulcher, doe bite one another cruelly, and by their great poyson, and furious rage, they never leave one another, from the moment that they have seized on one another . . . and finally killing one another, be stewed in their proper venome, which after their death, changeth them into living and permanent water; before which time, they loose in their corruption and putrification, their first natural formes, to take afterwards one onely new, more noble, and better forme.[67]

It was once assumed that the Venetian monk tried in the *Hypnerotomachia* to describe classical monuments he saw during his stay in Rome. This does not sound convincing because the architecture in his book does not seem to come from notes or sketches made during a journey. Today scholars believe that Colonna never visited Rome and knew its buildings only from his reading. According to G. Pozzi, the most important sources for his fantasies were the writings of Vitruvius and Pliny the Elder, as well as the architectural treatises by his contemporaries Alberti, Filarete, Flavio Biondo, and Feliciano.[68] The very first building explored by Poliphilo, a huge pyramid, turns out to be a reconstruction of the mausoleum in Halicarnassus as described by Pliny. Colonna enlarged its size and replaced the quadriga with an obelisk.[69] He also transplanted to it some elements from the mausoleum of Augustus in Rome, as it was described by Flavio Biondo in *Roma instaurata*. But the pyramid might have also been inspired by the fantastic "palace of vice and virtue" (*palazzo del vizio e della virtù*) mentioned by Filarete in the eighteenth book of his treatise on architecture. According to Erwin Panofsky, this building combines the architectural design of a university or a temple with that of a fancy restaurant or a brothel.[70] Filarete obviously translated into symbolic architecture Prodicus's metaphor of two paths leading through two different landscapes. The palace can be entered either through the "gate of virtue" (*porta areti*) or the "gate of pleasure" (*porta chachia*), and one can move in it either climbing up steep staircases or walking on comfortable platforms. The lower part of the pyramid can be reached through a huge portal situated at ground level; the way to the upper part leads through a smaller entrance that has the shape of the head of Medusa. Only through this entrance can one ascend as far as the obelisk.

Colonna's architecture transcends "geography and history,"[71] and its symbolic meaning is alluded to by innumerable inscriptions and hieroglyphs with which he covers his constructions. Some inscriptions are quotations from literature, the rest are games and puzzles invented by the monk himself. In the rump of the obsidian elephant (fig. 84), for instance, Poliphilo finds a black statue of a crowned man with the words: "I would be naked if the animal had not covered me. Search and you will find. Leave me alone." In the head of the elephant he discovers the statue of a woman pointing behind her to the inscription: "Whoever you are, take from this treasure as much as you want, but I warn you, take from the head and do not touch the body." The entire space in the elephant's body is organized with pairs of opposites: male and female, rump and head, man and beast, naked and covered.

During his journey Poliphilo is haunted by obelisks, and there is a great abundance and variety of these in the dreamland. Colonna praises them each time as "eminente," "excelso," "grande," "altissimo," or at least "magno obelisco." In one of the gardens the nymph Logistica shows Poliphilo a truly intellectual—and virile—building. It consists of a transparent cube with a trihedron placed on top of it, decorated with figures of nymphs carrying cornucopiae; this serves as the base for a golden obelisk, "straight, strong and indestructible," standing among delicious herbs and flowers. Poliphilo cannot take his eyes from this shiny phallus.

Sharp and pointed forms like the arrows of Amor penetrate delicate veils and flowers, enter soft openings, round enclosures, oval gates, doors, windows, cisterns and fountains. The most characteristic female construction is the round temple of Venus Physizoa situated at the seashore (fig. 85); it brings to mind the sanctuary of Aphrodite at Paphos in Cyprus, one of the most famous shrines of the ancient world. The temple, as shown on coins of the Imperial Age and models excavated from the royal tombs in Mycenae, has a façade surmounted by two doves. It is divided into three parts or chapels, of which the central one contains a white cone or pyramid, the sacred image of the goddess, and each of the side chapels holds a pillar or a candelabra-like object. The central cone is flanked by two columns, each terminating in a pair of ball-topped pinnacles, with a star and a crescent to be seen between the tops of the columns. In the Mycenae model one finds a supplementary element: horns crown the central superstructure. The sanctuary of Aphrodite was described by Herodotus (1, 105) and Pausanias (1, 14:7), and information about other personifications of the

Great Goddess and her temples was supplied by Diodorus Siculus (II, 4) and Lucian (*De dea Syria*, 14). At Ascalon she was worshiped as a mermaid under the name Derceto (a corrupt Greek form of Attâr, the Aramaic form of Astarte), to whom doves and fish were sacred. The cone represented Astarte at her shrine at Byblus and Artemis at Perga in Pamphylia. But at Emesa in Syria it was regarded as the emblem of the sun-god Heliogabalus. At certain festivals, the holy stones were anointed, like humans, with olive oil. Pausanias (10, 24:6) mentions that this was done, for instance, in the sanctuary of Apollo at Delphi.[72]

In Colonna's temple of Venus, elements of the sanctuaries of Aphrodite combine with those of astrology and alchemy. The walls, covered with golden mosaics representing the journey of the sun, the moon, and other celestial bodies through the signs of the zodiac, mirror the cosmos. The ceiling is formed by seven creeping vines made from gilded copper, a metal corresponding in alchemy to the planet Venus. In the middle of the temple a cistern is watered by rain that flows down through the columns. Above the cistern, called by Poliphilo "una fatale cisterna," a lamp filled with pure spirit ("spiritus") hangs from the center of the dome. The temple of Venus Physizoa is shaped in the image of a magnified philosophers' egg in which life is conceived and out of which it is hatched.

Hypnerotomachia Poliphili belongs to those works of art and literature that, because of their slight obscenity, are more widely circulated than one would expect. Colonna's influence on Beardsley was discovered by Mario Praz, who pointed to the almost identical descriptions and illustrations of fountains in the two books.[73] He singled out Beardsley's drawings that resemble the woodcuts of the *Hypnerotomachia* and mentioned the similar style of both authors. Beardsley must have known the work of the Venetian monk either in French translation[74] or in the Elizabethan version of the first book of the *Hypnerotomachia*, published in 1592 and reprinted in London in 1890,[75] which was dedicated to Essex and known to Shakespeare. Besides, copies of the original were available in England; one of them, for instance, belonged to Thomas Griffiths Wainewright (1794–1852), whom the English decadents regarded as their precursor. Praz suggested that Colonna's description of a sleeping nymph (fig. 86) inspired the passage concerned with the sleeping Lucretia Borgia in Algernon Charles Swinburne's *Chronicle of Tebaldeo Tebaldei* (1861), and he discovered a similarity between two epitaphs: one was seen by Poliphilo in a mysterious cemetery and read "cadaverib[us] amore furentium miserabundis"; the other was conceived by Faustine, Swinburne's heroine, who meant to put almost the same message on the tomb of the gladiator whose blood she had sucked out.[76]

Beardsley must have been both amused and moved by the way Colonna treated the figures of Venus and Amor, who, together with Polia and Poliphilo, form an erotic quadrangle in which one man can be exchanged with the other and the attributes of one woman can be transferred to the other. The hymen, for instance, symbolizes the virginity of Polia but belongs to Venus. It is torn apart by Poliphilo but with an arrow owned by Amor. All this smells of incest, and the ambiguity of the relationships is also reflected in the names. Poliphilo explains his name to the nymphs, telling them that it does not mean the lover (*phileo*—in Greek, "to love") of many (*polys*—in Greek, "many"), but the "lover of Polia." However *philo* can be easily distorted to *filio* (in Italian, "son") meaning the "son of Polia," whose eternal femininity is expressed by the very sense of "many" hidden in her name. While Venus and Amor are called by Colonna "la divina madre cum il dilecto filio," Polia and Poliphilo represent mother and son on the human level.

Besides those similarities already noted by Praz, there are a few others worth mentioning. For instance, the frontispiece of Beardsley's novel (fig. 87) might have been inspired by the scene of Poliphilo standing in front of three doors. Instead of three gates, Beardsley drew two windows of exactly the same shape as in the *Hypnerotomachia*, and he placed Venus between them to personify the third choice—entrance to the world of Mater Amoris; above her head he enclosed in a circle his initials and the date 1895. This unusual way of signing a drawing strongly suggests that he wished to indicate a connection between the mother of love and Abbé Aubrey, as he originally called Tannhäuser. Curiously enough, if one adds the numbers in the date of the *Hypnerotomachia*'s publication, 1499, and those in the date given by Beardsley, one obtains in both cases "23," Beardsley's age in 1895. This may be only a coincidence, but considering Colonna's playing with letters, words, and numbers, it may also be a coded expression of Beardsley's familiarity with the *Hypnerotomachia* and an acknowledgment of an inner link between himself and the Venetian monk. Beardsley's Venus is dressed in a loose Renaissance robe. A pair of doves is perched on a closed casket in front of her; a candle burns in the chandelier. Like the woman in his drawing *Autumn*, she stretches her hand tenderly toward a phallic chalice.

Even more striking is the similarity between a woodcut in the *Hypnerotomachia* entitled *Florido veris* (fig. 88) and Beardsley's cover for *The Yellow Book* (fig. 89). The first represents a female figure in the company of Cupid equipped with bow and arrows; the woman tears flowers to pieces and throws them into the fire burning in an antique tripod; three doves flutter over her head. In Beardsley's drawing a Renaissance lady is depicted next to a basket filled with flowers. Amor is replaced by two small boys, one of whom offers a flower to the woman; the other, naked on the floor, plays with petals. Both drawings emanate an ambiguous eroticism and point to "defloration." The banquet of Queen Eleuterilyda given for Poliphilo is echoed in a similarly wonderful reception organized by Venus in honor of Tannhäuser; and the scene with Adolphe could have been inspired not only by Apuleius and the legend of the unicorn but perhaps also by the remembrance of Colonna's sacrificial ass. But the greatest influence was certainly exercised by Colonna's imaginary architecture and his interest in erotic attributes such as the torch. Polia carries it through the underworld like a burning phallus, and the terrace on which Venus banquets with Tannhäuser "was lit entirely by candles. There were four thousand of them, not numbering those upon the tables. The candlesticks were of a countless variety, and smiled with moulded cochônneries. Some were twenty feet high, and bore single candles that flared like fragrant torches over the feast, and guttered till the wax stood round the tops in tall lances. Some, hung with dainty petticoats of shining lustres, had a whole bevy of tapers upon them, devised in circles, in pyramids, in squares, in cuneiforms, in single lines regimentally and in crescents" (VT, p. 35). The terrace of Venus displays another image from the *Hypnerotomachia*, as Praz already noted: a fountain consisting of "a many-breasted dragon, and four little Loves mounted upon swans," "grotesquely attenuated satyrs," and "a thin pipe hung with masks and roses, and capped with children's heads. From the mouths of the dragon and the Loves, from the swan's [*sic*] eyes, from the breasts of the doves, from the satyrs' horns and lips, from the masks at many points, and from children's curls, the water played profusely, cutting strange arabesques and subtle figures" (VT, p. 35).[77]

The chaos of bodies and forms, amorously connected to each other through water, recalls the birth of Aphrodite out of the waves of the sea as well as images of the Madonna with child rising out of a fountain that waters plants and provides drink for animals and humans—icons particularly popular in Byzantine art. Among the eleventh-century mosaics of the monastery at Daphni, near Athens, a truly living fountain, made of vegetable and animal shapes, is depicted in the middle of the scene showing the annunciation of Mary's Immaculate Conception to Anna and Joachim. But while the Christian images concentrate on the serenity of nature and architecture, grotesque authors and artists undermine the purity by alluding to the darker sides of sex; by injecting the ridiculous and obscene, by profaning the holy, and elevating the profane. In Beardsley's drawings ordinary flowerpots remind one at once of the mythical tree or plants of life[78] and of indecent dreams with an explicitly sexual character. And in his novel he leaves no doubt what gender should be attributed to "orange-trees . . . looped with vermilion sashes" as opposed to the "frail porcelain pots" (VT, p. 35) in which they grow.

At the core of the Venusland one finds a tiny "pavilion or boudoir," in which Venus and Tannhäuser first make love and then are put to sleep like two children, a reminder of the fancy Brighton pavilion, Colonna's Venus temple, and, perhaps, of Homeric architecture as well. In Chapman's translation the oxstall in which Venus and Anchises beget Aeneas is referred to as "the rich Pavilion of the Heroe."[79] "Scented with huge branches of red roses" and embellished with "folding screens painted by De La Pine, with Claudian landscapes," Beardsley's "sweet little place, all silk curtains and soft cushions" (VT, p. 52) has an octagonal shape, like the early Christian churches (eight was considered a holy number, standing for resurrection and regeneration), and is designed by the architect Le Con. All the names contain erudite and obscene allusions. "Claudian landscapes" point, of course, to Claude Lorrain and his ancient vistas. "De La Pine" seems to originate from "pineal" ("gland"), and "Le Con" combines, perhaps, homage paid to Colonna with "le con," a vulgar French expression for the vagina.

Cozy as a cocoon, Venus's heterogeneous boudoir evokes the features of pagan temples and Christian churches, of theaters and brothels, of casinos, museums, and curio cabinets and unites them into a timeless grotto shining "obscurely with gilt mouldings through the warm haze of candle light below" (VT, p. 52), where mirror images, paintings, and sculptures mix with living beings into an indistinguishable whole. While life is infused into "tiny wax statuettes dressed theatrically and smiling with plump cheeks, quaint magots that looked as cruel as foreign gods, gilded monticules, pale celadon vases, clocks that said nothing, ivory boxes full of secrets, china figures playing whole scenes of plays" (VT, p. 52), Tannhäuser "pale and speechless" (VT, p. 55) fades away and Venus's body, although "nervous and responsive" (VT, p. 55) loses its liveliness by being likened to a gem ("her closed thighs seemed like a vast replica of the little bijou she held between them" [VT, p. 55]) and to an entire street of pleasure: "the Rue Vendôme" (VT, p. 55).

In his essay on "Gradiva," a short story by W. Jensen, Freud analyzes the animation of ancient architecture and sculpture, on the one side, and the deadening of living beings (they either turn to stone or are not seen at all) on the other, as a device of fantastic literature and art that corresponds closely to the state of dreaming as well as of madness.[80] The schizophrenic hero of "Gradiva," a German archeologist, escapes from reality into the ruins and shadows of the past by means of his profession. His increasing capacity to ignore people stands in direct proportion to his power to animate statues. By being diverted from living to dead matter, his attention flows away from his best friends. He reduces them to shadows, to the remote stones of Pompeii where the young scholar searches, like Tannhäuser and Faust before him, for his ancient beloved. He simultaneously believes the imaginary girl Gradiva to have been killed by the eruption of Vesuvius and senses that she is alive amidst the ruins.

Freud recognizes the animating and deadening faculties of imagination as natural for a dreamer, extremely useful for an artist, and threatening to sanity for an ordinary person who, incapable of sublimating them into a work of art, begins to distort reality. Freud fails, however, to notice that the hero of "Gradiva" not only represents an artist à la Pygmalion and a pathological case, but that the story reflects an old European fantasy of antiquity regained, a dream that long ago had been turned into a grotesque stereotype prevailing in periods with archeological interests and escapist tendencies. Beardsley comments wittily on this childishly persistent desire to recover the lost paradise in one of his self-deprecating drawings. It shows him tied by his foot to the herm of a bearded Pan (fig. 82). The caricature clearly expresses a disbelief that the past can be retrieved or the ancient way of life revived. In a highly civilized world, nature is everywhere broken by culture, originality by a multitude of copies. Poliphilo gropes among ruins, Tannhäuser makes love amidst painted landscapes. Both Colonna and Beardsley are aware of the fact that, reflected in the endless mirrors of the past, their journeys and passions lack spontaneity and can only appear as slightly ridiculous repetitions. Overconscious of their obsessions, the authors and their heroes watch their own adventures from an ironic distance which permits them to see that the wish to recover paradise lost, if fulfilled, is doomed to produce infantilism and regression.

Return to Childhood

> Her robes slipped to her feet, and the true goddess
> Walked in divinity. He knew his mother,
> And his voice pursued her flight: "Cruel again!
> Why mock your son so often with false phantoms?"
> ——Aeneas to Venus in the *Aeneid*
> (Book 1).

Entering the mountain of love, Chevalier Tannhäuser worries about only one thing. Like a child returning home from his adventures, he is afraid that Venus may be upset by his untidy appearance. The subterranean world is governed by a mother whose powerful figure reduces Tannhäuser to a disobedient, naughty boy. She also plays the role of his sister, and in her boudoir both she and her lover are treated by Priapusa (her name suggests sex but her behavior is that of a governess) like two tots in a nursery school.[81] Beardsley's dream of the past coincides with the reverie of childhood. The fantasy follows many paths, dimly lit by vague and confused remembrances, leading to an imaginary state of infancy, a location and a season that precedes conscious existence. The Austrian poet Hugo von Hofmannsthal, Beardsley's contemporary, called this period and place "pre-existence,"[82] a chthonic and embryonic chaos of desires and fears in which all poetry originates. Indeed, Hofmannsthal wrote his best poems as a teenager, using intuition and ignoring constraints and taboos.

Adults tend to sentimentalize early childhood and to interpret it as an age of innocence—of goodness, purity, and beauty. Even Gaston Bachelard,[83] a sensitive explorer of daydreaming, who usually acknowledges the ambiguities and contradictions of poetical reverie, concentrates on sweet fables in his chapter concerned with childhood and overlooks all the obscenities and cruelties—the dolls cut to pieces, the drowned kittens, the wings of flies torn off. He neglects the incestuous and wolfish reverie of Georg Trakl[84] and the obscenity of Beardsley's novel. Bachelard is right to state that in a reverie of childhood the terms "life" and "death" are "too approximate," but he forgets to add that this very approximation, which is indeed a feature of the child's approach to reality as well as of the adult's fantasy about childhood, creates both loveliness and horror: spontaneous goodness and equally sudden evil. Without mentioning the darker side of infancy, Bachelard promotes the Christian stereotype, the "innocence incarnate" of the Christ child, and consequently of all infants, for whom the Church has even reserved a special place in the afterlife. Though religion has upheld this vision of childhood and imposed it on popular and poetical imagination, the ideal has been contradicted by reality and questioned and opposed by heretics for centuries. The apocryphal Thomas's Gospel of the Infancy of Jesus presents a shocking image of Christ, a youngster so passionate and arrogant that he does not hesitate to kill a boy who, running in the street, accidentally "knocked against his shoulder. . . . And the parents of the dead child came to Joseph and blamed him and said: 'Since you have such a child, you cannot dwell with us in the village; or else teach him to bless and not to curse. For he is slaying our children.' "[85] Jesus had performed the killing by word, by simply saying to the boy "You shall not go further on your way," and in a similar way he animated things as well. Playing "at the ford of a brook . . . he made soft clay and fashioned from it twelve sparrows . . . clapped his hands and cried to the sparrows: 'Off with you!' And the sparrows took flight and went away chirping."[86]

This picture of Jesus mirrors more accurately than the ideal biblical portrait the psychology of a child, an egocentric creature who identifies the said with the done, the named with the possessed, the thought with the achieved. The Gospel of Thomas expresses its concern with a child equipped with supernatural powers and points not to the innocent paradise of childhood but to the hell created for others by a selfish, juvenile god. As if unaware of good and evil, young Jesus takes advantage of his magical powers and behaves like a trickster. Like childhood itself, the reverie of it is characterized by ambiguities and contradictions. It is dominated both by the desire to regain the protected cocoon of repose, sleep, and death and the infantile wish to rule the world, to kill or to animate with one stroke or one word. The daydreamer combines the aspect of a helpless baby with that of an aggressive lover and magician, the passive wish to retire to the bosom of the mother (earth) with the desire to penetrate her womb in search of unlimited pleasure. As he proceeds to satisfy his instinctive drive, beauty gives way to ugliness, love is mixed with fear, the pure and the dirty combine.

In 1886 A. P. Sinnett, a theosophist and the author of *Esoteric Buddhism* and *The Occult World*, brought out in London *Incidents in the Life of Madame Blavatsky*, a compilation of information supposedly supplied by her relatives and friends but probably inspired by Blavatsky herself. Sinnett's narrative blends the semi-scientific with the purely fictional and fairytale-like in a manner characteristic of Blavatsky's own writings. Thus we learn that she was born in 1831 in the very special night between July 30th and 31st, in popular belief notoriously connected with witches and their deeds as well as with the domestic goblin ("domovoy"); that she was called by the serfs "Sedmitchka," meaning one connected to the magical number seven (July being the seventh month); and that

> she learned even in her childhood the reason why, on that day, she was carried about in her nurse's arms around the house, stables, and cow-pen, and made personally to sprinkle the four corners with water, the nurse repeating all the while some mystic sentences. These may be found to this day in the ponderous volumes of Sacharof's "Russian Demonology," a laborious work that necessitated over thirty years of incessant travelling, and scientific researches in the old chronicles of the Slavonian lands, and that won to the author the appellation of the Russian Grimm.[87]

Having started on this scholarly note, Sinnett changes his tone to that of a children's bookwriter by telling us that the future Madame Blavatsky (at that time still Mlle. Hahn) resided, as it were, among the demons studied by famous scientists: "Born in the very heart of the country which the Roussalka (the Undine) has chosen for her abode ever since creation—reared on the shores of the blue Dnieper, that no Cossack of Southern Ukraine ever crosses without preparing himself for death—the child's belief in these lovely green-haired nymphs was developed before she had heard of anything else." In this setting, a place depicted by Sinnett as so threatening that nobody, with the exception of the four-year-old Helena, dared to approach it without fear, the first miracle takes place, and the narrative seems familiar if one knows the Gospel of Thomas. "In one of her walks by the river side a boy about fourteen who was dragging the child's carriage incurred her displeasure by some slight disobedience. 'I will have you tickled to death by a roussalka!' she screamed. 'There's one coming down from the tree . . . here she comes . . . See, see!' " The boy takes to his heels and disappears—forever, of course. Several weeks later his corpse is found in the nets of the fishermen and his death is interpreted by the servants as not *"accidental* . . . but . . . one that had occurred in consequence of the child having withdrawn from the boy her mighty protection, thus delivering the victim to some roussalka on the watch."[88]

Chronicled in order to display the miraculous gifts possessed by the founder of theosophy even in her early childhood, the story proves interesting from several points of view. First of all, it represents an apocryphal and extraordinary image of infancy as an age rooted in the ancient, pre-Christian forces of nature—the nymphs living in the rivers and trees from the beginning of time. Second, it establishes a close alliance between the simple country folk (serfs, nurses, servants), believers in animism and magic, and the "wunderkind" Sedmitchka; they bring her in touch with their secret knowledge against the will of her wealthy, Westernized parents who "knew nothing of this side of the education of their eldest born, and learned it too late to allow such beliefs to be eradicated from her mind."[89] Third, Sinnett's account focuses on the primacy of femininity and infancy: the power of the four-year-old girl and of the water-nymph Roussalka, feared even by such strong characters as the Cossacks. Bridging folklore and magic, linking the remote past to early childhood, Sinnett offers not only a mythical description of Blavatsky's life but also the new perception of childhood that had been emerging in the second half of the nineteenth century.

While Romanticism cannot be imagined without the discovery of folklore, the late nineteenth century, the last phase of the "romantic agony," is unthinkable without its interest in childhood and in the culture of children. Biographers paid attention to the infancy of famous people, children's books were bestsellers, and the infantile was for the first time studied seriously by folklorists and anthropologists. At the end of the century articles on this subject could regularly be found in the periodicals of the British Folklore Society. Children's games received attention in two books by A. B. Gomme, *The Traditional Games of England, Scotland, and Ireland* (2 vols., 1894–98) and *Children's Singing Games* (1904), as well as in W. W. Newell's earlier volume, *Games and Songs of American Children* (1883). Kate Greenaway's (1846–1901) verses sound like nursery rhymes, and indeed this was certainly the source of her inspiration. Collections of children's songs appeared throughout the nineteenth century, starting with Robert Chambers's *Popular Rhymes of Scotland* (1826, reprinted 1870) and James O. Halliwell's *Nursery Rhymes of England* (1845). They were followed at the turn of the century by such scholarly publications as Lina Eckenstein's

Comparative Studies in Nursery Rhymes (1906), among others. Thus, the state of knowledge was certainly ready for Freud's discovery of the eroticism of children, something that had been strongly suggested by the studies of children's games and rhymes, which were seen as the last remnants of ancient customs and rites connected with fertility, rivalry, love, and marriage. Girls' games with a domestic character were considered to preserve better than the more flexible boys' contests the features of an older tradition. The interest in children's games is indicated quite clearly, for instance, by the inclusion of an entry on the subject in the 1910 *Encyclopaedia Britannica*, written by A. B. Gomme herself. She differentiates between the masculine "line" games, with two lines of players standing opposite each other and engaged in a struggle or contest, and the feminine "circle" form, where the players join hands to celebrate a common event—sowing or harvest, marriage or love. According to her, some of the "line" games, for instance "Nuts in May" and "Here come three dukes a-riding," reenact the early customary way of obtaining wives: marriage by capture. Gomme concludes her entry by stating that "the large majority of circle games deal with love or marriage and domestic life. The customs surviving in these games deal with tribal life and take us back to 'foundation sacrifice,' 'well worship,' 'sacredness of fire,' besides marriage and funeral customs."[90]

Stories written and illustrated for an audience of minors appear late in the history of European culture. They replace, to a large extent, the stories once told to children mainly by their mothers, nurses, and grandparents, and they express in words and pictures the spirit of children's games. Since Victorian times English authors have excelled in the field of children's books, and their style has been imitated all over the world. Intimate, personal, and witty, they contributed to the creation of a specific sensibility wherever they were read, and their influence on young readers may have been of greater importance than anyone suspected, although we know very little about this. However, Hofmannsthal mentioned his reading and liking Kate Greenaway's books,[91] and Marcel Proust, a great Anglophile, an admirer of Ruskin, and a re-creator of childhood, certainly read them as well. Of Greenaway's *Under the Window* (1879), 150,000 copies are said to have been sold, and French and German editions were issued. *The Birthday Book, Mother Goose* (fig. 90), *Little Ann,* and other of her "toy-books" were to be found in the bookshops of every capital in Europe as well as the cities of America. Greenaway was applauded by Ruskin and leading art critics throughout the world. In 1890 she was elected a member of the Royal Institute of Painters in Water Colours, and her illustrations, admired for their "infinite delicacy, tenderness, and grace,"[92] were compared with the paintings of Botticelli. Her idyllic world of dancing and singing infants dressed "in delightfully quaint costume"[93] promoted the reverie of childhood, nature, and the past and shaped the aesthetic taste of several generations.

The first drawings ever done by Beardsley were small figures copied from books by Greenaway. He liked best *Under the Window,* and Stanley Weintraub has suggested that its title might have inspired that of Beardsley's novel.[94] But the analogies between the two books are not limited to their titles. They have in common structures, ideas, motifs, and images. The figures of Venus and Tannhäuser move in a landscape whose basic features have been provided by Greenaway's book. *Under the Hill*—as *Under the Window*—expands into the paradise of childhood as it could never have been experienced by a boy with bleeding lungs, but therefore was more intensely dreamt by him. Flocks of sheep graze on green meadows, and tiny boys and girls play among flowers, herbs, and blooming trees. Greenaway drew children as androgynous and slightly pretentious elves and stylized the idyllic scenery after the playful yet melancholic rococo paintings, with courtiers dressed up as Pierrots or shepherds. Her illustrations dilute the French frivolities to sweet, slightly dull, pastel-colored and miniature, very English cartoons for children. They are a *Reader's Digest* of Watteau, produced for small Victorian people, the infantile equivalent of an evergreen island of play and love, where eroticism is hidden under nursery rhymes, old-fashioned hats, muffs, and umbrellas, and cats play men (fig. 91).

Under the Window is filled with masculine "line" competitions played in order to obtain a wife. Thus, girls encourage the boys in the following way:

> *Bowl away! bowl away!*
> *Fast as you can;*
> *He who can fastest bowl,*
> *He is my man!*

> *Up and down, round about,—*
> *Don't let it fall;*
> *Ten times, or twenty times,*
> *Beat, beat them all!*

And boys, in turn, ask them:

> *Will you be my little wife,*
> *If I ask you? Do!—*
> *I'll buy you such a Sunday frock,*
> *A nice umbrella, too.*

> *And you shall have a little hat,*
> *With such a long white feather,*
> *A pair of gloves, and sandal shoes,*
> *The softest kind of leather.*

And you shall have a tiny house,
A beehive full of bees,
A little cow, a largish cat,
A green sage cheese.[95]

Beardsley's frivolities sound like paraphrases of this nursery sexuality:

Fanfreluche and the rest of the rips and ladies tingled
with excitement and frolicked like young lambs in a fresh
meadow. Again and again the wine was danced round,
and the valley grew as busy as a market day. Attracted
by the noise and merrymaking, all those sweet infants I
told you of, skipped suddenly on to the stage, and began
clapping their hands and laughing immoderately at the
passion and the disorder and commotion, and mimicking
the nervous staccato movements they saw in their pretty
childish way.
    In a flash, Fanfreluche disentangled himself and
sprang to his feet, gesticulating as if he would say, "Ah,
the little dears!" "Ah, the rorty little things!" "Ah, the
little ducks!" for he was so fond of children. Scarcely had
he caught one by the thigh than a quick rush was made
by everybody for the succulent limbs; and how they tou-
sled them and mousled them! The children cried out, I
can tell you. (VT, p. 48)

In their singing and dancing games children impersonate objects, animals, other people. Beardsley's description of merrymaking takes the form
of a play—"a ballet for the evening's divertissement, founded upon De
Bergerac's comedy of 'Les Bacchanales de Fanfreluche,' in which the action
and dances were designed by him as well as the music" (VT, p. 43). The
ballet is indeed a childish parody of idyllic scenes in ancient art and literature, of the dainty Versailles tableaux and of the Greenaway pageants
(fig. 92):

To the music of pipe and horn, a troop of satyrs stepped
out from the recesses of the woods, bearing in their hands
nuts and green boughs and flowers and roots and whatso-
ever the forest yielded, to heap upon the altar of the mys-
terious Pan that stood in the middle of the stage; and
from the hills came down the shepherds and shepher-
desses, leading their flocks and carrying garlands upon
their crooks. Then a rustic priest, whiterobed and venera-
ble, came slowly across the valley followed by a choir of
radiant children. (VT, p. 44)

But here the infantile suggests something more sinister: children and cupids as symbols of death. After all, figures of children playing and fighting were frequently represented on Hellenistic sarcophagi (fig. 93), which since the Renaissance served as examples for European sculptors and painters. A children's merry-go-round symbolizes death in Hans Holbein's *Imagines mortis* (fig. 94), and, consequently, a similar meaning might have been carried in the scenes of cupids' bacchanals (fig. 95) particularly popular in the seventeenth and eighteenth centuries, even when this association was not directly stated in the titles. The depictions of children with hourglasses and skulls (fig. 96), however, are entirely explicit.

The ballet of Fanfreluche is set against "a scene of rare beauty, a remote Arcadian valley, and watered with a dear river as fresh and pastoral as a perfect fifth of this scrap of Tempe" (VT, p. 43). Here Arcady symbolizes not so much the idyllic *per se* as the lost serenity of a golden age. And from Panofsky we know that the famous ancient motto "Et in Arcadia Ego,"[96] words repeatedly quoted, interpreted, and illustrated in the European tradition up to the end of the nineteenth century (Beardsley had them inscribed on a monument or tomb in one of his drawings), has to be understood as spoken by Death. Entering Arcadia, Death transforms it into a cemetery.

Under the Window begins with the evocation of the serene and paradisiac:

> Under the window is my garden,
> Where sweet, sweet flowers grow;
> And in the pear-tree dwells a robin,
> The dearest bird I know.[97]

The poem is placed between the picture of a window where three children look out and that of a cup of roses at the bottom of the page (fig. 97). The window, which encloses the children, and the cup, which contains the flowers, are frequent images in Beardsley's illustrations, and both allude to the female worlds located "under the window"—inside the children's room and in the garden. Even if Beardsley was not aware of this symbolism as a child, he surely captured its essence when remembering *Under the Window* as he wrote his novel.

The motif of the rose is further elaborated by another of the Greenaway poems and the corresponding illustration, which shows a woman leaning out of the window and throwing a rose blossom to a baby (fig. 98).[98] The text and the image might well have inspired Beardsley's idea of a rose petal as the appropriate "passport . . . from the upper to the underworld" (VT, p. 26). It seems that the rose thrown down to Greenaway's "little baby" is caught upon the trimmings of Tannhäuser's "muff" as he is about to enter the Venusberg. Beardsley's narrative follows a familiar pattern established in Greenaway's books, in which motherly females dominate male babies. The older sisters hold, lead, and affectionately carry their younger brothers and playmates in their arms, and the latter are frequently described as eager to return to their female protectors when, by some misfortune, they are separated from them.

The image of a hill occurs twice in *Under the Window* and is each time associated with female figures. And in *Mother Goose* we read:

> *There was an old woman*
> *Lived under a hill;*
> *And if she's not gone,*
> *She lives there still.* (fig. 99)[99]

Interestingly enough, the composition of the picture that illustrates the poem reminds us of an alchemical miniature by the Italian artist Nicola d'Antonio degli Agli that depicts the Old Man (the alchemists called him Boaz, the farmer of Bethlehem) standing in front of a cave, the entrance to a mountain, where he was supposed to wed the female principle (his bride Ruth), their marriage representing the beginning of the alchemical opus (fig. 100). This hermetic meaning is further exemplified by the red castle on top of the hill, symbol of the fixed state, and the angel, symbol of the volatile state. In Greenaway's illustration a house stands on the right side of the hill, while two birds fly over its left side. I do not intend to suggest that Greenaway was inspired by the Italian miniature and its alchemical content; certainly if one disregards the hidden meaning, both pictures can simply be read as representations of people as seen against a mountain. What I want to propose is the hypothesis that by creating in her children's books an enchanted microcosm, pre-industrial and pre-adult, Greenaway could not but revive the legends and fairy tales, and their depictions, in which the curious fragments of an older world, a paradise lost, had been preserved. This made her popular not only with children but also with adults, who, among other things, must have appreciated the subtle allusions to their own childhood, since the children's clothing drawn by Greenaway did not reflect actual fashions of her day but rather the dresses worn by an earlier generation—the one whose infancy dated back to the beginning of the nineteenth century.

Greenaway's sweet and overdressed creatures look slightly grotesque because their ribbons, hats, ruffs, bonnets, muffs, umbrellas, sticks, and toys are out of proportion, too large or too small for them. This kind of "laboured niceness" is also a feature of Beardsley's figures, and especially of Tannhäuser (fig. 101), who with his ruff and stick looks indeed like an overgrown Tommy (fig. 102) coming out of a Greenaway rhyme:

> As I was walking up the street,
>   The steeple bells were ringing;
> As I sat down at Mary's feet,
>   The sweet, sweet birds were singing.
>
> As I walked far into the world,
>   I met a little fairy;
> She plucked this flower, and, as it's sweet,
>   I've brought it home to Mary.[100]

Both Greenaway and Beardsley make extensive use of adjectives referring to smallness, niceness, prettiness, etc. But in Beardsley's book grotesque effects are frequently achieved by breaking and reversing the sweet talk in a sudden turn from the childish to the obscene: "I'm just going to feed Adolphe,' she said, pointing to a little reticule of buns that hung from her arm. Adolphe was her pet unicorn. 'He is such a dear,' she continued; 'milk-white all over excepting his black eyes, rose mouth and nostrils, and scarlet John' " (VT, p. 63). It is enough to cut the last two words and the quoted passage would become acceptable for one of Greenaway's books.

The Story of Venus and Tannhäuser displays the grotesqueness of a kindergarten gone perverse and offers a parody of Victorian infantilism—all costume, repression, and baby talk. Beardsley derides Greenaway's closed and slightly oppressive mini-world "under the window," but he also pays tribute to her. Thus, the female author and illustrator of an infantile and motherly paradise and the creator of the grotesque reverie on the Venusland join hands. This is a curious alliance and one that reflects well the peculiar sensibilities of the late nineteenth century, with the focus turning away from grandiose masculinity toward the world of women and children; from heroic adulthood to intimate infancy; from high culture to the lowest level of folklore—that of nursery rhymes and children's games—where the research was mainly done by women and not easily admitted to the realm of "higher" and more "serious" subjects.

Freud's theories of children's eroticism were preceded by the pioneering work done by women folklorists. The great writers of the twentieth century (Hofmannsthal, Proust, Joyce, Musil, Nabokov) who were always or at some point of their lives deeply concerned with the exploration of childhood and the reverie of it were indebted to the predominantly female authors of their children's books and, more generally, to the particular sensitivity of women. Proust described in detail the emotions he experienced every time his mother read to him George Sand's *François le Champi*, and Nabokov's *Ada* seems to be modeled in part on the experience of the young Blavatsky, whose sister said that "no schoolboy was ever more uncontrollable or full of the most unimaginable and daring pranks and *espiegleries* than she was." She describes Helena as a child taking refuge in the catacombs of a large abandoned garden, reputed to be the "hiding-place for all the runaway criminals and deserters," as a charmer of living animals, putting birds to sleep "according to the rules taught in 'Salomon's Wisdom,' " the lover of "relics of fauna, flora, and historical antiquities, . . . antediluvian bones of stuffed animals and monstrous birds, . . . seals and stuffed crocodiles," as the protector and saver of "all those dark butterflies—known as *sphynxes*—whose dark fur-covered heads and bodies bore the distinct images of a white human skull. 'Nature having imprinted on each of them the portrait of the skull of some great dead hero, these butterflies are sacred, and must not be killed,' she said, speaking like some heathen fetish-worshipper." To the future prophetess "all nature seemed animated with a mysterious life of its own. She heard the voice of every object and form, whether organic or inorganic."[101]

The eroticism of children and the obscenities hidden in their games as well as in the books written for them are no news to anybody today. Putting aside the bulk of literature on the subject, I shall mention Arno Schmidt's book on Karl May, the German author of popular adventure stories about the Indians and the white explorers.[102] Schmidt shows how May's books mirror their author's homosexual inclinations, and he maintains that forbidden sexuality is subconsciously grasped and enjoyed by the readers, predominantly boys in puberty. May's adventures tend to culminate in secret encounters between beautiful Indians and their white friends, which usually take place in dark and foul-smelling caves—interpreted by Schmidt as a symbol of the anus. Schmidt goes into detail, pointing to the masculinity of May's grottoes as opposed to female cavities. It seems to me, however, that the gender suggested by these dwellings is only of secondary importance, because the eroticism of children is more vague and diffuse than adult sexuality and generally mixed with the affinity they feel with earth, animals, and vegetation. Children's fondness for caves transcends their erotic associations, for they identify the diverse grottoes with nature itself, into which they try to escape from a world controlled by adults. Children dig in the ground, explore cellars, ruins, dark rooms, and closets, and, fascinated with cabins, tents, and igloos, build their own miniature homes, repeating again and again the features of the original cave. The thrill experienced in such hideouts certainly has an erotic component, but it cannot be reduced to sexuality alone. It signifies the wish for regression and is thus closely related to the shadowy domain of the grotesque. When the infantile succeeds in dominating adult consciousness, the hidden archetypal layers of imagination are brought up to the surface and the world turns uncanny. This recovered infantilism is a source on the one hand of authenticity and originality and on the other hand of limitation and regression. Children are freer than adults but they are, of course, even more caught up in their own childish desires and dreams. Max Beerbohm expressed this wittily and cruelly in a caricature of Beardsley. It shows the artist as an infantile Faust, dragging behind him on a string a tiny toy poodle on wheels, and it replays a theme initiated by Beardsley himself, who in one of his vignettes from the *Bon-Mots* of Samuel Foote and Theodore Hook drew a winged naked boy with a tiny hat on top of his bald head as he holds a dressed-up dog on a leash (fig. 103).

Indeed, while he was dying in Menton at the age of twenty-six, Beardsley behaved like a child, asking his mother to bring him toys when she went out shopping. What at the end of the nineteenth century was regarded as grotesque degradation has meanwhile become a part of our reality. On 20 August 1984, I found in the Science section of the *New York Times* an article on changed sex roles illustrated by a picture of an effeminate man with a teddy bear in his hands.[103] Two days later, in the very same paper, I saw the photo of a female model in a fashion show parading a wooden elephant on a leash—a faint American echo of the feminist happening that the Austrian artist Valie Export performed in 1968 in the center of Vienna.[104] The event was called "From the Archives of Doggishness" and took place on the Kärtnerstrasse, where the artist walked her husband, crawling on all fours, on a leash.

In a world of equal opportunities for men and women, many features once regarded as typical of one sex are shifted to the other. The notions of masculinity and femininity become relative, and so does infantility. Once suppressed in men and attributed instead to women, childishness is recognized today as characteristic of many adult males. Not condemned or ridiculed any more, their infantile desires and attitudes seem not only quite natural but also enriching and charming. This modern shift of emphasis transforms some of the past grotesqueness into today's norm.

numifmati in circo. Vno facello cum patefacta porta, cum una ara i me-
dio. Nouiffimamente erano dui perpendiculi. Lequale figure i latino cu
fi le interpretai.

DIVO IVLIO CAESARI SEMP. AVG. TOTIVS ORB.
GVBERNAT. OB ANIMI CLEMENT. ET LIBERALI
TATE MAEGYPTII COMMVNIA ERE.S. EREXERE.

Similmente in qualúque fron
te del recenfito fuppofito qua-
drato, quale la prima circulata
figura, tale unaltra fe pftaua a li
nca & ordie della prima a la de
xtra planitie dúque mirai an-
cora tali eleganti hieroglyphi,
primo uno uiperato caduceo.
Alla ima parte dilla uirga dil-
quale, & de qui, & deli, uidi u-
na formica che fe crefceua i ele
phanto. Verfo la fupernate æ-
qualmente dui elepháti decref
ceuano in formice. Tra quefti
nel mediaftimo era uno uafo
cum foco, & dalaltro lato una
conchula cum aqua. cufi io li

PACE, AC CONCORDIA PAR-
VAERES CRESCVNT, DISCOR
DIA MAXIMAE DECRESCVNT.
interpretai. Pace, ac concordia
paruæ res crefcút, difcordia ma
ximæ decrefcunt.

FIG. 83 Hieroglyphs found by Poliphilo on ruins, in *Hypnerotomachia
Poliphili* (1499)

FIG. 84 From *Hypnerotomachia Poliphili* (1499).

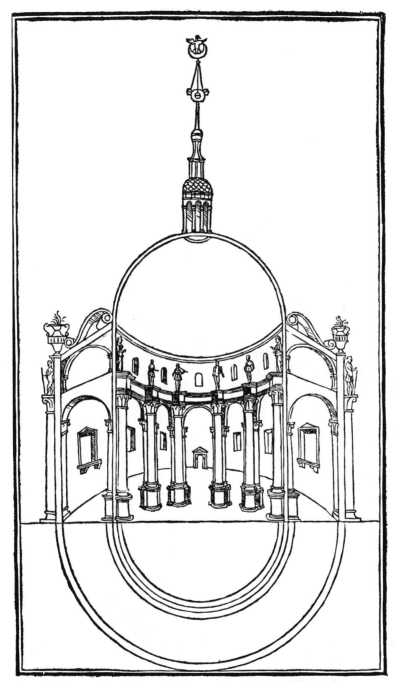

FIG. 85 The temple of Venus, in *Hypnerotomachia Poliphili* (1499).

FIG. 86 Sleeping nymph, in *Hypnerotomachia Poliphili*
(1499).

THE STORY OF VENUS AND TANNHAUSER, IN WHICH IS SET FORTH AN EXACT ACCOUNT OF THE MANNER OF STATE HELD BY MADAM VENUS, GODDESS AND MERETRIX, UNDER THE FAMOUS HÖRSELBERG, AND CONTAINING THE ADVENTURES OF TANNHÄUSER IN THAT PLACE, HIS REPENTANCE, HIS JOURNEYING TO ROME, AND RETURN TO THE LOVING MOUNTAIN. By AUBREY BEARDSLEY.

Fig. 87 Aubrey Beardsley, frontispiece and title page for *The Story of Venus and Tannhäuser*.

FLORIDO VERI ·S·

FIG. 88 From *Hypnerotomachia Poliphili* (1499).

FIG. 89 Aubrey Beardsley, front cover of *The Yellow Book* (1895).

FIG. 90 Title page of Kate Greenaway's *Mother Goose or the Old Nursery Rhymes* (1881).

THE CATS HAVE COME TO TEA.

FIG. 91 From Kate Greenaway's *Marigold Garden* (1885).

FIG. 92 From Kate Greenaway's *The Language of Flowers* (1884).

FIG. 93 Sporting children, front part of a sarcophagus, early third century A.D.

FIG. 94 Playing children as symbols
of death, in Hans Holbein's *Imagines
mortis* (1547).

FIG. 95 Lucas Faydherbe (or workshop), *Cupids in Bacchanalian Scene*, ivory, Flemish, seventeenth century.

FIG. 96 Child with hourglass and skull, probably Flemish, seventeenth century.

Fig. 97 From Kate Greenaway's *Under the Window* (1879).

LITTLE baby, if I threw
This fair blossom down to you,
Would you catch it as you stand,
Holding up each tiny hand,
Looking out of those grey eyes,
Where such deep, deep wonder lies?

FIG. 98 From Kate Greenaway's *Under the Window* (1879).

There was an old woman
Lived under a hill;
And if she's not gone,
She lives there still.

FIG. 99 From Kate Greenaway's *Mother Goose* (1881).

FIG. 100 Nicola d'Antonio degli Agli, Old Man in front of his cave, 1480.

FIG. 101 Aubrey Beardsley, *The Abbé*.

IT was Tommy who said,
  "The sweet spring-time is come;
I see the birds flit,
  And I hear the bees hum.

"Oho! Mister Lark,
  Up aloft in the sky,
Now, which is the happiest—
  Is it you, sir, or I?"

FIG. 102 From Kate Greenaway's *Under the Window* (1879).

FIG. 103 Aubrey Beardsley, Vignette.

Chapter 9 · Salome

In the twilight, at dusk of day,
at the time of the dark of night.
And lo! the woman comes to meet him,
robed like a harlot, with secret designs—

. . .

Her house is made up of ways to the nether world,
leading down into the chambers of death.
——Proverbs 7:9–10, 27

 The writers and artists of the late nineteenth century, pursuing visions of an anti-Christian and anti-heroic world in their works, revived the strong, legendary, and historical women of the past. The renaissance of Salome was especially significant. Helen Grace Zagona has dedicated an entire book to the legend of Salome as the great theme of art for art's sake—and more than a theme.[1] The Jewish princess was the symbol of *l'art pour l'art*, an icon set against the utility and positivism of modern times. Heine was the first poet to declare himself in love with Herodias;[2] and Mallarmé personified in her the perfect *oeuvre* and his ideal of an artist: an alienated Narcissus who creates out of the contemplation of his own reflection, out of the primordial depth hidden underneath the mirroring surface of the frozen water where death, "the eternal sister" of dream and trance, waits in silence.[3]

Salome represented the archetype of a terrible femininity and fin-de-siècle femme fatale, but her strange figure and story also symbolized the obscure paradoxes of unconscious desires and fears. The setting of her story and the juxtaposition of its chief protagonists, the saint who is kept underground and the princess in the banqueting hall who has him brought out in order to get his head—all this glitters obscenely like the metaphor of a forbidden wish emerging out of darkness or a dream one tries to forget after awakening. The odd and gruesome grotesqueness of the Salome legend, which had been preserved predominantly through folklore and was revived by the Romantics and decadents, functioned at the turn of the century as a parable of the chaos of emotions and as a fable of the artistic mind, fascinated by the ephemeral and irrational, transcending all boundaries of good taste and common sense.

Most of the late-nineteenth-century Salome tales as well as her representations in the visual arts are characterized by an extremely grotesque form: a style heavy with oxymorons and an imagery overburdened by quotations, allusions, parodies, and caricatures. Thus it is all difficult to take quite seriously, particularly the written works. One has to remember, however, that the function of such a style may be to hide what is forbidden. Certain things can be played only on a stage that looks like a worldly theater and not like someone's bedroom. Cruelties and obscenities are couched at a distance when they are attributed to a goddess, but then they are brought back, by means of wit, caricature, and parody, to touch and to pinpoint the obscene within the self. We shall see that the French and the English decadents devised a perversely ingenious technique, at once removing the subject almost to the moon and bringing it back, through some ridiculous phrase or ludicrous detail, to the very core of the ordinary psyche—in desire, agony, or anguish. They invented an absurd space that looks simultaneously like the universe and the black hole of a human soul. Once the love-story version of the legend of Salome became established by Heine and the monstrosity of her desire was fully explored, she grew into a goddess of the black waters and the night sky, a sacrilegious female Messiah or John the Baptist.

But there is not one Salome nor a single legend. Searching for her, one discovers a myriad of figures and a web of configurations: a complex, ambiguous iconography that was shaped by her awkward position, crossing from ancient to modern times, from paganism to Christianity, and influenced by the diverse and frequently contradictory mythology of John the Baptist as well as John the Evangelist, the author of the Apocalypse. Salome was not just a murderer. She participated in the destruction of John the Baptist, the precursor of Christ, and thus came to represent the enemies of the new faith. Among the female figures of the New Testament, both Herodias and Salome were particularly well suited to personify the perversions of late antiquity juxtaposed to rising Christianity. The early church fathers saw the dancing girl as an embodiment of the pleasure-seeking principle—and of the ruin voluptuousness led to.[4] Later, when the cult of the Baptist became popular at the time of the Crusades, ever more evil was projected onto Herodias and her daughter, and new details of cruelty added to the old story. In a medieval variation of the legend, for instance, Herodias allegedly cut one of John's dead eyes with a knife, as if to demonstrate the abyss of absurd abomination that was her lot (fig. 104). In folklore she was transformed into a witch, mixed up with other ancient demons, and blamed for various disasters.[5] As this process of vilification evolved, Herodias's and Salome's Jewishness became an important issue. Their crimes, like that of Judas, contributed to the stigmatization of the entire Jewish people. They functioned in the Christian culture as female counterparts of the betrayer of Jesus—as the attractive but bad, "real" Jewesses whom the anti-Semitic tradition perceived in contrast to the Holy Virgin. While the Herodian women were rooted in their sinful world, the semi-divine mother of Jesus was disassociated from the excesses of earthly femininity—and from her Semitic origins.

Mario Praz remarks in *The Romantic Agony* that Salome was beloved by the *à rebours* aesthetes, who in general delighted in her horrifying Medusan charm. But to this must be added that those who were fascinated by Herodias or Salome went against the grain not only from the aesthetic but also from the religious point of view; they made a heretical choice, meant to offend not only the philistines but also the Church.

Finally, one has to realize the psychological aspect of the Salome story, the fact that this female demon of Christian iconography came to be interpreted, particularly in the late nineteenth century, as an indication of women's hidden aggressiveness. At that time "female psychology" was, of course, the product of predominantly male fantasies which for millennia have likened woman to matter—the earth, the moon—and men to sources of energy—the spirit, the sun. Until recently masculinity has been conceived as a force which animates and illuminates passive, dark femininity, while woman was generally described as lacking something—spirit, mind, intelligence, reason, a name, or a penis. As the norms of female psychology were set and controlled by men, it seems likely that the theories of Freud, Jung, and Lacan illuminate only partly or not at all the fabric of the female psyche (if such a thing exists), but instead throw light on the male perception of women. Though these scholars meant to explore female peculiarities and regulate them, they may frequently have projected their own convictions and fantasies onto women, whose main frustrations were caused by this mixture of male mythologizing and social discrimination. On the other hand, the feminists who rightly fight what they assume to be a false male conception of femininity often come up with unconvincing theories of female psychology seen exclusively as the result of male oppression. Thus the inner life of woman (whether or not it is different from that of man) still remains *terra incognita,* and the psychology of both sexes still resides in the territory of legend and prejudice where all seems possible. For instance, do the figures of goddesses and great literary heroines reflect femininity, the male perception of it, or, perhaps, masculinity? Are Emma Bovary, Anna Karenina, and Effi Briest the fullest incarnations of the female principle, or are they simply Flaubert, Tolstoy, and Fontane? And who is Herodias or Salome? A historical figure? A fantasy of the Apostles? The mythical Hecate? The mother earth? The moon? The alter ego of the prioress Herrade of Landsberg, who painted Salome dancing on her hands? The anti-Madonna of Heine, a Jew? The real ego of Mallarmé, Wilde, and Beardsley? The notions of femininity and masculinity taken together form a slippery ground of the imaginary that, in order to be understood, has to be illuminated from all possible angles. An investigation of the grotesque can serve this purpose as well.

It is difficult to decide if the account of John's death in the Gospels is the original source for Salome's story or if the biblical version is already a remake of a much older legend—that of a god like Adonis or Attis sacrificed to a Great Goddess, the incarnation of mother earth. There are many suggestions that the latter hypothesis is correct. John's birthday on June 25 coincides with the summer solstice and his death on August 29 with the harvest. Curious customs which have survived to the beginning of the twentieth century in European folklore seem to reinforce this notion of John as a symbol for the death and rebirth of nature, associated with the cult of the sun. On the other hand, Herodias and her daughter are linked to demonic forces, to witchcraft and black magic. The strange popular beliefs and customs which the Church has always fought but never managed to eradicate are all strongly marked by sexuality; they allude to destruction caused by the passion of love, to marriage, defloration, and castration. They link women to severed heads, connect the sexual to the culinary, play with necrophilia and cannibalism. It is difficult to understand the complicated fabric of all the motifs and particular threads interwoven in the folklore of different European countries. It is equally hard to establish any direct relationship between the ancient cults, the biblical story and its slightly different renditions in the various translations,[6] and popular customs. But it is certain that the story has survived both in folklore and in literature and art because of its deep mythological *urgrund*, and that it has flourished throughout the centuries because of its complexities, ambiguities, obscenities, and, last but not least, because of the grotesque image of a woman bearing the head of a man on a dish. Herodias and Salome not only defeat the precursor of Christ, they also break some of the basic taboos of civilized humanity. They look as if they were ready to devour the head and make love to it. It is crucial to the story that the head is brought in during a banquet, like all the other dishes (fig. 105). The traditional equation between the consumption of food and sex opens wide the door for endless fantasies. The head, occasionally rendered as truly desirable (fig. 106), is likened to the penis; its bleeding becomes associated with the bleeding occurring during defloration and menstruation; castration is seen as the climax of intercourse with a powerful female or as her revenge. The image of John's death stimulates a deeply hidden erotic reverie in which everything is permitted and everybody desires everybody else, including the headsman, who in Cesare da Sesto's painting, for instance, seems to be in love with Salome (fig. 107).

The Choice of Herod

In the Bible, the court of Herod, a place of pleasure, excess, and brutal worldly power, symbolizes evil paganism as opposed to virtuous Christianity. But another important contrast is suggested as well. It concerns the sexes. While the tetrarch is described as not entirely inhuman but rather as a weak man, his wife Herodias and his stepdaughter Salome are truly devilish figures. Especially in the Gospel of Mark, all blame for the crime is attributed to the females, while Herod tends to be excused: he "feared John, knowing that he was a just and holy man, and protected him" (Mark 6:20). While the two men took to each other, "Herodias laid snares for him [John], and would have liked to put him to death, but she could not. . . ." The passage then proceeds:

> And a favorable day came when Herod on his birthday gave a banquet to the officials, tribunes and chief men of Galilee. And Herodias' own daughter having come in and danced, she pleased Herod and his guests. And the king said to the girl, 'Ask of me what thou willest, and I will give it to thee.' And he swore to her, 'Whatever thou dost ask, I will give thee, even though it be the half of my kingdom.' Then she went out and said to her mother, 'What am I to ask for?' And she said, 'The head of John the Baptist.' And she came in at once with haste to the king, and asked, saying, 'I want thee right away to give me on a dish the head of John the Baptist.' And grieved as he was, the king, because of his oath and his guests, was unwilling to displease her. But sending an executioner, he commanded that his head be brought on a dish. Then he beheaded him in the prison, and brought his head on a dish, and gave it to the girl, and the girl gave it to her mother. (Mark 6:19, 20–28)

Thus the second opposition lies between evil femininity—material and unclean—and the pure and spiritual masculinity of the Precursor. His virtue is recognizable to Herod, who is weak but still a man. At the banquet the tetrarch is given the opportunity to save the Baptist and thus to reverse the course of his so-far evil life; he has a chance to become the first Paul. But Herod lacks strength and tends to succumb to pleasure, so when he must decide between wrong and right, the immoral old world and the dawning new faith, he yields to Herodias's perfidy and Salome's beauty and adds to all his former crimes a decisive new one.

The Bible does not mention Salome by name; she is presented as the obedient daughter of Herodias, who uses the princess as a tool in her intrigue against the Baptist. Though young and still inexperienced, Salome functions as the mirror image of her voluptuous mother. The two women represent two ages and two aspects of sinful womanhood; they form together one allegorical figure split in two (fig. 108). This dramatizes the action and demonstrates that females (fig. 109), even when innocent-seeming, cannot be trusted. Salome is usually left out of the folk tradition, where all attention is focused on Herodias, the personification of a witch. However, the dancing girl who accepts from the executioner a charger holding John's head becomes a central figure, suggestive and picturesque, early in Christianity, through literature, and even more through the visual arts, and reaches finally in the late nineteenth century the cosmic proportions of a lunar goddess.

The biblical story not only links the mother to the daughter but also establishes a connection between the tetrarch and the saint. John is beheaded on Herod's birthday; thus the death of one man touches the beginning of the other's life. Popular imagination brought the destinies of the two men even closer. For instance Herod's defeat in the war with Aretas, the king of Arabia and the father of the tetrarch's first wife, was interpreted by the Jews "as a punishment of what he did against John."[7]

Of all the female figures of the New Testament, Herodias and her daughter are perhaps the two best suited to represent evil as the early Church saw it: as pagan, female, sensual, and beautiful. Thus the antagonism between the old immorality and the new faith could be likened to combat between the sexes, and the story of Herod, who was unable to choose the right way of life, served as an exemplar for ordinary Christian men, obligating them to withstand the temptations of corrupt femininity and their own weak flesh.

The Gospels link the death of John the Baptist to the immoral life in the Herodian court. The tetrarch and his wife are disturbed not so much by the general tone of John's preachings as by his direct attack on their sexual life: "For Herod had taken John, and bound him, and put him in prison, because of Herodias, his brother's wife. For John had said to him, 'It is not lawful for thee to have her' " (Matt. 14:3–4). The execution of the saint is interpreted as the revenge of Herod's wife, who regards John as a threat to her marriage. But eroticism not only causes the crime; its presence is evident in the Herodian palace, a hothouse of fleshly desires, where evil is born of too much eating, drinking, and fornicating. The biblical description of the obscene event reminds us of stories by the ancient masters of the grotesque, Lucian, Apuleius, or Petronius: "On Herod's birthday, the daughter of Herodias danced before them, and pleased Herod. Whereupon he promised with an oath to give her whatever she might ask of him. Then she, at her mother's prompting, said 'Give me here on a dish the head of John the Baptist.' And grieved as he was, the king, because of his oath and his guests, commanded it to be given. He sent and had John beheaded in the prison. And his head was brought on a dish and given to the girl, who carried it to her mother" (Matt. 14:6–11).

All this is pure voluptuousness, and that is what Herod chooses. He will be remembered by innumerable poets and artists who indulge in reverie about decadent antiquity and see him as an anti-hero, a negative image of Hercules at the crossroads. In *Hercules am Scheidewege* Erwin Panofsky analyzes the origins of the theme of choice between virtue and pleasure in the European tradition.[8] The story of Hercules, who chose virtue, has been attributed to Prodicus and was written down by Xenophon. Because of discrepancies in Xenophon's text, Panofsky suggests that he combined the version given by Prodicus with a slightly different account of the legend by Hesiod. In Prodicus the image of the two ways was meant as a metaphor; the ultimate goal was to attain happiness, and the two female figures, one personifying virtue, the other pleasure, were guides on the way. In Hesiod, however, the goal was either "virtue" or "pleasure," and both the two roads and the two women found at the end were portrayed as real. In Prodicus's story, Arete, a noble lady in a modest white dress, personified virtue; Kakia, a petulant courtesan wearing a seductive gown and covered with makeup and jewelry, stood for pleasure. Arete's way, a narrow, steep, and winding path, led to the right. The way of Kakia, a broad, easy, comfortable road, went to the left. The wanderer who attained Arete's heights found eternal life; the lover of pleasure ended up falling off a precipice.

Panofsky has shown how the legend of Hercules was adopted by Christianity and transformed by it. For instance, in the second century A.D., virtue, once incarnated by the modest but fair Arete, was represented by an ugly beggar-woman. She reflected the asceticism of a period which "could imagine an ethical plus only in the form of an aesthetic minus."[9] A repulsive appearance was thought to guarantee a beautiful soul. This poor and unattractive Virtus became a prototype for the medieval pictures of the good way of life; her rags were effectively opposed to both the rich clothes and the nudity of Voluptas, a common prostitute and a statue of Venus combined in one.

The motif of moral choice dominates the oldest representation of the Salome theme in art. In a Greek manuscript from Sinope that dates from the sixth century and illustrates the Gospel according to Matthew,[10] the princess is depicted at the moment of receiving the head, which is striking because of its size, considerably larger than the heads of all the other figures. Herod holds the banquet in the ancient way, reclining on a couch instead of seated at the table. The prison (with the Baptist's disciples taking care of his beheaded body) is depicted on the right side of the miniature. The two scenes are flanked by the figures of two prophets: one of them exhorts the pagans, the other praises the Christian martyrs. On the left, Moses displays a scroll: "Whoso sheddeth man's blood, by man shall his blood be shed; for in the image of God made He man" (Gen. 9:6). On the right King David's scroll reads: "Precious in the sight of the Lord is the death of His saints" (Ps. 116:15).

The next depiction of John's decapitation dates from the first half of the ninth century. The illustration in a Carolingian evangelary from Chartres focuses on Herod as he chooses between Virtus and Voluptas.[11] He is seated like a judge at the very center, behind the table, and has on one side John, who is being executed, on the other a dancing Salome. Thus, the martyrdom of the saint is opposed by a pleasurable activity. Choosing the latter, Herod takes the way of Kakia, which leads to damnation.

The introduction of the dance motif considerably influenced the further development of the theme. Instead of stressing moral indignation, medieval artists elaborated on the delightful and perverse details of the Herodian court. On the bronze door (eleventh century) of San Zeno's in Verona the sinuous line of the dancing princess's body likens her to a snake. In an English psalter from the beginning of the thirteenth century Salome is shown bent backwards like an acrobat, her long tresses touching the ground (fig. 110). But the most peculiar way of dancing was invented by Herrade of Landsberg, the famous prioress of the Sainte-Odile nunnery, who toward the end of the twelfth century illustrated the *Hortus deliciarum* (the manuscript was kept in Strasbourg and destroyed there in 1870, but it is known through copies).[12] She painted Salome dancing on her hands. This witty metaphor of a monstrous world standing on its head was taken up by other artists and writers. In Rouen the tympanon above one of the side entrances to the Cathedral of Saint John the Baptist and Saint John the Apostle shows the daughter of Herodias in exactly the same position as rendered by Herrade. Salome's ludicrous dance is contrasted with the terrible grotesque: the decapitation.

Like other personifications of luxury,[13] Salome was shown in the Middle Ages in lascivious poses, half naked and in the company of other providers of pleasure: servants, musicians, acrobats, and animals. The figure of a musician appears for the first time on Saint Bernward's column of Hildesheim cathedral (ca. 1022). And the anonymous *Roman de flamenca* describes Salome's dance as a circus performance.[14]

Another grotesque representation of Salome originated in the East. It shows the princess dancing before Herod with her bloody trophy. This can be seen for the first time on a silver plaque of Greek origin dating from the tenth or eleventh century.[15] The most famous interpretation of this motif is found among the fourteenth-century Byzantine mosaics of San Marco's in Venice (fig. 111). The sequence begins with Saint John, decapitated but still standing upright in the doorway of the prison; the vase at his feet contains his head. It continues with the executioner, who sheathes his sword, his eyes fixed on the princess; wearing an elegant long dress decorated with the feathers of a peacock, she performs a dance while carrying on her head a platter with the head of the Baptist. Similar scenes, dating from the beginning of the sixteenth century, cover the walls of the trapeza of Lavra and the catholicon of Dionysiou on Mount Athos.[16] A Bulgarian legend, published partly in Hugo Daffner's *Salome* (1912), describes this very episode.

With the passing of time Salome becomes visibly more involved in the crime. She not only takes the head into her hands but also places it on her head. Presented at first as completely manipulated by her mother, she grows into a voluptuous female with a sacrilegious activity of her own. The more the princess moves to the foreground, the less prominent become Herodias and the tetrarch. But the motif of the two ways of life does not disappear. It finds new expression in the diptychs, triptychs, and poliptychs of the late Middle Ages. They depict the life of John the Baptist by means of opposing his birth to his death and thus present the wicked Salome in contrast to the virtuous women: Elizabeth his mother, and Mary her cousin and the mother of Jesus, who was younger than John by six months.

The most complex and beautiful representation of this kind is the triptych painted by Rogier van der Weyden (fig. 9).[17] In accordance with Christian tradition, the central panel is dedicated to male spirituality. It shows Jesus in the very center being baptized by John, who stands at his right, and adored by an angel who kneels at left. On the wing to Christ's right the pregnant Mary stands with the baby John in her arms, facing Zacharias, Elizabeth's aged husband. Both are depicted as serious and modest people, well suited to symbolize domestic virtues. They are shown against the intimate background of the bedroom where John's mother, attended by a maid, recovers in bed after the delivery. The scene of birth and motherhood is contrasted on Christ's left with John's death, which has just occurred. The beheaded body of the saint lies on the floor between Salome and the executioner, who puts the head onto the platter held by the princess. Like Mary and Zacharias, Salome and the headsman also form a couple, but they turn away from each other and the severed head of the saint. Nevertheless, physically they are much closer to each other; they are "coupled" by the head, which he holds by the hair and she supports from below, where blood drips from the neck. The corpse of the saint lies between them like a bridge of their shared crime. The headsman still touches the dead body with his sword, and John's tied hands are turned toward Salome as if in supplication. The executioner is shown from the back; he has bare, hairy legs, and the sleeves of his shirt are crumpled. The position of his sword is such that it looks like an extension of his penis; it touches John's neck as if replacing the severed head. The attractive princess's snake-like attitude suggests dancing. The blood of the saint tarnishes the iron blade and flows into Salome's silver charger. The juxtaposition of the two women and the similar ways in which Mary carries the child and Salome holds the charger provide a focus on birth, the business of one woman, and death, the business of the other. The triptych emblemizes the circle of nature in which females preside at both the beginning and the end of life. John has just come out of his mother's womb; his dead head is placed in a deep, round bowl which evokes the femininity of the vessel.

Elizabeth's bedroom has one small window; it is a closed, simple, and homely enclosure that forms a contrast to the place of execution, a terrace situated at the border between architecture and nature. The killers' closeness to bestiality is accentuated by the half-naked figure of the executioner (while Zacharias is covered up with layers of clothes) and the serpentine line of Salome's body and dress (Mary's being entirely straight).

An analysis of this painting gradually uncovers different levels of meaning. First one realizes the moral and cultural opposition between the world of the Christian Virtus and that of the pagan Voluptas. Then one discovers that the path of evil coincides with death, the way of goodness with life. And finally, one comes to understand that the gentle virgin and the cruel Salome are deeply linked to each other through the handling of human blood, the juice of life that is spilt at birth and at death. Van der Weyden's triptych exposes not only the polarity between life-giving and life-taking femininity, but it points also to the opposition between the fleshly world of women and the domain of spiritual and divine masculinity represented by the saints, the messenger from heaven, the purifying waters of Jordan, and the vast sky above the river. This icon of the supreme male trinity is both flanked and enclosed by female nature commanding the circle of life and death. While the center of the triptych celebrates a male mystery of purification and immortality, the wings commemorate a physical transformation and transference of blood. Pregnancy is announced by a cessation of menstruation and thus the embryo seems to grow out of the mother's "preserved" blood. The blood of Elizabeth has been first transfused into the infant John and then deposited in the hands of Salome. Ideal, superior masculinity is baptized "with the Holy Spirit" (Luke 3:16), but real men are baptized with blood given by the maternal and taken by the deadly side of nature. When carefully studied, the triptych reveals itself as an illustration of Christ's words spoken to a woman by the name of Salome in the apocryphal Gospel of the Egyptians, as it was recorded by Clement of Alexandria: "Since then the Word has alluded to the consummation, Salome saith rightly, 'Until when shall men die?' . . . Wherefore the Lord answers advisedly, 'So long as women bear children,' i.e. so long as lusts are powerful."[18]

Van der Weyden depicted Mary and Zacharias in a simple and severe manner that has a classical quality; it is peaceful, balanced, and full of harmony. Compared with it, the execution—the coquettish princess turning her pretty face away from the monstrous platter, the half-naked headsman swinging his sword, and the both tortured and supplicating way in which the beheaded body is rendered—is devilishly fantastic. The scene to Christ's right stands for the familiar civilized order, the scene to his left for human bestiality. Thus in the very same triptych the classical and the grotesque are equally present. One stands for holy domesticity, the other for the forbidden garden of delights where middle-aged, pleasure-loving gentlemen enjoy themselves at the side of young dancing girls, but the saints lose their lives.

Eve of Saint John

And it was the full-moon season,
On St. John's Eve, when the hubbub
Of the Wild Hunt spilled out over
The Ravine of Ghostly Spirits.
———Heinrich Heine, *Atta Troll*,
in Hal Draper's trans.

The figures of John, Herodias, and Salome played an important role not only in religious art and literature but also in European folklore and in the superstitions and curious celebrations connected with the Eve of Saint John. This is the night of 24 June, considered the night before the birthday of the Baptist, who, according to the Bible, was born exactly six months before Jesus.

The systematic study of folklore began in the first quarter of the nineteenth century when the brothers Grimm published their *Kinder- und Hausmärchen* (1812–15) and *Deutsche Mythologie* [*Teutonic Mythology*] (1835), books which were to become a source of inspiration for writers and poets. Among those greatly indebted to *Teutonic Mythology*[19] was Heinrich Heine, and it was he who introduced into European literature the folkloric figure of a Herodias who had John beheaded because she loved him. In the epic poem

Atta Troll (1841) Herodias participates in the "wild hunt," a pageant of the dead, who in the Germanic folk tradition were believed to come to life for the duration of the night of Saint John. In the "mad cavalcade of spirits," hunters from different regions and ages ride alongside each other, and among them are three prominent ladies: Diana, who changed Actaeon to a stag (fig. 73), the lovely but cruel fairy Abunda, and Herodias:

> *In her hands she holds forever*
> *That bright charger with the head of*
> *John the Baptist, which she kisses—*
> *Yes, she kisses it with ardor.*
>
> *For she loved him once, this prophet:*
> *It's not written in the Bible,*
> *But the people guard the legend*
> *Of Herodias' bloody passion.*
>
> *Otherwise there's no explaining*
> *The strange craving by that lady:*
> *Would a woman ask the head of*
> *Any man she does not love?*[20]

The tone of Heine's poem is light, his imagery full of parody and caricature. He brings to life the shadows of the past and the ghosts of country folk in order to make fun of the grotesque inventions of fantasy and the language of romance. But behind Heine's pleasantries there is recognition that the pagan past lives on not only in folklore but also in a great many of the dreams of those who are only superficially civilized and Christianized. Of course, he is too witty and too intelligent to profess sadomasochism in the pathetic manner of a Sacher-Masoch or even de Sade. But he means it when he addresses Herodias:

> *Take me as your knight, O take me*
> *As your cavalier' servente,*
> *Bearing all your cloaks and also*
> *Bearing all of your caprices.*[21]

And he subsequently promises that, when the night is over, he will weep over her grave in Jerusalem, misleading Jews who will think that he mourns the destruction of the temple. Eroticism triumphs over religion, the old gods over the new ones. Churches are built on top of the old sanctuaries; mother nature pulsates under the shrines of the Savior:

Under ancient temple ruins
Somewhere in the old Romagna
(It is said) Diana's hiding
While Christ Jesus rules the day.[22]

The antiquity, depth, complexity, and diverse aspects of the Herodias, Salome, and John stories were only gradually discovered in the course of the nineteenth century by scholars of folklore, religion, and anthropology. Their studies disclose the pre-Christian roots of the biblical story. Simultaneously, partly independent of those works and partly under their influence, a new mythology of John's beheading was created in literature and art. To understand the transformation of this motif, one has to recall the richness of the European folklore concerned with the Eve of Saint John. Strange superstitions and various curious celebrations are well recorded in scholarly as well as popular magazines and books throughout the second half of the century. As late as the 1930s in some regions a visitor to the countryside could witness the diverse festivals of Saint John,[23] which shifted between the nights of June 21 and 24, and made scholars of European folklore realize that the celebrations of John's birth were in reality much older than the saint himself.[24] The Baptist's birth coincided with the summer solstice, which since time immemorial has been identified throughout the world as the moment of the sun's greatest potency. Thus the birth of the Precursor was projected onto the pagan festivals of the sun as it returned to the earth after the dark winter.

This solar symbolism played a crucial role in the early days of Christianity, when Jesus was likened to and represented as the invincible sun-god, the Sol Invictus rising from darkness into the sky. The same was true of John the Baptist, possibly to an even larger extent. While his birth marked the revival of nature, his death, celebrated by the Church on 29 August, coincided with the harvest, in which the cutting of grain suggested his beheading. Thus his death was perceived as a sacrificial and necessary one. He died to provide nourishment for the living and he was expected to be reborn the following spring.

The beliefs connected with Saint John's Eve and the celebrations which were still common in Irish, French, German, and Polish villages at the beginning of the twentieth century all shared certain features. Fire, water, and vegetation always played an important role; heads, crowns and wreaths of flowers, or, alternatively, skulls and heads of dead animals frequently appeared in the ceremonies. Singing and dancing was characterized by highly erotic as well as aggressive and destructive overtones, and there were many allusions to sexuality, loss of virginity, and/or life. The German scholar of folklore R. Wünsch suggested that the celebrations of Saint John's birth replaced the festivals of Adonis, which were celebrated in antiquity about midsummer.[25] And James Frazer elaborated on this subject in *Adonis, Attis, Osiris,* volumes five and six of *The Golden Bough.*[26]

Adonis, the "offspring of his sister and his grandfather"(*Met.* 10:521), was a doomed man—not unlike Jesus, the similar product of an incestuous relationship between the heavenly father and Mary, his daughter and wife. However, the Greek god did not die by human hands but rather in a hunt. He was killed by a wild boar which his hounds roused from its lair—in a scene of great dramatic beauty:

> *[Venus] recognized the groans of the dying Adonis from afar, and turned her white birds in his direction. As she looked down from on high she saw him, lying lifeless, his limbs still writhing in his own blood. Leaping down from her car, she tore at her bosom and at her hair, beat her breast with hands never meant for such a use, and reproached the fates. "But still," she cried, "you will not have everything under your absolute sway! There will be an everlasting token of my grief, Adonis. Every year, the scene of your death will be staged anew, and lamented with wailing cries, in imitation of those cries of mine. But your blood will be changed into a flower. Persephone was once allowed to change a woman's body into fragrant mint, and shall I be grudged the right to transform Cinyras' brave grandson?" . . . Within an hour, a flower sprang up, the colour of blood, and in appearance like that of the pomegranate, the fruit which conceals its seeds under a leathery skin. But the enjoyment of this flower is of brief duration: for it is so fragile, its petals so lightly attached, that it quickly falls, shaken from its stem by those same winds that give it its name, "anemone."*
> (*Met.* 10:718–39)

Like Persephone, who is allowed to leave Hades in the spring and to return to earth, Adonis appears to be a god of vegetation coming to bloom after the winter's sleep.[27] Accordingly scholars regard his metamorphosis as a version of the mystical marriage of the sun-god with the earth-goddess, which insures the fertility of nature, and as the synthesis of beliefs and customs concerning the early Phoenician kings of Paphos or their sons, who "regularly claimed to be not merely priests of the goddess but also her lovers, in other words, that in their official capacity they impersonated Adonis."[28]

Frazer ends his study of Adonis in Cyprus with the conclusion that among the Semitic people of antiquity Adonis was the divine lord of the city. Kings and male members of the royal family impersonated him and in this capacity were occasionally or periodically put to death. At festivals of Adonis held in western Asia and Greece, images of the god resembled corpses; they were carried out as for burial and thrown into the sea or into springs. Sometimes his revival was celebrated on the following day. At Alexandria, likenesses of Aphrodite and Adonis were displayed on two couches and surrounded with ripe fruit, cakes, and plants growing in flowerpots. On one day the marriage of the two was celebrated; on the other, women dressed as mourners carried the image of the dead Adonis to the seashore and threw it into the waves. In the temple of Astarte in Byblus the death of Adonis was celebrated annually with lamentation, but he was believed to return to life on the morrow and to ascend to heaven. The date of this festival depended on the discoloration of the river Adonis, which occurred in spring when the red earth, washed down by rain, made the water appear as if stained with the blood of the god, who was thought to have been killed by the boar on Mount Lebanon. Anemones sprang out of the same blood, and the name of the flower seems to originate from Naaman (darling), one of Adonis's epithets. The Arabs call the anemone "wounds of Naaman." A similar myth ascribes the red rose to the wounds of Aphrodite, who, rushing to the dying Adonis, stepped on a bush of white roses which at that very moment turned blood-red. As if alluding to Adonis's birth out of a myrrh tree, myrrh was burned as incense at his festivals. Like all the great mythological figures, Adonis eludes a single, precise interpretation. He is a sun-god and a holy king sacrificed to the Great Mother, a divinity of the emerging vegetation and of the harvest.

The image of a red flower growing from human blood is of course a metaphor for the knowledge that decomposing bodies serve to fertilize plants, that life continues in another form. This knowledge probably gave rise to images associating the spirits of the dead with diverse forms of vegetation, particularly with fragile flowers. In Athens the day of the dead was celebrated in the middle of March when all nature blossoms, and it was called the Festival of Flowers. Even today fresh flowers are brought to graves on the European day of the dead, All Souls' Day, 1 November. But the life of a plant served humanity also as an image: an old tree corresponds to old age, a flower that quickly loses its petals to a dead child or youth. Thus by planting long-lived trees or short-lived flowers one can symbolically allude to the lifespan of a deity or of a human being.

As a lover of Venus, Adonis was traditionally mourned by women, and women were also involved in growing the so-called "gardens of Adonis"[29]—baskets or pots filled with earth in which different crops, lettuces, and flowers were sown and cultivated for eight days. The plants grew quickly but, having no roots, also withered rapidly. Subsequently, at the end of the eighth day, they were carried out with the images of the dead Adonis and thrown into the sea or springs. The gardens of Adonis reflected the cycle of nature and were meant to secure the growth of corn and possibly also the supply of rain—therefore they were brought into contact with water.[30]

Fire, the counterpart of water, was equally important during the Saint John festivals. In Sweden, Bohemia, and Poland the festivities included the raising of a maypole or midsummer tree and burning it in a bonfire. In Russia the spirit of vegetation was represented in a double form, as a tree and as the straw effigy called Kupalo, reminiscent of the Adonis celebrations where the god was represented both by an image and a garden of Adonis. A 1927 survey by the Ethnographic Seminary of the University of Krakow brought to light very interesting and unusual customs practiced in the eastern regions of Poland.[31] In some villages people decorated the skull or head of a dead horse or cow with boughs and green leaves and then buried it in a bonfire.[32] At the Bug River, the bones, before being burned, were immersed in water by the oldest men of the community, who sprinkled all the people present with them three times. This custom seems to point to an association between the bones and the Baptist—a sacrificial sheep. It is also possible that the custom was derived from or influenced by a well-known Christian legend according to which the remains of John, which originally had been buried at the church of Sebaste, were removed in 362 by Julian the Apostate and other pagans, thrown into fire, and burned together with bones of animals.[33] (Gerard David [1460–1532] rendered this scene in a picture which is now in the Kunsthistorisches Museum in Vienna.) But one cannot dismiss the possibility that the legend of John's cremation was invented because of the burning of animal bones in connection either with his birth or his death.

The theme of the "wild hunt," elaborated by Heine, is also present in different forms in Polish folklore.[34] The peasants who were interviewed expressed the belief that during the night of Saint John evil spirits wander through villages and can be encountered at crossroads and fields.[35] While in German folklore of the Middle Ages it was explicitly Herodias who led the wild hunt, the witch recorded in the Polish version reminds us of the figure of Hecate,[36] who in Greek mythology presided over black magic. She was responsible, among other things, for war and tending cattle. On moonlit nights Hecate moved about the crossroads accompanied by the dogs of Styx and crowds of the dead. She presided over the birth and youth of wild animals, and over human birth and marriage. But she was also to be found near graves and on the hearth.

Another aspect of European folklore that points to the Baptist's association with a god of vegetation is the ritual search for certain herbs and flowers during the night of Saint John.[37] The Polish survey documents the custom of looking for the flower of fern ("the crock of gold"),[38] the only blossom in the entire forest that blooms only a single time—at midnight on Saint John's Eve. Whoever found the flower was supposed to have all his wishes fulfilled, but the expedition required great courage because evil spirits in the form of wild animals defended the plant and led those who approached it into the marshes. Different regions of Europe had various beliefs about collecting particular herbs on this very night and using them against evil spirits, spells, and illnesses. Small bouquets, wreaths, and crosses of flowers were stuck onto houses, put into holes and other openings to keep witches away. In Brittany the girls kept those flowers that were touched by the "fire of Saint John"[39] as a talisman and wore them around their necks.

The symbolism of the fire that was built on the Eve of Saint John is highly complex. It may stand for burning passion and destruction; however, it is obvious that in many cases it symbolizes the sun. In Languedoc it was believed that the sun danced with Saint John.[40] Accordingly, burning wheels were made and their rotation was further explained as signifying the movement of John in his mother's womb; he was turning toward Jesus in Mary's body during Elizabeth's visit to her cousin. According to another explanation, the turning symbolized the fact that when the Baptist reached the zenith, he had to begin to descend, like the sun, to give way to the new sun—the Savior.

All the legends and customs concerned with Saint John's Eve oscillate between birth and death, fire and water. There are hints that he might have been regarded as a new sun-god[41] as well as an offspring of the ancient water divinities.[42] The Baptist's connection with water is central to the doctrine of the Mandaeans, known also as Nasoraeans or Saint John's Christians. Members of this sect defined themselves as followers of Gnosis, and though their syncretic religion combined the Old and New Testament with diverse oriental ideas, they were deeply hostile both to Judaism and Christianity, rejecting all the saints of the Bible with the exception of John the Baptist, whom they recognized as the only true prophet.[43] They called him by the name of Yahya (the Arabic form of John) or John, son of Zacharias, and believed that he was an incarnation of Hibil, the supreme God. Yahya mistakenly baptized the false Messiah, was only seemingly executed, and after the completion of his mission on earth returned to the kingdom of light. Hatred against Jews and Christians found its fullest expression in the story of Hibil's brother Anosh Uthra, a contemporary of Yahya and the false Messiah, who descended from heaven in order to cause the crucifixion of Christ, the destruction of Jerusalem, and the dispersion of Jews who had killed Yahya.

The Mandaeans attributed great importance to the river Jordan, which stood for "sacred water" and denoted a spiritual and holy fluid pervading the world of light. "The great Jordan" emanated from Mana rabba, the king of light and the origin of all things. Similarly, the sky was imagined by the Mandaeans as an ocean of water upon which the stars and the planets sailed.

The teachings of Mandaeism are contained in several sacred books. The two most important are *Sidra rabba* and *Sidra d'Yahya*, or "Book of John."[44] The Baptist is depicted in it as the owner of a "ship of light" sailing on the Jordan and as the "fisher of souls," who is opposed to the "fishers of fish," "the eaters of filth."[45] Yahya's ship "shines by night like the sun" and from it the true prophet admonishes people, like Jokanaan in Wilde's *Salomé*, to "go into thy inner ground,"[46] to abandon the riches of life and to dedicate themselves to extreme asceticism: women are not to wear colorful dresses or jewelry and the representatives of both sexes are told not even to look at their faces in a mirror. The figure of Yahya, the Fisher and Sailor, might be a combination of the New Testament tradition with the ancient Babylonian, Chaldean, and Iranian mythology of the god Oannes, shaped as half man, half fish,[47] the father of Marduk. Oannes was believed to rise from the sea, his son to descend from heaven. The metaphor of a great fish also played an important role in the allegories of Judaism. For instance, Sheol, the underworld, was perceived as the belly of the Great Fish; Jonah was trapped inside the Leviathan, another sea monster. In the Torah, "fish" commonly symbolize the righteous Israelites who swim all their lives in the "waters" of the holy book.

In accordance with their glorification and adoration of John and the Jordan, the Mandaeans had their places of worship near running water and regarded baptism as the essential ritual of their religion. Baptism was usually carried out by total immersion in running water, and at the end of the second month of summer a five-day baptismal festival was celebrated, during which every Mandaean, male or female, had to dress in white and bathe three times a day. The baptismal practice places the Mandaeans with the sect of disciples of John who remained apart from Christianity. However, there are some hints that even in the West the Baptist took the place of a pagan water-god. For instance in Dunkirk as late as 1824 a festival of Neptune was celebrated between June 20 and 24; only later did it become the feast of Saint John.[48]

The fish is an ancient symbol for Christ, but also for the Precursor. Consequently, the two can be equated in this image, as can be seen in a miniature from the tenth- or eleventh-century evangelary of Bamberg (fig. 112). The illustration consists of two scenes: Above, Salome dances in front of the table over which Herod presides. The tetrarch wears a seven-branched crown and is surrounded by his courtiers. His left hand rests upon a knife, his right hand points toward the princess. In front of Herod, in the middle of the table, stands a bowl with a fish. The scene below shows the headsman with his sword, the huge, decapitated body of the saint placed within the walls of the Herodian palace (or Jerusalem), and Salome offering to her mother the head of the Baptist. The severed head lies in a bowl that is the exact counterpart of the one in the upper picture. While the face of the dead fish has a human expression, the head of the saint has a fish-like form. The bowl plays a double role: as a vessel containing food and as a funerary urn. However, there is more to it. Both the fish and the head have a certain embryonic quality. The fish, which once swam in water, swims now in its own juice as the head swims in its own blood. Consequently the image evokes both death and conception and leads to further associations and allusions. The bowl can be imagined as a womb or a ship, but it can also take the cosmic proportions of ocean and earth, the ultimate containers of life. Thus the head acquires another aspect: that of the sun moving above the earth, "sailing" on its waters, and disappearing in its depth at night. Two paintings exemplify this point beautifully. One, from the Milanese school of the sixteenth century, displays the head of John on a plate that reminds us of the disk of the earth (fig. 113). The other, from the Flemish school, shows his head upon a disk in the middle of the sky, with angels flying around and deploring his death (fig. 114).

Aquarium

Let us float down, where we will no longer feel the pulse of our consciousness.
      ——Jules Laforgue, *Salome,* in F. New-
man's trans.

The first full and accurate study of the beliefs and customs of the Mandaeans was published in Paris in 1880 by M. N. Siouffi.[49] It is not without significance that Laforgue's *Salome,* a tale in which the Jewish princess acquires the grotesque dimensions of a goddess of the underworld as well as of the night sky, appeared six years later. I do not mean to imply that Laforgue knew the book on the Mandaeans—though this possibility cannot be excluded—but to point out the growth at that time in the number of publications dealing with folklore, anthropology, and comparative religion. These works inspired speculation and new interpretations of biblical stories and revealed similarities in religious imaginings. What had been presented by official Catholic doctrine as Truth was gradually undermined and put into a different perspective through a better knowledge of heretic thought and sects as well as of ancient mythology. Recurring patterns were slowly discovered in the remote past as well as in the present, deeply hidden in the layers of the personal and collective unconscious. It seems that in the late nineteenth century both the mythologies of pre-Christian antiquity and the obscure semi-Christian currents (which, like the Mandaean, developed outside the mainstream of the Catholic church) were identified, at least in the minds of many writers and artists, with the depth of the unconscious and the subterranean power of archetypes. Artists proceeded to penetrate the darkest regions of the self by rewriting some of the well-known biblical stories as tales enacting the uncontrollable desires and fears within the unconscious. It is likely that they would hardly have been able to reinterpret those stories without all the information and inspiration provided by scholarly works and by the legends of the Baptist and John the Evangelist which Praz, Zagona, and other students of the Salome theme have not sufficiently explored.[50]

Heine had made it clear that the past resurrected during the night of Saint John was for him still alive; he recognized the cruel passions of paganism in himself and turned the biblical account into an eternally present event, a constant ingredient in human dreams. By introducing Herodias as a counterpart to Diana, Heine took an important step toward the deification of the wife of Herod. However, in *Atta Troll* she still has the character of a folkloric demon. Laforgue is inspired by Heine's poem but moves the scenery of his *Salome* to the elusive distance of the "Esoteric White Islands," where he gives Herod the name of the "Tetrarch Emerald-Archetypas," and replaces Herodias with her daughter. Laforgue makes Salome first appear in the hanging gardens, an ever green "jungle" which forms a part of the palace: "a monolith, which had been cut down, excavated, scooped out, laid out, and finally polished into a mountain of black basalt veined with . . . white."[51]

There is no doubt that the setting of *Salome* is meant to evoke the archetypal depth of the unconscious buried within the primordial mountain that rises out of the sea toward the sky. There are three main actors in this play of universal passion performed *sub specie aeternitatis*: Salome, who is a young girl, and two men, Archetypas and Jaokanaan, who are in each other's way. Herodias is not mentioned at all, and Salome plays in the beginning a role that is just the reverse of the biblical story: we are told that John is spared at first because of the "inexplicable intercessions" of the princess, whom Laforgue refers to as the tetrarch's daughter. In one breath incest and rivalry are both suggested. But meanwhile a tour of the black and white monolith leads the characters further and further down. The hanging gardens turn out to be a grotto behind a locked door that is "green with moss and with funguses" and discovered at the end of a hot and damp corridor. This humid enclosure "in the midst of the wide silence" is obviously a female cavity, and one is not surprised to encounter Salome there (p. 217). Like Diana, she is escorted by bats and greyhounds and moves against a background of "green slopes which brought dreams of dancing fauns" and "stagnant lakes where swans were engulfed in years and in boredom" (p. 218). Almost as in the Venus grottoes of the mad Ludwig, there is no end to the subterranean attractions; one first reaches a menagerie and then an aquarium, "a labyrinth of grottoes" where "a whole foetal flora, cloistered and vibrating, agitated by the eternal dream" lives without knowledge of day, or night, or seasons (pp. 219, 221). "O world of the satisfied," Laforgue makes one of the characters exclaim with envy, "you live in blind and silent blessedness, and we only dry up in super-terrestrial pangs of hunger. Why aren't the antennae of our senses bounded by Blindness, Opacity and Silence? . . . Why can't we incrust ourselves in our little corners to sleep off the drunken deaths of our own little Egos?" (pp. 221–22). And then he adds consolingly: "But, submarine watering-places, our super-terrestrial hungers give us two pleasures like yours: the face of the beloved asleep on the pillow beside us, with its damp bands of hair and its white teeth lighted by one of the Moon's aquarium rays" (p. 222).

After the aquarium comes the Gynaeceum filled with the smell of "melancholy old feminine fragrances" (p. 222). Then the path descends to the "little cell" of the imprisoned Precursor, and the first chapter of the tale ends. What follows is the banquet celebrating Archetypas's birthday, at which Salome not only dances but also sings. Like a sea-creature she emerges from the garden into the hall in a sheath of chiffon, with breasts covered only by mother of pearl to which peacock feathers are attached. The princess carries a "black lyre," the instrument of Orpheus, who went to the underworld to fetch his wife and was believed to enchant humans and animals with his music. Salome's performance foreshadows the fate of the Baptist, and it is described in terms both of eroticism and destruction. When "she drew blood from her black lyre" (p. 234), one remembers that Orpheus was a victim of female cruelty: he rejected the advances of the Thracian women and they tore him to pieces. Only his head and lyre floated to the shore of Lesbos, where the inhabitants buried the head, while his instrument was immortalized by the Muses, who carried it to heaven and placed it among the stars.

The fantastic song of Salome continues for pages and contains some interesting allusions to water as the element of the saint as well as the erotic female principle. The princess sings of "fatal Jordans, baptismal Gangeses, unsinkable sidereal currents, cosmogonies of Motherhood!" (p. 236). She proclaims love an "inclusive mania of not wanting to die absolutely," portrays women as "the little friends of your childhood," and "always unseizable Psyches," addresses "hydrocephalous theosophists," declares that "the Unconscious will function *da se*," and proposes to "float down . . . where we no longer feel the pulse of our consciousness" (pp. 235, 236, 239).

Upon finishing her performance, Salome promptly asks for the head of John. At this point Laforgue moves the scenery to the open air, suggesting that the daughter of Archetypas is responsible not only for the subterranean gardens and aquaria but belongs also to the black sky stretching endlessly above the mountain. Now the princess is called "a celestial creature." On the terrace she confers "with her twenty-four million stars" and in particular with Orion, her "little benjamin" who is present in dual form: as an astral configuration and as a jewel ("Orion's opal") in her crown (pp. 241–42).[52] The conference reaches its climax when the head of Jaokanaan is brought out "on a cushion and among the ruins of the ebony lyre." It shines "like the head of Orpheus—painted with phosphorus, bathed, rouged, curled, grinning" and inspires the princess to try "her famous post-decapitation experiments"; they consist of "electric caresses" and "kissing" of Jaokanaan's eyes. Then "for ten minutes" Salome "exposed her ripeness to the mystic nebulae" (p. 243) of her other lover, Orion, another victim of female cruelty.

The penetration of Orion's "ailing rays" (p. 242) into a virgin's womb introduces another topic: a mystical insemination. Laforgue refers to Salome not only as "the little Immaculate Conception" but finds an even more sacrilegious expression by calling her "the little Messiah with a womb" (p. 233). Thus he performs an outrageous confusion of sexes and values reminiscent of a black mass. Salome takes out of her crown the "troubled gold and grey opal," the symbol of the sacrificed and immortalized Orion, and, "like a sacramental wafer," lays it "in the mouth of Jaokanaan" (pp. 243–44). Then she kisses his mouth "mercifully and hermetically" and flings the head with both fists into the sea.

> The relic described a satisfactory phosphorescent parabola. Oh! the noble parabola! But the unlucky little astronomer had badly miscalculated her swing. She fell over the balustrade, and with a cry that was human at last, she toppled from rock to rock. With death rattling in her throat, and in picturesque anfractuosity which was washed by the waves, far from the sounds of her country's festivities, lacerated into nakedness . . . with her skull battered in, paralyzed by vertigo—in a bad way, as you might put it, she died for an hour. . . . So that was how Salome made the acquaintance of death—the Salome of the White Esoteric Islands. (pp. 244–45)

Laforgue mixes ancient mythological scenery with Christian figures and settings in a narrative so manneristic and ironic that it makes his tale read like a parody of the Greeks, the Bible, and the grotesque decadents. This is clearly one of his intentions; but there is another one as well. The absurd serves as a means to approach what is unspeakable and chaotic— the archetypes of the unconscious swimming in the watery and dark inner aquarium. The nonsensical style helps to weaken the horrors of incest, homicide, and necrophilia.

In Laforgue's prose, associations move freely, exaggerations are never too vast, caricatures never too overdrawn; the obscene is contrasted with the ornamental, the offensive diluted with wittiness. But strangely enough this confusing parody of mythology and religion reveals the paradoxical features of the human imagination, which both creates myths and derides them. This is particularly true with respect to legends directly inspired by the experience of sexuality with all its disturbing ambiguities. In order to hold society together, some of the most dangerous sexual desires are exiled: they become taboo, are transferred to the supposedly spiritual sphere (religion), and pushed into the unconscious. In this way one hopes to sweep away the evils of sexuality. However, as in real life, the exiles never leave those who expel them in peace and use every possible pretext to remind them of their exiled existence.

Biblical tales are meant to condemn evil. But in fact they acquaint us with it and then, through this very condemnation, arouse our sympathy for it. Because of this double-edged character, every condemnation must be reinforced by derision. But there is also a problem with deriding things— what is ridiculed is rendered familiar, all too familiar. While goodness is elevated to a distant heaven, evil tends to come right down to earth, to touch one's innermost being.

The authors of serious religious tales face problems not unlike those of pamphleteers making fun of religion. The first try to describe evil as terrible, ridiculous, and impotent and the good as heavenly, though not without a human touch; the latter want to present the good as suspect, grotesque, inhuman, or even nonexistent and to prove that evil is either wonderfully pleasurable or omnipresent and omnipotent. In both cases a dualistic scale of values is used in an effort to unbalance reality and to distort proportions. Consequently, two sets of myths are created: one about good, the other about evil. But nowhere is polarization so dubious and unrewarding as in sexuality. Thus the attempt to represent the sexuality of gods as absolutely pure must end with insurmountable paradoxes such as the Immaculate Conception. These dogmas inherently provoke the impulse to ridicule, and they are doomed to become targets of derision. But the need to ridicule may come from different sources and serve different purposes. One does it from affection and affinity as well as out of antipathy and hatred. If, like Karl Marx, one thinks of religion as the opiate of the masses, the jokes tend to be deadly; but if one has such an insatiable hunger for mythology as the decadents had, then it's another matter. Then the grotesque parodies of religion, such as Laforgue's *Salome*, read like mythological tales in reverse: while those who are good are omitted, those who are bad are given splendid costumes and the power to rule an ocean of blackness which extends from the underworld to the nocturnal sky. Laforgue calls Salome the "foster-sister of the Milky Way" and confines the

Precursor to a "little cell" below the Gynaeceum. He makes the princess play the lyre of Orpheus and robs the beheading of the Baptist of its pathetic uniqueness by connecting it to the misfortunes of other men equally victimized by women. Finally, he goes so far as to proclaim Herod's cruel daughter both an "Immaculate Conception" and a "Messiah with a womb." All this is meant as a joke. But what a joke! No wonder it helped establish the *à rebours* icon of Salome.

Woman in the Moon

The moon has a strange look to-night. . . . She is like a
mad woman who is seeking everywhere for lovers.
———Oscar Wilde, *Salomé*

Describing the setting of his play *Salomé* (1891), Oscar Wilde notes that it takes place at night and specifically that "the moon is shining very brightly" (fig. 115).[53] Indeed, while the first line of dialogue between a young Syrian soldier and the page of Herodias deals with the beauty of the princess Salomé, the second is already devoted to the moon, which is referred to as a "she." An intimate relationship is immediately established between the pale celestial body and the enchanting princess. At times Salomé and the moon are one; at times they are doubles, mirror reflections of each other. The moon functions as a milky looking glass showing Salomé's inner life or as a screen onto which her emotions can be projected. Thus the princess and the moon are the two main characters in a play that consequently takes place simultaneously in the sky and on earth or, more precisely, on "a great terrace . . . set above the banqueting-hall" (p. 1)— as if above the underworld. This parallel structure is maintained by Wilde throughout the play. It begins with the appearance of a silvery, veiled moon whose whiteness corresponds to Salomé, an innocent-looking maiden. When she begins to dance in order to obtain the head of the Baptist, the moon turns red; and when, after the execution of John, Salomé as well is put to death by Herod's order, "a great cloud crosses the moon and conceals it completely" (p. 36).

The nature of the moon, as seen from the earth, is a changeable one. As Eliade puts it, "the sun is always the same . . . never in any sense 'becoming.' The moon, on the other hand, is a body which waxes, wanes and disappears, a body whose existence is subject to the universal law of becoming, of birth and death. . . . For three nights the starry sky is without a moon. But this 'death' is followed by a rebirth: the 'new moon.' The moon's going out, in 'death,' is never final."[54]

Because of menstruation, women have always been regarded as subject to the cycle of the moon. Wilde's equation of woman and the moon was derived from lunar mythology. A quarter of a century after the publication of *Salomé*, Jung proclaimed that lunar legends present a lesson in female psychology. He maintained that in contrast with male eruptions of energy, the emotional life of the female has a much slower cycle, with feelings gradually growing and waning, moving obscurely back and forth between conception and decay like the moon in the night sky. To represent the unconscious, Jung, like many fin-de-siècle writers, spoke of men trapped in the "dark imperium of the mother" and a "sublunar world."[55]

The waxing and waning moon served humanity as its first calendar. The Greek Moirai,[56] the daughters of the earth-goddess Themis by Zeus, are spinners of human fate and lunar deities of time. In many cultures the moon is perceived as a girl baby and an old woman. For instance, to depict the growth of the Tantric lunar goddess Tripurasundari,[57] a ceremony was devised in which from the first day of the new moon through the whole fifteen days of moonlight she was represented by girls aged one to sixteen. In Greek mythology the moon-goddess was known as Hecate "before she had risen and after she had set; as Artemis (Cynthia, Diana, Phoebe) when in the open vault of heaven, the sister of sun; . . . as Selene (Luna) when the moonlight on the fields kissing the sleeping Endymion."[58]

The Hecate mythology[59] is particularly helpful in understanding the initial image of a dead woman looking for dead things and the sinister symbolism of Wilde's play. Hecate, a chthonic deity, might have been of Thracian or Hellenic origin. She was not mentioned by Homer but played an important role in Hesiod and was regarded as the queen of ghosts and the mistress of black magic. She kept the keys of Hades and together with Helios witnessed the rape of Persephone. With her mother she searched, torch in hand (a symbol of moon's light), for Demeter's lost daughter. Hecate was the mother of the sorceresses Circe and Medea, and she haunted graveyards and crossroads where, on the last day of the month, eggs and fish were offered to her. Black puppies and black she-lambs were also sacrificed to her (the victims offered to chthonic deities were usually black). Hecate was expected to be present at death, but she was also, like Artemis, a goddess of fertility and love. In the idyll of Theocritus (ii) she is asked to bring back a woman's faithless lover. To render her appearance as the new, the full, and the waning moon, she was represented in a fantastic shape ("triformis"), with three bodies standing back to back and six hands holding torches, or a snake, a key (to the underworld), a whip, or a dagger.

Hecate's features are shared with lunar divinities all over the world, and she is closely related, for instance, to Kali, the Indian goddess of death and destruction.[60] "Kala" in Sanskrit means "black," "dark," and "stained," but it also means "time." Kali is usually portrayed as a black woman with four arms, red eyes, and besmeared with blood. She may hold a cup made of a human skull, wear a necklace of skulls, and earrings made of dead human parts; her teeth protrude, her tongue drips blood, serpents wind around her, and she stands on the body of her husband, Siva. Victims sacrificed to her were always men. They were taken to her temple after sunset, imprisoned there, and found dead in the morning. It was believed that Kali, like a vampire, sucked their blood in the night. The British in India spread the news, frequently with exaggeration, of the bloody rituals of Kali, of not one but many young men being offered to her at once. Around the turn of the century some of these cruel festivals were forbidden in British territory.

There cannot be any doubt that in creating his *Salomé* Wilde must have been aware of both the Hecate and the Kali myths. The overpowering symbolism of these Great Goddesses encouraged him to inflate the figure of the princess as well as of her mother. But there are other influences to be recalled as well.

In Wilde's play all that happens on earth is prefigured by the moon. Just before Salomé begins to dance (on the blood of a young Syrian soldier who killed himself when he realized that she was in love with the Baptist), Herod exclaims: "Ah! look at the moon! She has become red. She has become red as blood. Ah! the prophet prophesied truly" (p. 28). However, what John foretells is nothing but his own death. And this depends solely on Herodias and Salomé. Holding in their hands the threads of his fate, they resemble the Moirai, the spinning women. When John exclaims "the time is come!" and Herod listens to these words with attention, his wife dismisses both men's competence to the domain of destiny by saying, "Can a man tell what will come to pass? No man knows it" (pp. 17–18).

The characters of Wilde's play do not take their eyes from the moon; they speak constantly about it and use metaphors concerned with it. The incantations to the goddess of the night are as monotonous as religious litanies and appear to be extremely artificial. However, Wilde's almost enervating style seems to correspond well to Eliade's scholarly observation that "the symbols which get their meaning from the moon *are* at the same time the moon . . . there can be no symbol, ritual or myth of the moon that does not imply all the lunar values known at a given time. There can be no part without the whole. . . . by wearing a pearl as an amulet a woman is united to the powers of water (shell), the moon (the shell a symbol of the moon; created by the rays of the moon, etc.), eroticism, birth and embryology."[61] Like a myth, Wilde's play evokes the totality of lunar symbolism. The moon illuminates the entire scene as well as each of its fragments; it clothes with its nebulous, silvery light every minute detail in this dramatic night of a double initiation: into love and into death.

When Salomé asks Herod for the head of John, the tetrarch in order to divert her offers three gifts all of which are in some mysterious way connected with the moon. White peacocks in whose midst the princess will look like "the moon in the midst of a great white cloud," are obviously lunar birds: "the moon shows herself in the heavens when they spread their tails" (p. 31). And so are pearls resembling "half a hundred moons caught in a golden net," and even more so "moonstones that change when the moon changes, and are wan when they see the sun" (p. 32).

Looking for the first time into the dark eyes of John, Salomé sees the "black lakes" of his pupils being "troubled" by her "fantastic moons" (p. 10). The metaphor is not new. Plato perceived the narcissistic mirroring of the self in the eyes of the beloved as an essential component of love, and this image has been used widely in European poetry.[62] However, the princess's reflection in the eyes of the saint is not the only lunar image. The Precursor, in her eyes, appears to be a moon-like creature as well: "an image of silver . . . chaste as the moon," "a shaft of silver," and a "moonbeam" (p. 10). Thus she perceives him as a reflection and a double of herself; as a mirror—and as another moon she desires.

Indeed, in *John and Salomé* Beardsley portrays the pair as lunar twins, two columns or shafts of light growing out of the ground (fig. 116). It is one of the few drawings in which man equals woman in size and the figures are perfectly balanced against each other. The mirror-like symmetry of this particularly mythical representation brings to mind another possible source of inspiration, both for Wilde and Beardsley: the mythology of the sun and the moon (fig. 117). In China yang, the male principle, was incarnated by the sun, the female yin by the moon. The emperor, regarded as the son of heaven, thus dwelt with the empress like the sun with the moon. On the fifteenth of every month, at full moon, the total union of yin and yang took place and accordingly the imperial couple was supposed to unite. Thus the full moon was considered the perfect mirror of sexual harmony while the broken mirror symbolized the separation of husband and wife.[63]

Many different cults of the sun and moon were common in late antiquity and reappeared in early Christianity. Sol Invictus, whose cult was enormously popular among the late Roman emperors, became identified with the image of Christ rising out of the tomb. Similarly the Virgin was perceived as a lunar goddess who yearned to be united with her son. But also the Church (ecclesia), God's bride on earth, and the individual human soul (anima), longing to become one with the divine beloved, were frequently described by the Christian mystics in terms of the moon desiring to join the sun.[64] In the Zohar, the main book of Jewish mysticism, the male and female aspects of God are pictured as sun and moon and their relationship is described in sexual terms. The female aspect, called the "Queen" or "Community of Israel," is likened to the moon as well as to an opaque mirror reflecting the light of the sun. It was believed that human wickedness caused the sun to withdraw its light from the moon, while righteousness restored the moon to its fullness.[65]

The different traditions of lunar symbolism are not reflected in Wilde's play or in Beardsley's drawings in any logical and systematic way, but as splinters of memory, as visual and literary remembrances randomly joined together. However, significantly, no allusion is made to the symbolism of the fire or the sun, either in connection with John or with Christ. The Baptist is not only regarded as entirely lunar by Salomé, but his chthonic character is stressed by the fact that he is kept in a cistern—a deep, humid hole. He appears to Salomé "covered with mire and dust"; his hair "is like a knot of serpents coiled round" his neck; and his mouth reminds the princess of "a branch of coral that fishers have found in the twilight of the sea" (p. 10). Furthermore, Jesus is described against a background of water: "in a boat on the sea of Galilee" (p. 13).

The moon rules not only the female cycle but also the tides. Thus it is conceived as responsible for fluids, particularly those of a female nature. In order to achieve the utmost consistency in *Salomé*, Wilde subordinated to the moon, the night, and water everything and everybody, including Christ, the god of light, who, indeed, was first symbolized by the fish. (Fish were offered to Hecate, as were lambs, the most common incarnations of the Precursor and the Savior.) Besides, there is an imaginary link between Christ in a ship (ship in English and many other languages is thought of as female) and the Baptist, who is first kept inside a cistern and whose head then swims in blood on Salomé's silver charger. In Wilde's fluid and obscure universe, desires creep and float around like silent reptiles at the bottom of the sea. Possibly he was fixed on Laforgue's vision of the aquarium. So it is not surprising that when Roland Holst, a minor Dutch artist, illustrated Wilde's play in 1900, he painted a triptych that looks like a submarine landscape in different shades of green with figures floating around.[66]

The continuous references to the moon give *Salomé* an oriental character. In ancient China the mandarins retired from the court to country houses designed in such a way that the wandering of the moon could be watched all night against many different backgrounds: over bamboos, between the branches of a cherry tree, or reflected in the pool. Chinese poetry and painting, Japanese novels and woodcuts are unthinkable without the presence of the moon, and this is true of Persian and Arabic verses as well. The poems of Firdusi and the ghazels of Hafiz enjoyed great popularity at the end of the nineteenth century, and their invocations to the moon were certainly remembered by Wilde. Beardsley, who read oriental poems and loved Japanese woodcuts, at once made fun of his friend and immortalized his female and narcissistic nature when he gave Wilde's features to the moon in his illustration of *Salomé* entitled *The Woman in the Moon* (fig. 115).

Seven Veils

> . . . *and the sun became black as sackcloth of hair; the whole moon became as blood. And the stars of heaven fell upon the earth, as the fig tree sheds its unripe figs when it is shaken by a great wind.*
>
> ——Revelation 6:12–13

> JOKANAAN. . . . the sun shall become like sackcloth of hair, and the moon shall become like blood, and the stars of the heaven shall fall upon the earth like unripe figs that fall from the fig-tree.
> . . .
>
> ——Oscar Wilde, *Salomé*

In a letter to the editor of the *Times* of 2 March 1893,[67] Oscar Wilde wrote that he waited with impatience to see Sarah Bernhardt play his Salomé in Paris, the center of the arts, where "religious" dramas are frequently performed. The designation of *Salomé* as "religious" may surprise all those who, like Mario Praz,[68] consider the play to be a parody of the entire decadent iconography and disregard its sacrilegious character—the result of mixture, distortion, exaggeration, and heretical interpretation of various biblical stories. But a close analysis shows how much *Salomé* owes, in its repetitive language, its daring metaphors, and its exalted tone, to the sacred writings of Christianity. In fact, the strange combination of the ecstatic, visionary, and hysterical was not invented by Wilde but largely derived by him from the Revelation. This most fantastic and controversial text of the New Testament was supposedly written by Saint John the Evangelist, the son of Zebedee, a Galilean fisherman, and of Salome, who was present at Jesus' death[69] and among those few women who first learned of his resurrection:

> And when the Sabbath was past, Mary Magdalene, Mary the mother of James, and Salome, bought spices, that they might go and anoint him. And very early on the first day of the week, they came to the tomb, when the sun had just risen. And they were saying to one another, "Who will roll the stone back from the entrance of the tomb for us?" And looking up they saw that the stone had been rolled back, for it was very large. But on entering the

tomb, they saw a young man sitting at the right side,
clothed in a white robe, and they were amazed. He said to
them, "Do not be terrified. You are looking for Jesus of
Nazareth, who was crucified. He has risen, he is not
here." (Mark 16:1–6)

The fact that the mother of John the Evangelist, one of Christ's first pupils, and the murderess of John the Baptist had identical names obviously did not escape Wilde's attention, since he put the words of the Evangelist into the mouth of the Precursor. This adds a new dimension to the play and brings to mind Freud's concern with the coincidence of names and slips of the tongue and the way they mysteriously point to sexual taboos and incestuous relationships. In *Salomé* the curses of the Evangelist, in particular those directed against the great whore of Babylon and Sodom, are uttered by the Precursor, but the visions of the Evangelist are shared by other characters as well. All the persons in Wilde's play tend to perceive Herod's birthday and the day of the Baptist's execution as signaling the approach of the apocalypse.

The Revelation was supposedly written by John the Evangelist on the island of Patmos, where he was banished after he had miraculously survived (at least according to the legend) immersion in burning oil. The book expresses a Manichean view of the universe as divided between good and evil. It reads like a dream of vengeance for a suffering so terrible that it can neither be forgiven nor sublimated. The tone and the metaphors used by the Evangelist burn with extreme emotions, and his outcry for the total annihilation of evil becomes deeply engraved in one's memory. This, perhaps the most dangerous text of the entire New Testament, has influenced European thought and imagination for centuries. The vision of a heavenly Jerusalem in opposition to an evil empire that encompasses almost the entire earth can be traced through Marxism, Fascism, and Nazism up to present-day declarations of political leaders.

The figure of an avenging Savior who liberates the world from evil by means of almost total annihilation, this nightmare of the twentieth century, indeed goes back to the Evangelist's horrifying fantasies.[70] His idea of two kingdoms and two rulers (Christ and Satan, "the prince of this world") is also tied to the perception of a dual femininity, one represented by the heavenly mother, the other by the earthly whore. The mother of God is described in the Apocalypse in accordance with the symbolism of the sun and the moon, the first dominating the second: she was "clothed with the sun, and the moon was under her feet" (12:1). Pregnant with a child, she is pursued by a great red dragon with "seven heads and ten horns" (12:3) who, like the serpent, is an incarnation of Satan. She is defended by Michael, who casts the devil down to earth. There, however, the dragon continues to run after the woman, who meanwhile has delivered a male child. In order to drown her, he spews water, flowing like a river, out of his mouth. But "the earth helped the woman, . . . opened her mouth and swallowed up the river" (12:16). Interesting enough, in the apocryphal *Protevangelium Jacobi* Elizabeth, fleeing with the future Baptist from Herod's assassins, is saved in a similar way. She cries in despair, "mountain of God, receive me, a mother, with my child" (chap. 22), and the mountain opens and receives her.[71]

Once the mother with the child is saved, the Evangelist proceeds with a description of the terrible side of femininity (fig. 118): "the great harlot who sits upon many waters . . . upon a scarlet-colored beast, full of names of blasphemy, having seven heads and ten horns" (17:1–3). She is "clothed in purple and scarlet, and covered with gold and precious stones and pearls, having in her hand a golden cup full of abominations and the uncleanness of her immorality. And upon her forehead a name written— a mystery—Babylon the great, the mother of the harlotries and of the abominations of the earth. And I saw the woman drunk with the blood of the saints and with the blood of the martyrs of Jesus" (17:4–6).

The harlot of the Revelation has her origin in the images of the ancient Great Goddesses of death and destruction. That she is a chthonic demon is made explicit by the Evangelist, who explains that "the seven heads are seven mountains upon which the woman sits; and they are seven kings" (17:9). The heads are first equated with mountains, the phallic protrusions of the earth, and then with men. The next metaphor leaves no doubt as to the obscene character of the passage: "And the horns that thou sawest are ten kings" (17:12). The beast on which the harlot sits represents both Satan and the earth. She copulates with the devil and with kings, his corrupted subjects, but she also fornicates with impure matter—the mountains. The powerful vision conveys John's disgust with all that is material. "The waters," he continues, "that thou sawest where the harlot sits, are peoples and nations and tongues. And the ten horns that thou sawest, and the beast, these will hate the harlot, and will make her desolate and naked, and will eat her flesh, and will burn her up in fire. . . . And the woman whom thou sawest is the great city which has kingship over the kings of the earth" (17:15–18), ". . . because all the nations have drunk of the wrath of her immorality, and the kings of the earth have committed fornication with her" (18:3).

The earth-prostitute is destroyed by the avenger, whom the Evangelist portrays as a "divine warrior . . . clothed in a garment sprinkled with blood" (19:11–13) and as a lamb. Christ, who is obviously present in all these allegories, proceeds now to wed the good woman; she "has been permitted to clothe herself in fine linen, shining, bright" (19:8). The wedding is followed by a hair-raising cannibalistic feast. "Come," the guests are invited, "gather yourselves together to the great supper of God, that you may eat flesh of kings, and flesh of tribunes, and flesh of mighty men, and flesh of horses, and of those who sit upon them, and flesh of all men, free and bond, small and great" (19:17–18).

John's exclamations—obscene, grotesque, and filled with unquenchable hatred—are eruptions of the darkest instincts, of humanity's animalistic past; they surpass the wildest dreams of Nero, the most perverse persecutor of Christians. At this point a paradox becomes apparent: one realizes that Wilde's story of the cruelty inflicted by the pagans on the representative of the new faith is inspired by appalling visions of Christian justice. In *Salomé*, exactly as in the Revelation, love equals annihilation. The princess kills the Baptist because she loves him. And the Baptist, out of his doctrine of love, preaches and prophesies not only the destruction of Herodias, her daughter, and all women who "imitate her abominations," but of the entire earth onto which stars will "fall like unripe figs." The message of the Apocalypse is accurately repeated in *Salomé* by the saint, for whom there is no other realization of love except through death—the mortification of flesh and the annihilation of the entire corrupt earth.

As in medieval morality plays each of *Salomé*'s characters is composed of different biblical figures. Jokanaan is a combination of two Johns who have frequently been brought together in the course of Christianity. Often churches were named after both of them, or both their figures were depicted in religious compositions. In Hans Memling's triptych in the Hôpital Saint-Jean in Bruges, for instance, the central panel shows the mystical marriage of Saint Catherine to Christ, but the beheading of the Baptist is portrayed on the wing to her right and the vision of the Evangelist on Patmos is painted on the wing to her left.

The tetrarch of Wilde's play is a mixture of the three Herods mentioned in the Bible, all of whom were renowned for their cruelty. Herod the Great (fig. 52) slaughtered the infants of Bethlehem (Matt. 2:16–18); his son Herod Antipas married Herodias, the wife of his brother Philip who resided in Rome; and Herod Agrippa I, the grandson of Herod the Great, was king of all Palestine from A.D. 41 to 44 and a persecutor of Christians (Acts 12:1ff.). Though Wilde combines all three Herods so that the tetrarch appears as a man heavily burdened with a sinister past, the wickedness is largely transferred from him to his wife. She is the one whom Jokanaan curses first, even before his attention is diverted to the evil lust of her daughter. Echoing the Revelation, in which the Evangelist accuses pagans of worshiping idols, Herodias is attacked for having seen "images of men painted on the walls" and having given herself "up unto the lust of her eyes" (p. 9). Immediately afterwards the Baptist proclaims from the depths of his cistern that she also made love to young men, and, finally, that she committed incest. Consequently she is a whore, and so is Salomé, whom he addresses forthrightly as the daughter of Babylon and Sodom and the "daughter of adultery" (p. 13). The tetrarch's wife and the princess are merged into one "harlot" with "golden eyes" and "gilded eyelids." The Baptist wants a "multitude of men" to stand up against her, to "take stones and stone her" (p. 22).

When Salomé agrees to dance for the tetrarch, she asks her slaves to bring her "the seven veils" (p. 27). In the spring of 1893, after the publication of his play, Wilde sent a copy of it to Beardsley with an inscription declaring that Beardsley was the only one besides himself who could understand and see the "invisible dance" of the seven veils.[72] The inscription was meant as a slightly obscene joke alluding to the veil as a popular symbol for the hymen. The veiling of women, an ancient custom observed to our day in Moslem countries, stands for the preservation of chastity. The veil prevents men from seeing and thus desiring women. A dance performed with veils has a highly erotic character: the veiling and unveiling of the different parts of the body increases its sex appeal and raises the expectations of the viewer. The oriental dance of the veils is the equivalent of the modern striptease, which is, indeed, usually combined with a dance or a pantomime and tends to leave some details of the naked body covered in order to excite the imagination. It is not surprising that by the end of Salomé's dance the tetrarch is in ecstasy. His incestuous love for his stepdaughter is mentioned in the course of the play, both by the dancing princess and Herodias. But now Herod is truly prepared to offer Salomé "whatsoever thy soul desireth" (p. 29).

The princess is introduced at the beginning of the play as a virgin, and therefore it seems quite appropriate to veil her. However, equipping her with not one but seven veils is one more device that helps to set the play against a universal background. The number seven is most commonly associated with the seven wonders of antiquity. But one also thinks of the seven sleepers of Ephesus—seven Christian youths who, in order to escape persecution, hid themselves in a cave and slept for two hundred years. Seven evokes the sense of completion because of the seven days of creation, and of the week, and it is an extremely popular number in mythology and religion. John the Evangelist is obsessed with it in his Revelation, and it is most likely that Wilde has taken the idea of seven veils from this very text. In the sixth chapter of the Apocalypse, the Lamb opens the seven seals. The sixth seal is the vision of the sun becoming black "like a sackcloth of hair." (In Wilde's play this is rendered as the prophecy of Jokanaan [p. 23]). And the seventh seal is concerned not with veils but with "white robes" worn by those "who have come out of the great tribulation, and have washed their robes and made them white in the blood of the Lamb" (7:13–14). Wilde was probably inspired by this paradoxical passage about robes becoming white after being washed in blood and took it as a point of departure for his own fantasies. He replaced the Christian martyrs dressed in white robes cleansed by blood with a pagan princess who in her seven veils dances on the blood of the man who has slain himself for her sake, in order to obtain the bloody relic of another man.

Before Salomé begins to dance, Herod already feels he is surrounded by blood. He slips in the blood of the young Syrian soldier, watches the moon become red like blood, and finally, in his apparent sexual excitation, likens the dance to the defloration of the desired girl. While the garland of roses on his forehead burns "like fire," the "red petals" appear to him as "stains of blood on the cloth" (p. 27). Philosophizing on this vision, the tetrarch remarks that "it were better to say that stains of blood are as lovely as rose petals" (p. 27). Though Herod resents the idea that Salomé, a virgin, is going to dance on the blood of another man, he desires so much to see her dance that he agrees even to that. Before the seven veils are brought in, a revealing exchange of words takes place between him and his wife:

> HERODIAS. *You are looking again at my daughter.*
> *You must not look at her. I have already said so.*
> HEROD. *You say nothing else.*
> HERODIAS. *I say it again.*
> HEROD. *And that restoration of the Temple about which*
> *they have talked so much, will anything be done?*
> *They say the veil of the Sanctuary has disappeared,*
> *do they not?*
> HERODIAS. *It was thyself didst steal it.* (p. 24)

The dialogue reads like a Freudian example of one erotic symbol being exchanged for another, like an allusion to the secrets of sex and the equally veiled mysteries of religion, and like a comparison between the profanation of a sanctuary and the loss of virginity. But Wilde's metaphor also refers to the very moment when Jesus "cried out with a loud voice, and gave up his spirit. And . . . the curtain of the temple was torn in two from top to bottom" (Matt. 27:50–51).

Though Wilde took the coincidence between the death of a saint and the torn veil of the temple from the New Testament, he made the symbolism more ambiguous and complex. In *Salomé* the "stolen veil" of the temple corresponds to the virginity of Salomé, which Herod would like to steal by deflowering her. Thus the "dance of seven veils" can be seen as an imaginary erotic intercourse, both for the tetrarch burning in his wreath of flowers and for the princess who with her veins filled "with fire" and "hungry" (p. 35) for the body of John moves around on blood. The end of the dance is the climax of the play and an orgasm (a small death) for the girl who danced and the man who watched her. For the absent lover, however, it means death or, more precisely, beheading—a symbolic castration. This equation of sexuality and destruction might have been suggested to Wilde by Mark's account of Christ's death.[73] John the Evangelist was the only one to mention Salome, the mother of John, in the passage immediately following Jesus' expiration and the tearing apart of the temple's curtain. Luke's description adds another phenomenon: the darkening of the sun,[74] and Matthew's report reminds us directly of the Revelation: "The curtain of the temple was torn in two from top to bottom; and the earth quaked, and the rocks were rent, and the tombs were opened, and many bodies of the saints who had fallen asleep arose" (Matt. 27:51–53). Similarly, once Salomé is given the head of the Baptist "the stars disappear. A great cloud crosses the moon and conceals it completely. The stage becomes quite dark" (p. 36). As in John's Apocalypse, corrupt female sexuality causes the universe to tremble and lose light.

Sacrilegious as they may sound, Wilde's parodies of the Bible create not only their own eroticism but also reveal the sexuality hidden behind the images in the Holy Scriptures; they point to eros and its rejection as a vital source of religious metaphors. Like the sevenfold fantasies of John the Evangelist, Salomé's dance of seven veils oscillates between love and hatred, between the hiding and disclosing of the inner ground of faith: a fabric woven of sexual dreams.

Curiously enough, Wilde's associations coincide with an obscene narrative contained in the apocryphal *Protevangelium Jacobi,* which he hardly could have known. There a woman by the name of Salome doubts the virginity of Mary after the birth of Jesus and, in order to test it, inserts her finger into the vagina of Christ's mother. She apparently finds the hymen but her "hand falls away . . . consumed by fire,"[75] and is restored to her only when the faithless, vulgar, and cruel woman touches in turn the newborn God.

Wilde was inspired not only by the New but also by the Old Testament. Salomé's kissing of the dead head recalls Original Sin. Following in the footsteps of Eve, who could not refrain from tasting the apple, the princess promises to bite his mouth "with my teeth as one bites a ripe fruit." And as the first woman was tempted by Satan in the shape of a snake, Jokanaan is accused by Salomé of being a demonic serpent. She compares his tongue to "a red snake darting poison" and to a "scarlet viper that spat its venom upon me" (p. 34).

Salomé loves and hates all at once. Her repetitive declarations of those opposite feelings imitate Solomon's Song of Songs, a collection of love verses commonly interpreted by the Church as a hymn in praise of the mutual love of God and the community of the faithful on the one hand, and the love between Christ and the Virgin on the other. The text has also been read as the portrayal of ideal human love and the sacredness of marriage. Salomé's monologues, directed first at the living saint and then at the dead head, are almost literally taken from Solomon's incantations. What makes them sound like a perverse parody is not the content or the wording but only the context: the fact that Salomé addresses her love song to the tortured prisoner who rejects her entirely and then to the head cut off from his body (fig. 119). Consequently, it is interesting to follow Wilde's borrowings from the Song of Songs not only in the words of the princess but also in the speeches of other characters. Here is a brief survey of the most obvious correspondences:

Song of Songs	*Salomé*
Let him kiss me with kisses of his mouth. (1:2)	SALOMÉ. Suffer me to kiss thy mouth. (p. 14) SALOMÉ. Ah! thou wouldst not suffer me to kiss thy mouth, Jokanaan. Well, I will kiss it now. (p. 34)
Ah, you are beautiful, my beloved, ah, you are beautiful! Your eyes are doves behind your veil. (4:1)	THE YOUNG SYRIAN. She is like a dove that has strayed. (p. 5) THE YOUNG SYRIAN. Her little white hands are fluttering like doves that fly to their dove-cots. (p. 4) HEROD. Thy little feet will be like white doves. (p. 28)
I am a flower of Saron, a lily of the valley. As a lily among thorns, so is my beloved among women. (2:1–2)	THE YOUNG SYRIAN. She is like a narcissus trembling in the wind. . . . She is like a silver flower. (p. 5) SALOMÉ. I am amorous of thy body, Jokanaan! Thy body is white like the lilies of a field that the mower hath never mowed. . . . The roses in the garden of the Queen of Arabia . . . [are not] so white as thy body. (p. 11) HEROD. Thy little feet . . . will be like white flowers that dance upon the trees. (p. 28)
O my dove in the clefts of the rock, in the secret recesses of the cliff, Let me see you,	SALOMÉ. Speak again, Jokanaan. Thy voice is as music to mine ear. (p. 10)

let me hear your voice,
For your voice is sweet,
and you are lovely. (2:14)

Your hair is like a flock of goats
streaming down the mountains of
Galaad. (4:1)

Your cheek is like a half-pome-
granate behind your veil. (4:3)

You are an enclosed garden, my
sister, my bride, an enclosed garden, a fountain sealed. (4:12)

Your neck is like David's tower
girt with battlements. (4:4)

Daughters of Jerusalem, come forth
and look upon King Solomon
In the crown with which his mother
has crowned him
on the day of his marriage. (3:11)

Let my lover come to his garden
and eat its choice fruits. (4:16)

I have come to my garden, my sis-
ter, my bride;
I gather my myrrh and my spices,
I eat my honey and my sweetmeats,
I drink my wine and my milk.
Eat, friends; drink! Drink freely of
love! (5:1)

SALOMÉ. Who is he, the Son of
Man? Is he as beautiful as thou art,
Jokanaan? (p. 11)

SALOMÉ. Thy hair is like clusters of
grapes, like the clusters of black
grapes that hang from the vine-
trees of Edom. . . . (pp. 11–12)
SALOMÉ. Thy hair . . . is a knot of
serpents coiled round thy neck.
(p. 12)

SALOMÉ. Thy mouth . . . is like a
pomegranate cut in twain with a
knife of ivory. (p. 12)
SALOMÉ. I will look at thee through
the muslin veils. (p. 8)

THE CAPPADOCIAN [*Pointing to the
cistern*]. What a strange prison!
(p. 4)

SALOMÉ. Thy mouth is like a band
of scarlet on a tower of ivory. (p. 12)

JOKANAAN. Back, daughter of
Sodom! Touch me not. Profane not
the temple of the Lord God. (p. 12)

SALOMÉ. I am athirst for thy beauty;
I am hungry for thy body; and neither wine nor apples can appease
my desire. (p. 35)

SALOMÉ. Thy body . . . was a garden full of doves and lilies of silver.
(p. 35)

They struck me, and wounded me,
and took my mantle from me,
the guardians of the walls.
I adjure you, daughters of Jerusalem, if you find my lover—
What shall you tell him?—
that I am faint with love. (5:7–8)

For stern as death is love, relentless
as the nether world is devotion;
its flames are a blazing fire.
Deep waters cannot quench love,
nor floods sweep it away. (8:6–7)

SALOMÉ. Neither the floods nor the great waters can quench my passion. . . . I was a virgin, and thou didst take my virginity from me. I was chaste, and thou didst fill my veins with fire. . . . Ah! ah! wherefore didst thou not look at me? If thou hadst looked at me thou hadst loved me. Well I know that thou wouldst have loved me, and the mystery of love is greater than the mystery of death. (pp. 35–36)

Comparison of Wilde's words with different biblical texts makes one see how much he is indebted to them and realize that he was right to perceive his drama as a "religious" one. What he did in *Salomé* was essentially to dismiss the Christian interpretation of all these writings, which, though they were filled with sensuality, passion, and fleshly desire, the Church had transformed into allegories of divine and spiritual love. In the case of the Song of Songs, for instance, Wilde either took the text literally or translated the images of gardens and architecture into what they were meant to be: metaphors for sexual topography. His procedure, by and large, resembles Freudian psychoanalysis, laying bare the eroticism behind the poetic figures of imagination or the artistic renderings of nature as well as the manmade world. Both Wilde and Freud brought back to earth symbols that Christianity had banished to heaven. The dove, for instance, has become in the Church the most popular icon of purity and spirituality. Incarnating the Holy Ghost, the dove in many paintings descends from the sky toward the womb of the Virgin in order to make visible the mystical conception of Christ. Frequently accompanying the Madonna, the white bird stands for salvation, purity of heart, innocence, modesty, and compassion. In antiquity, however, doves were birds not of divine but of sensual love and belonged to Aphrodite, whose carriage was drawn by them and by sparrows (fig. 47).

Another meaning of the dove was fixed by the Old Testament. When the flood began to recede, Noah let the bird out to seek land; and indeed, the dove returned with an olive branch in its beak, becoming thus a symbol of peace, hope, and new beginning. This very meaning was reversed by Wilde, who in his play changed the dove into a symbol not of a purity full of promise but one pregnant with mortal threat. The color white stands in

Salomé for coldness, sterility, and destruction. The princess is fashioned after the multitude of terrible virgins in fin-de-siècle literature,[76] young girls hiding behind the bodily façade of fragile buds but with passions that freeze men to death. Mallarmé and Barbey d'Aurevilly,[77] to name but two, elaborated with gusto on female chastity as a deadly trap—a kind of vagina dentata, a lunar wasteland. Through the constant repetition of "white," "silver," and "cold," Wilde creates in *Salomé* an inner landscape that is at once moon-like, wintry, and apocalyptic: frost flowers eat away the substance of life, and seven lunar veils sweep the earth clean.

Head and Maidenhead

> *A two-toothed mistress who remembers old Romulus*
> *is ready, amidst whose dark loins*
> *lies a cave hidden by a flaccid paunch,*
> *and, covered by skin wandering in yearlong cold,*
> *cobwebbed filth obstructs the door.*
> *She's ready for you, so that three or four times*
> *this deep ditch can devour your slimy head.*
> *Although you'll lie there weak, slower than a snake,*
> *you'll be ground repeatedly until—o wretch, wretch,*
> *you fill that cave three times and four times over.*
> *This pride of yours will get you nowhere, as soon as*
> *your errant head is plunged in her noisy muck.*
> ——Priapic poem in *Virgilian Appendix*,
> ed. Bücheler

> SALOMÉ. *It is for mine own pleasure that I ask the head*
> *of Jokanaan in a silver charger. . . .*
> HEROD. *It is not meet that the eyes of a virgin should*
> *look upon such a thing. What pleasure couldst thou*
> *have in it?*
> ——Oscar Wilde, *Salomé*

> *John the Baptist was a head.*
> ——*Encyclopedia of Graffiti*, ed. R. Reis-
> ner and L. Wechsler, 1974

In Wilde's play Salomé seems particularly monstrous because of her virginity. Men who desire her stress the innocent look of the princess, and she herself sees the reflection of her purity in the moon, "cold and chaste. I am sure she is a virgin. Yes, she is a virgin. She has never defiled herself. She has never abandoned herself to men" (p. 6). Salomé also does not give herself to anybody. Nevertheless, she accuses the Baptist of having taken her virginity not only by setting her blood on fire but also, in a more concrete sense, by spitting the "venom" upon her with his "red tongue." Thus she associates the red tongue with the penis and the venom with the semen of ejaculation as well as with the blood of defloration. Salomé's monologue, directed at John's head, sounds like sexual revenge, even more so when one remembers that in English "John" is a familiar word for the penis. Describing Adolphe, the beloved unicorn of Venus, Beardsley mentions his "scarlet John" (VT, p. 63). He reminds us also of another John, the womanizer Don Juan, and occasionally addresses Tannhäuser as "Don John."

Fantasies linking severed heads to the female sex, beheading to castration as well as to defloration or menstruation are well known to scholars of folklore and mythology. All over the world, legends, ceremonies, taboos, and linguistic expressions reflect this curious relationship. It is not easy to untie the complicated knot and to understand the exact meaning of these peculiar beliefs. It seems, however, that all of them have their origin in such basic and universal human experiences as the appearance of menstruation and initiation into sexuality on the one hand and the spilling of blood as a sign of destruction and death on the other. Besides, these experiences may be likened to the most imposing sight of great symbolic power: the daily setting and rising of the sun, which, like a big red ball, or head, seems to fall into the earth in the evening and to emerge from it in the morning. This spectacle may be translated by the imagination in many different ways. It may inspire fantasies of death followed by rebirth or erotic visions of penetration and of a climax followed by a rupture—a kind of "small death," a temporary darkness.

The festivals of the summer solstice, which coincide with the celebrations of the birth of Saint John the Baptist, are imbued with eroticism; they evoke the initiation and consumption of love. Heads and wreaths of flowers play a central role in some traditions. In Poland, for instance, on the Eve of Saint John, young girls made wreaths of flowers and floated them down the Vistula. What looks like an innocent spectacle acquires more meaning when one remembers that the Polish word for "wreath," *wianek,* also signifies "maidenhead." *Straciła wianek* (she lost her wreath—as well as her virginity) corresponds to the English phrase "she flung her cap over the windmill." Both expressions are obviously derived from a similar likening of the maidenhead to the covering over a girl's head, the wreath being the more evocative of the two because of its obvious association with defloration. In both cases, however, what once adorned and protected a young girl's head is thrown away and becomes a plaything for such energetic elements as water and wind. Lorenzo Lotto's (ca. 1480–1550) painting *Venus and Cupid* (Metropolitan Museum, New York) exemplifies this symbolism charmingly and perversely. A naked Venus, with her belly covered with rose petals and a shell over her head, confers a blessing upon a bride. She is approached by Cupid, who expresses the consummation of the marriage by urinating on his mother through a myrtle wreath, an attribute of classical and Renaissance wedding ceremonies.

Most cosmogonies mention the marriage between the sky and the earth. The superior male principle is further identified with the rain, which fertilizes the earth, with the sun and sunlight, and with the wind, which carries the seeds. In mythology the sun is rendered sometimes as a disk with a penis, hands, and feet, and the wind as a tube hanging down from the sun. In medieval paintings of Christ's conception, the Holy Spirit descends from above in the shape of a dove aiming at Mary's womb. The psychiatrist Honnegger mentions the fantasies of an insane man who saw the sun as an "upright tail" similar to an erect penis; when he swayed his head back and forth, the sun-phallus also swung back and forth and out of that arose the wind.[78]

But the meaning of the Polish and English expressions cannot be grasped fully without recalling the features of the hymen. This tiny membrane has either a circular form with a central aperture, or it is in the shape of a half moon. It can easily be imagined as a veil covering the sight of the vagina, similar to the veil covering a girl's face. As if admonishing Salomé to keep her virginity, that is, to keep away from him, Jokanaan tells her to "cover thy face with a veil" (p. 10). The female membrane is torn apart by the penetrating penis, a tiny head which causes a woman to bleed when it pushes through the hymen. The blood appearing on the skin and the bedding reinforces the notion of annihilated purity and the stained maiden. Likened to the petals of the destroyed flower, blood plays its part in the creation of the word "defloration." The painful process transforms a sexual initiation into a traumatic exchange: the hymen is given away for blood and semen; the presence of a tiny male head replaces maidenhead and foreshadows the head of a future child. The baby comes out of the vagina with its head first, covered with blood.

During defloration female genitals look like a wound. But also the penis, slightly stained with blood, may produce a frightening effect. Because it is connected to the spilling of blood, initiation becomes deeply engraved in the memory of both partners. The woman, visibly hurt, becomes linked both in her own imagination and in that of the man with a human victim or an animal wounded during the hunt. Such an association must have been absolutely common in all primitive cultures based on the hunt, but one encounters it also in modern thought. For instance, José Ortega y Gasset, when writing about Judith and Salome, remarks that these two women represent a perversion; instead of "falling a prey" to men as "normal women" do, they get the males.[79]

The notion of sexuality as being connected to hunting and killing, blood and revenge was obviously in the air at the turn of the century. Freud, for instance, approached the problem in a way that may not be valid today but echoes the art and literature of his time. In "The Taboo of Virginity" (1917) he analyzes the reasons for defloration's being perceived as dangerous and horrifying by the majority of primitive peoples. He points to the "horror of blood among primitive races who consider blood the seat of life,"[80] and suggests further that primitive man fears defloration much as he fears any other situation that differs in any way from the usual, that involves something new, not understood, uncanny. Primitive men not only fear the spilling of blood; they also experience deep anxiety when faced with sexuality in general and with women in particular. Femininity as such represents for them in many ways a taboo; it is unfamiliar ground on which they sense a latent hostility.

Freud mentions that he obtained some insight into woman's spontaneous wish "to castrate her young husband" from one of his newly married patients. But it seems more likely that he derived his ideas mainly from anthropology, mythology, and literature. He quotes in particular Friedrich Hebbel's tragedy *Judith* (1841) and a short story by Arthur Schnitzler, his Viennese contemporary, entitled "Das Schicksal des Freiherrn von Leisenbogh." Hebbel transformed the patriotic heroine of the Old Testament, a widow who murdered the Assyrian general, into a virgin whose maidenhead was "protected by a taboo."[81] Her first husband was paralyzed on the bridal night and never touched her. Thus, when Holofernes deflowered her, she revenged herself by striking off his head, a substitute for the penis. Freud sees the tragedy as a symbolic castration. He does not realize, however, that Hebbel made Judith a virgin possibly because of an affinity between her and Salome. Both stories display similar details that point to the obscene as well as the culinary. While the daughter of Herodias asks for the head to be brought to the banqueting hall as if it were a dish, Judith, according to the Book of Judith, "rolled his head off the bed, and pulled the canopy down from the pillars, and after a little while she went out and gave Holofernes' head to her maid, and she put it into her bag of food" (Jth. 13:10–11). Significantly, the image of this bedcloth covered with blood, which suggests the hymen and the holy curtain of the temple, returns at the end of the tale. What Judith "had taken for herself from his bed chamber she gave as a gift to God" (Jth. 16:19).[82] The present was not inappropriate: it brings to mind bedsheets stained with blood, which only a few years ago were still hung out of windows in Spanish villages after the bridal night—visible proofs of the consumed maidenhead.

Schnitzler's story reads even more like the Salome legend. The dying lover of an actress "creates a sort of new virginity for her."[83] He puts a curse of death on the man who would dare to possess her after his passing away. And indeed, a man to whom she grants her favor dies of a stroke when he learns the motive behind her love.

Nowhere is the motif of revenge for a sexual offense more passionately expressed than in the paintings of Artemisia Gentileschi (1590–?1642), who as a young girl was raped by a friend of her father. Obviously she used the image of Judith beheading Holofernes, a subject that she treated with unique vehemence in several pictures, as a vehicle for expressing her rage. A similar exchange of head for maidenhead in Shakespeare's *Measure for Measure* has been studied by Jan Kott, who explains that for Isabella, as for Salome, "sex is a pollution and she compares the horror of defloration to blood spilt during an execution. . . . Even if her brother had twenty heads, says Isabella, it would be better to deposit them on twenty blocks than to have his sister yield her body to such abhorred pollution (II, IV, 182)."[84]

Defloration usually occurs only after sexual maturity has arrived, after the first menstruation. The monthly bleeding represents another traumatic experience; it causes pain, associates sexuality with suffering, and, later, reminds the woman of defloration and male cruelty. In men, the sight of blood on female genitals brings back the shock of defloration and points to all the wounds they might have inflicted on other living beings. Early anthropologists observed that in some primitive societies the taboos imposed on menstruating women were identical with the restrictions imposed on women in childbirth, on young men at the initiatory rites that celebrated the attainment of puberty, and on warriors in their first campaign.[85]

The taboos imposed on menstruating women require in the first place their strictest separation from men. The reasons for this are complex and manifold[86] but certainly one of them may be guilt. Men, who spill blood at defloration, in the hunt, and in war, don't want to be reminded of their deeds and therefore tend to isolate the menstruating women, for whose bleeding they subconsciously feel responsible. The idea that menstruation is incited by a male is clearly expressed, for instance, in the Zoroastrian myth of the Whore whom Ahriman (the destructive spirit of the universe) kissed on her head. After the kiss "the pollution which is called menstruation appeared on the Whore."[87] The presence of blood at defloration, menstruation, and birth, as well as at violent death may be one of the factors determining the widespread conception of sexuality as dirty and evil. In religious beliefs, Satan in the shape of a serpent first initiates humans into love and then into death. Moreover there exists in mythology a particular affinity between snakes and menstruating women. Snakes are thought to be lunar animals, and women who have their period are considered to be under the influence of the moon. Magic and superstition build upon this connection; goddesses in primitive cultures as well as in ancient Greece (Artemis, Hecate, Persephone) were often represented with snakes in their hands. According to a Central European superstition, if one buried some hair which had been pulled out of the head of a menstruating woman, the hairs would turn into serpents.[88] The mythological figure of a woman with the tail of a snake instead of feet also alludes to menstruation. In some legends she looks normal for the larger part of every month and transforms herself into a monster only at the end of it; in this period it is strictly forbidden for men to be in her company.[89]

The serpent's nature, like that of many other important symbolic figures, is bisexual. As a male, frequently of demonic character, it enters women, causing defloration, menstruation, and pregnancy; as a female it observes the cycle of the moon and sheds its skin in a process likened to the monthly bleeding. One has to remember this dual nature of a serpent to realize that the severed female head of Medusa, with snakes instead of hair, has a different meaning from the severed male heads of Orpheus, Holofernes, or John the Baptist. Freud fails to recognize this,[90] although the story of Medusa as told by Ovid makes it evident. Medusa, once a lovely girl, was transformed by Minerva into a female monster with snakes instead of hair after the goddess had watched her being raped. This happened in Minerva's temple, so not only was the maiden robbed of her virginity but the sanctuary of the goddess was violated as well. To punish the girl for a deed for which she, being the victim, could hardly be held responsible, Minerva first turned her into a snake-woman and subsequently helped Perseus kill the monster.

After Medusa's death, Minerva wore her terrible likeness on her shield. Reading this tale carefully, one suspects that Medusa represents the menstruating aspect of the Great Goddess, who, to defend her chastity, scares men away by wearing on her breast the sign of her own impurity. Of course, the notion of castration as revenge for making a woman bleed is incorporated into this image, but it is more ambiguous than in the motif of a male head severed by female violence. Freud suggests that Medusa's snakes mitigate the horror because they are interpreted as penises and, accordingly, offer a substitute for the castrated member.[91] But it seems to me that, on the contrary, they heighten the terror by transforming Medusa's head into a kind of horrible entrance into a fleshly hell and underworld out of which there is no escape; the snakes are ready to coil around a man and to drag him into the dreadful mouth—a symbol of vagina dentata. Significantly, the head of Medusa is commonly placed on doors, over gates, at the entrances into caves. The counterparts for this image are not the heads of Orpheus, Holofernes, or John, but rather those of lions or, as in grotesque Venetian architecture, of diverse fabulous animals and, finally, of Satan, prince of this world. All of these heads represent the destructive aspect of nature—a female or animalistic monster ready to devour everything.

The severed heads of men, all victims of female violence, have a different meaning. Orpheus's head is carried by the waves; the head of Holofernes is thrown by Judith into a food basket; the head of John is served on a silver charger. They are horrible to look at, but not threatening. Associated with penises as well as with embryos, these heads do not mean to devour; they are returning to where they have come from: to the womb of nature.

Claude Lévi-Strauss analyzed the relationship between male heads and female genitals in a structuralist way. Studying the link between decapitation and menstruation, between the woman "stained with blood below" and the sculpted man "stained with blood above," he came to the conclusion that "not only in North America, but also throughout the world, the philosophy of head-hunting, either ritually or by direct representation, suggests the same tacit affinity between trophy-heads and the female sex."[92] According to Lévi-Strauss, it was the custom for Indian women all over North America to perform a dance before receiving the scalps (Salome also dances for Herod in order to obtain the head of John). On this occasion, they often had blackened faces and were dressed as male warriors.

From his studies of mythology and primitive customs Lévi-Strauss derives the idea that because head-hunting is imaginatively linked to hunting for women, there is a direct equivalence between war and marriage. But he neglects the equation established between the severed male heads and penises, which is obvious in his story (cited here in the notes) of women going to bed with a scalp as well as in the legends of Holofernes and John the Baptist, the enemy-lovers whose cut-off heads symbolize the defeated male superiority and constitute, as metaphorical phalluses, objects of sexual desire.

A similar symbolism can be suggested by skulls brought together with young, attractive, and naked women. Associating the biblical Eve with the Greek Pandora, Jean Cousin painted her in a grotto and with a skull (fig. 10). In alchemical manuscripts one finds curious images of a naked Eve who, herself reclining on the ground, points to a large skull placed on top of a sarcophagus. These compositions symbolize the mortification of Eve, the feminine aspect of the prima materia, but they also make one think of the absent Adam whom the skull seems to represent. Eroticism is even more pronounced in the renderings of Magdalen with a skull. A close disciple of Jesus, Mary Magdalen went with him on his last journey to Jerusalem, witnessed the Crucifixion, followed the burial, prepared spices, and was the first one to find the tomb empty and to speak to the risen Christ. The Gnostic Gospel of Philip tells us that "[Christ loved] her more than [all] the disciples and used to kiss her [often] on her [mouth]."[93] Georges de la Tour's *Penitent Magdalen* (Metropolitan Museum, New York) shows a seated young woman who rests her hands on a skull in her lap.

She faces away from the viewer toward the mirror and the burning candle which, standing in front of the glass, is reflected in it. In his *Repentant Magdalen* (National Gallery, Washington), the girl while looking into the mirror gently touches with her left hand the skull that is placed on top of a book, presumably the Bible. This time the candle is covered by the skull, and only the top of the flame rises above it. The glass does not reflect the candle but the skull illuminated by it. In both paintings, as well as in de la Tour's four other versions of the Magdalen theme that have survived either in the original or in copy, Christ is present in his dual nature: as a mortal and as an immortal, as the skull resting in the ground and as the flame of life. Like all images of fire, the candle stands universally for life and love, but in Christianity it also symbolizes the Savior. Accordingly, the candle extinguisher in Spain is called "the hand of Judas," and an ancient church festival commemorating Christ's presentation in the temple is named "candlemas" (in Latin, *festum candelarum sive luminum*). But Jesus can be also represented by the cross, a truly phallic object in Francesco Hayez's *Magdalen* (fig. 120).

In legends and erotic tales derived from them, the image of the skull is occasionally hidden in the innocent form of a ball, and the sexual drive is camouflaged as the "ball game." Dorothy Epplen Mackay presents in her excellent book several folk stories in which the skull is first stolen from the cemetery or found near a grave and then used for playing ball or some other disrespectful activity.[94] This offense against the dead makes them rise, visit the living, and punish them for this disturbance of their peace. All legends of this kind contain a moral lesson; they teach the living that they should refrain from contact with the dead, from all "playing" (intercourse) with a corpse. Of course a skull signifies not only a dead body but in a more general way the dead past, and in the case of Christianity it denotes paganism, which should not be exhumed. The themes of the forbidden past and of the flying ball/head, of Pygmalion and Tannhäuser are tied together in popular medieval legends of Venus and her ring.[95] The first version of this legend was written down by William of Malmesbury in his *Chronicles of the Kings of England* (ca. 1125). In his story a young Roman nobleman who has just married goes out after the wedding feast to play a game of ball with his friends; for safekeeping he puts the wedding ring on the outstretched finger of a bronze statue of Venus. When he tries to get it back, the finger is clenched fast. During the following nights a cloud-like appearance of Venus hinders him in embracing his wife and whispers that he is now wedded to her and that she will never surrender the ring. She is finally forced to return it by a priest skilled in black magic. But before this happens the young man sees Venus in her "true" shape: participating in a wild hunt, she rides in the night on a mule while making indecent gestures.

Twenty years later the first variant of the story appeared in the German collection of tales known as the *Kaiserchronik*. There it is stressed that the incident occurs in the early days of Christianity and that the two noble brothers playing ball with their friends are still under the influence of paganism. One of the brothers, by the name of Astrolabius (in Greek, one who takes a star) throws the ball into the walled-in ruins of a dilapidated temple, climbs over the wall, and perceives in the deserted garden a statue of Venus. When he approaches her, the statue moves to him as well. Attracted by her charm, Astrolabius declares his love for Venus and pledges himself to her by presenting her with his ring. When his brother finally removes him from the enchanted place, Astrolabius begins to waste away in amorous agony. He recovers from his fervor when his ring is brought back by a priest who descended to hell for it. To prevent further temptation, the pope himself orders the statue of Venus to be taken from the garden to the Castel Sant' Angelo; there it is exorcised and consecrated to the memory of the archangel Michael. Out of gratitude, Astrolabius, his brother, and his friends are baptized and become Christians.

The story displays beautifully many motifs discussed so far. In this second version the ball, an image which suggests a flying penis, acts as the carrier of Astrolabius's hidden desire for forbidden love—and faith. "Taken" by Venus, the pagan "star," the youth commits a double offense: like Pygmalion, he pledges his love to a statue (inanimate matter—corpse) and proves to be attracted by the "dead" religion. This criminal passion affects him mortally: he wastes away and finally can be saved only by tearing himself from his subterranean beloved, by exchanging the forbidden old goddess of sensual love for the new god of spirituality—and sexuality for abstinence. The story of Venus and her ring, like that of Tannhäuser, demonstrates the difficult task of Christianity: to strike dead the animated and eroticized pagan world of unlimited metamorphoses—the core of the grotesque.

At this point, however, it makes sense to remember that a ball in the hands of a man can be also interpreted as a female globe, the earth (fig. 121), or the planet Venus. This adds to the legendary ball game another dimension, and a further warning: do not play with nature that does not respect the human norm.

Beardsley's Salomé

Beardsley's illustrations to Wilde's *Salomé* provide the European tradition with a formidably epigonistic epilogue, tying together remembrances of an archaic earth-and-moon goddess with the caricatures of a fin-de-siècle femme fatale. Oscillating between the universal and the local, the obscene and the sacrilegious, Beardsley mixes together distinct times and cultures in a unique pursuit of grotesque heterogeneity. His illustrations transcend the territory delineated by Wilde's apocalyptic drama. Beardsley's Herodias and Salomé do not so much incarnate the Babylonian whore as they impersonate a more universal goddess of voluptuousness and vanity who combines elements of Venus and Hecate, Nyx and Astarte with shapes and attributes taken from Indian divinities and Japanese geishas, rococo ladies-in-waiting and nineteenth-century French courtesans. In some drawings the clarity of outlines is inspired by Greek vases, in others the exquisite play of black and white is suggested by Japanese woodcuts; some satirical features go back to eighteenth-century French prints, others to the shadow theater of the East. The black mass, celebrated by Wilde through his use of passages echoing the Bible, is represented in Beardsley's drawings with far greater explicitness and strength. In *Enter Herodias* (fig. 122), Beardsley shows the wife of the tetrarch, her long black hair covered with moon crescents, as the center of a grotesque trinity. On her right side she is flanked by an obscene embryo who, dressed in a loose robe embellished with roses, lifts Herodias's veil with his finger. On her left stands a naked old eunuch with a powder box, a puff, and a mask in his hands, his effeminate face resembling Wilde's, whose likeness one also finds in the figure placed below. Equipped with Mercury's wand and an owl-mask, the author of the sacrilegious play points with his right hand to the central candle, a wax phallus growing out of a horned head standing on tiny feet, as if in front of an altar. The same motif is further elaborated in *The Eyes of Herod* (fig. 123), where the tetrarch and his wife are presented in a way that is strongly reminiscent of a bearded God the Father with the Madonna. However, the Christian hierarchy is reversed, with Herod placed lower and on the traditionally female side and Herodias presiding over him. They are separated by the flames of candles burning in the floral candelabrum which is held by two putti posed like Eros and Anteros struggling for the palm of victory. Indeed, the scene is about rivalry, the woman overpowering the man. Her dominance and his defeat are reflected below in the features of the two boys: the one standing on Herodias's side has a lively young face, the other, situated below Herod, is a disgusting aged dwarf. His sinister face seems to foreshadow death and is almost identical with that of the dwarf kissing the hand of Christ in Beardsley's *The Kiss of Judas* (fig. 125). Where Herodias's skirt disappears in the ground, a peacock emerges out of a rose-hedge—a symbol of her as well as of her daughter's worldly splendor. Beneath the bird, its tail glittering with moons, three mutilated trees suggest the subject of Herod's quarrel with his wife: the execution of the Baptist and his imminent martyrdom (in *The Kiss of Judas* dead trees speak of Jesus' end).

The Stomach Dance removes the scene from Judea to the Far East. The fantastic phallic creature playing the vaginal instrument seems to have stepped out of an Indonesian shadow play, while the "deflowered" princess dancing on rose petals makes one recall the dancing Indian gods—and Blavatsky's account of her visit to the cave of an Indian witch.[96] Likened by the author to a prima donna performing in an open-air opera, the witch danced among rose-like flowers, burning candles, children with aromatic powders, and a priest dressed in garlands of roses who played an instrument that reminded Blavatsky of a violin; she drank the warm blood of the sacrificial animal and in ecstasy cut its body with a knife. The witch, a grotesque creature with a small head looking like the skull of a dead child and adorned with a golden snake, is described by Blavatsky as a "living mummy" and "death herself." During the dance the seven sisters or incarnations of the goddess whom she served took possession of her body. The chapter in Blavatsky's book following the one about the sorceress has the description of two children becoming engaged to each other, the prenuptial rites culminating in the decapitation of a goat.

In *The Dancer's Reward* (fig. 119) the dualistic setting of the *John and Salomé* (fig. 116) drawing is repeated, with the saint having been meanwhile reduced to his head. Placed on a plate, the head is supported from below by a hairy column, trunk, or penis. But Beardsley deflates the horror of the scene by placing at Salomé's side a pair of slippers that, as they convey domesticity and fetishism, question the seriousness of John's beheading and of her necrophilia. In contrast, in *The Climax* (fig. 124), the last full-page illustration to Wilde's play, Beardsley almost totally abandons the grotesque in favor of mythical pathos. Placed within the white quarter circle, Salomé, the woman in the moon, with locks of her hair dancing like two snakes, holds close to her face the head of the Baptist. She is depicted above black waters. Where the white flux coming out of John's head touches the water's surface, a white lily grows out of the dark depth. Did Beardsley remember the anemone springing up from the blood of Adonis, the lover of Venus? Or is this an allusion to the Song of Songs, in which the beloved is likened to a lily? Or the white narcissus, the flower evoked by Wilde? Or, most likely, the lotus, the theosophical symbol of life mystically renewing itself, a flower rendered by Kupka in an early drawing depicting the blossom in the middle of a black pond with an embryo among its petals. Whatever its origins, the delicate plant that perpetuates the life of a man sacrificed to the Great Goddess perfectly completes the ancient mystery.

It looks as if Beardsley was himself overpowered by this and therefore avoided disturbing the great synthetic design with any of his jokes. Instead, he shook the pathos off in the last drawing, the small but extremely grotesque *Cul de lampe*. It shows Salomé being buried by a bearded, horned satyr-devil and a masked clown whose head resembles the moon. The two lower her slim, naked body into a roundish sarcophagus, decorated with roses and inscribed "FIN," that not only looks like a powder box but obviously is one, since the puff, larger than the body of the princess, lies in front of it. This huge, fluffy "moon" brings the primordial drama not only down to earth but straight into a French boudoir and to Salomé's dressing table, where, next to *La terre* and *Fleurs du mal* stand *Nana, Manon Lescaut,* and *Les fêtes galantes.*

FIG. 104 Salome presents to Herod the head of John the Baptist and Herodias prepares to cut his eye with a knife, French school of the North (Amiens?), fifteenth century.

FIG. 105 *Salome with the Head of Saint John the Baptist,* Spanish, Catalan, middle fifteenth century.

FIG. 106 Andrea Solario (ca. 1460–1524), *Salome with the Head of Saint John the Baptist*.

FIG. 107 Cesare da Sesto (1477–1523), *Salome*.

FIG. 108 Master of Astorga, *Salome and Saint John's Head*, 1530.

FIG. 109 *The Beheading of Saint John the Baptist*, Spanish, Catalan, middle fifteenth century.

FIG. 110 Dance of Salome and beheading of Saint John,
miniature in an English psalter, early thirteenth century.

FIG. 111 Dancing Salome, Baptistery of San Marco, Venice, fourteenth century.

FIG. 112 Dance of Salome and beheading of Saint John, miniature
in the evangelary of Bamberg, tenth or eleventh century.

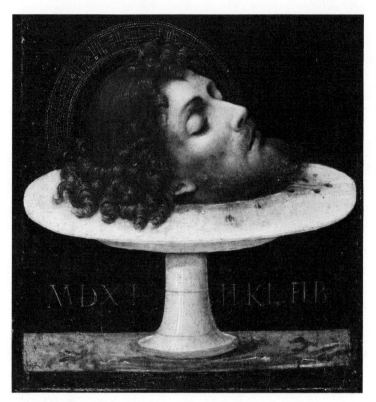

FIG. 113 Follower of Leonardo, *The Head of John the Baptist*, Milanese school, sixteenth century.

FIG. 114 Jan Mostaert (1499–1601), *Angels Deplore the Death of Saint John the Baptist*, Flemish school.

FIG. 115 Aubrey Beardsley, *The Woman in the Moon*.

FIG. 116 Aubrey Beardsley, *John and Salomé*.

FIG. 117 Sun and Moon, Benedictine Abbey, Charlieu,
France, twelfth century.

FIG. 118 An angel shows Saint John the Evangelist the damnation of the great
harlot seated on the seven-headed beast, French Ms, thirteenth century.

FIG. 119 Aubrey Beardsley, *The Dancer's Reward*.

FIG. 120 Francesco Hayez (1791–1882), *Magdalen*.

FIG. 121 Emperor Octavius Augustus as a fifteenth-century personage with the earth in his hand, in Suetonius, *Lives of the Twelve Caesars*, ca. 1433.

FIG. 122 Aubrey Beardsley, *Enter Herodias*.

FIG. 123 Aubrey Beardsley, *The Eyes of Herod*.

FIG. 124 Aubrey Beardsley, *The Climax*.

Chapter 10 · Judas

Judas was the most prominent villain of the New Testament, the abominable traitor onto whose figure hideous grotesque features could be freely projected. His surname, "Iscarioth," was usually interpreted as meaning "man of Kerioth," an explanation that made him the only non-Galilean among the twelve Apostles. In Christian tradition Judas had become the incarnation of a Jew, providing the best example of the Church's ability to focus on the Jewishness of "bad" Jews and to deemphasize the Jewish identity of the "good" ones by concentrating on their Christian nature. As a result, even today anti-Semitic Catholics, when asked to explain their dislike of Jews, give as a reason the fact that Jews crucified Jesus, as if he were not one of them.

The difference between a classical-looking Christ and a fantastic-looking Judas can be studied in many medieval paintings and sculptures. Judas's Semitic features and expressions, an enormous nose, curly red hair and beard, and his rather short body, created a demonic caricature which could be clearly associated with the devil. In contrast to Christ's modest outfit, Judas frequently wore expensive and foolishly extravagant clothes. Sometimes these were a dingy yellow color that symbolized the sulfuric fumes of hell, deceit, jealousy, degradation, and contagion (Jews and heretics were forced to wear yellow, and in times of plague contaminated areas were marked with this color as well). Judas's most popular attributes were his thirty pieces of silver, a bag of money, and a rope. He was related to Cain (fig. 135), shown in the company of devils, and represented as Satan himself. The kiss with which Judas indicated Jesus was compared to the bite of a scorpion.

Judas's suicide was described in obscene terms in order to provide a contrast with Christ's expiration and to deny the sinner a last chance for confession. Without that he was condemned for eternity to the worst infernal circles and made the plaything of the most sadistic devils. But to some dreamers of torture even this did not suffice, and they invented two hells, one unbearably hot, the other unbearably cold, between which Judas was constantly moved.[1]

The alien and distorted figure of Judas belonged to the officially sanctioned vocabulary of the horrible bizarre. But he also inhabited the heretical underground, where he played a relatively subordinate role because of his masculinity. In the omnipotent female cave not even a distinguished male criminal could pass for more than a dwarf or an infant. The subterranean Judas presented himself as a character altogether different from the one described in the Bible. In his apocryphal biography, shaped after the lives of Oedipus and Moses, his adulthood at the side of Christ was preceded by a long prehistory of exile, murder, and incest. Seen from this perspective, the Judas kiss acquired a surprisingly ambiguous meaning which resulted from a combination of the archaic and the erotic. This mixture was rendered with macabre humor by Beardsley in his drawing *The Kiss of Judas*.

The Kiss of Judas

> *"When I have before me one of your drawings I want to drink absinthe, which changes colour like jade in sunlight and makes the senses thrall, and then I can live myself back in imperial Rome, in the Rome of the later Caesars."*
>
> *"Don't forget the* simple *pleasures of that life, Oscar," said Aubrey. "Nero set Christians on fire, like large tallow candles; the only light Christians have ever been known to give," he added languidly.*
>
> ——A conversation between Oscar Wilde and Aubrey Beardsley

One of Beardsley's most intriguing drawings bears the title *The Kiss of Judas* (fig. 125). It appeared in July 1893 in the *Pall Mall Magazine*, where a note, signed X. L., says that it represents a Moldavian legend: "They say that Children of Judas, lineal descendants of the arch traitor, are prowling about the world seeking to do harm, and they kill you with a kiss. 'Oh! how delightful!' murmured the Dowager Duchess."[2]

Kenneth Clark is right that the tone of the text sounds like Beardsley himself.[3] It seems very likely that Beardsley invented the note with the intention to mystify readers as well as to distract attention from his sacrilegious depiction of one of Christianity's most dramatic moments: the betrayal of Christ by Judas Iscariot, one of the twelve Apostles. I doubt that, without the pseudo-explicatory "footnote," a drawing with such a title, clearly written by Beardsley in the right bottom corner, would have appeared in a magazine when less shocking allusions to Jesus were purged from books.[4] While the fictitious note was meant to provide a temporary alibi, the title was given a prominent place inside the drawing, as if to remind the future public how to read the strange scene correctly: a naked putto kissing the hand of a hermaphroditic youth who, leaning against an obscenely mutilated tree, has fallen asleep. What supports this assumption is the fact that all inscriptions on Beardsley's drawings are generally used to make a point that might otherwise have been overlooked by the viewer. Disconnected from the misleading note, the drawing represents what the title says: The Kiss of Judas.

Clark compares the composition of the drawing with that of *A Platonic Lament,* an illustration in *Salomé;*[5] it shows the page of Herodias bent in grief over the body of the young Syrian who killed himself because of the princess's passion for the Baptist. In Wilde's play the Syrian's sacrifice foreshadows the victimization of the Precursor. However, Clark fails to recognize a resemblance between the sleeping figure kissed by the naked dwarf and that of the Baptist as rendered in the drawing *John and Salomé* (fig. 116). Obviously misled by Beardsley's clever maneuver, Clark inter-prets the sleeping figure not as a youth but as a woman. Not only do the sleeper and John look like twins, but the two scenes—the kiss of Judas on the one hand, and the first encounter between the Baptist and Salomé on the other—also have a hidden content in common: the touch of death. The princess ordered the saint to be taken out of the cistern; the moment her eyes catch sight of John, Salomé falls in love with him and declares that she has to *kiss him.* Rejected by him, Herodias's daughter will have him killed in order to obtain the desired kiss, a central "token" of Wilde's play. Salomé repeats her wish to "kiss thy mouth, Jokanaan" *eight* times, with ever more threatening passion; and when she finally gets his head, she exclaims: "Ah, thou wouldst not suffer me to kiss thy mouth, Jokanaan. Well, I will kiss it now" (pp. 12–14, 34). If the *Pall Mall* text was indeed written by Beardsley, it is the voice of Salomé we hear when the "Dowager Duchess," after being told that "they kill you with a kiss," exclaims: "Oh! how delightful!"

Salomé's desire for a kiss destroyed the life of the Precursor. This original idea of Wilde's "religious" play was probably inspired by the kiss of Judas, which ended the life of the Savior. This analogy could not have escaped Beardsley's sensibility. He associated the two kisses and, while working on the *Salomé* illustrations, drew also the scene of Jesus' annihi-lation through Judas as a situation of obscene ambiguity. The setting of *The Kiss of Judas* resembles *The Dancer's Reward,* a drawing in which Salomé holds the head of John by the hair, and *The Climax,* in which she draws her face close to his. In *The Kiss of Judas* both gestures are present: the naked dwarf, whose voluptuous face reminds us of Salomé's morbid expression, raises the hand of the sleeping figure in order to kiss it. This macabre eroticism is supported in the background by the outlines of three mutilated trees and four rosebushes brutally penetrated by black sticks.

The drawing, although in itself uncanny, becomes truly shocking when connected with the title, which brings to mind both the traditional representation of the kiss of Judas as it is treated in the visual arts and the biblical description of the dramatic event. However, when one overcomes the initial surprise, one realizes that Beardsley's drawing renders justice to at least some of the accounts in the Gospels. Entitled "The Agony in the Garden," these accounts also stress the motif of sleep, which symbolizes human weakness and foreshadows death. While Jesus tries in vain to keep the good Apostles awake in the garden (which evokes the lost paradise), the bad Apostle does not sleep but prepares for his Lord's extermination in the city. Passive virtue falls prey to the aggressiveness of evil. Behind the back of Christ and his faithful disciples, Judas makes his transaction. Similarly, Salome demands the head of the Baptist on a silver charger as payment for her dance.

I have already mentioned the mixture of the erotic and the culinary in the scene of Herod's banquet. The very same combination is contained in the kiss, an act which has long been regarded by anthropologists as a remnant or a transference of the primitive desire to incorporate into the self anything that feels good.[6] The Eucharist is based upon the idea of eating the body of the beloved, and this has been occasionally interpreted in truly cannibalistic terms. For instance Jacques Bénigne Bossuet, the bishop of Meaux, mentions first "the ecstasy of human love" in which "we eat and devour each other . . . carry off even with our teeth the thing we love in order to possess it, feed upon it, become one with it," and then adds: "That which is frenzy, that which is impotence in corporeal love is truth, is wisdom in the love of Jesus: 'Take, eat, this is my body': devour, swallow up not a part, not a piece but the whole."[7]

As a counterpart to the *Salomé* illustrations, *The Kiss of Judas* occupies such a central position in Beardsley's work that it is worthwhile to recall the biblical narrative:

> Then Jesus came with them to a country place called
> Gethsemani, and he said to his disciples, "Sit down here,
> while I go over yonder and pray." And he took with him
> Peter and the two sons of Zebedee, and he began to be
> saddened and exceedingly troubled. Then he said to them,
> "My soul is sad, even unto death. Wait here and watch
> with me." And going forward a little, he fell prostrate
> and prayed, saying, "Father, if it is possible, let this cup
> pass away from me; yet not as I will, but as thou
> willest."
>
> Then he came to the disciples and found them sleep-
> ing. And he said to Peter, "Could you not, then, watch
> one hour with me? Watch and pray, that you may not

*enter into temptation. The spirit is willing, but the flesh
is weak." Again a second time he went away and prayed,
saying, "My Father, if this cup cannot pass away unless
I drink, thy will be done." And he came again and found
them sleeping, for their eyes were heavy. And leaving
them he went back again, and prayed a third time, saying
the same words over. Then he came to his disciples, and
said to them, "Sleep on now, and take your rest! Behold,
the hour is at hand when the Son of Man will be betrayed
into the hands of sinners. Rise, let us go. Behold, he who
betrays me is at hand."*

*And while he was yet speaking, behold Judas, one of
the Twelve, came and with him a great crowd with
swords and clubs, from the chief priests and elders of the
people [fig. 126]. Now his betrayer had given them a
sign, saying, "Whomever I kiss, that is he; lay hold of
him." And he went straight up to Jesus and said, "Hail,
Rabbi!" and kissed him. And Jesus said to him, "Friend,
for what purpose hast thou come?"* (Matt. 26:36–50)[8]

Jesus' question is a rhetorical one. He knows the cup of abomination that he is meant to drink. But another question forces itself upon the observer of this pathetic scene. How is it that Jesus, a local celebrity, has to be kissed in order to be recognized? This intrigued medieval scholars who suggested that the kiss was necessary because of the great resemblance between Christ and another Apostle, his brother James.[9] The explanation does not sound very convincing. It seems that the kiss, not mentioned at all in the Gospel of John, does not have a practical purpose, but has the character of a symbolic act, expressing a low, dark, and destructive passion. Material and fatal, the kiss of Judas stands for the very opposite of the spiritual and animating kiss of peace with which the Lord greeted his disciples during his lifetime and which took the form of breathing when he appeared to them after his death (John 20:21–22).[10] The scene recalls that moment in Genesis (2:7) when God animated the earthly body of the first man with his breath.

Babies are welcomed into life by parents kissing them; relatives and friends kiss the dying beloved goodbye. Kisses revive (Poliphilo is kissed back to life by Polia), return enchanted monsters to human shape,[11] and restore health; parents warmly kiss children who have hurt themselves. But the positive features of a kiss are counteracted by its dangerous and poisonous qualities. In the context of eroticism the kiss is viewed with the same mixture of delight and fear as sex itself. In imitation of ancient lovers, King Wenceslaus of Bohemia sang of his beloved that "just as a rose that opens its calyx when it drinks the sweet dew, she offered me her sugar-sweet mouth."[12] But, in contrast, Lucian described in his *True History* a vineyard where all the vines were plants below, and above they had the shape of women. They kissed the travelers on the mouth and made them lose consciousness. In the tight female embrace men were changed into boughs and twigs. When illustrating Lucian's book, Beardsley chose to depict this very scene—whose traces can be found in many European legends of venomous women killing with their embraces, breath, and kisses. This image of horror combines the notion of contagious illnesses with that of poisonous fumes emanating from the earth, as from the terrible lake at the entrance to the underworld in the *Aeneid*.

These obscene fantasies arise because the mouth is identified with other cavities of the body, in particular the vagina and the anus, as well as with the earthly grotto. The Latin *osculum* (kiss) combines, accidentally, *os* (mouth) with *culum* (ass). This provides humorous wordplay for the married Roman lady who, when asked for a kiss, replied that she already gave the first syllable to her husband, but the other was still available:

> *Syllaba prima meo debetur tota marito,*
> *Sume tibi reliquas, non ero dura, duas.*[13]

The identification of the native ground with the mother is the basis for the ancient custom of kissing the earth. The Danish satirist Ludvig Holberg (1684–1754) made fun of this sentimental habit in his comedy *Ulysses of Ithaca*, where, upon kissing the ground, the hero remarks ironically that somebody has been there before him.

Die Erde küssen is a German euphemism for dying that corresponds closely to *den Pfennig küssen* (to kiss the penny, common in English as "penny-kisser"), an idiom that might have been derived from the combination of Judas's avarice and his kiss. The "kiss of peace" (*osculum pacis*) with which the members of the early Christian Church greeted each other is the root of the Irish *pōc* (kiss, from the Latin *pax*) and the medieval Spanish *paz* (kiss). In the Middle Ages there even existed an osculatorium, or *tabella pacis*, a metallic disk with a holy picture, which was passed around the church to be kissed and occasionally served as a profane intermediary between lovers. In *The Voyage of Saint Brandan* Judas admits that, pretending to love Jesus, he gave him the "kiss of peace" and thus used this symbol of reconciliation to sow the seeds of discord.[14]

One is not surprised to hear that the devil was supposed to be kissed by witches on his *culum* and that this was practiced as admission into certain secret societies and during black masses and other orgiastic and sacrilegious events. In German, the idea of the second, obscene "face" is reflected in the expression "er kann mich küssen da, wo ich keine Nase habe" (he can kiss me there, where I have no nose); and the reply "kiss my ass!" is readily uttered in most languages.

Beardsley's obscene figure of Judas is undoubtedly derived from all these playful, indecent, and terrible ambiguities that a kiss in general, and the kiss of Judas in particular, carry in the European tradition. As if remembering Judas, who got thirty pieces of silver for the kiss of his Lord, the seventeenth-century English poet John Lyly made Cupid play with his beloved "at cards for kisses."[15] She won and Amor lost everything, including both his eyes. (With this idea the poet cleverly explained the popular figure of blind Amor.) The notion that one has either to pay or to be paid for a kiss occurs frequently in erotic poetry and literature, and many lovers declare, like Christopher Marlowe's Doctor Faustus, that no price is too high for them.

Judas as Cupid

The depiction of Judas as a putto with an aged face strikes us as absurd only as long as it is seen in the context of traditional Christian art. The image loses its shocking aspect when it is compared to the ancient stelae and sarcophagi on which the dead are frequently shown as sleeping figures attended by putti who touch and kiss them gently (fig. 127). There even exists a Roman sarcophagus which so closely resembles Beardsley's drawing that one is tempted to think the English artist saw a sketch or a photograph of it.[16] But if this was not the case, other sarcophagi in the collection of the British Museum display the theme as well. Franz Cumont interprets the tiny boys on the Roman sarcophagi as erotes.[17] Indeed, when we recall that Eros shoots his own mother as well as other lovers with his arrows, we can regard the penetration as a deadly wound. In accordance with this symbolism, Christian martyrs equated the arrows that caused their torture and death as instruments of love.

In her analysis of the Boston Throne, a fifth-century B.C. Greek relief from southern Italy which uses for the central figure a young winged boy holding the scales, Emily Vermeule observes that he seems to be a fusion of Eros and Thanatos "enticing Sleep or Death, a young Eros, a final Thanatos, an iconographic fusion of two superficially incompatible aspects of divinity which . . . came to seem inseparable, like mirror images of two big human experiences."[18] Antiquity knew other fusions and mirrorings as well. To express the reciprocal character of love, the Greeks created the double figure of two identical tiny boys struggling for the palm of victory: Eros and his twin brother, Anteros. Near the Acropolis in Athens an altar to Anteros as Alastor (the avenger of unreciprocated love) once commemorated the legend of Meles, who rejected the love of Timagoras and pushed him into death by forcing him, in order to prove his passion, to jump down from the Acropolis; then, in remorse, Meles dashed himself into annihilation. The story brings to mind the ending of Laforgue's *Salome,* with the princess throwing the head from the rock into the sea and then falling down herself. The motif is indirectly repeated by Wilde, whose play ends with Herod ordering the slaying of Salomé. Thus her death follows that of the man whose mouth she desired to kiss. In the Gospel of Matthew, Judas rejects the love of Jesus, brings about his death and then, repenting, kills himself: "Then Judas, who betrayed Him, when he saw that He was condemned, repented and brought back the thirty pieces of silver to the chief priests and the elders saying, 'I have sinned in betraying innocent blood.' But they said, 'What is that to us? See to it thyself.' And he flung the pieces of silver into the temple, and withdrew; and went away and hanged himself with a halter" (27:3–5). The version told by Matthew is slightly contradicted by Acts, where Peter reports that Judas was "hanged, burst asunder in the midst, and all his bowels gushed out" (1:18). In this description the death of Judas is presented as a vulgar parallel to the tacit noblesse with which the Savior expired on the cross.

The connection between love and death explains the presence of erotes on the ancient sarcophagi and of the strange Judas-putto in Beardsley's drawing. However, the symbolism is more complex because the twins Eros and Anteros are complemented as well as contradicted in Greek and Roman imagery by the brothers Hypnos and Thanatos.[19] These two were represented in the visual arts as an almost identical pair of winged male babes; however, monstrosity rather than playfulness was attributed to them. They were believed to cut locks of hair from the heads of the deceased and to drink the blood of sacrificial victims. Hypnos and Thanatos were the sons of Nyx,[20] the personification of the night, who was born, like her brother Erebus (the underworld), from Chaos. She lived in a cave, drove a carriage through the night sky, and was depicted in a black dress covered with glittering stars and with black wings. The moon was the eye of Nyx and her features combined the restful and peaceful with the terrible and murderous. Pausanias (5:17–19) describes the figure of a motherly Night with Hypnos and Thanatos in her arms as represented on the famous "chest of Cypselus"[21] at Olympia. This image might have served as a prototype for such sarcophagi as that of the Roman matron attended by two putti, one seated on her pillow, the other sleeping at her feet. One can see in them Eros and Anteros,[22] but it may make more sense to interpret the figures as Thanatos and Hypnos. Christian artists translated the winged cupids and souls into angels (fig. 128) and used the figures of Eros and Anteros, Thanatos and Hypnos as prototypes for the holy infants Jesus and John the Baptist as well (fig. 129).

Obsessed in their works by the mysterious femininity of the Night, and by Sleep and Death, with whom they often identified themselves, the German Romantics revived the ancient figure of Nyx with her twins. In *The Night with Her Children* Asmus Jakob Carstens (1754–98) drew a young woman who, unveiling her naked body, reveals the blond twin Hypnos, leaning in deep slumber against her hip, two poppy-heads in his hand, and Thanatos, sleeping standing, his dark head on her knee and an extinguished torch in his hand. Pursuing a similar theme, Philipp Otto Runge (1777–1810), spiritual father to the archaic and infantile microcosm of nineteenth-century children's books, depicted Night as a queen of elves seated on poppy-stalks. He complemented *The Night* with *The Morning* (fig. 130) and *The Day*: picturing a woman with naked infants in a blooming earthly cavity (fig. 131).

The German Romantics illustrated what the Greeks had already recognized: the enormous erotic drive of the male child toward his mother. Their concept of Eros as a three- or four-year-old boy resulted from this understanding. In an equally "psychoanalytic" manner they seem to have equated death with the wish to regress by returning to the infantile state and to the motherly cave. Therefore they imagined Thanatos as the twin brother of Eros, a tiny boy who appears at the moment of transition from the upper to the lower world. In the light of this symbolism, one begins to understand how Beardsley could portray the figure of the "arch traitor" as an amor who in the uncanny garden of roses and dead trees kisses the sleeping Jesus. Remembrances and dreams intertwine in this strange location that combines the features of a rose garden, the earthly paradise of Venus, with those of Golgotha, as three mutilated trees stand for three crosses. It is a place of love, sleep, and death, reminding us of Ovid's cave of Hypnos, where "in the midst of the cavern stands a lofty couch of ebon wood, dark in colour, covered with black draperies, feather soft, where the god himself lies, his limbs relaxed in luxurious weariness" (*Met.* 11:607–9), and of the garden of Gethsemane, where the Apostles could not keep awake.

A strange plant grows in the center of the garden, exactly underneath the figure of Judas; its character may be purely ornamental but I suspect that it is not. In any case, it is connected with Judas in a dual manner. At the top, his right foot is covered by the flowers; at the bottom a straight line, a prolongation of the letter "A" in the word "Judas," points back to the plant. This association makes one perceive the bush as a "flower of evil," a plant similar to that which seems to threaten the Baptist in Bosch's depiction of the Precursor (fig. 132). Indeed, several plants were named after Judas. The most popular among them is the "Judas tree" (*Cercis siliquastrum*), a native of the Mediterranean basin. It has the shape of a handsome low tree with a flat spreading head. In spring it blossoms with purplish-pink flowers which appear before the leaves (they are eaten in a salad or made into fritters). In earlier times herbalists frequently drew the tree, and a twelfth-century French relief from the Cathedral of Saint Lazare in Autun shows Judas being hanged on it by devils (fig. 133). In Germany there exists a garden flower called "Judasborze"; the lunaria annua is called "médaille de Judas" in French, "Judasgeld" in German, and "money-flower" in English; mushrooms growing on an old tree carry the name "auricula Judae." It seems very likely that Beardsley's centrally located bush refers to the idea of a plant of Judas. Moreover, the stylized flowers (there are twenty to thirty of them) resemble coins or pouches filled with seeds.

Female Jesus, the Fusion, and the Twins

The femininity of the sleeping figure in *The Kiss of Judas* allows the seemingly sacrilegious interpretation of Jesus as a woman. However, far from being invented by Beardsley, this strange idea can be found elsewhere, for instance in Augustine's writings on divine love. There Christ appears in the female personification of Sophia (Wisdom), whose contact with her "amatores" is described in erotic terms: she "receives all her suitors without arousing jealousy in them; she is shared by all, and with each she is chaste. No one says to another: get back so I may approach, take your hands away that I may embrace her. All cling to her, all hold her at the same time."[23]

Because of the presence of the strange cupid, Beardsley's female-seeming Jesus can be interpreted in several ways: as Venus with her son, as the Virgin with the baby Christ, and as Psyche with Amor. The last couple is often mentioned in connection with the kiss that unites the lovers into one being, and so they are often depicted as kissing (fig. 134). Their image reflects the desire for psychic fusion and is frequently evoked in Christian times with respect to Jesus uniting with the Holy Spirit or Mary becoming one with her own soul. In a Gnostic text belonging to the group known as *Pistis Sophia* we read that the Virgin interpreted the words "justice and peace shall kiss" (Ps. 84:11) by telling the story of a nebulous double of her son who appeared before her and asked for the baby Christ as if he were his brother.[24] When the two saw each other, they kissed, became one being—the phantom turning out to be the Holy Spirit, the divine Pneuma, occasionally portrayed as Christ's beloved and bride. In a Bohairic manuscript from the sixth century the assumption of the Virgin is described in a similar way. When Mary died, Christ descended to earth and carried her soul to heaven. Then he came down another time, with his mother's soul already seated in his lap in the form of a physical double. Arriving at the tomb, he asked Mary's body to rise. It appeared and "embraced [kissed] its own soul, even as two brothers who are come from a strange country, and they were united one with another."[25] The author of this text also quotes Psalm 84:11.

The Judas theme first appeared in Christian art during the second half of the fourth century, and the scene of the kiss was rendered frequently on Theodosian sarcophagi. Then, however, Judas's figure was not yet semitized or demonized and resembled closely that of Jesus. On a marble sarcophagus from the end of the fourth or the beginning of the fifth century (school of Ravenna, in the crypt of San Giovanni's in Vale, Verona) a handsome young Judas caresses Christ, also a youth. This tradition can be traced later as well. For instance in Giotto's *Kiss of Judas* (Scrovegni Chapel, Padua), Jesus and his betrayer fuse, like two lovers, into one. Standing at Christ's left, Judas puts his arm around the body of the Lord, covering it with his yellow coat. Their faces, although dissimilar in character and expression, are shown in perfect symmetry with each other. Such images reflect a long history of speculations concerned with the relationship of Jesus and Judas. In particular the Gnostic writings interpret the two men in the dualistic terms of the eternal twins as they are known in Zoroastrianism. The bad one, like Ahriman, stands for darkness and destruction, the good one, like Ohrmazd, for light and life. In the Bible the traitor is called a devil by Christ and the other Apostles. Thus he could be identified with Satan or considered as Satan's servant. In the Syriac Acts of Thomas, Judas is bribed to betray Jesus by the same serpent which enticed Eve, moved Cain, and hardened the heart of the Pharaoh.[26]

The concept of a doublet, a coincidence of opposites, was also nourished by several confusions. First of all, the author of the biblical Epistle of Saint Jude the Apostle claimed to be "the brother of James." At the time when he wrote his epistle there was no one of prominence in the Church with the name of James except the Apostle James the Less, who is referred to as one of the "brethren of the Lord" (Gal. 1:19). He had a brother named Jude (Matt. 13:55; Mark 6:3), and a "Jude of James" is also given in Luke's list of the Apostles (Luke 6:16; Acts 1:15). On the other hand, one of the twelve Apostles was Thomas, whose Aramaic name or surname was translated by John into Greek as Didymus (twin). According to the Acts of Thomas he was the twin brother of Jesus himself. This tradition seems to be derived from the name Judas Thomas, which he bears in an Edessene legend,[27] and implies the identification of Thomas with Judas, the twin brother of the Lord.

But Beardsley's female-looking Jesus can also be defined as hermaphroditic. This presents us with another fusion—the fusion of two sexes into one. The Chinese yin and yang form a sphere. A perfect, original being is described by Plato (*Symposium* 89:193) as spherical and bisexual. When it was split into two halves, love came into existence: the two halves pursuing each other eternally in the desire to merge into one.

Androgyny has been attributed to gods in many religions. Bisexual divinities are frequently worshiped in Eastern religions and they populate the Indian pantheon. The Greek cult of the Hermaphroditus can be traced back to the East; it coincided with the cult of Aphrodite and had its oldest seat in Cyprus. There the bearded statue of a male Aphrodite, Aphroditus, was worshiped and apparently identified with the moon; at his celebrations men and women became transvestites, exchanging their clothing with each other.[28] Hermaphroditus originally meant Aphrodite in the form of a herm, a quadrangular pillar topped with a head or a bust. However, later legends explained the name as meaning the son of Hermes and Aphrodite. This version was popularized by Ovid's *Metamorphoses*, in which the child was called Hermaphroditus because he resembled both his father and his mother. The naiads brought up the boy in a cave on Mount Ida and delighted in his beauty. The nymph Salamis fell in love with the charming boy and, when he was bathing in a stream, fell upon him, raped him, and prayed to the gods to be forever united with him. They granted her the favor, and thus the boy and the girl grew into each other, becoming one bisexual being—an obvious illustration of the Greek concept of love.

In the metaphoric language of the Christian writers, Jesus as well as God the Father could change sex or, when united with the Virgin or the diverse female personifications (anima, ecclesia), they could be viewed as androgynous. The Christian mystics and heretics delighted in the idea of a bisexual God, as did the Jewish Kabbalists and, following in their footsteps, the Romantics and the decadents. Jakob Böhme (1575–1624), the heretical German mystic, regarded all perfect beings, Christ as well as the angels, as androgynous. He believed that the deprivation of the original hermaphrodite happened while it was asleep, and he expressed the hope that through Christ's sacrifice humans would be able to regain their lost bisexuality. Böhme's ideas influenced the German Romantics, for whom androgyny was an ideal. Franz Xaver von Baader (1765–1841) saw in the sacrament of marriage the restitution of heavenly and angelic bisexuality and proclaimed that androgyny, which had existed at the beginning of time, would return at its end. Similarly, in his essay "Über die Diotima," Friedrich von Schlegel called for the reintegration of both sexes until androgyny could be achieved.[29] In England Swinburne declared that in the art of late Hellenism there existed nothing more charming than the figures of the sleeping hermaphrodite;[30] and the French satanist Joseph Péladan wrote a hymn to the androgynous god, praising him as the pinnacle of beauty and perfection.[31] Beardsley's representation of Jesus as a beautiful sleeping hermaphrodite fits into this tradition and perhaps also alludes to the fact that while it was worshiped in religion, art, and poetry, in real life the hermaphrodite was regarded as either a freak of nature or as a passive and impotent, sleepy "saint," predestined to become the victim of violence and cruelty. Unaware of any thirst for the opposite sex, the androgyne incarnated total innocence and thus attracted passionate, sadistic lovers who, like the nymph Salamis, the princess Salome, and the Apostle Judas, desired to consume the hermaphrodite with a kiss. Beardsley drew the Baptist and Christ as victims of insatiable, obscene love and obviously saw the figures of Salome and Judas as related to each other. Although he was certainly unaware of it, such an analogy had already been made. In the play *La vida y muerte de Judas* the seventeenth-century Spanish playwright Damián Salustio del Poyo made Judas the son of Herod and Herodias![32]

The ambiguous and perverse eroticism of Beardsley's *Kiss of Judas* reflects, of course, the homosexual speculations that have probably surrounded Jesus and his disciples ever since the remarks of Paul, who in his second Epistle to the Corinthians wrote to the brothers that he betrothed them to "one spouse" (God) so that they might be presented to Christ as "chaste virgin[s]" (11:2). In the world of male intimacy, as depicted, for instance, by Leonardo in his *Last Supper* (Maria delle Grazie, Milan), Judas differs from the other Apostles only in having his face obscured by a shadow.

Judas's Apocryphal Life

The Arabic *Evangelium infantiae Jesu Christei* tells of Judas, a child possessed by the devil, who is brought to the small Jesus in order to be exorcised by him.[33] On this occasion the bad boy tries to bite the good one. He does not succeed but instead strikes Jesus on the right side, the very same spot which was opened by the lance of the Roman soldier after Christ's expiration on the cross (John 19:34). The apocryphal scene represents a counterpart to the popular Christian depiction of Jesus and John the Baptist as two baby angels, and it sheds light on Beardsley's horrible Judas-putto. While official illustrations of the Bible always rendered Judas as an adult, medieval legends display a profound interest in the rest of his life and strongly emphasize his earliest childhood.[34] They also remove from the traitor the heavy burden of responsibility by pointing out that Judas was as much predestined to play his evil role as Jesus was to become the Savior. The legendary biography which achieved the greatest popularity was written in the thirteenth century by the Genuese monk Jacobus of Voragine.[35] His account, based on older sources and frequently copied and imitated by later writers, displays many stereotypes frequently found in the mythologized lives of famous people. Judas's birth, like that of the Savior, is prophesied in advance. Not, however, by the appearance of a heavenly messenger, but in a dream. Cyborea, the mother of Judas, learns about her bad luck in the darkness of the night. She dreams that the son with whom she is pregnant will become a menace to his own father, to God, and to the entire Jewish people. Unable to kill the child, she gets rid of it in a way rooted in ancient tradition. The baby is given the name Judas, put in a basket, like Romulus and Remus as well as Moses,[36] and thrown into the sea. The basket floats to the island Iscariot[37] and is found on the shore by the local queen. Being childless, she decides, upon seeing a fair infant, to adopt Judas and to raise him as her own son. However, soon afterwards she becomes pregnant and gives birth to her own male child. The boys grow up together and are marked, of course, by very opposite traits of character. The meek-hearted true prince is constantly tortured by his wicked brother. Finally, in accordance with the Cain-Abel pattern, Judas kills him and flees from Iscariot to Jerusalem. There he enters into the service of Pilate[38] and strikes up a friendship with the governor of Judea, who, one day seeing ripe apples in the neighboring garden, orders Judas to fetch them. Like Eve, who by listening to the serpent caused the fall of humanity, Judas precipitates his own crime by obeying Pilate's words. The garden belongs to Judas's father, Simeon (or Ruben), who surprises the thief and is killed by him. But the anonymous author(s) are not satisfied with the slaying of a brother and a father. They turn Judas into an Oedipus as well. Pilate presents the murderer with the garden and the widow. Judas marries Cyborea and they live happily together until the day when, by telling each other about their earlier lives, they discover the horrible truth. In despair, Judas decides to do penance. He joins Jesus, attains his confidence, and is made responsible for his finances. He steals as much as he can and finally sells his Lord for thirty denarii.

In his analysis of grotesque elements in *Wuthering Heights* Geoffrey Harpham interprets Heathcliff as the impersonation of a negative force, a demon, coming out of nowhere and bringing chaos into the normal course of events.[39] His appearance, like that of Judas, makes things turn obscene, incestuous, deadly. A riddle and a bastard, he incarnates the mythical figure of the eternal disturber of the peace—and promotes the grotesque.

Among the crimes committed by Judas, incest appears to be particularly interesting because of its parallel in the life of Jesus. Mary, the product of an Immaculate Conception, is the daughter of a mortal woman and God the Father, who makes her pregnant by infusing into her the Holy Spirit. The Savior is conceived through the union of Mary with her Father or, alternatively, with the Holy Spirit. Christ's mother is simultaneously his sister, and she is also viewed as his bride and spouse, thus acting as the beloved of the entire Holy Trinity. Saint Ambrose, the bishop of Milan, was the first to coalesce the Virgin, the Church, and each Christian soul with the beloved Shulamite of the Song of Songs.[40] He was followed by the medieval mystics. Amadeus, the twelfth-century bishop of Lausanne, admonishes the Virgin to hurry in preparing the bed in which she will receive her bridegroom, the Holy Spirit.[41] Announcing that her creator will also become her husband, Amadeus describes how she will be embraced, kissed, and fecundated by the divine lover. Similarly, the mystics saw the soul become pregnant through divine infusion. Saint Aelred of Rievaulx speaks of the Annunciation as a marriage of the Son and the Virgin, with the angel acting as best man and the incarnated Christ coming out of Mary's womb like a bridegroom from the bedroom.[42] In all these fantasies, obscene as they sound, incest is a vehicle of sublimation; it elevates human females to the sphere of the divine, spiritual, and eternal; it promotes the Christian ideal of sexual purity and is considered a sanctified miracle and an example of chastity. In the thirteenth-century homily *Holy Maidenhead*, the delights of a mystical marriage to Christ are contrasted with the horrors of physical marriage to men.[43] To promote the vision of an even more virginal Immaculate Conception, a late medieval legend proclaims that Mary was conceived not *ex coitu* but *ex osculo*—through a kiss.[44]

Incest among humans, on the other hand, is denounced as much as possible. It remains, however, an intriguing fact that in the stories of both Jesus and Judas, those who actively initiate and engage in incest perform a killing: God delivers his son, his rival; and Judas murders his father to become the suitor of his mother. It seems that the legendary lives of Christ's betrayer touch upon the hidden obscenity of the biblical story. They reflect also the recognition that the son who submits to the authority of the father is—a saint; the son who gets rid of the father in order to possess the mother—a villain; the first fits into the paternal design, the second disturbs it. The image of the crucified Savior is projected onto the divine male screen of the sky; it is transfused with light, composed of sublimating metaphors. The grotesque picture of the traitor is depicted against a material and maternal background, with spilt blood and faecalia (gushing out of his bursting stomach). On the margin of a fourteenth-century manuscript,[45] little Judas is represented with a naked bottom, squatting indecently before the Iscariot queen, who punishes him for his bad behavior. This crude image is the reverse of the icon of the Madonna, who may proudly and solemnly disclose the genitals of her son but never show the viewer his anus.

Beardsley's figures of Salomé are fashioned after the ancient goddesses of earth and night. The dwarfish, naked Judas appears as the child of this underground Venus: a messenger of sleep and death. Both in the illustrations to Wilde's play and in *The Kiss of Judas* the heroic new gods of light are subdued by the ancient forces of darkness—by powerful females and their infant sons. This vision of a subordinated Judas is reflected in several legends that explain his wicked deeds as inspired by a woman. In a thirteenth-century English ballad,[46] for instance, Judas sets out on Thursday for Jerusalem to buy food with thirty pieces of silver. On his way he meets his sister, who derides him for believing in the false prophet and induces him to go to sleep with his head in her lap; upon awakening he discovers that the silver has been stolen. To recover his loss, he makes a bargain with a rich Jew by the name of Pilate, to whom he sells his Lord for thirty stolen pieces of silver. The idea of female responsibility was derived from Gnostic apocrypha. For instance, in the Coptic Gospel of the Twelve Apostles it is the wife of Judas who incites his villainy.[47] A woman of insatiable avarice, she makes her husband steal from his Lord's bag and, not satisfied with small sums, suggests the treachery to Judas (who listens to her like Adam to Eve) as a way of obtaining a larger profit. By being connected with femininity, the avarice of Judas is thus further debased and put into striking contrast with Jesus' extreme generosity. However, grotesque travesties of Christ's sublime character occasionally reflect common sense. In the Huldreich text of the *Toldoth Jeschu* (*Historia Jeschuae Nazareni*, 1705)[48] Jesus, Peter, and Judas stop in an inn on their journey from Rome to Jerusalem. They are very hungry but cannot find anything to eat except for a goose that is not sufficient for three people. Jesus then decides that the one who has the best dream would be entitled to devour the bird. In the morning it turns out that the Lord, indeed, had dreamed something amazing. But when he looks for the goose he cannot find it because Judas had arisen in the night and consumed it himself.

In Beardsley's *Kiss of Judas* the sleeping Jesus leans against a tree so twisted that it looks about to be transformed into a cross. Whether consciously or not, the artist seems to allude to the widespread and frequently illustrated ancient legends that identify Christ with Adam and the paradisiac tree of knowledge with the cross. In the sixth-century Syrian version of the Adam and Eve story which C. Bezold published in 1883 under the title *Schatzhöhle,* the tokens from paradise—gold, incense, and myrrh—are buried together with the corpse of Adam in the cave of treasures to which the parents of humanity were exiled. When the flood occurs, God instructs Noah to bring with him the body of Adam and the souvenirs from the garden. Later the corpse and the treasures are buried in the center of the earth—at Golgotha. From this new cave the three holy kings take the gold, incense, and myrrh and present the tokens from paradise to the Jesus child.

The ancient motif was elaborated by Gottfried of Viterbo in his complicated story of the money with which Judas was rewarded.[49] The thirty pieces of silver were coined by Ninus, the legendary Assyrian king, and passed into the hands of Joseph's brothers, who sold him into Egyptian slavery. Through the intermediary of Sheba and Solomon, the coins came into the possession of the three kings who gave them to the Jesus child. However, fleeing to Egypt, the Virgin left the silver behind. It was found by shepherds and for thirty years kept by an Armenian who returned the treasures to Jesus. The thirty coins were offered by the generous Christ to the temple in Jerusalem and, after his betrayal, paid to Judas. Thus pure gold of paradise was degraded into dirty money—a vehicle of evil.

Rehabilitation and Transformation of Judas

The transformation of Judas from a villain to a hero was promoted by heretical writings. Irenaeus (1.31.1), Epiphanius (38.1.3), and Theodoretus all mention the existence of the *Evangelium Judae Ischariotis,* which was used by the Gnostic sect of the Cainites. They regarded the treachery of Judas as a positive deed because it led to the Crucifixion, through which the salvation of humanity could alone be attained. Similarly, Thomas de Quincey, in his famous essay "Judas Iscariot" (1852), portrayed Jesus as a man who had to be "precipitated into action by a force without," and Judas as the one who "supposed himself executing the very innermost purposes of Christ." Judas hoped that "when at length actually arrested by the Jewish authorities, Christ would no longer vacillate; he would be forced into giving the signal to the populace of Jerusalem, who would then have risen unanimously, for the double purpose of placing Christ at the head of an insurrection movement, and of throwing off the Roman yoke."[50]

Hebbel, after he published three tragedies dealing with religious material (*Judith,* 1841; *Maria Magdalene,* 1844; *Herodes und Mariamne,* 1850), planned to write a play that would have rehabilitated the figure of Judas. Read during his lifetime only in the intimate circle of his friends, his preliminary sketches for the drama display a concept similar to Goethe's *Faust.* Faust was to be replaced by Christ, Mephisto by Lucifer, while Judas was to personify the zealot who, as the only Apostle, understood God's prophecy and promoted the death of Jesus in order to immortalize him. Wagner also considered writing a *Jesus-Drama* (1843) in which Judas was to be portrayed as an ardent patriot. And around 1848, when movements of national liberation shook Europe, the figure of Judas was frequently interpreted in the context of political struggle.[51]

A century earlier another approach was taken by Friedrich Gottlieb Klopstock, who throughout his life was fascinated by the relationship between the Lord and his pupils. While still in school, he drafted the plan of his *Messias* and continued to work on this epic poem during his study of theology at the university in Jena. The first three cantos of the *Messias* were published anonymously in 1748 in the magazine *Bremer Beiträge,* the last five appearing twenty-five years later. Hypersensitive, solitary, and melancholic, Klopstock developed a passion for Judas. He defended the betrayal as an act of jealousy, despair, and vengeance for the secret and unrequited love that Judas felt for Jesus while the Lord favored John.[52] The motif of jealousy was taken up by Joseph Ernest Renan in his *Life of Jesus* (1863).

The Christian practice of portraying Judas as the typical Jew was derided by Heine, who remarked ironically: "As I know the Jews, the personality of this disciple of the Savior has always remained incomprehensible to me. What he did is as little a part of Jewish character as incendiarism and brigandage; I would hesitate to issue a certificate of marital faithfulness to Madame Iscariot, his mother, especially since the Roman centurions, as Josephus claims, were very partial to those beautiful Jewesses."[53]

Interested neither in history and politics nor in Judas's biography, the decadents pushed to extremes the erotic motifs of his story and interpreted the figure of the traitor in terms of morbid infantile homosexuality which mixed love with death. Curious, phantasmal links between Judas and Jesus were established in the grotesque "Ballad of Judas Iscariot" by the English poet Robert Buchanan (1841–1901). The poem was written in the years 1878–83 and its imagery and tone are typical of the last quarter of the nineteenth century. The "Ballad" begins with a vision of the traitor as a double figure. Judas is split into a dead body and a living soul, which is referred to as "he":

> Black was the earth by night,
> And black was the sky;
> Black, black were the broken clouds,
> Tho' the red Moon went by.
>
> 'Twas the body of Judas Iscariot
> Strangled and dead lay there;
> 'Twas the soul of Judas Iscariot
> Look'd on it in despair.[54]

Like a loving Antigone, the soul decides to bury the body, and in order to find a suitable place for it, begins to walk through the world carrying the corpse:

> For months and years, in grief and tears,
> He walked the silent night;
> Then the soul of Judas Iscariot
> Perceived a far-off light.[55]

When the soul approaches the lit house, the world turns wintry. "The ghost of the silvern Moon" arises "holding her yellow lamp," and the scene of the Last Supper is remembered:

> And the icicles wore on the eaves,
> And the walls were deep with white,
> And the shadows of the guests within
> Pass'd on the window light.

The shadows of the wedding guests
Did strangely come and go,
And the body of Judas Iscariot
Lay stretch'd along the snow.
....

And of every flake of falling snow,
Before it touched the ground,
There came a dove, and a thousand doves
Made sweet sound.

'Twas the body of Judas Iscariot
Floated away full fleet,
And the wings of the doves that bore it off
Were like its winding-sheet.

'Twas the Bridegroom stood at the open door,
And beckon'd, smiling sweet;
'Twas the soul of Judas Iscariot
Stole in, and fell at his feet.

"The Holy Supper is spread within,
And the many candles shine,
And I have waited long for thee
Before I poured the wine!"

The supper wine is poured at last,
The lights burn bright and fair,
Iscariot washes the Bridegroom's feet,
And dries them with his hair.[56]

After the body of Judas has been carried away by doves—the symbol of the Holy Spirit, the Virgin, and Aphrodite as well— the "Ballad" ends with a reversal of the Last Supper, at which it was Jesus who washed the feet of the Apostles. But the long hair of the Judas-soul brings to mind other biblical scenes. In the Pharisee's house an anonymous fallen woman (confounded with Mary Magdalen, to whom the anointment has been traditionally attributed) "brought an alabaster jar of ointment; and standing behind him at his feet, she began to bathe his feet with her tears, and wiped them with the hair of her head, and kissed his feet, and anointed them with ointment" (Luke 7:37–38). Asked why he allowed this sinner to touch him, Christ answered the owner of the house: "I came into thy house; thou gavest me no water for my feet; but she has bathed my feet with tears, and has wiped them with her hair. Thou gavest me no kiss; but she, from the moment she entered, has not ceased to kiss my feet. . . . Wherefore I say to thee, her sins, many as they are, shall be forgiven her, because she has loved much" (Luke 7:44–47).

Matthew, Mark, and John tell a slightly different story. They mention that the disciples were indignant that the entire jar of precious ointment, which could have been sold in order to give money to the poor, was wasted on Jesus (Matt. 26:7–9; Mark 14:3–5). In John's narrative the anointment occurs twice and is performed by Mary of Bethany (equally confounded with Mary Magdalen), the sister of Lazarus, whom Jesus raised from the dead (John 11:1–3). At the second anointment, six days before Passover, Mary took "a pound of ointment, genuine nard of great value, and anointed the feet of Jesus, and with her hair wiped his feet dry. And the house was filled with the odor of the ointment. Then one of his disciples, Judas Iscariot, he who was about to betray him, said, 'Why was this ointment not sold for three hundred denarii, and given to the poor?' Now he said this, not that he cared for the poor, but because he was a thief, and holding the purse, used to take what was put in it. Jesus therefore said, 'Let her be—that she may keep for the day of my burial. For the poor you have always with you, but you do not always have me' " (John 12:3–8). It is, of course, this passage which inspired Buchanan, who, at the end of his poem, transferred the action of Mary, a loving woman, to the soul of Judas, the very disciple who was angry with her for wasting the precious perfume on the Lord. Before it inspired the English poet, the biblical passage had influenced many medieval legends in which Judas sold Christ to recover the loss caused by Mary's extensive care.[57]

Buchanan transformed the traitor's soul (an animus and not an anima) into the effeminate, loving male bride and combined in the Judas figure reminiscences of Eros and Anteros, Thanatos, Hermaphroditus and Psyche as well as echoes of Christ's ambiguous relationship with Judas and the Savior's erotic union with women and souls. His perverse Judas is close to the Beardsley putto, and the difference between the poet and the artist consists chiefly in the sentimentality of the first as opposed to the irony of the second. The nocturnal and wintry landscape of the poem seems to foreshadow the lunar scenery of Wilde's *Salomé* and the Jewish princess's pursuit of another saint.

During the late nineteenth century, references were made to Judas outside of England as well.[58] He played, for instance, a significant role in satanism and black magic (fig. 135). But in no other country was he represented in the equally grotesque form of a libidinous Amor. What was the reason for this extremely daring vision? Beardsley knew. When asked why the English decadents and dandies surpassed all others in their sacrilegious extravagances, he pointed out that no other country had achieved a similar degree of puritan bigotry, and thus a forceful reaction was bound to occur.[59]

Indeed, the iconography of English literature and art at this time is strong stuff, and all against the grain. So it seems that it was not for nothing that Victorian poets and artists explored the obscure grotto of the past. Obviously they learned there how to answer simple orthodox questions: with riddles.

FIG. 125 Aubrey Beardsley, *The Kiss of Judas.*

FIG. 126 *Judas Entering the Garden of Gethsemane to Betray Christ*, high relief, Flemish or German, fifteenth century.

FIG. 127 Sarcophagus with Selene and Endymion, Roman, first half of second century A.D.

FIG. 128 François Augier (1604–69), the funerary representation of Jacques de Souvré.

FIG. 129 Joos van Cleve (1485–1540/41), *The Infants Jesus and Saint John the Baptist*.

FIG. 130 Philipp Otto Runge (1777–1810), *The Morning*.

Fɪɢ. 131 Philipp Otto Runge, *The Day.*

FIG. 132 Hieronymus Bosch (ca. 1450–1516), *John the Baptist.*

FIG. 133 The hanging of Judas, Cathedral of Saint Lazare, Autun, twelfth century.

FIG. 134 Antonio Canova (1757–1822), *Psyche Re-animated by the Kiss of Amor.*

FIG. 135 Henry de Malvost, *The Evocation of the Devil*, in
Jules Bois's *Le satanisme et la magie* (1896).

FIG. 136 Aubrey Beardsley, *The Black Cape*.

FIG. 137 *Miss Prattle Consulting Doctor Double Fee about Her Pantheon Head Dress,* anonymous English engraving, early eighteenth century.

FIG. 138 Aubrey Beardsley, *Lucian's Strange Creatures*.

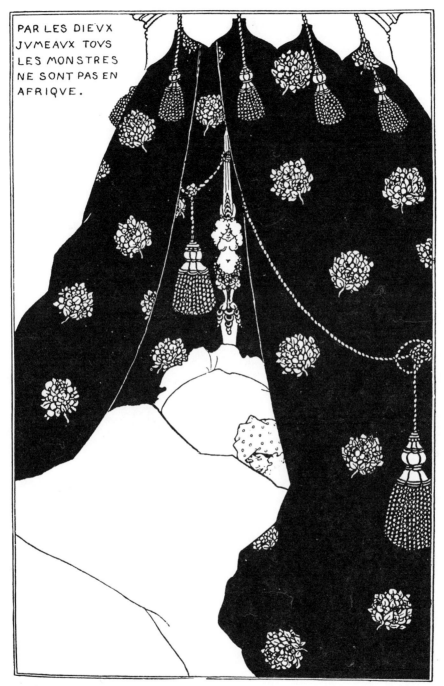

FIG. 139 Aubrey Beardsley, *Portrait of Himself*.

FIG. 140 Workshop of Lorenz or Stephan Zick,
Standing cups and covers, seventeenth century.

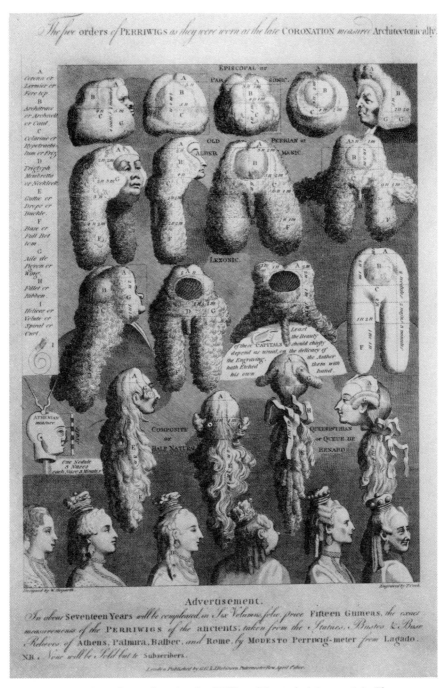

FIG. 141 Engraving after a drawing by William Hogarth (1697–1764), *The Five Orders of Perriwigs as They Were Worn at the Late Coronation Measured Architectonically.*

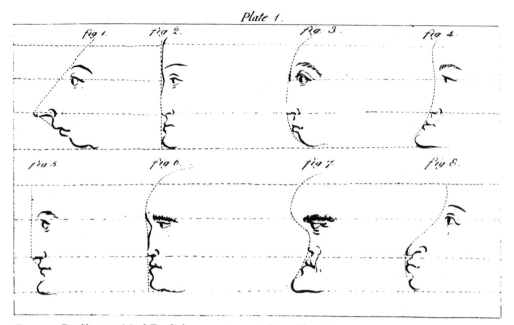

FIG. 142 Profiles, satirical English engraving, eighteenth century.

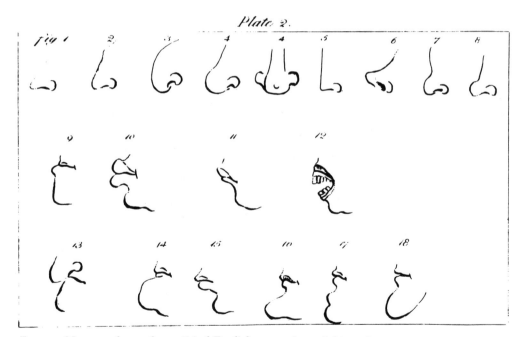

FIG. 143 Noses and mouths, satirical English engraving, eighteenth century.

FIG. 144 Aubrey Beardsley, Initial V.

FIG. 145 Aubrey Beardsley, Initial M.

FIG. 146 Franz von Pocci (1805–76), *Jewish Merchants*.

FIG. 147 Aubrey Beardsley, *The Death of Pierrot*.

Brief Survey of Techniques of Grotesque Art

Chapter 11
Distorting Techniques

The foregoing analysis of iconography suggests formal procedures which grotesque artists used in their work. The key words are debasement, distortion, displacement, and heterogeneity, but it makes sense to look systematically at exactly what they did.

Separation, Mixture, and Reassembly

In the grotesque, as in an anatomical theater, whole entities and parts of reality, cultural icons, and, in short, any things that belonged together were separated, dissected, torn apart, and dispersed. Fantastic creatures and exotic pictures, as well as parts of them, could also undergo separation. But this was of secondary importance because of the viewers' inability to notice distortions in something already unusual while it was experienced as a shock when what was popular and traditional was broken to pieces. The separated elements were recombined into new entities which might seem absurd but usually were not. One could read their messages if one had the right key, which was symbolic and mythological, secret and unorthodox.

Antiquity had possessed a fixed repertoire of mixed beings, satyrs, sirens, harpies, centaurs, sphinxes, winged souls, and cupids, that was assimilated by the grotesque, becoming its most conventional source of heterogeneity. Androgyny, a favorite subject of grotesque artists, also implied mixture, as did such themes as that of Salome, a woman with the incongruous head of a man in her hands, or that of the world as a theater-stage where heroes and heroines from different periods and cultures mixed with each other in one play, where costumes, masks, attributes, and vistas distant in space and time were combined in a single scene.

Duplication and Multiplication

The techniques of duplication and multiplication can partly be seen as a subgroup of the previous category. For instance, a necklace made of a human skull or head results from separation and rearrangement. The same is true when the necklace, like that of the Indian goddess Kali, consists of many heads which clearly serve to multiply horror. But when several heads are shown growing out of the same body, the grotesque effect is of a different order; it is associated not with dismemberment but with uncontrolled spontaneous fertility as characteristic of the gemmation of lower organisms and suggests the uncontrolled procreative power of nature. Duplication and multiplication can be found frequently in the ancient images of divinities responsible for birth and child-raising as, for instance, the statue of Diana of Ephesus, furnished with many breasts, or that of the Japanese Kannon of Hase, with its small heads on top of one colossal head. Although the dancing Indian divinities with multiple hands convey chiefly the optical illusion of movement, a sense of natural richness and power is also emanated through them, as it is in the multitude of tiny figures protected by the mantle of a Madonna in the medieval representations of the "Schutzmantelmadonna" type: wooden statues which open like boxes and disclose a crowd of humans hidden like embryos between the folds of the Virgin's coat.

Idols with multiple heads, hands, and feet were popular in oriental religions, which flooded the late Greco-Roman world. Early Christianity fought fiercely against pagan pansexuality; so, not surprisingly, it regarded multiplication as an obscene monstrosity. In John's Revelation the great whore of Babylon (fig. 118), "the mother of the harlotries and of the abominations of the earth" (17:5), sits on a beast with seven heads and ten horns (17:3). This monster turns out to be the entire material earth and the fleshly and corrupt part of humanity opposed to heavenly Jerusalem and Christ's followers, who reject matter and believe in the victory of the spirit. Befitting this tradition, the multiplication of bodily parts was seen in the Christian world as a sign of beastly fertility, and the multiple forms were reserved mainly for the inhabitants of hell or the messengers of the apocalypse. Working against cultural norms, the artists of the fantastic and grotesque delighted in this procedure.

Elongation and Compression, Enlargement and Miniaturization

Techniques of elongation and compression, enlargement and miniaturization can be applied to every particular element of a composition or to the whole object or image. The elongation and compression of a two-dimensional figure was probably suggested as early as prehistoric times by the changing character of a shadow, man's earliest companion. Beardsley was a master of this kind of shadow-like enlargement and compression, and thus the character of these transformations can best be understood when one considers a few of his drawings in detail.

In *The Black Cape* (fig. 136) Salomé is lost in her overwhelmingly large black dress; and her enormous chignon, inspired by the exaggerated fashion of the eighteenth century (fig. 137), makes her head look as small as a child's fist. In fact it is fifteen times smaller than her body. In *The Peacock Skirt* her dress is so long that it overflows the edges of the picture and makes her look even more enormous. A small peacock in the background, whose proportions resemble those of the princess, emphasizes Salomé's animalistic nature. In other drawings similar manipulations of proportion combine with zoomorphic elements or patterns (wings, scales) to transform Herodias's daughter into a flying serpent, a moth, or a mantis.

Beardsley's ideal of female beauty is personified by the naked girl in *The Mysterious Rose Garden* (fig. 69). Her head is one-fourteenth of the figure and her proportions are identical with those of Venus as described in Beardsley's novel: "From the hip to the knee twenty-two inches; from the knee to the heel twenty-two inches, as befitted a Goddess" (VT, pp. 30–31). If we apply these measurements to the *Rose Garden* girl, she turns out to be 192 cm—quite a size for a woman! A further elongation of the female body in other drawings makes it appear like a flower on a stem.

Most men in Beardsley's drawings are smaller and plumper than his women. The most handsome among the boys have a head-to-body proportion of 10:1 or 11:1, but perspective as well as size makes them look insignificant. They are rarely in the foreground or in the center of a picture, and obviously they fulfill a subordinate function. Thus we see a monumental sleeping Salomé who looks like a mountain and is attended by small boys (fig. 57). Beardsley miniaturizes men even in drawings of romantic couples, and the only male figures who get to be as tall and dominating as women are those who imitate them, like Abbé (fig. 101), the hero of *Venus and Tannhäuser*, and Albert, the effeminate lover of the masculine Mademoiselle de Maupin. The difference in size between female and male becomes increasingly disturbing in those drawings where the male principle is represented by dwarfish and embryonic creatures whose heads are larger than their bodies (fig. 138). These monsters greatly resemble the ancient grylli, the walking heads.

The absurd character of Beardsley's figures is further accentuated by the way he distorts body parts. Tiny heads, hands, and feet make women look like birds, reptiles, and insects; huge hands and feet transform men into apes. While enormous coiffures make the women even taller, the same hair style on dwarfs reduces them even further. Long noses become hawkish beaks; small eyes and a beakish nose transform a puffy face into an owl head. Beardsley also changes the proportions of objects, architecture, and landscape. Pompous ladies dominate their gardens, but they, in turn, are sometimes overshadowed by monstrous flowers. Beardsley's self-portrait presents him in a huge canopied bed, his head engulfed by an enormous turban, his body swallowed up by large pompoms (fig. 139). In another self-portrait the artist is tied to a herm which has been miniaturized, but under his arm he has a disproportionately long stick (fig. 82). Nowhere is Beardsley's attitude towards proportion more striking than in his illustrations to Aristophanes' *Lysistrata* (fig. 80). There, short men with huge penises become phallic counterparts of the female genitals transformed in *Venus and Tannhäuser* into a subterranean landscape.

Reversal

Reversal has to be understood in the broadest possible sense. Entire figures or only parts of them, whole images or only fragments of them can be reversed. Left and right, up and down can be exchanged for each other, the negative can be made positive, shadow turned into light, black into white. What should be clothed appears naked, and vice versa. For instance, in Beardsley's *Mysterious Rose Garden* (fig. 69), a travesty of the Annunciation,[1] the angel wears a flowery female dress while the Virgin is completely naked. Often where one expects a man, a woman shows up, as in Félicien Rops's famous *Crucifixion*, in which a voluptuous female is nailed to a cross.[2]

A particularly interesting case involves the reversal or play with dimensions. In drawing and painting, three-dimensional objects can be rendered either as flat figures or, through the use of chiaroscuro, as full bodies. Grotesque artists liked to upset the commonsense concept of what should look flat and what should have volume. For instance, they might flatten the human figure but depict embroidery as three-dimensional. A similar procedure was also applied to sculpture, in which convex surfaces replaced the concave and vice versa.

All of the procedures described so far reflect universal capacities of the human imagination and can be found in all cultures and times. However, since the inventions of camera obscura, glass mirrors, and mirrored cabinets, optical distortions have become an important source of inspiration for artists interested in fantastic images. This has been studied by Jurgis Baltrušaitis, one of the first scholars to examine the influence discontinuous picture planes and curious perspectives had on art (fig. 140).[3]

Simplification and Overcrowding

One can strengthen grotesque effects either by leaving out details, concentrating on the essential features of a figure and isolating them from the rest, or by multiplying forms, lines, and dots as if plagued by a pathological horror of vacuum. A good example of the first procedure is Beardsley's *Black Cape* (fig. 136). Here Salomé has been reduced to a black, S-shaped piece of armor, slightly split in the middle, which reveals a small fragment of a quasi-human body. Thus the serpentine monstrosity of the princess is achieved through the use of a simple outline and the suggestion of a fleeting shadow. In contrast, Beardsley's *Cave of Spleen* (fig. 64) looks as if it is overgrown by tissue. Like the inside of an organism, there is no end to complications and multiplications; every enclosure seems to breed new homunculi. While overcrowding as such makes fantastic effects, simplification per se does not. It must be added therefore that the simplification mentioned here is of a special character: it aims not at simple beauty but at simple monstrosity.

Fantastic Interpretation
and Projection

A cloud resembles a camel or a weasel. The moon reminds us of a face. Two hillocks look like female breasts. A pebble has the form of an ear; a piece of wood that of a man with outstretched arms. Spots on the wall suggest to one person a landscape, to another the profile of a bearded man. William Hogarth's obscene periwigs allude to sexual organs (fig. 141). The tendency to connect accidental shapes and designs with concrete objects and images, to distort familiar figures (figs. 142, 143), and to project one thing onto another lies at the bottom of all art. Cracks in the wall and veins in a stone can suggest a lot to an imaginative person and even more to a great artist. Although Leonardo noted this fact in his diaries, most of the serious European artists cared little for this kind of fantasy. They occasionally let their imaginations go while representing, for instance, strange "landscapes" on the surface of a marble floor, but rarely let the suggestive lines and spots be the center of their vision. However, for the masters of the fantastic and grotesque the interpretation of accidental shapes and contours always played an essential role. Monsters engraved on ancient gems and creatures on medieval margins illustrate this process which seems to lie between daydream and poetry. Like a true artist of the grotesque, Freud discovered the shape of an eagle in the skirt of the Madonna whom Leonardo depicted in the lap of Saint Anna.[4] Looking at Bosch's paintings, I remember games played in childhood with the aim of finding an ever better similarity for some common object—a pear, for instance. What does it look like? Like my mommy; like my bear; like a shoe; like the yellow dress of my sister, etc. To represent mommy, the pear was equipped with feet; to stand for the bear, it was furnished with two ears; to resemble the sister, it was supplied with a ribbon; and in order to look like a shoe, with laces. An inventive mind can explode with similes at the sight of an insignificant spot which other people completely overlook.

The faculty of fantastic association is possessed to a high degree by children and is frequently reflected in primitive art: one can see clearly how the shape of a pebble suggested a seal to an Eskimo. Among ordinary people a heightening of associative faculties may be promoted by exceptional situations that make them blind to the normal order of things and give them instead a new sensibility which makes them see the fantastic in the ordinary. Before going crazy, dying, or committing a crime, one may, like Hamlet, discover an animal in a passing cloud, or remark, like a Hemingway heroine at a decisive moment of her life, that "hills look like white elephants."[5] Strange images come to one's mind and lips when one steps off the common path, crossing over to the uncanny and forbidden. In Max Frisch's novel *Homo Faber* (1957) the incestuous love of a father and a daughter reaches its climax on the last night they spend together on a deserted Greek beach, as if they had returned to an archaic past. Walking along the sea, they compete in finding extravagant comparisons for the night sky, the white rocks, the waves, the trees. The girl does far better than the man, and this alone seems to mark her out for death.

What ordinary people experience so strongly in their agonies, fantastic artists use all the time. There is no end to what a hole, a basket, or a sphere can suggest to an artist like Bosch. Beardsley interprets the protrusions on a head as female breasts (fig. 51); he sees a face in the hump of a hunchback and another head in the stomach (fig. 50). Similarly, a person's rear end can easily be regarded as a face without eyes and nose. At the bottom of all these fantastic interpretations lies the ability to associate, exchange, transform, and project the appearance of one object onto the shape or surface of another, to manipulate perception and memory freely.

Distorting techniques are used by different artists in varying degrees and are not limited to the creation of fantastic and grotesque art; they form a part of every creative process. What makes a work of art strange and uncanny is only the predominance of these tendencies. However, they do not all have to occur at the same time. It is the intensity which determines the various ways and degrees our perceptions are upset and mystified. Fantastic pictures blur borderlines and make it difficult to decide what is what and who is who or to differentiate between living and dead matter. Furnished with parts of humans or animals, objects look animated; and vice versa, bound to things, living creatures seem partly dead. However, the feeling of animation prevails over that of death because of the human tendency to interpret the dead as animate rather than the contrary. This peculiarity may well be inherited from the age of animism (repeated in everyone's childhood), when the difference between animate and inanimate was disregarded and the entire cosmos was perceived as a breathing creature.

Each artist possesses to a different degree the gift of creating extravagant new forms by means of the procedures mentioned above, but most are much more likely to imitate existing fantastic forms than to invent them. They take inspiration from literature and study the monstrosity in the world by exploring the appearances of those humans and creatures, places and situations which contradict established norms and ideals.

Chapter 12
Form and Color

All the distorting procedures listed so far involve the manipulation of form alone. Color, of course, adds a new dimension to any work of art, and consequently a grotesque painting is perceived as different from a grotesque drawing. Although color can by itself create alienating and surprising effects, it does not affect the structure of the grotesque, which is determined largely by the drawing. Color may, as in the paintings of Bosch, make the spectator realize the peculiarities of his vision even better, but it may also obscure and diffuse attention by providing far greater aesthetic pleasure than black and white can achieve. Kayser has already remarked that drawing seems to be the ideal medium for expressing the grotesque because of the directness with which a hand, like a seismograph, transmits to paper the flow of the unconscious.[1] This observation, however, does not exhaust the problem of the predominantly graphic character of the grotesque. To come closer to it, one has to ask two questions: (1) In what respect does color differ from black and white? (2) What is the difference between a line and an area of color?

Black and White,
Darkness and Light

Black and white were originally, and to some extent still are, regarded as synonymous for darkness and light. *Melan* signified in Greek not only darkness and blackness but was also associated with dirt, impurity, and opacity. Aristotle identified *leukon* and *melan* with light and darkness and considered them the principal colors from which all others were derived.[2] Indeed, other colors are secondary in the sense that they become visible only in the light. In darkness one cannot see but can discern only the contours of objects through touch. Birth equals the coming out of darkness, death the return to it. In the world of light the newborn baby only gradually learns to recognize different colors. They add to the sense of richness and beauty in the perceived world and offer aesthetic pleasure. In contrast to this pure and disinterested joy, the experience of light and darkness (of day and night, awakening and falling asleep) is of a different order; it represents an experience of great existential depth which forever remains attached to the trauma of birth and the fear of death. Plato (*Philebus*) regarded the perception of color as the source of pure joy which he saw in opposition to sensual pleasure.

The contrast of darkness and light evokes the personal genesis and is enacted again and again in religion and philosophy, literature and art. Cosmogonies depict creation as the separation of darkness and light and/or the appearance of light: "Darkness covered the abyss, and the spirit of God was stirring above the waters. God said, 'Let there be light,' and there was light. God saw that the light was good. God separated the light from the darkness, calling the light Day and the darkness Night. And there was evening and morning, the first day" (Gen. 1:2–5).

While light can be called "good" in the sense that it allows seeing and promotes growth and development, there is no reason to attribute this goodness to the color white. While darkness can be regarded as negative, there is nothing evil about the color black. However, the metaphorical transference of the features of light to white and those of darkness to black has provided humanity with a powerful duality that ever since ancient times has been applied to moral and aesthetic judgments and even today plays a role in religion and ideology, in racism and theories of beauty. For the most part neglecting to indicate colors, the Bible frequently mentions light and darkness as morally antagonistic ways of life. Homer, who has an equally limited range of color, often attaches a positive sense to light, a negative one to darkness. The same can be observed in ancient Indian writings and in mythologies all over the world.[3]

Along with black and white two other basic colors of the Greeks were red, the symbol of blood and fire, of sex and war, of death and worldly majesty, and yellow, or rather ochre, the color of earth. The Greek vases were executed in these four colors, and their exquisite linear depictions became a source of inspiration for all future European draftsmen. Pliny (*Hist. nat.* 35:50; 35:92) enumerates these four colors as those used by the ancient painters. They are identical with the colors of the four castes mentioned in Sanskrit. The Paleolithic cave paintings were also executed in red and yellow ochre, white and black.

In antiquity white pigment was obtained from chalk and lead pits. The most famous white came from the chalk rocks in Melos, Samos, and Crete; lead white was found in Selinunte, Sicily. Black, however, was not taken from nature but was a by-product of destruction. It was obtained from the burning of various organic substances, of ebony (elephant black) or of grapevines (wine black.) It is important to remember this fact, as it played a role in the symbolism of black and white. Aristotle, for instance, liked best of all paintings "leukografesos eikona," pictures made in white.[4]

The Line

Humanity's earliest visual documents consist of lines and outlines inscribed onto different surfaces. Lines drawn on the walls of caves or cut into stone, bone, or wood precede all other forms of visual communication. In pre-classical and early classical Greek painting only outlines were drawn, and color was applied flatly to the surface divided by them. Therefore accuracy of line was considered the essential feature of beauty. Dionysus of Halicarnassus deplored the introduction of chiaroscuro;[5] it made possible the rendition of depth and distance, but at the same time diverted attention from the simplicity, precision, and perfection of the line. The introduction of light and shadow modulation as well as the introduction of colors obscured the clarity of contours and rendered it difficult to "read" the image properly. It is not surprising that ancient writers and philosophers favored drawings and monochromatic pictures over colorful paintings.[6]

When we speak today of having something "in black and white" we are usually referring to a written document. Before writing was invented, drawn and incised marks and signs, pictographs from which all writing was developed, played the role of such documents. Even today a mark made of a few dark lines on a light background (or vice versa) is thought of as a sign with a message rather than as an image to be admired for purely aesthetic reasons. We still tend, in accord with an archaic tradition and the black-on-white character of our writing, to "read" a black-and-white drawing, engraving, or photograph with far greater attention than we do a color image. The more sensitive a person is to color, the less likely he is to "read" carefully the content of a splendidly colorful painting or photograph, and, vice versa, people insensitive to color decipher its meaning more readily. Color, unless applied with economy and an obvious symbolic intention, leads away from content to aesthetic enjoyment. To sum up, one can say that the psychological response to the black-and-white image is determined on the one hand by the experience of light and darkness, on the other by the habit of reading signs and letters.

There exists, however, a basic difference between the perception of a black-and-white image like the photograph, made of the modulation of light and shadow, and that of a linear drawing or print. The first is seen more as a factual, the second more as a symbolic representation. One assumes that a photo or a naturalistic drawing reproduces a fragment of reality at a given time, or a momentary inner vision. The linear rendition, on the other hand, is expected to reflect rather the underlying scheme or structure, the position of objects and people in relation to each other, distances, sizes, etc. It contains some of the characteristics of a map or a plan.

Reading ordinary writing, the eye progresses in a linear way in order to grasp the meaning. In a drawing the meaning is constituted in a different way. The eye does not assign a particular meaning to every form it encounters. It jumps around, trying to comprehend the image as a whole, and only subsequently begins to discern and interpret the details. Outlines are associated with objects recognized from visual perception and from literary description. But this is not all. While reading, one tends to ignore the straightness of an "I," the roundness of an "O," or the doubling of a "W." However, in a drawing at least some meaning is attached to the appearance and direction of a line: when it goes up, it is spontaneously associated with rising; when it goes down, it is perceived as falling. Straight lines and rectangular forms evoke crystals and manmade constructions; round and oval lines and shapes designate the organic world. Stick-like characters penetrating roundish apertures are likely to be perceived in terms of sexuality (everyone understands the obscene grafitti in public toilets or baths, which are exactly the same all over the world).

A linear black-and-white drawing is something of a pictograph, a rebus, and a written word. It contains a grain of the universal symbolism out of which first pictographs and then alphabets developed. I suspect that certain signs found among Egyptian hieroglyphs or ancient Chinese pictographs still provoke in us a psychological response similar to that which determined their meaning. We can still "read" the Egyptian hieroglyphs

flat land	
sun	
conciliation, peace, rest, setting	
mouth	
slope of earth	

as well as the archaic Chinese pictographs for

sun	
moon	
mountains	
eye	

Calligraphy occupies an intermediary position between writing and drawing and represents an important source of the grotesque. In illustrated manuscripts and books the fantastic, semi-calligraphic frames mediate between the pictures and the text; obscenities and monsters intertwine the initial letters, exploring the peculiarities of their shapes and suggesting the existence of a secret meaning hidden between the lines. Indeed, when put together, the initials of chapters may supply the reader with unexpected information, as in *Hypnerotomachia Poliphili.*

Beardsley's three display initials for *Volpone* are charged with meaning. "V," the first letter of "Volpone" and *vir* (man), points down with the aggressivity of an arrow (fig. 144). The "V" is depicted against the background of a priapic herm—an enormous phallus which dominates the entire landscape. The herm consists of both the bearded, horned head of a monstrous satyr and his muscular bust, changing in its lower part into garlands of ripe fruit hanging down the column; instead of arms there is a slight suggestion of wings. The "V" points to the earth, out of which the herm emerges, and it fits into the letter "M," the first letter of the word *mater* (mother). The display initial "M," consisting of two "Vs" turned upside down like a roof, shelters a couple: an opulent Venus and a tiny Amor who approaches her tenderly with outstretched arms (fig. 145). The "M" is flanked on both sides by female columns with multiple breasts which remind us of the statue of Diana of Ephesus.[7] The drawing is packed with obsessive female symbolism, and all the forms are depicted against a black background. Beardsley executed this drawing shortly before his death. More than any other of his works, it makes one think of a return to the primordial grotto. Stripped of frivolity and irony, this portrayal of the mother of love and her son is saturated with tenderness, horror, and sacredness. The child, ready to reenter her womb, brings to mind such places of the childbirth cult as, for instance, the Kannon temple in Hase, Japan.[8] Built over a grotto, it enshrines the feminine-looking image of the deity responsible for raising children. The ground around the temple is covered by tiny statues of children. These replicas of real infants are brought by parents who wish Kannon to take care of them.

Penetration into the belly of a female creature is suggested also by the third display initial, another "V," in *Volpone.* Like the former two it is obviously inspired by the *Hypnerotomachia,* and in particular by Colonna's description of the black elephant (fig. 84) inside of which Poliphilo discovers the statues of a man and a woman. The elephant is worshiped in India as a god of fertility, and in Beardsley's drawing it stands at once for a phallic idol and for the symbolic vessel in which life is hatched and buried. Unlike the previous one, this "V" is situated not on the surface of the earth but underneath a vault. Darkness is suggested by the presence of a candle, a masculine sign standing to the right of the elephant. To its left, a curtain forms the female background for the trunk and the horns of the animal.

Beardsley's three display initials are white, outlined with black. Their straightness and sharpness stand in contrast to the unusual materiality of the pictures that surround them. In contrast with his early work, Beardsley in these late drawings uses fine shades of black and white to make bodies swell and seem to burst with vitality. The penetrating "V" and the sheltering "M" together constitute a mental coincidence of opposites. They are abstractions projected onto the dark, mixed background of nature. Duality in the initials is achieved not so much through the play of positive and negative, light and shadow, male and female, as through the contrast between the constructs of the mind and the complexity of organic life.

Doodles and Ornaments

Black-and-white drawing and linear engraving are both related to doodles, the quasi-automatic writing-drawing which seems to bring to the surface a heterogeneous mixture of visual remembrances and hidden, unarticulated inner conflicts. Doodles do not seem to originate in the need for artistic creation and they are not intended for aesthetic pleasure. Now highly structured, now extremely chaotic, doodles, because of their uncontrolled character, like fingerprints and signatures reflect all at once personal uniqueness, the universal features of the human brain, and the deeply engraved patterns of culture. But doodles are also related to ornaments, in which automatism and spontaneity are overshadowed by the remembrance and imitation of existing patterns. The grotesque on the margins of books, in architecture, on the surface of furniture or utensils oscillates between a doodle and an ornament, between automatic writing-drawing and the reproduction of traditional patterns. In this way the present becomes interwoven with the past, the personal with the typical.

Sculpture and Architecture

Along with drawing and printing, sculpture has to be seen as another domain of the grotesque play of light and shadow. In particular, reliefs and sculptural bands on walls or along roofs are likely to be "read." Fantastic architecture has had a constant influence on the other media. Bosch was inspired by the drolleries and gargoyles of the Cathedral of Saint John in 's Hertogenbosch, and the Roman frescoes suggested a mixture of humans, animals, plants, and architecture. This brings us back to the problem of deadening and animation. In grotesque art and literature stones seem to breathe, while humans, falling asleep among ancient ruins, easily turn into marble statues. The play of light and darkness is thus translated into a drama of life and death. At the core of the grotesque lies the figure of Pygmalion next to the lovely female statue who is coming to life. From Colonna to Beardsley, female matter is magically animated and made dead by men—dreamers and artists, lovers and archeologists.

Shadow Theater

In his famous metaphor of the cave Plato likens human perception of the world to the watching of a shadow play in an artificially lit subterranean grotto. What humans regard as reality is presented as a flat black-and-white projection thrown onto the wall of the cave, their only screen, by a true world which is high above the underground spot. The relation of the true world to the two-dimensional performance is that of a splendid, colorful original to a black-and-white reproduction.[9] This suggestive image is borrowed by Pliny (*Hist. nat.* 35:15) to explain the connection between reality and art that began with the shadow of a man being outlined on the wall by a woman. Neoplatonists translated Plato's shadow metaphor into the metaphor of the mirror. Similarly, the notion of art as the mirror of nature replaced Pliny's concept of the shadow, which was not very suitable in respect to painting. But the vision of life as a shadow play performed in a cave fits exceedingly well both shadow theater and grotesque art in black and white. Both are reductionist media which, by leaving out superficial details, outline with great clarity the contours of figures and indicate the relationship of figures to each other.

Interestingly enough, the history and character of Turkish shadow theater throws light on some essential features of the grotesque: its nature at once ephemeral and symbolic as well as coarse and vulgar. The development of Turkish shadow performance was prompted by the religious orthodoxy of the Ottoman Empire,[10] whose rigid morality was similar to that of the Counter-Reformation in Europe. Moslem iconoclasts viewed with suspicion the popular puppet theaters with their three-dimensional, quite realistic marionettes and trivial, worldly plays. This led at the beginning of the seventeenth century to the replacement of puppets by the less substantial flat figures which, instead of appearing on the stage, were projected onto a screen. In order to satisfy (and mystify) potential critics, all plays were preceded by a truly Platonic prologue, a stylized sequence not connected with the play itself, in which the recitation of a "poem of the curtain" occupied a prominent place. Written in the style of a ghazel, the poem expressed the belief in an ideal world hidden behind the mere "shadows" of reality:

> To the eye of the uninitiated this curtain produces [only]
>   images.
> But to him who knows the signs, symbols of the truth.
>   . . .
> Behold the meanings which are hidden under this [play]!
> It is a show of subtlety intended for the expert ones to
>   understand its subtle points.[11]

After the elevated prologue a more or less rough action followed, frequently taking place in brothels, mental asylums, or hell and displaying monstrosity, madness, and degraded sexuality. The absence of naturalism did not prevent the performances from being explicitly indecent. Shown in shadow, a hunchback, for instance, appeared not less but even more deformed, and tails, horns, huge penises, stomachs, breasts, and buttocks were clearly visible. It seems very likely, because the shadow was identified with obscure secrets of the night, that the shadow plays surpassed the puppet theater in obscenity.

In Europe, a medium related to the puppet and shadow theater involved the cutting out of silhouettes. In this the Germans excelled, and Luise Duttenhofer, a contemporary of Goethe, has to be regarded as the undisputed master of the "Scherenschnitt." Pairing unconventional irony with mythological and embryonical qualities, her cut-out arabesques are ancestors of Beardsley's vignettes. On a less sophisticated level, the German silhouettes played the role of satire and caricature and expressed primitive, popular humor (fig. 146).

Shadow theater brings to mind another primordial spectacle: observation of the moon, the first television, as Nam June Paik called it.[12] Beardsley's illustrations of *Salomé,* a lunar play, reflect his fascination with Japanese woodcuts, an art that seems to be deeply indebted to the play of shadows and contemplation of the night sky. But the motif of life as a play of marionettes or a commedia dell'arte occurs frequently in Beardsley's other drawings as well. The vision obviously comes from his life in a sickbed and his position there as a spectator. But it reflects also a more general attitude that is often adopted by artists of the grotesque: their refusal to take the world seriously. They tend to consider it a mere play of fleeting shadows, a children's game, or a narcotic danse macabre performed on a darkening stage.

As one of his last subjects Beardsley chose the butterfly-like figure of Pierrot. Dressed in a white, loose costume, a combination of nightgown and baby dress, this infantile and androgynous boy with an uncanny and exhausted face functions as the self-portrait of the artist—the dying clown.[13] Beardsley represented him in the cemetery-like settings of a lost Arcady, playing musical instruments, contemplating his pale features in a mirror or holding an hourglass in his left hand: its upper half about to be empty, the lower one to be full. He also drew him buried in the white linen of his bed in a room that is entered by his fellow comedians; walking on their tiptoes, they perform the pantomime of death in his honor (fig. 147).

Epilogue

The grotesque can be grasped only when studied in the context of the erotic and heretic, the apocryphal and sacrilegious. It can only be understood in terms of animosity between Christianity and antiquity and, more generally, in terms of opposition between the official culture and the subculture that fought, negated, and ridiculed it. But the grotesque, unlike satire or caricature, was concerned less with the derision of concrete institutions and events, more with paganism as an anti-image of the Christian world—an overall animated continuum with no ruptures between plants, animals, and humans, a place of transition and transformation. This material, female entity, a chaos of floral, zoomorphic, and anthropomorphic creatures in eternal pursuit of each other, was denounced by Christianity as beastly and corrupt, lacking in spirit and soul. Christ was sacrificed to this evil world in order to redeem it, to liberate it from its fleshly passions by establishing a strict new order—ascetic and puritan. To achieve this goal the Church demonized the old divinities, in particular the goddesses of fertility, the chief antagonists of the new god of love, and the diverse mixed creatures which were all, with the exception of winged cupids and souls transformed into angels, suspected of sodomy. While classical and humanistic aspects of antiquity were incorporated into the new faith, the pagan monstrosity was banished, if not to hell, at least to the outskirts of Christian culture.

The grotesque could not have developed without antiquity. But it was not the Apollonian principle, to speak with Nietzsche, which inspired it but the darker, Dionysian face of the old world. Having its origins in the remains of bestial antiquity, the grotesque in turn was to become concerned with excavation of all that was against the grain, against the canons of religion and the laws of the state, against academic art and sanctioned sexuality, against virtue and holiness, against established institutions, ceremonies, and officially celebrated history. The artists of the grotesque unearthed obscure folk legends and secret doctrines and never tired of exploring the realms of the obscene and criminal, that which was shadowy, subterranean, and macabre.

Having its origins in the symbolism of the natural as well as the artificial cave, the grotesque came to represent a place of passage between nature and culture. The grotto, as described in this book, stood both for a real location—the earthly and bodily cavity—and for its diverse metaphors: boxes, vessels, closets, rooms, buildings, ruins, and tombs. The cave acted for centuries as a powerful symbol that influenced philosophy and literature, visual arts and architecture, alchemy, anatomy, and many other disciplines of European culture. Certain aspects of cave symbolism changed with time; others persisted.

The image of the cave can be viewed as an archetype resulting from the predominantly male erotic reverie (women probably dreamt of the grotto as well but because of their silent history we know little about their dreams) that compared the earth with the female body and its cavities with the female genitals. Thus one understands why the fantastic and obscene art found in the Roman ruins was connected to the grotto of Diana; why the grotesque became associated with a particularly suspect part of the past, and with sex, the forbidden zone of Christianity. The symbolism of the cave suited heterosexual as well as homosexual men because the grotto could function not only as a vagina and a uterus but also as an anus. Dreams of penetration, incest, and regression could be projected onto this sexualized landscape. Finally, both sexes perceived the dark and watery cavity as the internal space enclosed by the body, as the seat of the organic impurities common to all humans, and as the residence of one's unique mind, spirit, or soul. The fact that the soul was conceived in the European tradition as a volatile female added further complexity to the symbolism of the cave and led to the creation of metaphors which linked sexual drive to the exploration of one's own or another person's self. This colored the language of mystics, philosophers, and poets with eroticism and made the masters of the grotesque deride with obscene terms the search of a man for his muse or anima.

The moving force of the grotesque world was eros. It was injected into landscape and architecture, and, allegorized in different ways, it appeared as a winged boy or a horned satyr, a chevalier or a beast, a dwarf and an embryo who explored the female garden, island, or planet of love, a subterranean paradise. In this setting stones breathed and water was omnipresent, supplying fantastic images of sea monsters and, on the formal level, wave-like, serpentine lines. In the nineteenth century this dark stream was connected to the flow and the depth of the unconscious. Thus the decadents saw in the grotesque the reflection of an obscure inner "aquarium" and used the particular symbolism of this genre as a means for approaching submerged territories.

Occupied with the extremes of love and death, the artists of the grotesque oscillated between sadism and masochism but had a stronger inclination for the second. This probably resulted from the imagery of global femininity by which they felt surrounded—and imprisoned. From this point of view they had no other choice but to represent men as inferior and dependent beings, as children or tiny old men soon to be returned to the place of birth. Perceived as two sides of the same coin, love and death were always in danger of turning into one another. While grotesque artists depicted the uninterrupted chain of growth and dissolution, they derived their shocking effects by questioning the existence of heavenly eternity and the ultimate victory of light over the forces of darkness. Openly disputing this victory, they brought the most cunning enemies of the Christian faith to the foreground as winners and heroes—as figures quite different from their representations in canonical writings and pictures. Not the paganism of Herod but the passion of Salome caused the head of Christ's precursor to roll off his neck. And Judas betrayed Jesus not out of greed but out of obscene voluptuousness. Satan, the undisputed prince of the grotesque world, ruled it effectively by making love not war.

The fantastic erotic reverie flourished for ages, in spite of or perhaps because it was repressed. Similarly, the grotesque, although it was kept away from the center and viewed as a degraded decoration (even in the eyes of Adolf Loos ornament was equivalent to crime), became with time virtually omnipresent, gaining access to churches, palaces, bourgeois homes, and books. The fact that "shapely shapelessness" stimulated indecent dreams was recognized by Saint Bernard. The same point was made by Ruskin and later by Hofmannsthal, who in his early plays and short stories described wealthy young men who, trapped in their overly ornamented homes, were doomed to have their lives consumed by idle fantasizing. The recognition of this danger was astute, but there was another side to it as well. Grotesque ornamentation, because of its affinity with the complicated structure of organic life and the opaque and highly eroticized nature of the inner self, offered a refuge for ambiguous, unverbalized feelings and helped to keep in touch with the vital flow of nature. Undoubtedly, the grotesque could stimulate animalistic instincts and criminal forces within the self, but it could also prevent inner ossification—the freezing in an over-civilized outer shell—by reminding people of the beast sleeping within themselves, and of the subterranean labyrinth underneath a splendid culture.

The preoccupation with images of bloodthirsty men and women and with monsters certainly satisfied sadistic and masochistic desires; the vision of forces of darkness ridiculing and subduing innocence and goodness served to justify evil. But, on the other hand, the apocryphal and heretic versions of official doctrines and their fantastic interpretations drew people's attention to the hidden complexity of life itself and induced their own reasoning and imagination. In this respect the grotesque could act as a vehicle for emancipation and, significantly, exploded in times of unrest and spiritual crisis. At these historical moments the goats to the left rebelled against the sheep to the right, and females, infants, and animals triumphed over the heroes of Church and State. The liberating aspect of the grotesque can best be understood when one realizes that in our times women and children have been indeed on the move and snatching power away from men.

For centuries the grotesque reflected the chemistry of imagination, the fluid and volatile alchemy of dreaming. It mirrored the internal rhythm of life, answering escapist tendencies, and engaged in indecent masquerades. In spite of these ahistorical and apolitical features, there was a conflict between grotesque artists and the authorities, who at all times were unwilling to tolerate an autonomous subculture promoting vice instead of virtue, infancy rather than maturity. But the subterranean was too authentic and thus too strong to be eradicated. Although it bothered the authorities, it also served them by stressing the private rather than the public. The masters of the fantastic and grotesque were revolutionaries of sexuality and morality. But to those engaged in direct social and political struggle, they looked like reactionaries. Thus they were considered by the rulers as less dangerous than the satirists and caricaturists confronting issues of the day.

My deliberate concentration on the obscure contents of the grotesque required an interdisciplinary approach which at times might have provoked in the reader a feeling of too much heterogeneity. But mixture is the guiding principle of the grotesque, and thus one cannot escape mythology and anthropology, folklore and children's literature while working on this subject. Grotesque artists were lovers of the esoteric, scholars of the hermetic, and specialists of the absurd and obscene. Their wild fantasies were nourished by curio cabinets and rare books, and they indulged in secret codes and hieroglyphs. Respecting nothing, they assembled in their strange works fragments of the highest and the lowest achievements of literature and art, bits taken from different cultures and times. Of course, all artists do this, and the private and collective memory can easily be viewed as a curio cabinet or a half-natural, half-artificial grotto. But while the serious, classical, and academic artists restrained the flow of their fantasies, checked, balanced, and clarified their visions, the creators of the grotesque let their imaginations go. Therefore the sources of their inspirations are difficult to trace, and it is easy to blunder. The grotesque dealt with a lot of nonsense, and this has to be kept in mind as well. Writing about it one should not take oneself too seriously, become too pedantic, as justice has to be done both to the uncanny material and the peculiar character of the grotesque artists, their unscholarly, encyclopedic erudition centered on sacrilegious eroticism, and their heated minds which jumped back and forth between antiquity and modernity, Europe and the other continents.

The study of grotesque iconography suggests formal procedures for which the artists of the grotesque have the greatest predilection. The illustrations provided in this book show clearly how themes concerned with dissection and mixture, debasement, distortion, and fantastic interpretation were formulated. Consequently, one begins to understand why particular forms were needed to represent the world to which the ordinary rules of order and hierarchy could not be applied, where people, animals, plants, and inanimate objects grew out of each other, were ready to dismember and to devour each other or to fuse into one another. Subjects which directly involved dissection were in great demand and often led to duplication and multiplication. To stress the strange contours of particular figures, artists frequently simplified and isolated them from the whole. But on the other side they accentuated the complexity of the grotesque world—an organism ruled by the *horror vacui* of growing and decaying nature.

While realist painters preferred the cool and stable northern light, it can be assumed that the artists of the grotesque tended to work, like Beardsley, in the night or in rooms with covered windows and artificial light. They locked themselves away from the business of life, withdrawing into their own inner space. This space lacked color, subtlety, and distant perspectives. The fixation on darkness and night, illuminated by the moon and the light of burning torches, candles, and lamps, implied the predominance of shadows floating around, changing, disappearing, and easily turning to monsters. While painters opened new vistas into the visible world, grotesque artists projected obsessions, captured enigmas, fixed obscure signs and hieroglyphs. Colors were contemplated and enjoyed, but grotesque creations in black and white surprised and shocked. Of course, certain aspects of the grotesque were present in all European art. But everything is a question of degree. In painting, the ridiculous, obscene, and terrible was softened by color; in grotesque drawing it confronted the viewer.

The grotesque was a reductive form that derived its strength from its very reduction. Made out of compressed and distilled obsessions and repressions, it was filled with a peculiar intensity—an intensity broken by irony and paradox—which reached into the depth of existence and suggested a hidden richness. The essence of the grotesque is best visible in drawings, prints, and reliefs. They oscillate between black and white, shadow and light, being and non-being, are at once strictly personal and highly universal, and can be captured instantly but understood only in a broad context. Incongruous and contradictory, the grotesque can perhaps be designated, both from the point of view of the artist and the spectator, as an "inner realism"—of the premodern world.

Notes

Introduction

1. John Ruskin, *Stones of Venice* (London and Boston: Faber, 1981 [1851–53]), vol. 3; Arthur Clayborough, *The Grotesque in English Literature* (Oxford: Clarendon Press, 1965); Nicole Dacos, *La découverte de la Domus Aurea et la formations des grotesques à la Renaissance* (London: The Warburg Institute, University of London, 1969); Lee Byron Jennings, *The Ludicrous Demon: Aspects of the Grotesque in German Post-Romantic Prose* (Berkeley: University of California Press, 1963); Mario Praz, *Belleza et bizzarria* (Milan: Il Saggiatore, 1960); Lech Sokół, *Groteska w teatrze Stanisława Ignacego Witkiewicza* (Wrocław, Warsaw, Krakow, Gdansk: Ossolineum, 1973); Eva Wydra Hoffman, "The Grotesque in Modern Fiction" (Ph.D. dissertation, Harvard University, 1975); Geoffrey Galt Harpham, *On the Grotesque* (Princeton, N.J.: Princeton University Press, 1982).

2. Wolfgang Johannes Kayser, *Das Groteske: Seine Gestaltung in Malerei und Dichtung* (Oldenburg: G. Stalling, 1957); all quotations after the English translation *The Grotesque in Art and Literature*, trans. Ulrich Weisstein (New York: Morningside, 1981).

3. Mikhail Bakhtin, *Rabelais and His World*, trans. Hélène Iswolsky (Cambridge: M.I.T. Press, 1968), originally published as *Tvorchestvo Fransua Rable* (Moscow: Hudozestvennaya Literatura, 1965); Bakhtin, *Problems of Dostoevsky's Poetics*, trans. R. W. Rotsel (Ann Arbor, Mich.: Ardis, 1973), originally published as *Problemy tvorchestva Dostoevskogo* (Leningrad: Priboi, 1929).

4. Johann Fischart, *Geschichtklitterung* [*Gargantua*], ed. U. Nyssen (Dusseldorf: K. Rauch, 1963–64 [1590]), p. 20. Author's translation.

5. Jurgis Baltrušaitis, *Le Moyen Age fantastique* (Paris: A. Colin, 1955). See also by the same author *Réveils et prodiges: Le gothique fantastique* (Paris: A. Colin, 1960).

6. Ewa Kuryluk, *Wiedeńska apokalipsa* [*Viennese Apocalypse*]: *Eseje o sztuce i literaturze wiedeńskiej około 1900* (Krakow: Wydawnictwo Literackie, 1974); Kuryluk, *Salome albo o Rozkoszy: O grotesce w twórczości Aubreya Beardsleya* (Krakow: Wydawnictwo Literackie, 1976).

Chapter 1 · The Norm

1. See, for example, the ideology of Elijah Muhammad as described in *The Autobiography of Malcolm X* (New York: Grove Press, 1965), pp. 165–68.

2. Ibid. On the ideology of the racist Adolf Lanz, the teacher of Hitler, see Wilfried Daim, *Der Mann, der Hitler die Ideen gab* (Vienna: Hermann Böhlaus Nachf, 1985); Georg Lanz von Liebenfels, *Theozoologie oder die Kunde von den Sodoms-Äfflingen und dem Götterelektron* (Vienna, Leipzig, Budapest: Moderner Verlag, 1904); and Kuryluk, "The Other Vienna," *Formations* 2 (Fall 1985): 41–52.

3. See Dacos, *La découverte de la Domus Aurea.*

4. Vitruvius, *De architectura*, trans. and ed. Frank Granger (Cambridge: Harvard University Press, 1962), 2:105.

5. Leone Battista Alberti, *Ten Books on Architecture*, trans. Cosimo Bartoli and James Leoni, ed. J. Rykwert (New York: Transatlantic Arts, 1966), 9:5–6. Parenthetical references hereafter are to this edition.

6. F. de Hollanda, *Quatro dialogos da pintura antiga* (1538), after Dacos, *La découverte de la Domus Aurea*, p. 128.

7. Ghirlandaio, Giovanni da Udine, Filippino Lippi, Perugino, Pinturicchio, and Luca Signorelli also delighted in the grotesque.

8. Ruskin, *Stones of Venice*, vol. 3.

9. Emanuele Tesauro, *Canocchiale Aristotelico* (Venice: Pier Giò di Pauli, 1702 [1654]).

10. Leo Steinberg, "The Sexuality of Christ in Renaissance Art and in Modern Oblivion," *October* 25 (1983): 6–9.

11. Baltrušaitis, *Le Moyen Age fantastique.*

12. Lilian M. C. Randall, *Images in the Margins of Gothic Manuscripts* (Berkeley: University of California Press, 1966).

13. J. P. Migne, *Patrologia Latina* (Paris, 1878–90), 182: 915; for full translation see Elizabeth G. Holt, *A Documentary History of Art*, 2 vols. (Garden City, N.Y.: Doubleday, 1957–58), 1:19–22.

14. Ibid., coll. 916.

15. In a French manuscript of the fifteenth century, Pluto and Proserpina, dressed in contemporary outfits and placed in Hades, remind one of a sinful couple condemned to reside forever in hell; their chamber is depicted, in the style of Hieronymus Bosch, as the mouth of an owl-like monster. Bibliothèque Nationale, ms.fr.143 (*Le livre des echecs amoureux*). The miniature is reproduced in Jean Seznec, *The Survival of the Pagan Gods* (Princeton, N.J.: Princeton University Press, 1972), p. 196.

16. The earliest known Last Judgment is preserved on the lid of a sarcophagus now in the Metropolitan Museum, New York. It illustrates Christ's prophecy of the end of the world spoken to his disciples on the Mount of Olives: "But when the Son of Man shall come in his majesty, and all the angels with him, then he will sit on the throne of his glory; and before him will be gathered all the nations,

and he will separate them one from another, as the shepherd separates the sheep from the goats; and he will set the sheep on his right hand, but the goats on the left" (Matt. 25:31–33). The same image can be seen in the upper mosaic frieze (ca. 500–526) in the nave of Sant' Appolinare Nuovo in Ravenna. A third representation, in the apse at Fundi, has not been preserved but is mentioned by Paulinus of Nola (*Epistola*, 32.17). See also *Age of Spirituality* (exhibition catalogue of the Metropolitan Museum of Art, ed. K. Weitzmann, 1979), plate 501, p. 558; W. F. Volbach, *Early Christian Art* (Mainz am Rhein: Von Zabern, 1976), plate 151.

17. The number eight symbolizes the eighth day of the week, on which Christ rose from the dead. The Resurrection happened on the day of the sun, the Sol Invictus, whose cult was strong among the late Roman emperors and their legions. The significance of this number is reflected in the octagonal form of many early churches. In the catacomb of the Julii, under Saint Peter's Basilica in Rome, an octagonal panel in the center of a field of intertwined grapevines on a gold background shows the figure of Christ-Helios in a chariot pulled by four white horses. The early Church took advantage of the widespread adoration of the Sol Invictus and projected the image of Christ, the new god of light, onto the old icon. Because creation had been finished on the seventh day, the eighth was also regarded as a potential new beginning and therefore associated with universal regeneration. Five stands for evil and death because Christ was crucified on Friday, the fifth day of the week if one starts counting not on Sunday but on Monday, the first working day after the holiday. This way of numbering the weekdays is reflected in the Slavonic languages, in which Friday is called the fifth day of the week (*pyatnitsa* in Russian, *piątek* in Polish). The Friday of Christ's death was a day dedicated to the planet Venus, a goddess who was to be regarded by Christianity as the personifion of female wickedness and carnal sin. Friday is still "Venusday" in Romance languages (*venerdi* in Italian, *vendredi* in French). In English, Friday is named after the northern goddess of love, Frig, whom the old Norse sources call the "darling of gods."

On the earliest known representation of the Last Judgment eight and five not only represent polarities but together they form a unity which reflects the cycle of nature, of birth and death. On both ends of the relief half a scallop shell is shown in such a way that, if the ends were joined together to form a circle, the symbol of completion and perfection, the two halves would become a whole. In Greek mythology Venus was born out of a scallop shell, which subsequently was regarded as a symbol of fertility. Because of their aqueous origins, shells are universally regarded as representations of life, birth, and femininity. For the symbolism of numbers see U. Holzmeister, *Chronologia vitae Christi* (Rome, 1933); H. Rahner, *Griechische Mythen in Christlicher Deutung* (Zurich: Rhein Verlag, 1945), pp. 141–77; E. Hulme, *History, Principles, and Practice of Symbolism in Christian Art* (New York: Gordon Press, 1976), p. 15. About Frig see P. Rawson, *Primitive Erotic Art* (New York: G. P. Putnam's Sons, 1973), p. 44.

18. Jesus explicitly applied to himself the title of the "Good Shepherd," and in the Epistle to the Hebrews he is called the "great Shepherd of the Sheep" (13:20). In the Gospels of Luke (15:3–7) and John (10:1–16) he is characterized as a shepherd who loves his flock and will bring the soul to salvation as a shepherd retrieves lost sheep. The model is derived from Greek bucolic scenes. A ram-bearing shepherd personified philanthropy, and when shown on funerary monuments implied the promise of salvation. In the pagan mystery cults Orpheus is sometimes represented as a shepherd. John the Baptist announced Jesus as "the Lamb of God" and in the Revelation he is called "lamb" twenty-nine times. *Age of Spirituality*, plates 464–66, pp. 520–22. According to a Pishdadian legend, the earliest legendary history of

Iran, Yima, the third ruler of the world, was called Yima Kshaeta, the Good Shepherd. *Songs of Zarathustra: The Gathas*, trans. Dastur Framroze Ardeshir Bode and Piloo Nanavutty (London: George Allen and Unwin, 1952), p. 59.

Christ's words have contributed to the iconography of the devil with goat-like attributes. But the metaphor reflects an old tradition of demons and females equipped with horns, symbols of the phallus, of male fertility as well as aggressivity. Some of the prehistoric figures of the Great Mother, for instance the famous Venus of Laussel (Salutrian, Museum of Bordeaux), have horns in their hands. Pan, one of the prototypes of the Christian devil, is half man, half goat. In a marble group from Herculaneum (first century B.C.) he is sculpted in copulation with a goat which submits to him like a woman. In the "Villa of the Mysteries" in Pompeii a female satyr suckles a young goat. One of the most fantastic monsters of antiquity is the Chimera, usually depicted with the head and body of a lion, a fire-spewing goat head growing out of its back, and a serpent's tail.

19. John the Baptist is frequently shown in art as bearing a lamb on his shoulders. On Saint John's Day in Venice a boy used to impersonate him. He was clothed in a sheepskin tied around his body and a lamb accompanied him. Hulme, *History, Principles, and Practice of Symbolism in Christian Art*, p. 163.

20. For instance on the sarcophagus of the Roman prefect Junius Bassus (ca. A.D. 359), in the grottoes of Saint Peter in Rome. The image of Jesus as a lamb reappeared in the Middle Ages and was made famous by Jan van Eyck's *Adoration of the Lamb* in Saint Bavon's Cathedral in Ghent.

21. The engraving is reproduced in Dacos, *La découverte de la Domus Aurea*, plate 95, fig. 158.

22. This pattern is visible in the earliest representations of Original Sin: tracing of the fresco from the baptistery of Dura Europos, with Good Shepherd and Adam and Eve, second or third century, New Haven, Yale University Gallery; sarcophagus with the Original Sin, Rome, ca. 315–25, Vatican City, Monumenti, Musei e Galerie Pontificie, Museo Pio Christiano Lat. 161; sarcophagus of Junius Bassus, Vatican, grottoes of Saint Peter, ca. A.D. 359; several Spanish sarcophagi from the Constantinian period: of Layos, Toledo, in Museo Marés, Barcelona; of San Justo de la Vega, Astorga, Leon, in National Archeological Museum, Madrid; sarcophagus in the Provincial Archeological Museum, Cordova. By the eighth century the serpent starts to change from a male into a female monster. Thus the tempter is henceforth frequently shown with a female head, long hair, and a female bust, and resembles the nereids and sirens. In this form it alludes to the pagan past and wicked animalistic femininity.

The motif of the tree of life appears in many cultures. In *Vetalapanchavimshati* [*Twenty-five Tales of a Vetala*], a cycle of stories embedded in the eleventh-century Indian epic known as the *Ocean of Story* by Somadeva, there is a "wishing-tree" rising out of the sea, with boughs of gold, glittering with sprays of coral, with fruits and flowers of jewels. On the trunk of that tree sits a maiden whom a traveling man approaches. Indian miniatures depict the scene in a way highly reminiscent of the representations of Original Sin: the man stands at the right of the tree, the girl at the left. *Parabola* 2 (1977): 49. The left side is universally regarded as female.

23. Philippe Ariès, *Western Attitudes toward Death from the Middle Ages to the Present*, trans. Patricia M. Ranum (Baltimore: Johns Hopkins University Press, 1974), pp. 34–46.

24. For instance, in Baldung's *Rider with Death and a Maiden*, Louvre, and *Vanity*, Kunsthistorisches Museum, Vienna.

25. Ariès, *Western Attitudes*, p. 57.

26. Erwin Panofsky, *Hercules am Scheidewege und andere antike Bildstoffe in der neueren Kunst* (Leipzig and Berlin: B. G. Teubner, 1930).

Chapter 2 · The Cave

1. Harpham, *On the Grotesque*, pp. 58–69.

2. Naomi Miller, *Heavenly Caves* (New York: Braziller, 1982), pp. 7–28.

3. As Freud suggests, "Perhaps this dread is based on the fact that woman is different from man, for ever incomprehensible and mysterious, strange and therefore apparently hostile. The man is afraid of being weakened by the woman, infected with her femininity and of then showing himself incapable." Sigmund Freud, "The Taboo of Virginity" (1917), in *The Standard Edition of the Complete Psychological Works*, ed. and trans. James Strachey and Anna Freud (London: The Hogarth Press and the Institute of Psychoanalysis, 1957), 11:198–99.

4. Frobenius discusses a possible source of this fear: "Perhaps in connection with the blood-red sunrise, the idea occurs that here a birth takes place, the birth of a young son; the question then arises inevitably, whence comes the paternity? How has the woman become pregnant? And since this woman symbolizes the same idea as the fish, which means the sea, (because we proceed from the assumption that the Sun descends into the sea as well as arises from it) thus the curious primitive answer is that this sea has previously swallowed the old Sun. Consequently the resulting myth is, that the woman (sea) has formerly devoured the Sun and now brings a new Sun into the world, and thus she has become pregnant." As quoted by C. G. Jung, *Psychology of the Unconscious* (New York: Moffat Yard, 1916), p. 237. On the symbolism of the mother-earth, mother-sea, mother-sea monster, etc., and the birth of a sun-hero see pp. 191–341.

5. Almost every country has caves associated with some kind of suspect eroticism, as, for instance, the grottoes situated in England under the West Wycombe hill. They are connected with the mock-religious ceremonies of the Knights of Saint Francis of Wycombe (Sir Francis Dashwood), the pleasure-loving Georgian gentlemen who, disguised as Franciscan monks, enjoyed themselves in the company of their "nuns." The Wycombe caves, completed ca. 1752, were, of course, dedicated to Venus, and each of them bore the words of Rabelais, "Fay ce que voudras."

6. See Erwin Rhode, *Psyche: Seelencult und Unsterblichkeitsglaube der Griechen* (Freiburg, 1894); in English, *Psyche: The Cult of Souls and Belief in Immortality*, trans. W. B. Hillis (New York: Harper and Row, 1966); Maxime Collignon, *Essai sur les monuments grecs et romains relatifs au mythe de Psyché* (Paris, 1877).

7. Mircea Eliade, "Homo-Humus," in *Patterns in Comparative Religion*, trans. R. Sheed (New York: New American Library, 1974), pp. 253–54.

8. In his *Genio e follia* (Padua, 1877) Cesare Lombroso tells the story of two insane artists who created the world by reproducing it from the rectum. One of them painted himself in this act of creation, the world coming forth from his anus; his penis was in full erection; he was naked and surrounded by women. Freud and Jung report similar cases and, consequently, write about the importance of the toilet. "The 'locus' is known to be the place of dreams where much was wished for and created which later would no longer be suspected of having this place of origin." Jung, *Psychology of the Unconscious*, pp. 211–15.

Some modern artists have made a particular point in stressing the excremental character of their work. The excrements of the German artist Dieter Roth are in collections of several European museums of art. Carl Andre, a New York artist, remarked that his work consisting of bricks and flat pieces of metal and wood lying on the floor deliberately alluded to excrement. Similarly, contemporary women artists have exhibited sanitary napkins and sheets stained with menstrual blood. The Austrian artist Friederike Pezzold impressed her bleeding genitals on a white bedsheet on every consecutive day of her period. There is also some evidence suggesting that the imaginary connection established between a spiritual emanation, the female bleeding, and the *hemodrosis* of Christ contributed to the creation of the legend of Veronica's miraculous cloth. See Ewa Kuryluk, "Mirrors and Menstruation," *Formations* 1 (Fall 1984): 64–77.

9. M. Delcourt, *L'oracle de Delphes* (Paris, 1955).

10. Alexander Pope, *The Odyssey of Homer*, Books 13–24, ed. M. Mack (London: Methuen; New Haven, Conn.: Yale University Press, 1967). Parenthetical references hereafter are to this edition.

11. *The Aeneid of Virgil*, trans. Rolfe Humphries (New York: Charles Scribner's Sons, 1951), Book 6, pp. 151–52, 157. Parenthetical references hereafter are to this edition.

12. After Amy Richlin, *The Garden of Priapus: Sexuality and Aggression in Roman Humor* (New Haven, Conn.: Yale University Press, 1983), p. 130.

13. Flaubert was inspired by the painting of Jan Brueghel the Elder. Not by chance did Flaubert work simultaneously on the fantasies of the Egyptian monk and those of the protagonist in *Madame Bovary* (1857), exploring at the same time the erotic cave of a man and the depths of a female psyche with which he professed to identify ("Madame Bovary c'est moi"). The first fragments of *The Temptations* were published as early as 1857, but altogether Flaubert worked on the book for twenty-five years and sent the entire manuscript to press only in 1874. In no other project was he more passionately involved, throwing himself into *The Temptations* whenever personal and public problems overwhelmed him, as he mentions in his letters: *Lettres à Georges Sand* (Paris, 1884), pp. 137–38; p. 23; p. 132.

14. G. D. Painter, "The Hypnerotomachia Poliphili of 1499. An Introduction on the Dream, the Dreamer, the Artist and the Printer," *Hynerotomachia Poliphili*, facsimile edition (London: Eugrammia Press, 1963), p. 6.

Chapter 3 · Alchemy

1. Linda Fierz-David, *Der Liebestraum des Poliphilo: Ein Beitrag zur Psychologie der Renaissance und der Moderne* (Zurich: Rhein-Verlag, 1947).

2. M. P. E. Berthelot, *Les origines de l'alchimie* (Paris, 1885).

3. *Catalogue des manuscripts alchimiques grecs*, ed. J. Bidez, F. Cumont, J. L. Heiberg, and O. Lagercrantz (Brussels: M. Lamertin, 1924).

4. G. L. Figuier, *L'alchimie et les alchimistes* (Paris, 1856).

5. C. G. Jung, *Psychology and Alchemy*, 2d ed., ed. Gerhard Adler et al., trans. R. F. Hull (Princeton, N.J.: Princeton University Press, 1968).

6. Fierz-David mentions the great popularity of the *Roman de la rose* in Italy. Some scholars attribute its translation into Italian, entitled *Fiori*, to Dante. *Der Liebestraum des Poliphilo*, p. 27.

7. A. Raphael, *Goethe and the Philosophers' Stone* (New York: Garrett Publications, 1965).

8. Such as Goethe's *Die Wahlverwandschaften* (1809); in English *Kindred by Choice*, trans. H. M. Waidson (London: John Calder, 1976).

9. Jung reproduced many of these stunning images in *Psychology and Alchemy*.

Chapter 4 · Anatomical Theater

1. *Fasciculo di medicinae* [*The Anatomical Bundle*] (1493) includes the text by Mondino de Luzzi (ca. 1275–1326).

2. Jacopo Berengario da Carpi (ca. 1460–ca. 1530), *Isagogae breves* [*A Short but very Clear and Fruitful Introduction to the Anatomy of the Human Body, Published by Request of his Students*] (1522).

Chapter 5 · Satire, Death, and Traveling

1. In modern times Menippus has been imitated by the authors of the well-known *Satyre Menippée* (1593), which was reprinted in Paris in 1882, and by Justus Lipsius, the author of *Satyra menippaea* (1637).

2. In the treatise *De dea Syria* (Mylitta, the Semitic Aphrodite, a moon-goddess), Lucian describes miraculous events in Syrian and Palestinian temples, the self-imposed privation of manhood practiced by the Galli, and curious rituals and sacrifices. In *Lucian in Eight Volumes*, trans. A. M. Harmon (London: W. Heinemann; New York: Macmillan, 1913–67), 4:337. Lucian also wrote his own version, satiric and obscene, of a narrative contained in the *Metamorphoses* by Lucius of Patrae, which was also imitated by Apuleius, a contemporary of Lucian, in his *Golden Ass*.

3. In *The Carousel or the Lapiths*, a dialogue between Philo and Lycinus, a banquet attended by philosophers achieves its climax when Zonothemis tries to secure for himself a fatter fowl than that served to his neighbor. In *Lucian in Eight Volumes*, vol. 1.

4. Even in the 1910 edition the entry for "anthropology" in *Encyclopaedia Britannica* was illustrated by a grotesque picture of apes transforming themselves into humans. Vol. 2, plate 1 (fig. 1), opposite p. 112.

5. Freud interpreted the affinity of adults to animals (particularly strong in dreams) as a regression to infantile memory material. "That which once ruled in the waking state, when the psychical life was still young and impotent, appears to be banished to the dream life, in somewhat the same way as the bow and arrow, those discarded, primitive weapons of adult humanity, have been relegated to the nursery." Freud, *Traumdeutung* (1900), quoted after Jung, *The Psychology of the Unconscious*, p. 27. Jung points in this context to sodomy and mentions the Egyptian shrine of the goat-god, the Greek Pan, where the Hierodules prostituted themselves with goats (p. 33).

Chapter 6 · The Fantastic, the Grotesque, and the Metaphorical

1. Wilhelm Fraenger, *Hieronymus Bosch* (1975). Epiphanius and Augustine are quoted after the American edition (New York: Putnam, 1983), p. 17ff.

2. Ibid., passim. See also W. Fraenger, *Von Bosch bis Beckmann: Ausgewählte Schriften* (Cologne: DuMont, 1985), pp. 15–33.

3. Charles van Beuningen, *The Complete Drawings of Hieronymus Bosch* (London: Academy Editions; New York: St. Martin's Press, 1973), p. 7.

4. Reproduced in Fraenger, *Hieronymus Bosch*, p. 40.

5. For the iconography of the Domus Aurea, see Dacos, *La découverte de la Domus Aurea*, pp. 9–40. Roman frescoes were also discovered at the Colosseum, in Hadrian's villa in Tivoli, and in the vicinity of Naples. Pompeii and Herculaneum were not yet unearthed.

6. Ruskin *(Stones of Venice)* stressed the difference between the northern and the southern grotesque. But he did not analyze the varying iconography. Instead he praised the northern artists for their noble feelings, and called the Romans and Italians vulgar and degenerate.

7. Roland Barthes, *Arcimboldo* (New York: Rizzoli, 1980), p. 16.

8. *The New Science of Giambattista Vico*, rev. and trans. T. G. Bergin and M. H. Fisch (Ithaca, N.Y.: Cornell University Press, 1968), II.2, 2 and II.2, 4.

9. Thomas Aquinas (ca. 1227–74), *Expositio super librum Boethii De Trinitate*, ed. Bruno Decker (Leiden: E. J. Brill, 1955).

Chapter 7 · *Grotesque Tendencies in the Late Nineteenth Century*

1. These words were spoken by Beardsley in an interview he granted Arthur H. Lawrence, who quoted them in his article published in the *Idler* 9 (March 1897).

Chapter 8 · *The Planet Venus*

1. The first three chapters of Beardsley's novel were published in January 1896 in the first number of the *Savoy*, a periodical of which Beardsley was artistic editor. They were published under the title *Under the Hill*, with three illustrations by the author. Beardsley had been intrigued by the Tannhäuser legend for some time. As early as 1894 John Lane announced the publication of *The Story of Venus and Tannhäuser* by Aubrey Beardsley, and Beardsley included a copy of his not-yet-written book, along with volumes of Dickens and Shakespeare, in an unused design for the front cover of *The Yellow Book* (fig. 89). The names of the chief protagonists were changed for the *Savoy* serialization, Tannhäuser to the more sacrilegious and autobiographical-sounding "Abbé Fanfreluche" (originally "Abbé Aubrey"), and Venus to Helen. But, more importantly, the text was purged of erotic allusions and descriptions. The second number of the *Savoy*, for April 1896, contained chapter 4 of *Under the Hill* and two further illustrations, as well as an explanatory note by Leonard Smithers, the publisher of the magazine, that owing to his illness Beardsley was unable to finish one of the full-page illustrations. The third number, for July 1896, appeared without any additional text or illustrations by Beardsley. With his health quickly deteriorating, he left London in the spring of 1897, moving first to Dieppe and Paris and then, in November 1897, to Menton. He died there on 16 March 1898 with his "romantic story," as he called his novel, still unfinished. It was left in two sets, the unexpurgated manuscript version in ten chapters describing Tannhäuser's pleasures in the Venusberg, and the censored *Under the Hill* of the *Savoy*. In 1904 John Lane republished *Under the Hill* in a collection of Beardsley's writings, observing the deletions made for the sake of decency. Finally in 1907 Smithers issued the original manuscript in a limited private edition of three hundred copies which did not, however, include the illustrations and omitted two passages from chapter 7. The Smithers version was reprinted in New York in 1927, privately and without the two missing passages. This volume, absurdly, was not illustrated by Beardsley's own work but by the banal drawings of Bertram Elliot. In 1959 Olympia Press brought out an even more senseless edition which not only departed in many minor but unreasonable ways from the Smithers edition but attempted to present the unfinished novel as a finished one, its completion being done by John Glassco. Finally in 1974 the Academy Editions in London and St. Martin's Press in New York jointly brought out the so far most faithful and coherent edition of *The Story of Venus and Tannhäuser*. Based on the Smithers version of 1907, it restores

the two missing passages. All the quotations come from this edition, which is abbreviated VT.

2. *Two Books of Adam and Eve*, also called *The Conflict of Adam and Eve with Satan*, were originally written in Arabic in Egypt at an unknown date. In the sixth or seventh century A.D., probably, they were translated into Ethiopic. In 1882 the Ethiopic version was translated into English by S. C. Malan. He worked from an edition by E. Trumpp of the University of Munich, who had access to the Arabic original. "Two Books of Adam and Eve or the Conflict of Adam and Eve with Satan," trans. S. C. Malan, in *The Forgotten Books of Eden*, ed. R. H. Platt (Cleveland: World Pub. Co., 1927; reprinted New York: Bell, 1980). There also exists a Syriac version of Adam and Eve's story, entitled "The Cave of Treasure." Assigned to the sixth century, it was written by a Christian and translated into German by C. Bezold. *The Apocrypha and Pseudepigrapha of the Old Testament in English*, ed. R. H. Charles (Oxford: Clarendon Press, 1913), 2:126.

3. Porphyrius (A.D. 233–ca. 304), *De antro nympharum* [*The Cave of the Nymphs in the Odyssey*] (1518), rev. and trans. Seminar Classics 609 (Buffalo: State University of New York at Buffalo, 1969).

4. In *Chapman's Homer*, ed. A. Nicoll, Bollingen Series no. 41 (New York: Pantheon, 1956), 2:579.

5. *The Metamorphoses of Ovid*, trans. Mary M. Innes (Harmondsworth: Penguin, 1955). Parenthetical references hereafter are to this edition.

6. Vitruvius (*De architectura*, 5.6.9) describes the grotto as part of the scenery of satyric plays. See also "Grotto as Theatre" in Miller, *Heavenly Caves*, pp. 21–22.

7. Apuleius, *The Golden Ass*, trans. W. Adlington, rev. S. Gaselee (London: W. Heinemann, 1915), p. 203. Parenthetical references hereafter are to this edition.

8. W. Pater, *Marius the Epicurean: His Sensations and Ideas*, ed. H. Bloom (New York and Toronto: New American Library, 1970 [1885]), p. 58.

9. Jung suggests that women portray their souls as masculine (animus), but because of the scarcity of their literary or artistic production there are too few examples to prove this. In one of her poems Emily Dickinson addresses "Death" in a loving way as a "He" (*Selected Poems and Letters*, ed. R. N. Linscott [Garden City, N.Y.: Doubleday, 1959], p. 151), but Angelica Kaufmann, for instance, painted her inspiration not as an apollonic youth but as a sisterly looking muse. (Her painting is now in the Kenwood Museum in London.)

In this context it is interesting to note that while traditionally it is the man who enters the grotto in search of love, inspiration, and/or death, E. M. Forster in his *Passage to India* reverses the pattern and, using the grotto as a Freudian metaphor for the frightening depth of the repressed self, sends two English ladies into the fantastic Indian caves. Besides symbolizing the unconscious, the caves also represent India, a country perceived by the cool and rational Britons as an unlimited female reverie and a primordial chaos made of hallucinations and dreams. The caves embody the essence of the mythical Indian soul, which cannot be captured by Western reason, and the darkened fabric of an occupied country which has gone underground, mad, and, like the female who is discriminated against, become all soul. Humiliated by its colonizers, India has turned irresponsible, moody, hysterical—at once submissive and aggressive. Thus it appears grotesque to the energetic, well-educated, and pragmatic English women. Their common sense breaks down only during the visit to the caves, where they are confronted with their own repressed desires and fears. The younger woman is overwhelmed by sexuality, the older one paralyzed by a vision of death. Both lose their sense of superiority and begin to drown in a sea of passion and pain, despair and destruction. In the grottoes they have touched a deeply buried inner ground, fantastic and threatening, and they now fear for their civilized egos.

10. After Jack Finegan, *The Archeology of the New Testament* (Princeton, N.J.: Princeton University Press, 1969), p. 23.

11. S. Aurigemma, *Villa Adriana* (Rome: Instituto poligrafico dello Stato, 1961).

12. Pater, *Marius the Epicurean*, p. 91.

13. G. Bachelard, "La Coquille," in *La poétique de l'espace* (Paris: Presses Universitaires de France, 1958), pp. 105–29.

14. Baltrušaitis, *Le Moyen Age fantastique*, p. 56.

15. H. Egger, "Ergänzende Bemerkungen zur Ikonographie der Fresken von Stift Altenburg," in *Groteskes Barock*, exhibition catalogue, Altenburg, 17 May–26 October 1975, p. 57. Author's translation.

16. After M. Mack, *The Garden and the City: Retirement and Politics in the Later Poetry of Pope, 1731–1743* (Toronto: University of Toronto Press, 1969), p. 44.

17. Ibid., pp. 46–47.

18. Cited in Mack, *The Garden and the City*, p. 47.

19. Egeria is also mentioned by Juvenal: "We went down to Egeria's Vale and the caves, all artificial now. How much nearer the water-nymph's presence would be felt if green grass bordered the water, instead of marble slabs that insult our native rock!" *Satires*, 3:10, in *Juvenal and Persius*, trans. G. G. Ramsay (Cambridge: Harvard University Press, 1979).

20. Mack, *The Garden and the City*, p. 241.

21. *The Works of Alexander Pope* (London, 1871), 2:168–69.

22. Beardsley might have seen pictures of bottled embryos at the home of his grandfather who was a surgeon-major. But the artist certainly studied them in anatomical and alchemical illustrations as well, as he had a passion for rare books.

23. At the turn of the century many literary works took place in or referred to morbid cities dominated by water (Venice, Bruges, St. Petersburg), for instance, Georges Rodenbach's story *Bruges-la-morte* or Hugo von Hofmannsthal's unfinished novel *Andreas oder die Vereinigten*, set against the hallucinating background of Venice.

24. Elis, the hero of Hofmannsthal's play *Das Bergwerk zu Falun* [*The Mines of Falun*], becomes a miner to be closer to the "black lady." The play was inspired by a short story by E. T. A. Hoffmann with the same title. Hofmannsthal started it in 1899 and finished it in 1918. Also, in his short story "Das Märchen von der verschleierten Frau [The Fairytale of the Veiled Woman]" (1900), the miner Hyacinth abandons his wife and disappears in the underworld of the "veiled lady."

25. See Kuryluk, *Viennese Apocalypse*, pp. 215–62.

26. For instance, in the paintings of Egon Schiele.

27. J. Siebert, *Der Dichter Tannhäuser: Leben—Gedichte—Sage* (Halle/Salle: M. Niemeyer, 1934), p. 240. Author's translation.

28. Beardsley's earliest drawing of Tannhäuser dates from 1891 (*Tannhäuser*, Rosenwald Collection, National Gallery of Art, Washington). He drew Max Alvary as Tannhäuser in 1892.

29. Steven Marcus, *The Other Victorians: A Study of Sexuality and Pornography in Mid-Nineteenth-Century England* (New York: Basic Books, 1974), pp. 271–72. On the homosexual cave, the symbol of the anus, see A. Schmidt, *Sitara und der Weg dorthin: Eine Studie über Wesen, Werk und Wirkung Karl Mays* (Karlsruhe: Stahlberg, 1963).

30. Marcus (*Other Victorians*, p. 272) mentions the growing and shrinking of the female cavity.

31. Beardsley's satirical drawings for the *Aeneid*, which he studied at school in 1886, show a tiny Aeneas and a huge Venus. He also wrote a limerick about Aeneas traveling by balloon. The drawings are published in *Collected Drawings of Aubrey Beardsley* (New York: Crown, 1969).

32. Homer, *Hymn to Venus*, in *Chapman's Homer*, 2:572. The epigraph to this section is from the short poem "To Venus," *Chapman's Homer*, 2:586.

33. *Eros: I capolavori della letteratura amorosa VI A.C.-XX secolo* (Milan: Sormani, 1953).

34. Pater, *Marius the Epicurean*, p. 93.

35. Ibid., p. 52.

36. Ibid., pp. 53–54.

37. Beardsley might have read the bilingual edition, *The Romaunt of the Rose*, from the Glasgow Ms, parallel with its original *Le roman de la rose*, ed. M. Kaluza (London, 1891), or in French: *Le roman de la rose*, ed. F. Michel (Paris, 1864).

38. This was already noted by B. Brophy, *Black and White: A Portrait of Aubrey Beardsley* (New York: Stein and Day, 1970), p. 24.

39. According to D. J. Gordon, Beardsley's friends knew that he meant the drawing to represent the Annunciation. D. J. Gordon, "Aubrey Beardsley at the V and A," *Encounter* 27 (October 1966): 13.

40. E. Dowson in the anthology *The Victorian Verse*, ed. G. Mac Beth (Harmondsworth: Penguin Books, 1969), p. 401.

41. Rossetti translated and published many unknown Italian poets. In a letter to Charles Eliot Norton of July 1853 he writes that some of them had never before been available to a broader public, not even in Italy. In J. Ruskin, *Rossetti: Preraphaelitism, Papers 1854 to 1863*, arr. and ed. W. M. Rossetti (London, 1899), p. 202.

42. In a letter to King of 12 July 1891, in A. W. King, *An Aubrey Beardsley Lecture* (London: R. A. Walker, 1924), p. 63.

43. The tapestry *Pilgrim in the Garden* could also illustrate other medieval writings, such as the thirteenth-century poem by the Italian poet Paolo Lanfranchi of Pistoia, in which Love visits the dreaming lover and presents him with a flower that has the face of his beloved:

> L'altr'er, dormendo, a mi se venne Amore,
> desedòmi e disse: "Eo so'mesazo
> de la tua dona che t'ama di core,
> se tu, plu che non sòy, se'fatto sazo."
> Da la sua parte mi donò un flore,
> che parse per semblanti'l so visazo.

In C. Kleinhenz, "The Interrupted Dream of Paolo Lanfranchi da Pistoia," *Italica* 49 (Summer 1972): 188.

44. *Hymn to Venus* in *Chapman's Homer*, 2:571, 572, 578–79.

45. Ibid., 2:579, 571. In the garden of Aphrodite we find all the elements that constitute the archetypal dwelling of a Great Goddess, who, across all ages and cultures, except in the polar regions, is represented amidst rich vegetation, water, and animals. For instance, Xochiquetzal (Precious Flower), the Aztec goddess of love, dwelt on the top of a mountain and was surrounded by dwarfs, musicians, dancers, and animals. On the pattern of "goddess-tree-mountain-heraldic-animals," see Eliade, *Patterns in Comparative Religion*, p. 286.

46. There is an excellent entry on the unicorn in the *Encyclopaedia Britannica* (1910), 27:581–82. It shows that the legendary beast, whose symbolism is today largely forgotten, still played a significant role in popular imagery and superstition at the beginning of the twentieth century.

47. Ctesias of Cnidus, *Ancient India*, trans. J. W. McCrindle (Calcutta, 1882). The earliest representation of a unicorn that I have seen was a wooden Chinese statuette, "Chi'i-Lin with bowed head" (first or second century A.D.), unearthed in 1959 in We-wei, Kansu province and shown in the exhibition of Chinese art in the Museum of Applied Art in Vienna (23 February–20 April 1974). *Archäologische Funde der Volksrepublik China*, exhibition catalogue, Vienna, Museum für Angewandte Kunst, No. 208 on p. 106.

48. L. Germain, "La chasse à la licorne et l'immaculée conception," *L'espérance* (1897); F. Pesendorfer, "Tiersymbolik und Religion," *Christliche Kunstblätter*, No. 71–73 (1930–32); P. Albert, "Die Einhornjagd in der Literatur und Kunst des Mittelalters, vornehmlich am Oberreihn," *Schau-ins-Land* 25 (1898).

49. For the two latter items of information, see *Encyclopaedia Britannica*, under "Unicorn."

50. In a German church song from the sixteenth century, God hunts Mary with the help of the archangel Gabriel, who, "blowing the little horn," makes the Virgin "full of grace":

> *Es wolt gut Jäger jagen*
> *wol in des Himmels thron,*
> *was begegnet ihm uff der Heyden?*
> *Maria die Jungfraw schon.*
>
> *Den Jäger den ich meine,*
> *der ist uns wohl bekant*
> *err jagt mid einem Engel*
> *Gabriel ist er genant.*
>
> *Der Engel bliess ein Hörnlein*
> *es laut sich also wol:*
> *Gegrüsst seyest du, Maria,*
> *du bist aller Gnaden voll.*

After H. von der Gabelentz, "Die Einhornjagd auf einem Altarbild im Groszherzoglichen Museum zu Weimar," *Sonderdruck aus dem Jahrbuch der Königlichen Pruszischen Kunstsammlungen* 3 (1913).

51. L. Preller, *Griechische Mythologie* (Berlin, Zurich: Weidmannsche Verlagsbuchhandlung, 1964), 1:381.

52. Ibid., 1:379–84.

53. Clement of Alexandria, *Exhortation to the Greeks*, trans. G. W. Butterworth (London: W. Heinemann, 1919). Parenthetical references hereafter are to this edition.

54. The names of the dogs are taken from the Bible: "Misericordia et veritas obviaverunt sibi; iustitia et pax osculatae sunt" (Ps. 84:11). The white dog is called "misericordia," the red "iustitia," the gray "pax" and the yellow one "veritas." They all appear on the Weimar painting analyzed by von der Gabelentz, "Die Einhornjagd."

55. Preller, *Griechische Mythologie*, 1:314.

56. See Leopold von Sacher-Masoch's letters, in Wanda von Sacher-Masoch, *Meine Lebensbeichte* (Berlin and Leipzig: Schuster and Loeffler, 1906), pp. 328–29 and 294–95.

57. Leopold von Sacher-Masoch, *Venus in Furs*, trans. F. Savage (n.p.: privately printed, 1921), p. 41.

58. Ibid., pp. 42–43.

59. Ibid., p. 208.

60. W. von Sacher-Masoch, *Meine Lebensbeichte*.

61. This is an expression that Beardsley used in letters to L. Smithers (nos. 42 and 17), *Letters from Aubrey Beardsley to Leonard Smithers*, ed. R. A. Walker (London: The First Edition Club, 1937).

62. According to Hippolytus, the Corybantes come out of the ground like trees. In art they were usually represented executing their orgiastic dance in the presence of the Great Goddess, her lions, and Attis. For more information on Corybantes and Dactyli, see Preller, *Griechische Mythologie*, 1:641–42, 655–58.

63. Ibid., 1:735–37.

64. I use the facsimile of the 1499 Venetian original of *Hypnerotomachia Poliphili* (London: Eugrammia Press, 1963). Quotations in English hereafter are my translations from this edition.

65. M. T. Casella and G. Pozzi, *Francesco Colonna: Biografia e opere*, 2 vols. (Padua: Editrice Antenora, 1959).

66. Giovanni Pozzi, for instance, believes that Colonna made sketches for some of the woodcuts (Ibid.).

67. Nicolas Flamel (ca. 1330–1418), *Le livre des figures hiéroglyphiques: Le sommaire philosophique, Le desir desire*, ed. M. Préaud (Paris: Denoël, 1970), pp. 104–5. English translation quoted after Stanislas Klossowski de Rola, *Alchemy: The Secret Art* (London: Thames and Hudson, 1973), p. 11.

68. Casella and Pozzi, *Francesco Colonna*, 2:52.

69. Ibid., 2:57.

70. Panofsky, *Hercules am Scheidewege*, p. 192. See also G. Pozzi and L. Ciapponi, "La cultura figurativa di Francesco Colonna e l'arte veneta," in *Umanesimo europeo e umanesimo veneziano* (Florence: Sansoni, 1964).

71. Casella and Pozzi, *Francesco Colonna*, 2:52.

72. J. G. Frazer, *Adonis, Attis, Osiris*, vols. 5 and 6 of *The Golden Bough*, 3d ed. (New York: Macmillan, 1935), 1:33–36.

73. M. Praz, *The Romantic Agony*, trans. A. Davidson, 2d ed. (London and New York: Oxford University Press, 1951), pp. 342–43. M. Praz, "Some Foreign Imitators of the 'Hypnerotomachia Poliphili,' " *Italica* 24 (1947): 20–25. The woodcuts of the *Hypnerotomachia* inspired many famous paintings, for instance, *The Nymph of the Fountain* (1534) by Lucas Cranach, Walker Art Gallery, Liverpool.

74. *Le songe de Poliphile ou Hypnérotomachie de frère Francesco Colonna*, trans. C. Popelin (Paris, 1883).

75. F. Colonna, *The Strife of Love in a Dream. Being the Elisabethan Version of the First Book of the Hypnerotomachia* (London, 1890 [1592]).

76. Praz, "Some Foreign Imitators."

77. Mario Praz ("Some Foreign Imitators") suggests that Beardsley's fountain was inspired by the nymphaeum of Queen Eleuterilyda. And Stanley Weintraub has noted that Tannhäuser frolics in the pool with young boys like Nero in Suetonius's

Twelve Caesars. Beardsley: A Biography (New York: G. Braziller, 1967), p. 169. Weintraub's book (p. 61) is the source of the epigraph to the first section of chapter 10 of this book.

78. The mythical plant or tree of life is universally connected with water. For instance the soma, a miraculous plant in Indo-Iranian mythology, is represented in the Rig Veda in the form of a spring, a torrent, or a plant of paradise. In the Vedic and post-Vedic texts it grows out of a vase and secures life, fertility, and regeneration. See Eliade, *Patterns in Comparative Religion,* p. 281. The equation between the tree of life and the source of water is also common in Christianity. Four rivers, corresponding to the four directions, may originate from the roots of the tree of life. See for instance the apocryphal *Two Books of Adam and Eve,* I, 9:2.

79. *Hymn to Venus* in *Chapman's Homer.* 2:571.

80. "Der Wahn und die Träume in W. Jensens 'Gradiva' " (1907), in *Gesammelte Schriften* (Leipzig: Internationaler Psychoanalytischer Verlag, 1924–34), 9:273–367.

81. This has been noted already by Brophy, *Black and White,* pp. 22–26.

82. H. von Hofmannsthal, *Aufzeichnungen: Gesammelte Werke in Einzelausgaben,* ed. H. Steiner (Frankfurt am Main: Fischer-Verlag, 1959), p. 217.

83. G. Bachelard, "Reveries toward Childhood," in *The Poetics of Reverie,* trans. D. Russell (New York: The Orion Press, 1969), pp. 97–141.

84. Georg Trakl is obsessed with sinful, incestuous, and criminal childhood, perhaps because of his love for his sister Margarete. See, for instance, the poem "Passion" in G. Trakl, *Dichtungen und Briefe: Historisch-Kritische Ausgabe,* ed. W. Killy and H. Szklenar (Salzburg: O. Müller, 1969), 1:393, 369.

85. "The Account of Thomas the Israelite Philosopher Concerning the Childhood of the Lord" in Edgar Hennecke, *New Testament Apocrypha,* ed. W. Schneemelcher (Philadelphia: Westminster Press, 1963), 1:393.

86. Ibid., 1:392–93.

87. A. P. Sinnett, *Incidents in the Life of Madame Blavatsky* (London, 1886; reprinted New York: Arno Press, 1976), p. 21.

88. Ibid., pp. 22–24.

89. Ibid., p. 23.

90. A. B. Gomme, "Children's Games," *Encyclopaedia Britannica* (1910), 6:141.

91. H. von Hofmannsthal, "Age of Innocence" (ca. 1893), *Prosa I, Gesammelte Werke in Einzelausgaben,* ed. H. Steiner (Frankfurt am Main: Fischer-Verlag, 1956), p. 147.

92. "Kate Greenaway," *Encyclopaedia Britannica* (1910), 12:537.

93. Ibid.

94. Weintraub, *Beardsley,* p. 6.

95. Kate Greenaway, *Under the Window: Pictures and Rhymes for Children* (London: G. Routledge; New York: McLoughlin Bros., n.d.), pp. 42 and 16.

96. Panofsky, "Et in Arcadia Ego," in *Hercules am Scheidewege.*

97. Greenaway, *Under the Window,* p. 15.

98.
> *Little baby, if I threw*
> *This fair blossom down to you,*
> *Would you catch it as you stand,*
> *Holding up each tiny hand,*
> *Looking out of those grey eyes,*
> *Where such deep, deep wonder lies?*

Ibid., p. 53.

99. Kate Greenaway, illus., *Mother Goose* (London: Frederick Warne, n.d.), p. 11.

100. Greenaway, *Under the Window*, p. 27.

101. Sinnett, *Incidents*, pp. 32, 33, 34–35, 36–37, 35.

102. Schmidt, *Sitara oder der Weg dorthin*.

103. Daniel Goleman, "As Sex Roles Change, Men Turn to Therapy to Cope with Stress," *New York Times*, 20 August 1984, p. C1.

104. The woman with the elephant was Sallie Dornan. *New York Times*, 22 August 1984, p. A16.

Chapter 9 · Salome

1. Helen Grace Zagona, *The Legend of Salome and the Principle of Art for Art's Sake* (Geneva: Librairie E. Droz; Paris: Librairie Minard, 1960).

2. In Heine's poem *Atta Troll* (1841). H. Heine, *Complete Poems*, trans. H. Draper (Boston: Publishers Boston, Inc., 1982), p. 462.

3. The poem *Hérodiade*, which Mallarmé began in 1864, at the age of twenty-two, and had on his mind till his death in 1898. See chapter 3 of Zagona, *Legend of Salome*, pp. 41–88.

4. Saint Gregory of Nazianzus (329–89), Saint John Chrysostom (ca. 347–407), and Saint Jerome (ca. 340–420) all disapproved of Salome's dancing—a corrupt amusement. See Blaise Hospodar de Kornitz, *Salome: Virgin or Prostitute?* (New York: Pageant Press, 1953), p. 37.

5. In Catalania, for instance, it was believed that the dancer-killer drowned herself in one of the local rivers, and so did Herod as well. In times of flooding, she was the one to be blamed for devastation. The legend, mentioned in J. Collin de Plancy's *Dictionnaire infernal* (Paris, 1844), obviously reflects how water, the attribute of the Baptist, was transferred to his killer and turned from a good, life-giving element that is evoked by the baptism to an evil, life-taking one.

6. For instance, I was initially at a loss as to which English translation of the Bible should be used in this book. As it deals with the apocryphal and popular tradition, and with inspirations taken from older rather than newer books, from rare and curious texts rather than from established ones, it did not seem appropriate to use the Authorized Version. Therefore I originally opted for the Rheims-Douay Version, a translation executed under the reign of Queen Elizabeth and published at Douay in 1609–10. However, its vernacular, at times hardly understandable, would have presented problems and distanced the reader from the visual imagery so important in this context. The revision of this text, done in the mid-eighteenth century by Challoner, was still too ambiguous. Thus I have finally settled for the Confraternity Version, a revision of the Challoner-Rheims-Douay Version published in 1962 by the Episcopal Committee of the Confraternity of Christian Doctrine, which preserved some flavor of the sixteenth-century version but freed it from a stilted literalness. Of course, this is a compromise, and as such it is far from ideal. But as this book deals with art and literature from different periods and countries, and with the products of artists, writers, and simple folk who read the Bible in Greek, Latin, French, Italian, German, English, Polish, etc., there is no real solution to the problem. However, intuitively, the translation used here seems to fit the material I am dealing with. The problem of the biblical text as a source of literary inspiration is particularly serious in the case of Wilde's *Salomé*, which was originally written in French. However, one cannot tell if Wilde read in connection with his work a French or an English Bible (and which version) or adapted for his purpose, as

writers frequently do, some cheap, inadequate, and popular biblical summary or excerpt, either in French or in English. Very likely he did not read anything at all but just remembered vaguely and mixed up reminiscences of childhood and school-day readings or occasional visits to a Mass. Similarly, it does not seem very probable that when Wilde's young lover, Lord Alfred Douglas, sat down to translate the play into English, he did it in a very scholarly way. Most likely he never compared a French to an English Bible nor bothered to look up the quotations in the Authorized Version. It was Wilde's style he cared for, mixed up with his own re-membrances of the Holy Scriptures. Strangely enough, what he came up with can be well grasped when one compares his translation with the revised Challoner-Rheims-Douay Version (did the Catholic scholars of the Episcopal Committee read his *Salomé*?). The spelling, at times unusual (for instance "Gethsemane" is spelled "Gethsemani" and "Sharon" "Saron"), comes from this edition.

7. Flavius Josephus, *Works,* trans. William Whiston (London, 1894), p. 540.

8. Panofsky, *Hercules am Scheidewege,* p. 43.

9. Ibid., p. 52. Author's translation.

10. Now in the National Library, Paris. See also Walter Lowrie, *Art in the Early Church* (New York: W. W. Norton, 1969), p. 190.

11. Now in the National Library, Paris.

12. J. Walter, "Aurait-on découvert des fragments de l'Hortus Deliciarum?" *Archives alsaciennes d'histoire de l'art* 10 (1931): 1–8.

13. Panofsky studied them in his *Hercules.*

14.
> Alors se lèvent les jongleurs. . . . L'un joue de la harpe, l'autre de la viole, l'un de la flûte, l'autre du fifre, l'un de la gigue, l'autre de la rote, l'un dit les paroles, l'autre les accompagne. . . . Il en est qui jonglent avec des couteaux, l'un rampe à la terre et l'autre fait la culbute, un autre danse en faisant la cabriole. . . .

After Alexandre Masseron, *Saint Jean Baptiste dans l'art* (Paris: Arthaud, 1957), p. 120.

15. Ibid., p. 114.

16. Ibid., p. 115.

17. Städelsches Kunstinstitut, Frankfurt am Main. A copy of this triptych can be found in the Dahlem Museum, West Berlin. Occasionally it has been suggested that both paintings are not originals but mere copies: see *Kindlers Malerei Lexikon* (Munich: Deutscher Taschenbuch Verlag, 1976), 12:269.

18. *Stromateis,* III.64, after Hennecke, *New Testament Apocrypha,* 1:167. It is unclear if this is Salome, the mother of John the Baptist, who was also considered the sister of the Virgin, or some other woman by the same name.

19. Jacob Grimm, *Teutonic Mythology,* trans. J. S. Stallybrass (London, 1883), 3:927–50.

20. Heine, *Atta Troll* (19:6) in *Complete Poems,* pp. 458–59.

21. Ibid., p. 462.

22. Ibid., p. 461.

23. René Ancely, "Une tradition régionale: Les herbes de la Saint-Jean," *Bulletin de la société des sciences, lettres et arts de Pau,* 3d series, 6 (1946): 79–90; "Zwyczaje świetojańskie na zachodnim Polesiu," *Lud Słowiański* 1 (1929–30): B76–B88.

24. Abbé J. Corblet, ed., "Culte et iconographie de Saint-Jean-Baptiste dans le diocèse d'Amiens," *Revue de l'art chrétien* 8 (1864): 452–73; Abbé Pardiac, "Les feux

de Saint-Jean," *Revue de l'art chrétien* 16 (1873): 115–40; J. M. Le Maine, "Origin of the Festival of Saint-Jean-Baptiste. Quebec: Its Gates and Environs," *Morning Chronicle* (1880); Benjamin Sulte, "La Saint-Jean-Baptiste 1636–1836," *Proceedings and Transactions of the Royal Society of Canada*, 3d series, 10 (1916): 1–8; E. Debacker, "Un cortège de la St. Jean à Dunkerque au XVIII siècle," *Mémoires de société dunkerquoise* 56 (1913): 7–26; J. L. André, "Saint John the Baptist in Art, Legend and Ritual," *Archeological Journal* 50 (1893): 1–19.

25. R. Wünsch, *Das Frühlingsfest der Insel Malta*, after Frazer, *Adonis, Attis, Osiris*, 1:246.

26. The following is a summary of Frazer's research on Adonis, *Adonis, Attis, Osiris*, 1:3–287, and of other relevant texts:

The main sites of the Adonis cult were Byblus, on the coast of Syria, and Paphos in Cyprus. These places were also the centers of the cult of Aphrodite, who was celebrated there as the Semitic goddess Astarte. Byblus was once her religious capital, where in the great sanctuary the rites of Adonis were also celebrated. In fact, the whole city was sacred to him and the river Nahr Ibrahim bore in antiquity the name "Adonis" (Frazer, 1:13–14).

In the different versions of the Adonis legend various parents are given for him: Phoenix and Alphesiboea, Cinyras and Metharme (the daughter of Pygmalion), and Zeus, who is said to have begotten him, like Athena, without the help of a female. However, in the most popular and also presumably the most ancient version, Adonis is the product of incest between the king of Byblus, whose name is given either as Theias or as Cinyras, and his daughter Myrrha. Ovid describes in detail the forbidden passion of the princess, who tries in vain to love her father "but as my father" (*Met.* 10:336), without becoming his mistress and her mother's rival. Burning with desire, Myrrha wants to commit suicide but is prevented from it by her old nurse, who, unable to bear the sufferings of her darling, arranges for her to meet the king by telling him "of the girl who was in love with him, altering nothing but her name" (*Met.* 10:439). It is worth recalling Ovid's description of this erotic encounter because of its closeness to the moonlit scenery of Oscar Wilde's *Salomé*.

When Myrrha set out to join her father, "the golden moon fled from the sky, black clouds concealed the stars as they shrank from sight. Night was robbed of its starry fires, Icarus being the first to cover up his face, and Erigone, raised to heaven by her devoted love for her father. Three times an unlucky stumble checked Myrrha's steps, three times the funereal screech-owl gave its ominous warning, with fatal croaking, but still she went on, and the darkness and shadows of the night lessened her feeling of shame. . . . The father welcomed his own flesh and blood into that bed of horror, soothed her girlish fears, and encouraged her when she was afraid. It may well be that he used the name appropriate to her age, and called her 'daughter,' while she called him 'father,' so that even the names were not wanting to complete their wickedness" (*Met.* 10:450–70).

When, finally, after a great many incestuous encounters, the king, anxious to see the girl with whom he made love, brought in a lamp and, recognizing his own daughter, wanted to kill her, Myrrha fled the home. She wandered for nine months "across broad lands of her father's kingdom" and, tortured by her expulsion, asked to be changed "into some other form." Her prayers were heard and a metamorphosis took place: she turned into a tree. In due time its "trunk split open" and Adonis, a lovely boy, was born out of it. The baby grew into a beautiful youth who became the darling of Venus: "The goddess of Cythera, captivated by the beauty of a mortal, cared no more for her sea shores, ceased to visit seagirt Paphos, Cnidos rich in fishes, or Amathis with its valuable ores. She even stayed away from heaven, preferring Adonis to the sky" (*Met.* 10:530–33).

27. This connection with the cycle of nature is further stressed through a detail given by Ovid, who points out that the first incestuous encounter between Cinyras and his daughter took place at the time of harvest and abstention "when all married women were duly celebrating the annual festival of Ceres, at which, dressed in garments of snowy white, they offer her garlands made of corn ears, the first fruits of the crops, and for nine nights hold love and all male contact in the category of forbidden things" (*Met.* 10:430–43).

28. Frazer, *Adonis, Attis, Osiris*, 1:49. In this sense Cinyras was but a double of Adonis. Frazer connects the story with the legend of Pygmalion, the Phoenician king of Cyprus, who fell in love with a statue of Aphrodite and went to bed with it (Arnobius, *Adversus nationes*, 6:22). In some versions of the Adonis story, Pygmalion is the father-in-law of Cinyras and thus seems to be one more of Adonis's doubles—a divine lover who perhaps had to play the role of Aphrodite-Astarte's bridegroom in a symbolic marriage with a statue, or at certain festivals had to mate with the sacred prostitutes at the temple of the goddess. Frazer tends to stress Adonis's character as the corn-spirit or Adon (Lord) of each individual plant rather than a personification of the entire vegetable life, and Mannhardt believes that the corn-spirit was once impersonated by human victims annually slain in the fields during the harvest (W. Mannhardt, *Mythologische Forschungen* [Strasbourg, 1884], p. 1ff.).

29. Frazer, *Adonis, Attis, Osiris*, 1:236–59.

30. In the nineteenth-century villages of Sardinia "the gardens of Adonis" were planted by a girl who was asked by a boy to be his *comare* (sweetheart), while he offered to become her *compare*. At the end of May the girl filled a pot with earth and sowed wheat and barley in it. The grain grew rapidly and had "a good head" by Saint John's Eve. The pot was called Erme or Nenneri and was carried by the young man and the girl, accompanied by a pageant, to a church outside the village. They broke the pot by throwing it against the door. Then they rested in the grass, playing music, eating eggs and herbs, joining hands and singing "Sweethearts of Saint John" *(compare e comare di San Giovanni)*. At the village of Ozieri the pots were richly adorned and displayed on the Eve of Saint John on the windowsills draped with cloth. On each pot there was a doll dressed as a woman, or a Priapus-like statuette made of paste. After the villagers had admired the pots, they made a fire and those young people who wished to become "Sweethearts of Saint John" joined hands by each taking one end of a long stick which they passed three times back and forth across the fire. In Sicily pairs of boys and girls became "sweethearts" by each taking a hair from the other's head, tying them together and throwing them into the air (Frazer, *Adonis, Attis, Osiris*, 1:244–45).

In different parts of Europe people bathed in rivers and springs on the Eve of Saint John in order to wash away their sins and diseases; they believed in the healing properties of the dew which fell on Saint John's Night so they collected it in vessels in order to wash themselves with it; they drank water from springs. Petrarch happened to visit Cologne on Saint John's Eve and he described (*Epistolae de rebus familiaribus*, 1:4) the sight of women, girt with herbs, who knelt on the banks of the Rhine and washed their hands in the river; they believed that this would preserve them from misfortune. Even today in some Polish villages the girls on this night make flower wreaths (*wianki*) and throw them into the river.

31. "Zwyczaje świetojańskie," pp. B76–B88.

32. In the village of Rybna the dead head was placed over the cattle in the cowshed in order to protect the animals from evil spirits. In the village of Uhlany, Kupalo was celebrated on Saint John's Eve with a bonfire over which the heads, skulls, or bones of horses and cows were hung. The fire was usually made near a river or a lake, and people danced around it and sang. Finally, one of the young men made the bones fall into the fire. When they were burned, the ashes were collected and thrown into a deep and flowing body of water. The heads and bones belonged to animals which had died of some disease, and it was believed that this washed away with the water. However, in the village of Uhlany not only bones but also a "witch" made by the girls and boys from straw and old clothes was burned in the fire. Once this was done, the boys started to jump over the fire, attacking the girls, pretending that whomever they catch they would burn "like the witch." All songs sung on this occasion dealt with Kupalo and the witch. While the bones, the heads, and the straw figures burned, people watched closely for glowing coals that spit out of the fire and carefully put them back; otherwise the evil spirits were believed to be resurrected. When the fire was over, the ashes were thrown into water. Ibid.

33. Abbé Corblet, ed., "Culte et iconographie," p. 452. Bones of animals were burned in many regions of France and in Paris; even as late as the seventeenth century 144 caged cats were burned alive and the crowds enjoyed their agony. Abbé Pardiac, "Les feux de Saint-Jean," pp. 134–35.

34. "Zwyczaje świetojańskie," pp. B85–B86.

35. They were supposed to appear in different forms—as witches, usually dressed in white, or as Kupalo, and were believed to steal the milk from the cows. Occasionally, to prevent this, the heads and horns of the cattle were wreathed with green branches and nettles; nettles were also stuck into windows, doors, and all openings to prevent evil spirits from entering the buildings. Sickles were hung at the entrance to the cowshed in order to wound the witch who would try to get in. Women cooked the cloth for straining the milk over a fire, believing that this would force the witch to come out of hiding. If an animal (a cat or a chicken) appeared by the fire just then, they caught it and cut its claws. Ibid.

36. *Dictionary of Folklore, Mythology and Legend* (1949), under "Hecate." *Encyclopaedia Britannica* (1910), under "Hecate."

37. Ancely, "Une tradition régionale," p. 80.

38. "Zwyczaje świetojańskie," p. B86.

39. Abbé Pardiac, "Les feux de Saint-Jean," p. 139.

40. Ibid., p. 130.

41. K. Müller-Lisowski, "La légende de St. Jean dans la tradition irlandaise et le druide Mog Ruith," *Études celtiques* 3 (June 1938): 57.

42. There is a rather obscure paper arguing that John the Baptist belonged in the family of hereditary rainmakers. Hugh J. Schonfield, "Onias the Rainmaker," *Search Quarterly* 2 (1932): 267–78.

43. Wilhelm Brandt, *Die Mandäische Religion* (Leipzig, 1889).

44. M. Lidzbarski, *Das Johannesbuch der Mandäer*, 2 vols. (Giessen: A. Töpelmann, 1905–15).

45. G. R. S. Mead, *The Gnostic John the Baptizer* (London: J. M. Watkins, 1924), pp. 72–74.

46. Ibid., p. 72.

47. Ibid., p. 17.

48. Debacker, "Un cortège de la St. Jean," p. 22.

49. M. N. Siouffi, *Études sur la religion des Soubbas, ou Sabéens, leurs dogmes, leurs moeurs* (Paris, 1880).

50. H. Bren, "Die Gestalt der Salome in der französischen Literatur. Mit Berücksichtigung der nicht französischen Versionen des Salomestoffes" (Ph.D. dissertation, University of Vienna, 1950).

51. Jules Laforgue, *Salome* (1886), in *Six Moral Tales*, ed. and trans. F. Newman (New York: H. Liveright, 1928), p. 206. Parenthetical references hereafter are to this edition.

52. Orion, in Greek mythology a hunter of great strength and beauty, perhaps corresponding to the "wild huntsman" of Teutonic mythology. Sometimes he is described as having sprung from earth. He was slain by Artemis, who, in some versions of the legend, was angry with him because he did violence to her or challenged her power; in others because she loved him and was deceived by Apollo to shoot him by mistake. Apollodorus 1:4; Hyginus, *Poet. astron.* 2:34; Horace, *Odes*, III, 4:71.

53. Oscar Wilde, *Salomé*, trans. A. Douglas (London: Elkin Matthews and John Lane; Boston: Copeland and Day, 1894). Quoted after the 1964 American edition (Boston: Bruce Humphries), p. 1. Parenthetical references hereafter are to this edition.

54. Eliade, *Patterns in Comparative Religion*, p. 154.

55. C. G. Jung, *Symbolik des Geistes* (Zurich: Rascher Verlag, 1948), pp. 41–42.

56. *Der Kleine Pauly. Lexikon der Antike* (Munich: Deutscher Taschenbuch Verlag, 1979), under "Moira"; Eliade, *Patterns in Comparative Religion*, p. 181.

57. Eliade, *Patterns in Comparative Religion*, p. 177.

58. Gertrude Jobes, *Dictionary of Mythology, Folklore and Symbols* (New York: Scarecrow Press, 1961), under "Moon."

59. *Encyclopaedia Britannica* (1910), under "Hecate"; *Der Kleine Pauly*, under "Hecate."

60. *Encyclopaedia Britannica* (1910), under "Kali."

61. Eliade, *Patterns in Comparative Religion*, pp. 157 and 156.

62. Herbert Grabes, *Speculum, Mirror und Looking-Glass* (Tübingen: Max Niemeyer Verlag, 1973), pp. 89–91.

63. Michel Soymié, "La lune dans les religions chinoises," *La lune. Mythes et rites. Sources orientales* (Paris: Seuil, 1962), pp. 298–99.

64. Rahner, "Das christliche Mysterium von Sonne und Mond," in *Griechische Mythen*, pp. 125–224.

65. Maurice Simon, Appendix to *The Zohar*, trans. H. Sperling and M. Simon (London: Soncino Press, 1931–34), 5:396–97.

66. Now in the Prints and Drawings Collection of the Art Institute of Chicago.

67. *Times* (London), 2 March 1893, p. 4, after O. Wilde, *Salomé* (New York: Dover, 1967), p. XIV.

68. Praz, *Romantic Agony*, p. 298.

69. "And some women were also there, looking on from a distance. Among them were Mary Magdalene, Mary the mother of James the Less and of Joseph, and Salome" (Mark 15:40).

70. Adolf Lanz, a Viennese ex-monk and the spiritual teacher of the young Hitler, for instance, "retranslated" the Bible at the turn of the century into a completely

dualistic and apocalyptic book concerned solely with the struggle against evil and the ultimate victory over it brought about by a new savior, a pure Aryan and a god of light. See Daim, *Der Mann, der Hitler die Ideen gab.* On the Manichean aspect of Catholicism, see also F. Heer, *Der Glaube des Adolf Hitler: Anatomie einer Politischen Religiosität* (Munich, Esslingen: Bechtle Verlag, 1968). The Revelation provided a basis for Elijah Muhammad's hatred of the white race. He taught his followers that the first humans were black people; they founded the holy city of Mecca and lived happily until about sixty-six hundred years ago, when Mr. Yacub was born. He came to the world to create disorder, had an unusually large head, and became a great scientist. He was able, among other things, to breed a new race. Because of his agitation against the authorities, Mr. Yacub was banished from Mecca with his 59,999 followers to the island of Patmos. Embittered toward Allah, he decided there to bring upon the earth a devil race—bleached-out white people. He could achieve this by recognizing that black people's bodies contained two germs, one black, the other brown; he cultivated the brown one and, with time, managed to make it lighter and lighter in a process of extermination: black babies were killed, brown survived. After the death of Mr. Yacub his followers continued to bleach out people; thus, gradually, the brown race was changed into the red, the red into the yellow and the yellow into the white race of "cold-blue-eyed devils—savages, nude and shameless . . . [who] walked on all fours and . . . lived in trees. . . . this devil race had turned what had been a peaceful heaven on earth into a hell torn by quarreling and fighting." Seeing the wickedness of the whites, the blacks exiled them into the caves of Europe where the white race slowly rose to power. Like John before him, Elijah Muhammad preached the end of white rule and the coming of a savior who would avenge the black people. His name was Master W. D. Fard, and he appeared to Elijah Muhammad. Little, *Autobiography of Malcolm X*, pp. 165–69.

71. After Hennecke, *New Testament Apocrypha*, 1:387.

72. The inscription bears the date "March 93" and is to be found in the copy of *Salomé* which is now in the Sterling Library, University of London.

73. ". . . Jesus cried out with a loud voice, and expired. And the curtain of the temple was torn in two from top to bottom. Now when the centurion, who stood facing him, saw how he had thus cried and expired, he said, 'Truly this man was the Son of God.' And some women were also there, looking on from a distance. Among them were Mary Magdalene, Mary the mother of James the Less and of Joseph, and Salome. These used to accompany him and minister to him when he was in Galilee—besides many other women who had come with him to Jerusalem" (Mark 15:37–41).

74. "It was now about the sixth hour, and there was darkness over the whole land until the ninth hour. And the sun was darkened, and the curtain of the temple was torn in the middle. And Jesus cried out with a loud voice and said, 'Father, into thy hands I commend my spirit.' And having said this, he expired" (Luke 23:44–46).

75. After Hennecke, *New Testament Apocrypha*, 1:385.

76.　　　　*J'aime l'horreur d'être vierge et je veux*
Vivre parmi l'effroi que font mes cheveux
Pour, le soir, retirée en ma couche, reptile
Inviolé sentir en la chair inutile
Le froid scintillement de ta pâle clarté
Toi qui te meurs, toi qui brûles de chasteté,
Nuit blanche de glaçons et de la neige cruelle!

Stéphane Mallarmé, *Hérodiade*, in *Oeuvres complètes* (Paris: Pléiade, 1945), p. 44. The poem was first conceived in 1864 but occupied his mind till his death in 1898. In 1865 he wrote to a friend that he was reserving *Hérodiade* for "the cruel winters" and complained that this work, concerned with female sterility and destructiveness, had "sterilized" him. Letter to Cazalis, June 1865, after Zagona, *The Legend of Salome*, p. 43, author's translation. *Hérodiade* undoubtedly inspired Oscar Wilde.

77. See for instance Barbey d'Aurevilly's *Le rideau cramoisi*, in *Les diaboliques* (Paris, 1874).

78. After Jung, *Psychology of the Unconscious*, pp. 108–9.

79. J. Ortega y Gasset, *Facciones del amor* (1926–27), in *Obras completas* (Madrid: Revista de Occidente, 1950–52).

80. Freud, "The Taboo of Virginity," in *Complete Psychological Works*, 11:197.

81. Ibid., 11:207.

82. The Book of Judith is quoted not after the Confraternity Version but, exceptionally, after *The Apocrypha*, trans. Edgar J. Goodspeed (New York: Vintage Books, 1959). This translation is based directly upon the Greek text and it uses the expression "bag of food," important in this context, while the same passage in the Confraternity Version reads "wallet."

83. A. Schnitzler, "Das Schicksal des Freiherrn von Leisenbogh," in *Gesammelte Werke* (Frankfurt am Main: Fischer Verlag, 1961–67).

84. Jan Kott, "Head for Maidenhead, Maidenhead for Head: The Structure of Exchange in 'Measure for Measure,'" *Theatre Quarterly* 31 (1978): 22.

85. J. G. Frazer, *Taboo and the Perils of the Soul*, vol. 3 of *The Golden Bough* (London: Macmillan, 1914), pp. 156, 158.

86. Kuryluk, "Mirrors and Menstruation."

87. R. C. Zaehner, *The Teachings of the Magi* (New York: Oxford University Press, 1975), pp. 46–47, 69.

88. H. H. Ploss, *Das Weib in der Natur- und Völkerkunde* (Leipzig: Th. Grieben, 1905).

89. Claude Gaignebet, "Veronique ou l'image vraie," *Anagrom* 7–8 (1976): 55–60.

90. Freud, "Medusa's Head," in *Complete Psychological Works*, 18:273.

91. Freud, "Medusa's Head."

92. Claude Lévi-Strauss, *The Origin of Table Manners*, trans. J. and D. Weightman (New York: Harper and Row, 1978), pp. 349, 399. Lévi-Strauss differentiates between those cases in which the scalps were given to warriors' wives or their wives' relatives and those in which they went to blood relatives such as the mother, aunt, or sister. He maintains that in the one instance the man transformed his sister into "a perpetually menstruating woman, thus symbolically taking her away again from her husband" (p. 400). In the other instance he himself, as a husband, recognized "that a wife is never given without some hope of return: each month, during the space of a few days, menstruation deprives the husband of his wife, as if relatives were reasserting their rights over her, and as if the tension between givers and takers, correlative to this re-appropriation, could be resolved by the presentation of a blood-stained trophy in exchange for that other blood-stained trophy, a menstruating wife" (p. 400). Lévi-Strauss cites several examples of North American myths concerned with this exchange. For instance, after cutting off the ogre's head, the false wife leaves the hut, pretending that she is menstruating. Consequently, the blood dripping from the head is understood by the victim's mother not as male, but as female. In a Winnebago myth the hero retrieves his father's scalp from the

enemies and presents it to his mother and to a co-wife asking them to go to bed with it. They refuse, saying that they cannot make love with a scalp, "thus adopting an attitude symmetrical with that of a man whose wife is menstruating" (p. 400).

93. After Elaine Pagels, *The Gnostic Gospels* (New York: Vintage Books, 1981), p. 77.

94. Dorothy Epplen Mackay, *The Double Invitation in the Legend of Don Juan* (Stanford: Stanford University Press, 1943), p. 12, and passim.

95. For an extensive treatment of this subject see Theodore Ziolkowski, *Disenchanted Images: A Literary Iconology* (Princeton, N.J.: Princeton University Press, 1977).

96. H. Blavatsky, *From the Caves and Jungles of Hindostan* (London, 1892), chap. 7.

Chapter 10 · Judas

1. In *Navigatio sancti Brendani Abbatis*, the imaginary travel of Saint Brandan, an Irish monk, of which the oldest Latin manuscript goes back to the ninth century. *Visio Tundali*, one of the books which inspired Bosch, was derived from this source, as well as the *Voyage of Saint Brandan* by the twelfth-century Anglo-Norman poet Benedeit, the most successful adaptation of this fantastic travelogue. See Benedeit, *Le voyage de Saint Brandan*, text and trans. Ian Short (Paris: Union Générale d'Éditions, 1984), pp. 95–111.

2. After Kenneth Clark, *The Best of Aubrey Beardsley* (New York: Doubleday, 1978), p. 74.

3. Ibid.

4. Beardsley combined the features of an ancient Hermaphrodite, Eros, and Christ in the drawing *Mirror of Love*. It was meant as a frontispiece to Marc André Raffalovich's collection of poems *The Thread and the Path* (London: D. Nutt, 1895). G. Mattenklott, who dedicated an entire essay to the analysis of this drawing, thinks that it was purged from the book edition because of these hidden analogies. G. Mattenklott, *Bilderdienst: Ästhetische Opposition bei Beardsley und George* (Munich: Rogner und Bernhard, 1970), pp. 119–41.

5. Clark, *Best of Aubrey Beardsley*, p. 74.

6. P. d'Enjoy, "Le baiser en Europe et en Chine," *Bulletin de la société d'anthropologie*, series 4, 8 (1897): 181; R. Briffault, *The Mothers: A Study of the Origins of Sentiments and Institutions* (London: Allen and Unwin, 1927), 1:120; B. Malinowski, *The Sexual Life of Savages in North-Western Melanesia* (New York: Halcyon House, 1929), p. 333.

7. Jacques Bénigne Bossuet, *Oeuvres complètes* (1862), 6:369, after N. J. Perella, *The Kiss Sacred and Profane* (Berkeley: University of California Press, 1969), p. 3.

8. The version given by Mark and Luke does not differ much from that of Matthew. However, Mark (14:32–46) does not mention the question, while Luke (22:48) mentions it in a slightly different form: "Judas, dost thou betray the Son of Man with a kiss?" John (18:4–5), however, does not mention the kiss at all. In his version it is Christ himself who asks the arriving cohort " 'Whom do you seek?' They answered him, 'Jesus of Nazareth.' Jesus said to them, 'I am he.' Now Judas, who betrayed him, was also standing with them."

9. W. Patrick, *James, the Lord's Brother* (Edinburgh: T. T. Clark, 1906).

10. See also Perella, *The Kiss*, pp. 18–23.

11. A frequent motif of fairy tales (the prince who has been transformed into a frog can regain his original form when kissed by the princess). See also Kristoffer Nyrop, *The Kiss and Its History*, trans. W. Harvey (London: Sanda & Co., 1901), p. 95.

12. Nyrop, *The Kiss*, p. 11.

13. Ibid., p. 130.

14. Benedeit, *Le voyage de Saint Brandan*, p. 97.

15. John Lyly, "Cards and Kisses," in *The Kiss in English Poetry*, ed. W. G. Hartog (London: A. M. Philipot, 1923), p. 2.

16. The sarcophagus of a Roman matron in the Vatican Museum. Reproduced in Franz Cumont, *Recherches sur le symbolisme funéraire des Romains* (Paris: Fondation Carrière, 1942; reprinted Paris: Librairie Orientaliste Paul Geuthner, 1966), plate 52, no. 3, p. 400.

17. Ibid., pp. 400–443.

18. Emily Vermeule, *Aspects of Death in Early Greek Art and Poetry* (Berkeley: University of California Press, 1979), p. 162.

19. In Homer's *Iliad* (16.454, 672, 682) the twins Hypnos and Thanatos carry the dead Sarpedon to Lykia. In Hesiod's *Theogony* (211ff.) Hypnos, Thanatos, and the dreams are children of Nyx and live in the underworld. *Der Kleine Pauly*, 2:1279; 5:648.

20. C. Ramnoux, *La nuit et les enfants de la nuit dans la tradition grecque* (Paris: Flammarion, 1959).

21. Cypselus, tyrant of Corinth (ca. 657–627 B.C.), was meant to be killed by the Bacchiadae, a ruling family, because they had been warned by an oracle that he would ruin them. But his mother concealed him in a chest.

22. Pausanias (1. 30, 1) calls Anteros the "third" Eros of the "third" Venus. In *Description of Greece*, with an English translation by W. H. S. Jones (Cambridge: Harvard University Press, 1926–54).

23. *De libero arbitrio*, II.xiv.37, after Perella, *The Kiss*, p. 47.

24. Carl Schmidt, ed., *Koptisch-gnostische Schriften* (Leipzig: J. C. Hinrichs, 1905; reprinted Berlin: Akademie-Verlag, 1954), p. 78.

25. "The Discourse of Theodosius" in *The Apocryphal New Testament*, trans. M. R. James (Oxford: Clarendon Press, 1924; corrected edition 1955), p. 199. See also Perella, *The Kiss*, who quotes both texts and more on the subject, pp. 18–23.

26. "Acta Thomae" in *Apocryphal Acts of the Apostles*, ed. and trans. W. Wright (London and Edinburgh, 1871), 1:172–333.

27. Eusebius, *History of the Church*, trans. G. A. Williamson (Baltimore: Penguin Books, 1965), 1.13:10.

28. In a letter to John Lane, Beardsley confesses that he intends to go to the St. James restaurant dressed as a woman. The letter was accompanied by a drawing showing him in feminine clothes. J. L. May, *The Path through the Wood* (London: G. Bles, 1931), p. 49.

29. Friedrich von Schlegel, "Über die Diotima," in *Sämmtliche Werke* (Vienna, 1846).

30. Algernon Charles Swinburne, *Notes on Poems and Reviews* (London, 1866), after R. L. Peters, *Victorians on Literature and Art* (New York: Appleton-Century-Crofts, 1961), p. 231.

31. Joseph Péladan, *L'androgyne* (Paris, 1891).

32. J. E. Gillet, "Traces of the Judas-Legend in Spain," *Revue Hispanique* 65 (1925): 330.

33. In *Evangelia apocrypha*, ed. C. Tischendorf (Leipzig, 1876), pp. 181–209.

34. Paul Lehmann, "Judas Ischarioth in der lateinischen Legendenüberlieferung des Mittelalters," *Studi medievali* 2 (1929): 289–346.

35. Jacques de Voragine, *Légende Dorée* (Paris, 1843), 2:27–29. For earlier versions of the legend see E. K. Rand, "Medieval Lives of Judas Iscariot," *Anniversary Papers by Colleagues and Pupils of G. L. Kittredge* (Boston and London: n.p., 1913), pp. 305–16.

36. The story is particularly indebted to the description of the birth of Moses (Exod. 1:15–2:10), whose wife's name, "Sepphora" (Exod. 2:21), suggested the name "Cyborea." This association might have occurred because of Moses' appearance at Jesus' transfiguration: "And these were Moses and Elias, who, appearing in glory, spoke of his death, which he was about to fulfill in Jerusalem" (Luke 9:31). See also Matt. 17:3.

37. In a twelfth-century legend "Iscariot" is not the name of the island to which Judas floats in his basket, but the name of the village near Jerusalem where he was born. He floats to Butrito in Epirus, is brought up by fishermen and educated in Greek arts and sciences. He intends to participate in the Olympic games, and only upon being rejected learns the fact of his being a bastard and so returns to Palestine. The rest of the story coincides with Voragine's version. Lehmann, "Judas Iscarioth," pp. 298–99.

38. In the Greek imitations of the Voragine version Judas is not a servant of Pilate but of Herod. V. Istrin, "Die Griechische Version der Judas-Legende," *Archiv für Slavische Philologie* 20 (1898): 605–19.

39. Harpham, *On the Grotesque*, pp. 79–105.

40. Marina Warner, *Alone of All Her Sex* (New York: Random House, 1983), p. 126.

41. Amédée de Lausanne, "Huit Homélies Mariales," *Sources Chrétiennes* 72 (1960): 174.

42. Aelred of Rievaulx, "Sermo VIII in Annuntiatione Beatae Mariae," in Migne, *Patrologia Latina*, 195:254.

43. Warner, *Alone of All Her Sex*, p. 127.

44. Perella, *The Kiss*, p. 73.

45. In a German lectionary (finished 1330) in the collection of the Stadtbibliothek Schaffhausen, Switzerland. Reproduced in Lehmann, "Judas Iscarioth," p. 314.

46. P. F. Baum, "The English Ballad of Judas Iscariot," *PMLA* 31 (1916); reprinted n.s. 24 (1963): 181–89.

47. *Patrologia orientalis*, 2, 2; *Les apocryphes Coptes*, ed. and trans. E. Revillout (Paris: Firmin-Didot, 1904), 1:156–57.

48. See P. F. Baum, "English Ballad," p. 187.

49. Gottfried of Viterbo, "Pantheon" (finished before 1191), in J. Pistorius, *Germanicorum scriptorum Tomus II* (1584), pp. 549ff. See also Lehmann, "Judas Iscarioth," p. 292.

50. Thomas de Quincey, *Writings*, 20 vols. (Boston, 1850–55), 16:149, 151.

51. Gert Buchheit, *Judas Iskarioth: Legende, Geschichte, Deutung* (Gütersloh: Rufer Verlag, 1954), pp. 52–53.

52. Ibid., p. 41.

53. After Israel Tabak, *Judaic Lore in Heine* (Baltimore: Johns Hopkins University Press, 1948), p. 64.

54. R. Buchanan, "The Ballad of Judas Iscariot," *The Poetical Works* (London: Chatto and Windus, 1884), pp. 494–96.

55. Ibid., p. 494.

56. Ibid., pp. 495–96.

57. Rand, "Medieval Lives," pp. 305–16.

58. In Russia V. S. Solovyov published in 1895 a "Historical-Literary Essay on the Legend of Judas the Traitor"; and W. Doroschevitch interpreted the life of Judas in a short story which appeared in New York: *Judas Iscariot and Other Stories* (G. Bruno, 1919), pp. 5–12. The Polish painter Edward Okuń illustrated the poem *Judasz* by Jan Kasprowicz for the magazine *Chimera* n.s. 4, 10–12 (1901): 163. It shows Judas's head, rising above the horizon like the sun and wearing a crown of thorns which spreads over the entire landscape. In the same year he also painted Judas wearing a crown of coins against the background of Jerusalem. See *Symbolism in Polish Painting 1890–1914*, exhibition catalogue, the Detroit Institute of Arts (1984), p. 84.

59. In the interview given to the *Idler* (March 1897).

Chapter 11 · Distorting Techniques

1. Arthur Symons calls the drawing a "terrible annunciation of evil." In *Aubrey Beardsley* (London: John Baker, 1967), p. 25.

2. The engraving is mentioned by Freud as an example of the repressed wish of the monk who, escaping the temptation of the flesh, flees to the crucifix and projects onto it his unfulfilled desire. "Der Wahn und die Träume in W. Jensens 'Gradiva'," *Gesammelte Schriften*, 9:302–3.

3. Jurgis Baltrušaitis, *Anamorphoses, ou Perspectives curieuses* (Paris: O. Perrin, 1955); *Aberrations: Quatre essais sur la légende des formes* (Paris: O. Perrin, 1957). For illustrations see F. Leeman, *Hidden Images*, trans. E. C. Allison and M. L. Kaplan (New York: Harry W. Abrams, 1976).

4. Freud, "Eine Kindheitserinnerung des Leonardo da Vinci" (1910), *Gesammelte Schriften*, 9:430.

5. E. Hemingway, "Hills like White Elephants," in *Men without Women* (New York: Scribner's, 1927).

Chapter 12 · Form and Color

1. Kayser, *Das Groteske*, pp. 18, 39.

2. Aristotle, *On the Soul, Parva Naturalia, On Breath*, trans. W. S. Hett (Cambridge: Harvard University Press, 1964), pp. 225–26. See also M. A. Tonnelat, *L'évolution des idées sur la nature des couleurs* (Paris: Université de Paris, 1956), pp. 6–7.

3. H. Magnus, *Die Geschichtliche Entwicklung des Farbensinnes* (Leipzig, 1877); A. Marty, *Die Frage nach der Geschichtlichen Entwicklung des Farbensinnes* (Vienna, 1879).

4. A. Reinach, *Recueil des textes grecs et latins, rélatifs à l'histoire de la peinture antique* (Paris: Klincksieck, 1921), p. 63.

5. Ibid., p. 48.

6. See, for instance, Petronius (*Satyricon*, 84) and Quintilian (*Institutio oratoria*, 10, 3, 46).

7. The statue dates from the first century A.D. and represents Diana as the goddess of childbirth. In the Villa d'Este (1565–72) in Tivoli a copy of this famous statue stands in a grotto and serves as a fountain; water runs through the body of the goddess and flows out of her breasts. It is possible that the source of this structure is to be found in Colonna's design of the temple of Venus Physizoa.

8. Kannon is identical with Avalokiteśvara Bodhisattva, a Buddhist deity which was mistaken by the Europeans for a goddess of mercy because its images, looking

sweet and female, reminded them of the Madonna. The name means "the hearer of the voices of all the people of the world." The statue of Kannon in the temple of Hase is about thirty feet tall and dates from the eighth century A.D.

9. The theme of the upper and lower world is also discussed in *Phaedo* (111), where the region above is described as "fairer in colour than our highly-valued emeralds and sardonyxes and jaspers, and other gems, which are but minute fragments of them. . . . The reason is, that they are pure, and not, like our precious stones, infected and corroded." *The Dialogues of Plato,* trans. B. Jowett (New York: Random House, 1937), p. 495.

10. A. Tietze, *The Turkish Shadow Theater and the Puppet Collection of the L. A. Mayer Memorial Foundation* (Berlin: Mann, 1977), p. 18.

11. Ibid., p. 31.

12. In the 1970s the Korean-born artist even created a videotape entitled "Moon—the first television."

13. The figure inspired Arnold Schönberg's *Pierrot Lunaire,* a piece performed for the first time in Vienna in a Beardsley-like setting. On Beardsley as Pierrot see also Symons, *Aubrey Beardsley,* pp. 18–20.

Notes and References for the Illustrations

1. Detail from *Wisdom Vanquishing the Vices,* courtesy of the Louvre, Paris, photo by E. Kuryluk.

2. Detail from a fragment of the sarcophagus representing Dionysus discovering the sleeping Ariadne, St. Médard d'Eyrans (Gironde), courtesy of the Louvre, Paris, photo by E. Kuryluk.

3. Brass, cast and chiseled, courtesy of the Metropolitan Museum of Art, the Jack and Belle Linsky Collection, 1982.

4. God seated on the rainbow, his feet on the globe. To his right the Virgin and the Elected ones, to his left Satan with a female sinner. *Chants royaux sur la conception couronnée du Puy de Rouen,* 1519–28, French Ms 1537, Folio 106, courtesy of the Bibliothèque Nationale, Paris.

5. The separation of the sheep from the goats, marble, courtesy of the Metropolitan Museum of Art, Rogers Fund, 1924.

6. *Imagines mortis, Duodecim imaginibus,* fourth edition (1547). Images by Hans Holbein, blocks by H. Lützelburger, pp. 2–3, courtesy of the Princeton University Library.

7. Baltimore, 1791, courtesy of the John Carter Brown Library at Brown University.

8. "This *Life* is a *way,* or a *place divided into two ways,* like *Pythagoras's Letter* Y. broad, 1. on the left hand track; narrow, 2. on the right; that belongs to *Vice,* 3. this to

Vertue, 4. Mind, Young Man, 5. imitate *Hercules;* leave the left hand way, turn from Vice; the *Entrance*, 6. is fair, but the *End*, 7. is ugly and steep down. Go on the right hand, though it be thorny, 8. no way is unpossible to vertue; follow whither vertue leadeth through *narrow places* to *stately palaces*, to the *Tower of honour.*" John Amos Comenius, *Orbis pictus* (first published in Nuremberg in 1657; Syracuse, N.Y.: C. W. Bardeen, 1887), p. 136, photo by E. Kuryluk.

9. Oil on wood, courtesy of the Städelsches Kunstinstitut, Frankfurt am Main.

10. Oil on wood, courtesy of the Louvre, Paris. According to Hesiod (*Theog.* 570–612), Pandora, the first woman, was fashioned by Hephaestus out of earth. Zeus gave her a jar, the so-called "Pandora's box," containing all kinds of evil, which she opened.

11. Nature holding Mary. *Chants royaux sur la conception couronnée du Puy de Rouen*, 1519–28, French Ms 1537, Folio 102, courtesy of the Bibliothèque Nationale, Paris.

12. Oil on canvas, courtesy of the Metropolitan Museum of Art, Gift of J. Pierpont Morgan, 1917.

13. Oil on canvas, courtesy of the Frick Art Museum, Pittsburgh, photo by Carl M. Martahus.

14. *Apocalypse historiée*, French Ms 403, Folio 40, courtesy of the Bibliothèque Nationale, Paris.

15. Courtesy of the Princeton University Library, G. Kane Collection.

16. Courtesy of the Princeton University Library, G. Kane Collection.

17. *Michaelis Majeri . . . Secretioris naturae secretorum scrutinium chymicum, per oculis et intellectui accuratè accommodata, figuris cupro appositissimè incisa, ingeniosissima emblemata, hisque confines, & ad rem egregiè facientes sententias, doctissimaque item epigrammata, illustratum* (Frankfurt: G. H. Oehrling, 1687). (This book was first published in 1618 under the title *Atalanta fugiens*.) Emblem XXX, p. 88, inscribed: "Sol indiget Lunâ, ut gallus gallinâ." Courtesy of the Princeton University Library.

18. Ibid., Emblem XXIII, p. 67, inscribed: "Aurum pluit, dum nascitur Pallas Rhodi, & Sol concumbit Veneri." While the alchemical fire burns to the left, Sun and Venus, on the right side, copulate with each other, assisted by Amor. The god of love is also standing on a postument and overlooking the scene. Over the tent of the lovers gold is raining, in allusion to Jupiter's encounter with Danaë. Courtesy of the Princeton University Library.

19. Ibid., Emblem XXXVIII, p. 112, inscribed: "Rebis, ut Hermaphroditus, nascitur ex duobus montibus, Mercurii & Veneris." Courtesy of the Princeton University Library.

20. Cod. Pal. lat. 1066, courtesy of the Biblioteca Apostolica Vaticana, Rome.

21. "Perfect solution" is the moment in the first opus in which the solid matter is dissolved by the volatile spirit within it (represented by the winged figure in the neck of the glass), and unites with the liquid or volatile contents of the vessel. Ms 975, Folio 13, courtesy of the Bibliothèque de l'Arsenal, Paris.

22. Ibid., Folio 14, courtesy of the Bibliothèque de l'Arsenal, Paris.

23. Courtesy of the Prado, Madrid.

24. *Antastrologo; Das ist, Die unfelig gewisest practica practicarum, auff das yetzig und nachfolgende jar auss grund der grossen coniunction, langer erfarnuss und steter übung mit vergleichung der siben jrrdischen planeten und zwölff himlischen zaichen beschriben . . .* (Ingolstadt, 1567), courtesy of the Princeton University Library.

25. *Andreae Vesalii Bruxelensis icones anatomicae* (Bremen: New York Academy of Medicine and University Library, Munich, 1934), plate 1–98, courtesy of the Princeton University Library.

26. Courtesy of the Louvre, Paris.

27. *Theodori Kerckringii. . . . Opera omnia anatomica* (Leiden: T. Haak and S. Luchtmans, 1729), third edition, frontispiece plate, courtesy of the Princeton University Library.

28. *Anatomische Tabellen* (Danzig, 1725), plate I–II, courtesy of Stadt- und Hochschulbibliothek, Bern, photo by Fotoatelier Gerhard Howald, Bern.

29. Adrian van der Spieghel (1578–1625), *De humani corporis fabrica* (Venice: Evangelista Dehuchino, 1627), bound with Giulio Casserio (1561–1616), *Tabulae anatomicae* (Venice: Evangelista Dehuchino, 1627), and Spieghel, *De formato foetu* (Padua: Giovanni Battista de Martinis and Livio Pasquato, 1626), courtesy of the Houghton Library, Harvard University, Mr. and Mrs. Arthur Vershbow Collection.

30. *Andreae Vesalii*, plate V35–39, courtesy of the Princeton University Library.

31. *Theodori Kerckringii*, p. 301, courtesy of the Princeton University Library.

32. *Andreae Vesalii*, plate 1–98, courtesy of the Princeton University Library.

33. *Theodori Kerckringii*, plate XVIII, p. 112, courtesy of the Princeton University Library.

34. *Judas der Erzschelm*, copper engraving, courtesy of the Yale University, Medical Library, Clemens Fry Collection.

35. Ms Hunter 208, Folio 276 recto (detail), courtesy of the Glasgow University Library.

36. Not used in *Lucian's True History* (London: Lawrence and Bullen, 1894) but published in *An Issue of Five Drawings Illustrative of Juvenal and Lucian* (London: Leonard Smithers, 1906), plate 255. In Greek mythology Dionysus was born from Zeus's thigh. There he was transferred from Semele's womb at the moment of his human mother's destruction by Zeus, his divine father.

37. Ed. Théodore de Bry, with illustrations by J. White (Frankfurt am Main, 1590), plate XVIII, courtesy of the Princeton University Library.

38. Ibid., plate III, courtesy of the Princeton University Library.

39. *Le livre des merveilles*, a collection of accounts of travels made by Marco Polo, Oderico de Pordenone, Guillaume de Boldensele, Jean de Mandeville, Hayton and Ricardo de Montecroce, illustrated by the Master of Boucicaut and the Master of Bedford, French Ms 2810, Folio 194, courtesy of the Bibliothèque Nationale, Paris.

40. This is the translation of *Histoire générale des drogues* (Paris, 1694), courtesy of the Princeton University Library.

41. Bacchiacca (Francesco d'Ubertino), oil on wood, courtesy of the Metropolitan Museum of Art, the Jack and Belle Linsky Collection, 1982.

42. In the left upper corner God gazes at the world holding an open book. Courtesy of the Prado, Madrid.

43. Courtesy of the Prado, Madrid.

44. Marble, courtesy of the Metropolitan Museum of Art, Gift of J. Pierpont Morgan, 1917.

45. Oil and tempera on panel, courtesy of the Art Institute of Chicago, Wilson L. Mead Fund.

46. Statuette, bronze, Padua or Ravenna, courtesy of the Metropolitan Museum of Art, Fletcher Fund, 1925.

47. Carved gilded bronze, Louis XV period, courtesy of the Yale University Library, Gift of Archer M. Huntington.

48. Carved gilded bronze, Louis XV period, courtesy of the Yale University Art Gallery, Gift of Archer M. Huntington.

49. Courtesy of the Yale University Art Gallery.

50. Vignette for p. 187 in *Bon-Mots* of Charles Lamb and Douglas Jerrold (London: J. M. Dent and Company, 1893), repeated on p. 153 in *Bon-Mots* of Samuel Foote and Theodore Hook, ed. Walter Jerrold (London: J. M. Dent and Company, 1894), plate 246.

51. Vignette on p. 148 in *Bon-Mots* of Samuel Foote and Theodore Hook.

52. Formerly attributed to Arcimboldo by Benno Geiger, oil on canvas, courtesy of the Paride Accetti Collection, Milan.

53. The satirical grafitto was discovered in 1856 in the ruins of the imperial palace on the Palatine hill in Rome. After Georg Ott, *Die ersten Christen ober und unter der Erde; oder Zeugnisse für den Glauben, die Hoffnung und Liebe unserer heiligen Mutter, der Kirche. Ein Buch des Trostes und der Ermuthigung für die Katholiken und der Belehrung für ihre Gegner* (Regensburg, New York, Cincinnati, 1879), p. 130, photo by E. Kuryluk.

54. Pahari school, Basohli (?), courtesy of the Musée Guimet, Paris.

55. *Michaelis Majeri,* Emblem II, p. 4, inscribed: "Nutrix ejus terra est," courtesy of the Princeton University Library.

56. Jules Bois, *Le satanisme et la magie,* with a study by J.-K. Huysmans (Paris, 1896), photo by E. Kuryluk.

57. First version, intended for illustration in *Salomé,* trans. from the French of Oscar Wilde by Lord Alfred Douglas (London: Elkin Mathews and John Lane; Boston: Copeland and Day, 1894), not used. Courtesy of Mr. Edward James Matthews, New York.

58. Illustration facing p. 48 in *Salomé.*

59. Drawing intended to illustrate *The Story of Venus and Tannhäuser,* not completed, courtesy of Mr. F. J. Martin Dent, London.

60. *Pastor Sang,* the drama of *Over Aevne* by Bjørnstjerne Bjørnson, trans. W. Wilson (London and New York: Longmans, Green and Company, 1893).

61. Courtesy of the Princeton University Library, G. Kane Collection.

62. Courtesy of the Yale University Art Gallery, Marion N. Kemp und in memory of her brother Arthur T. Kemp.

63. The drawing is inscribed:

> Vom Rätselrachen der Welt umfangen
> Sitzt die arme Menschenseel in Fürchten und Bangen,
> Das Ungeheuer kann sie ja spielend verschlingen,
> Und möchte doch jede ihr fröhliches Lebenslied singen.

After W. Fraenger, *Deutscher Humor aus fünf Jahrhunderten* (Munich: R. Piper, 1925), 2:1, photo by E. Kuryluk.

64. Illustration facing p. 24 in *The Rape of the Lock,* an heroi-comical poem in five cantos written by Alexander Pope, embroidered with nine drawings by Aubrey Beardsley (London: Leonard Smithers, 1896).

65. Design for a tailpiece in the periodical *St. Paul's,* vol. 1, no. 1, March 1894. The drawing was reproduced in plate 94 of *The Early Work of Aubrey Beardsley* (London: John Lane, 1899), courtesy of the Graphische Sammlung, Albertina, Vienna.

66. Heading of chapter 14, book 7 (p. 244 of vol. 1) in *Le Morte Darthur* (London, 1893–94).

67. *Emblemata nobilitati* (Frankfurt: by the author, 1593), an *Album amicorum,* text followed by engraved escutcheons alternating with emblematic plates. Courtesy of the Houghton Library, Harvard University, Mr. and Mrs. Arthur Vershbow Collection.

68. Illustration to chapter 4 of *Under the Hill,* published on p. 189 in the *Savoy,* no. 2, April 1896.

69. Design for a plate that was reproduced in *The Yellow Book,* vol. 4, January 1895. Courtesy of the Grenville L. Winthrop Bequest, Fogg Art Museum, Harvard University. Brian Reade comments upon the drawing: "The messenger with the winged slippers of Mercury is whispering a message at dusk to a young girl evidently pregnant, wandering in a garden with a background of symbolic roses on trellises. . . . The form of the girl is sufficiently like that of Beardsley's sister, Mabel, for us to suspect that . . . the underlying association was with her." B. Reade, *Aubrey Beardsley* (London: Studio Vista, 1967), p. 347.

70. Illustration to the Sixth Satire of Juvenal, 1896. Published in *An Issue of Five Drawings Illustrative of Juvenal and Lucian.*

71. The Garrett Ms of Marcanova is a fifteenth-century copy of Parisianus 5825F, which is in turn a copy of the famous Modena Codex, Garrett Medieval and Renaissance Ms No. 158, Folio 12, courtesy of the Princeton University Library.

72. Courtesy of the Louvre, Paris.

73. Courtesy of the Metropolitan Museum of Art, Samuel D. Lee Fund, 1941.

74. Mechanism for propulsion in base, silver, silver-gilt and jewels, German metalwork, Augsburg, courtesy of the Metropolitan Museum of Art, Gift of J. Pierpont Morgan, 1917.

75. Reproduced in *A Book of Fifty Drawings by Aubrey Beardsley* (London: Leonard Smithers, 1897).

76. Reproduced in *Six Drawings Illustrating Théophile Gautier's Romance Mademoiselle de Maupin by Aubrey Beardsley* (London: Leonard Smithers, 1898).

77. Vignette on p. 23 in *Bon-Mots* of Sydney Smith and R. Brinsley Sheridan, ed. Walter Jerrold (London: J. M. Dent and Company, 1893), repeated on p. 156 in *Bon-Mots* of Samuel Foote and Theodore Hook.

78. No. 1, January 1896, courtesy of the Grenville L. Winthrop Bequest, Fogg Art Museum, Harvard University.

79. Courtesy of the Princeton University Library, G. Kane Collection.

80. Illustration facing p. 50 in *The Lysistrata of Aristophanes* (London: Leonard Smithers, 1896).

81. The satirical engraving displays the ancient symbolism of the left and right, female and male, passive and active. The four then-known continents, Europe, Asia, Africa, and America, are represented as four women on a pier. Dark clouds and a devil with female breasts holding a clock can be seen over them; underneath sits a dog inscribed "True English Breed." The females are approached by men riding on grotesque animals and representing the politicians of Great Britain, France, Spain, Russia, Turkey, Germany, Italy, Holland, and Corsica. Thus the ancient image of the hunt and conquest of women is used to depict the new era of colonialism. Courtesy of the Princeton University Library.

82. Illustration on p. 185 preceding the installment of *Under the Hill* in the *Savoy*, no. 2, April 1896.

83. Courtesy of the Princeton University Library, G. Kane Collection.

84. Courtesy of the Princeton University Library, G. Kane Collection.

85. Courtesy of the Princeton University Library, G. Kane Collection.

86. Courtesy of the Princeton University Library, G. Kane Collection.

87. Intended for the frontispiece and title page of Beardsley's unfinished novel, reproduced as plate 92 of *The Early Work of Aubrey Beardsley* (London: John Lane, 1899).

88. Courtesy of the Princeton University Library, G. Kane Collection.

89. Vol. 4, January 1895.

90. Title page (London and New York: Frederick Warne, n.d.), courtesy of the Princeton University Library.

91. (London and New York: Frederick Warne, n.d.), p. 40, courtesy of the Princeton University Library.

92. (London: George Routledge, n.d.), p. 2, courtesy of the Princeton University Library.

93. Courtesy of the Louvre, Paris, Collection Borghese, photo by E. Kuryluk.

94. *Imagines mortis*, pp. 50–51, courtesy of the Princeton University Library.

95. Courtesy of the Metropolitan Museum of Art, Bequest of Mary Clark Thompson, 1924.

96. Statuette, ivory, courtesy of the Metropolitan Museum of Art, Bequest of Mary Clark Thompson, 1924.

97. (London: George Routledge; New York: McLoughlin Bros., n.d.), p. 13, courtesy of the Princeton University Library.

98. Ibid., p. 50, courtesy of the Princeton University Library.

99. P. 11, courtesy of the Princeton University Library.

100. Cod. Urb. lat. 899, courtesy of the Biblioteca Apostolica Vaticana, Rome.

101. Intended for illustration to *Under the Hill*, reproduced on p. 157 in the *Savoy*, no. 1, January 1896.

102. P. 42, courtesy of the Princeton University Library.

103. *Bon-Mots* of Samuel Foote and Theodore Hook, design accompanying half-title after the Introduction on p. 15.

104. Oil on wood, courtesy of the Musée Granet, Musée de Beaux-Arts et d'Archéologie, Palais de Malte, Aix en Provence, acquisition Fauris de Saint Vincens, photo by Bernard Terlay.

105. Tempera on canvas, courtesy of the Metropolitan Museum of Art, Bequest of Michael Friedsam, 1931, the Friedsam Collection.

106. Oil on wood, Italian, Milanese, courtesy of the Metropolitan Museum of Art, Bequest of Michael Friedsam, 1931, the Friedsam Collection.

107. Cesare da Sesto has chosen for the scene a particularly grotesque setting. The leg of the table has the shape of an obscene sphinx, and a jewel in the form of a grotesque head, almost a miniature replica of John the Baptist's head, dangles between the breasts of the extremely seductive Salome. Courtesy of the Kunsthistorisches Museum, Vienna.

108. Oil on panel, courtesy of the Art Institute of Chicago, Gift of Mr. and Mrs. Chauncey.

109. As in the representations of the Fall men line up to the left, women to the right. Tempera on wood, courtesy of the Metropolitan Museum of Art, Bequest of Michael Friedsam, 1931, the Friedsam Collection.

110. Courtesy of the Bayrische Staatsbibliothek, Munich.

111. A detail from *The Banquet of Herod*, a mosaic in the Baptistery of San Marco, Venice, photo by Ditta Osvaldo Böhm, Venice.

112. Courtesy of the Bayrische Staatsbibliothek, Munich.

113. Courtesy of the National Gallery, London.

114. Courtesy of the National Gallery, London.

115. Frontispiece to *Salomé*.

116. Excluded from the 1894 edition of *Salomé* and published as plate VIII in *A Portfolio of Aubrey Beardsley's Drawings Illustrating "Salome" by Oscar Wilde* (London: John Lane, 1907).

117. Courtesy of the Atelier du Regard, Orsay.

118. *Apocalypse historiée*, French Ms 403, Folio 33, courtesy of the Bibliothèque Nationale, Paris.

119. Illustration facing p. 56 in *Salomé*.

120. Oil on canvas, courtesy of the Galeria d'Arte Moderna, Milan, photo by Saporetti, Milan.

121. This manuscript was executed by the Visconti of Milan, courtesy of the Princeton University Library.

122. Proof of the first state of an illustration facing p. 24 in *Salomé*. In the second state of this illustration a fig-leaf was shown tied to the male figure in the background; this was the state printed in the 1894 edition of *Salomé*. Courtesy of the Princeton University Library.

123. Illustration facing p. 32 in *Salomé*.

124. Illustration facing p. 64 in *Salomé*.

125. Drawing for the plate prefixed to the story "A Kiss of Judas" in the *Pall Mall Magazine*, July 1893, p. 339.

126. Judas, wearing a fools' cap, to Christ's left. Wood, carved, polychromed and gilded. Courtesy of the Metropolitan Museum of Art, Gift of J. Pierpont Morgan, 1916.

127. Marble, courtesy of the Metropolitan Museum of Art, Fletcher Fund, 1924.

128. From Jacques de Souvré's marble tomb at the church of Courtenvaux, courtesy of the Louvre, Paris.

129. Oil on canvas, courtesy of the Art Institute of Chicago, Charles H. and Mary F. S. Worcester Fund Income.

130. Brush, black ink, courtesy of the Nationalgalerie, Berlin.

131. Etching, courtesy of the Kupferstichkabinett, Dresden.

132. Courtesy of Museo de la Fundacion "Lazaro Galdiano," Madrid.

133. Courtesy of the Atelier du Regard, Orsay.

134. Marble, courtesy of the Louvre, Paris, photo by E. Kuryluk.

135. Jules Bois, *Le satanisme et la magie*, photo by E. Kuryluk.

136. Illustration facing p. 8 in *Salomé*.

137. English caricature printed for Carington Bowles, Map & Print Seller in St. Paul's Church Yard, courtesy of the Princeton University Library.

138. Not used but published in *An Issue of Five Drawings Illustrative of Juvenal and Lucian.*

139. Reproduced in *The Yellow Book,* vol. 3, October 1894, p. 51.

140. Ivory, German, Nuremberg, courtesy of the Metropolitan Museum of Art, Gift of Robert Gordon, 1910.

141. Engraved by T. Cook, London, 1800, courtesy of the Princeton University Library.

142. Courtesy of the Princeton University Library.

143. Courtesy of the Princeton University Library.

144. *Ben Jonson his Volpone: or the Foxe* (London: Leonard Smithers, 1898), p. 147.

145. Ibid., p. 83.

146. Cut-out silhouette from *Die Münchner Bilderbogen,* after W. Fraenger, *Deutscher Humor,* 2:67.

147. The *Savoy,* no. 6, October 1896, p. 33.

Index

Page numbers in italics indicate illustrations.